"They'll attack behind the smoke," Starke warned. "Be ready."

The smoke from the fire the Indians had started bore down on the men, filling their throats and burning their eyes.

Gunfire from the surrounding bluffs redoubled. Somebody screamed in agony. The soldiers heard yelling. The drumming of horses' hooves shook the ground.

"Fire!" Starke shouted. "Pour it on, boys. If they get in here again, we'll be overrun!"

Harry Winston fired blindly. The smoke was suffocating. For a moment Harry couldn't breathe. He fought down panic. He reloaded his carbine and fired again. Ghostly arrows hummed out of the smoke. All around were the crash of weapons and the yelling of men. Now and then the smoke parted, and Harry glimpsed painted Indians, like wraiths, advancing toward him on horseback. . . .

Also by Robert W. Broomall
Published by Fawcett Books:

THE BANK ROBBER
DEAD MAN'S CANYON
DEAD MAN'S CROSSING
DEAD MAN'S TOWN
TEXAS KINGDOMS
CALIFORNIA KINGDOMS

K COMPANY

Robert W. Broomall

FAWCETT GOLD MEDAL • NEW YORK

A Fawcett Gold Medal Book
Published by Ballantine Books
Copyright © 1992 by Robert W. Broomall

Library of Congress Catalog Card Number: 92-90151

ISBN 0-449-14662-6

Manufactured in the United States of America

First Edition: August 1992

Part I

WINTER

1

The blizzard roared out of Canada, blasting the Kansas plains with its fury. The small detachment of soldiers struggled along, heads averted to avoid the stinging flakes. Ahead of them, breaking a path through the snow, was a six-mule wagon, driven by a civilian teamster.

There were ten privates in the detachment. They were recruits, unarmed. Riding alongside them were a first lieutenant and a sergeant. The privates and the lieutenant were replacements for the garrison at Fort Pierce, the westernmost fort protecting the road from Independence, Missouri, to Denver. The men had detrained at Fort Hays, terminus of the Kansas Pacific Railroad. There they had been met by the sergeant and the wagon, which was to carry their baggage. The lieutenant, whose name was Starke, had purchased a horse at Fort Hays, but the privates were forced to walk to their new post.

The weather had been unusually mild for late November. The men had marched in easy stages, fifteen miles a day, camping under the stars. Lieutenant Starke had shot game to supplement their rations. Then, this morning, the sky had darkened to the northwest. The wind had picked up. The temperature had plummeted.

"We're in for what the Texicans call a blue norther," said the teamster, Pennington, spitting tobacco juice. Almost before he'd finished speaking, the first flakes of snow had fallen. There had been no sheltered place to camp. There had been no choice but to continue on.

Now it was late afternoon, and the little column was lost in a howling wilderness of white. Visibility was about thirty

3

feet. "How far to the fort, Sarge?" one of the recruits shouted, as they tramped in the wagon ruts.

The sergeant's name was Cronk. He was a shortish, muscular fellow, with high cheekbones and a big nose. "Ten miles, maybe."

There was a chorus of groans.

"Close up, there!" Cronk ordered. He had a deep, rough voice, like shifting bedrock. "You men in the rear—you fall behind in this, and you'll never catch up again. They won't find your bodies till spring."

"What's the difference?" wailed a jowly ex-grocer named Barker to the man beside him. "We're all going to die out here, anyway. Harry, I'm scared."

Harry Winston said nothing. He tried to look brave, but he was scared, too. He had considered the possibility of death when he'd joined the army, but until now he'd never seriously believed it could happen to him, and certainly not like this, on the way to his first duty station.

Barker was crying. The tears froze on his pudgy cheeks. "This is all Susan's fault. If she hadn't left me, I never would have joined the army. I wouldn't be in this mess."

Again Harry said nothing. He could blame no one but himself for his predicament. Harry was twenty-one, the minimum age for enlistment. He was tall and skinny, with blue eyes and a mop of dark brown hair. He was frozen to the bone, colder than he could have dreamed possible a month ago. The gusting wind tugged his flimsy forage cap against its chin strap. His ill-made shoes had raised blisters on his feet, so that for the last few days it had been painful to walk; but now his feet were so cold, they had become like blocks of wood, and he no longer felt the blisters. His caped overcoat looked warm, but the cloth was cheap, and it provided little protection against the elements. The men had not been issued gloves, so Lieutenant Starke had made them put their spare socks over their hands to protect them. Like most of the men, whitish patches on Harry's ears and cheeks showed where he was developing frostbite.

In front of Harry, his friend Kevin Daugherty suddenly wandered out of line. He stumbled a few steps to the side, then collapsed on his knees in the drifting snow.

Harry broke ranks. "Kevin!" He, Daugherty, and Barker had come through the cavalry depot at Jefferson Barracks together.

Sergeant Cronk rode over, his horse's hooves scattering snow. "Get back in ranks," he told Harry, cutting him off.

Harry pointed at Daugherty. "But—"

"Get back!"

Harry returned to the line. Cronk started to yell at Daugherty, but Lieutenant Starke rode over. "It's all right, Sergeant," he told Cronk.

Starke dismounted beside Daugherty. The lieutenant's overcoat cape flapped in the wind. He held his hat down tightly. He had broad shoulders and narrow hips, and a horseman's slightly bowed legs. His curly blond hair was cut short, and he wore a moustache. To Cronk, he said, "Keep the men moving, Sergeant. We'll catch up."

"Very good, sir," Cronk said. He turned and shouted, "What are you people looking at? No one told you to stop. Keep moving."

Starke squatted beside Daugherty. He spoke quietly. "What is it, Corporal?" Before the war, Daugherty had been a pipe fitter, but work had been hard to find when he'd returned home, so he'd joined the Regular Army. Because of his previous military experience, he had been made acting corporal.

Daugherty looked up. His eyebrows were rimmed white. His cheeks were red from the stinging snow. There was a hopeless look in his eyes. "Me feet are froze, sir. They hurt something fierce. I can't take no more. Go on, leave me here to die."

When they'd broken camp that morning, Daugherty had wet his shoes in the stream to break them in, an old campaigner's trick. The shoes—and Daugherty's feet—had still been wet when the storm struck.

"Now, Corporal," Starke told him, "nobody's going to die. You can make it through this. It's just a little snow."

"Just a little snow," Daugherty muttered. "Faith, and Shiloh was just a little battle."

"Were you at Shiloh?" Starke said.

"Yes, sir, that I was."

"Then I'm surprised. A veteran like you, you're supposed to set an example for these men. What if they all decided to be like you, and gave up? You'd have their deaths on your hands. Would you want that?"

Daugherty said nothing.

"Of course you wouldn't," Starke told him.

"But me feet . . ."

"You're not the first man to have frostbitten feet, Corporal, and you won't be the last. Think of the others, if you don't want to think of yourself."

Daugherty hung his head. After a second he tried to rise.

"Good man," Starke told him. He helped the Irishman up. "After all, there's going to be an Indian war in the spring. It's the old sweats like you we'll be depending on."

"Yes, sir," Daugherty mumbled. He had bitten through his lip in pain. There was a frozen dribble of blood on his chin.

Starke considered letting Daugherty ride his horse, but walking—however cruel it seemed—would keep the Irishman's circulation going. If he rode, he'd freeze to death.

"All right, Corporal. Fall in."

"Yes, sir." Daugherty hobbled forward on his frozen feet.

Starke caught up to the column, walking alongside, leading his horse. "Keep moving, men. Before your enlistments are up, you'll see it a lot colder than this. I've been on the plains before. Wait till you've experienced a summer out here. You'll wish you had the cold back."

There were moans of disbelief. To Harry, going on seemed like postponing the inevitable. He fought down a sudden panic. Barker was right. They were all going to die. The intense cold was seductive. It would be so easy to give in to it. Harry knew that had he been alone, he would never have made it this far. It was only the example of the others that kept him going.

Up ahead, the wagon stopped. Sergeant Cronk halted the little column.

"Lost the road!" the teamster Pennington yelled back. His words were snatches on the howling wind.

Lieutenant Starke came up beside Cronk. "Night's comin' on, sir," the sergeant observed.

Starke nodded. "We won't make Fort Pierce today. We'll have to camp here. The temperature's falling faster than the value of Confederate bonds. These thin blankets will never keep the men alive through the night."

"No wood for a fire, sir."

"We'll burn the wagon."

Cronk grinned, showing big teeth. "Mr. Pennington won't like that."

The news was relayed to the tobacco-chewing teamster, who said, "I'm responsible for this here wagon, Lieutenant. I'll need some kind of authority, else Uncle Sam'll make me pay for it."

"Draw up the papers," Starke told him. "I'll sign them."

To Cronk, Starke said, "Sergeant, post your guard. Detail two men to take the axes from the wagon and break it up. Another two men to start the fire. Two more to butcher one of these mules. The men will have a hot meal tonight."

"Yes, sir," Cronk said.

"The guard will be in charge of the fire," Starke went on. "Tell them to use the wood sparingly. If the fire goes out before dawn, we'll freeze to death. I wish to be summoned each time the guard is relieved."

"Yes, sir."

Sergeant Cronk told off the guard. "Why do we have to stand guard?" complained a private named Walsh. "Indians ain't gonna attack us in this shit."

Cronk confronted him. "You'll stand guard because that's what we do in the army."

Walsh was a self-styled tough guy, big and beefy, with a chip on his shoulder. He had lied about his age to join up. He was only nineteen, but the army needed men, and the recruiters had passed him through. "Maybe I don't want to," he told the sergeant, with a smirk.

A blow from Cronk's fist sent Walsh onto his back in the snow. "You'll do as you're told," Cronk said.

Walsh got up. His narrow eyes burned with defiance. "I know the regulations," he said. "You ain't allowed to do that."

Cronk knocked him down again. "Do what? I didn't do anything. Did any of you men see me do anything?"

No one spoke.

"Of course you didn't. Why are you lying in the snow, Walsh? You'll catch your death of cold. Get up."

Walsh climbed to his feet once more, holding his jaw. This time he had nothing to say.

Under Cronk's sharp eye the novice soldiers hauled their canvas utility bags from the wagon. While two men chopped the wagon to pieces, two more broke up the splintered wood and splashed coal oil over it. Pennington watered and fed his mules, selecting the one to be butchered. A couple of ex-farm boys handled that job. When the wood was ready, Lieutenant Starke lit it from a box of sulfur matches, cupping his hands against the wind.

As darkness fell, the half-frozen men huddled around the fire, wrapped in their gray blankets, roasting mule steaks on the ends of sticks, while falling snow floated into the flames. Starke and Cronk had made the men remove their wet shoes and socks and bind their feet with layers of wool cut from their spare trousers.

Hungry as they were, Harry and some of the others were hesitant about eating roast mule. "Go ahead," Lieutenant Starke told them. "You'll get the habit of mule meat before your time's up. You'll think it's a treat." He munched his own happily.

Harry took a tentative bite. The meat was stringy, but it was hot and filling. Harry gnawed some more. Suddenly he found himself wolfing it down. A month ago he could not have imagined himself eating mule meat, much less liking it. He caught the juices on a square of hardtack, ate the hardtack, and washed it all down with hot coffee.

Then it was Harry's turn for guard. He walked around the camp, now and then adding wood to the fire. The icy wind whipped his face. Alone with his thoughts, he had plenty of time to reflect on how he'd gotten here . . .

"You'll never make it, Harry. You can't be a soldier. You don't have what it takes."

Harry could still hear his older brother, Ed, taunting him. All his life Harry had been in Ed's shadow. Ed was successful at everything—school, games, girls. Harry had never been successful at anything. He was ineffective, gangly, a dreamer. Unlike Ed, who had a future with their father's newspaper mapped out, Harry had no idea of a career. He could follow them into the newspaper business, maybe, but the thought hadn't really excited him.

What had excited him had been the life of a soldier. Since he was a child, Harry had been fired with a vision of glory and adventure, of bugle calls and splendid uniforms, of gallant charges against hordes of feathered Indians, who considerately allowed themselves to be killed.

When the Civil War had broken out, Ed had gone off to fight, and of course he had been a hero. Just as Harry had become old enough to join up, the war had ended. Ed had come home, and Harry had listened to his boasts, until finally he could take no more. He had decided to join the Regular Army. He had decided to stop dreaming and prove that he could do something on his own. Ed's goading had tipped him over the edge.

His parents had been horrified, but he'd already signed the papers when he told them. It had been too late to back out. His brother Ed had just laughed.

"You'll never make it, Harry. You can't be a soldier. You don't have what it takes."

"I *can* do it," Harry had sworn angrily. "I'll show you . . ."

When Harry's two-hour shift was over, he and his replacement were inspected by Lieutenant Starke. Then Harry was dismissed.

Harry lay down near the fire, beside Daugherty and Barker, both of whom were asleep. He wrapped himself in his blanket. Nearby, someone was snoring. Daugherty moaned softly.

Harry stared into the fire. He could almost pretend it was the parlor fire at home, on a cold winter's night. Yes, he thought, as his eyelids fluttered with sleep, it was as if he were back home, warm and safe and snug. . . .

2

Someone was shaking his shoulder. It must be his mother. He could almost smell her hot apple turnovers baking in the kitchen. Harry murmured with content and rolled over. He opened his eyes and stared into the unshaven face of Sergeant Cronk.

Cronk stood and spoke to Lieutenant Starke. "Here's another one still alive, sir. That's all of them."

It was barely dawn. Everything was seen in muted shades of gray. The snow had stopped, but the bottom had fallen out of the thermometer, and the whistling wind made it seem even colder. They were miles from anywhere. There was not a landmark in view on the horizonless plain.

Around Harry, men were struggling out of their frozen blankets. They flapped their arms and stamped their feet, trying to get warm. The teamster Pennington was building up the fire, melting a bucket of snow to make water for coffee.

"All right," Cronk rasped. "Off your butts. Inspection and roll call in five minutes."

With fingers stiff and clumsy from cold, the men unwrapped their feet. They put on their dried shoes and socks. They had slept with them under their coats, to keep them warm and supple. Kevin Daugherty's feet were so swollen that he could not lace his shoes. Harry and Barker helped him stand.

Harry said, "How are you making out, Kevin?"

Daugherty shrugged. Through gritted teeth he said, "I'll make it." Then he laughed. "Faith, I've no choice, have I?"

The men fell into a double line, shivering and grumbling. Their breaths were like crystalline ice on the frozen air.

"What do they need roll call for?" said an Irishman named Hennessy. "They know we're here. Where else could we go?"

Cronk walked down the line, muffled in overcoat, scarf, and gauntlets. "No talking in ranks! Straighten those lines. Arm's length apart. You, there"—he spoke to Barker—"square away that cap."

Under his breath Barker muttered to Harry, "Here we are, freezing to death, and all he can do is worry about my hat."

Cronk kicked Barker hard in the ankle. "Ow!" Barker yelled.

"I said, no talking!" Cronk told him. He faced the formation. "Squad—atten-tion!"

The men complied.

Cronk called the roll. Some of the men replied listlessly, some with spirit. When Cronk was done, he did an about-face in the snow and saluted Lieutenant Starke smartly. "Squad all present, sir."

Starke returned his salute. "Very good." The lieutenant was haggard but cool. If he was worried, he didn't show it. "How's the feet, Corporal Daugherty?"

Daugherty forced a grin. "Better, sir. Pain's gone. I can't feel them at all no more."

Starke and Cronk exchanged an apprehensive glance. Then Starke said, "Very well. Sergeant, dismiss the men for breakfast. We move out in thirty minutes."

"Yes, sir."

Starke saluted and walked off. Cronk turned to the men. "Squad—dismiss."

The men hurried to get something to eat. They fried the rest of the mule meat. They warmed their sock-covered hands on tin cups of boiling coffee. They wrapped the strips of wool from last night around the outsides of their shoes. There was ice on their eyelids, ice on their whiskers. Their noses and ears were frostbitten. Their teeth felt hollow from the cold, and the hot coffee made them hurt.

"Fall in. Prepare to move out."

The men poured the rest of the coffee down their throats and crammed the tin cups in their utility bags, with what was left of their extra clothing. They shouldered the bags and fell into a double line, many still chewing pieces of hardtack or meat.

The teamster Pennington, who, unlike the soldiers, wore a warm buffalo robe coat and heavy gauntlets, mounted one of his mules. He led the rest.

"Why can't we ride?" Hennessy grumbled.

"They don't want to strain the mules," said his friend Mack. "They're more valuable to the army than we are."

Cronk faced them, on horseback. "Squad," he bellowed, "atten-tion! Right—face. By twos, forward—march!"

The detail marched out, leaving behind the charred and smoldering remains of the wagon. The snow was calf deep, deeper where it had drifted. The bitter cold had frozen the crust, and the men had to punch their way through. It took all the effort they possessed, especially as they no longer had the heavy wagon to break a path for them. Harry was so cold that he wanted to cry. He would have given anything to get warm again.

"Close up there," Cronk said. "No straggling."

Once an hour Lieutenant Starke fired off three rounds from his hunting rifle, in case a relief party from the fort was searching for them.

Overhead, the clouds cleared away and the sun came out, though the temperature remained well below freezing. Around the little party was a wasteland of white. The sun's glare hurt the eyes.

The hours dropped away. The column's pace was agonizingly slow. Half the men no longer knew where they were, or why. "They won't last much longer, most of them," Sergeant Cronk told Starke.

The lieutenant nodded grimly.

Ahead of Harry, Daugherty stumbled, breathing deeply. Harry took Daugherty's utility bag. Then he and Barker each took Daugherty under one shoulder, and the three of them slogged on through the snow.

For the fifth or sixth time Lieutenant Starke fired his hunting rifle. The flat reports drifted over the plain.

Daugherty lifted his head weakly. "Listen . . . what's that?"

There was a distant popping sound.

"Gunshots," said Hennessy, and his voice grew excited. "Somebody's heard us!"

Mack shook his head. "Nah, it's just an echo."

"Not unless echoes shoot pistols," said Daugherty. "I developed an ear for firearms during the war."

There were three more of the distant shots. Suddenly revived, the men plunged on, helping each other through the snowdrifts.

Soon, a column of mounted figures appeared on the horizon.

"Soldiers," said Sergeant Cronk, shading his eyes with his hand.

"Did you hear that? We're saved!" The men began cheering with what strength they had left. Several were actually jumping up and down.

"Enough of that!" said Lieutenant Starke sharply. "You men are soldiers, and I expect you to act like it. When that relief party gets here, I want you lined up and squared away."

The men re-formed their line. Harry and Barker let go of Daugherty and shouldered their utility bags. The relief column consisted of an officer and a dozen men, along with two ambulances. The officer was a well-bred second lieutenant, boyishly handsome, with an expensive uniform. He saluted Starke as he rode up, then extended his hand.

"Tom Conroy, K Company."

"Jim Starke. Glad to see you."

"Captain Hayes—the post commander—thought this storm might have put you in difficulty. He sent us out to find you."

"I was hoping he would," Starke said.

The frozen recruits climbed into the ambulances. It was still cold, but at least there was some protection from the wind. They sat on the floors with their backs against the sides. Harry was between Barker and Daugherty. Daugherty stared blankly ahead; Barker fell into an exhausted sleep.

The ambulances and their escort started off. Harry looked out the back of the vehicle as they jolted across the snow, but there wasn't much to see. The view out the front was blocked by the driver. Harry loosened the grommets holding down the canvas cover. He lifted the cover and peered out the side. Across from him, Mack and Hennessy did the same.

"Flat, ain't it?" Mack said.

"It's that flat you could play billiards on it," Hennessy said.

On they went, across the endless expanse of white. Distant trees marked the Smoky Hill River. Then, away from the trees, Harry saw a flagpole and a low line of buildings.

"There's your new home, rookies," said the ambulance driver, looking back over his shoulder. "That's Fort Pierce."

3

Fort Pierce had been named for Brigadier General Benjamin H. Pierce, killed at the battle of Kennesaw Mountain. The post was home to one company of cavalry and one of infantry. Harry Winston had expected a fort like the kind he had seen in books—a palisade of sharpened logs, with loopholed blockhouses and guards walking the parapets. Instead, he found a group of low buildings grouped around a central parade ground, with a tall flagpole. There was no palisade, no entrenchments of any kind; the fort was defended by nothing but the vastness of the prairie. Most of the buildings were constructed of logs or frame. Some had canvas roofs. A few were made of limestone, and piles of that material showed that future construction was planned. A small stream ran by the fort. Across the stream, connected to the post by a bridge, was a shantytown. On this frigid day only a few people stirred on the town's narrow streets. Tendrils of smoke rose from tin chimneys.

The ambulances and their escort were passed through the fort's main gate by white-gloved guards. On the parade ground the infantry company drilled to the barking of sergeants. Soldiers and civilians came and went on various errands. A line of men moved through the stable area, picking up trash. Harry could smell the stables. He smelled baking bread.

The ambulances halted before post headquarters, a ramshackle frame building with a canvas roof. There, Conroy and Starke reported to the Officer of the Day, an infantry lieutenant named Gottfried.

To Starke, Lieutenant Gottfried said, "I'll have the orderly show you to your quarters. After that, report to the post commander, Captain Hayes. He's also C.O. of I Company, Third Infantry. The orderly will show you. Then you can see your company commander, Captain Bannerman. Don't be surprised if Bannerman's out of sorts, though—he's got a young son who's extremely ill."

"I'll remember that," Starke said. "Thanks."

To Cronk, Gottfried said, "Sergeant, take these men to the post hospital. I'll send for Dr. Dudley."

"Yes, sir," Cronk replied, saluting.

The cavalry escort returned to the stables, while Sergeant Cronk led the ambulances around the snowy parade ground, past the drilling infantrymen.

The ambulances drew up before the post hospital. A white-jacketed surgeon hurried up from Officers Row to meet them. He said, "Bring these men inside, Sergeant."

The men climbed from the ambulances and filed inside. The hospital was a low, log structure, with cots along the walls. Two sheet-iron stoves gave off what some might have considered heat. There was a strong smell of rubbing alcohol and lye soap. A few of the beds were occupied, and these men greeted the newcomers with jeers and catcalls.

"Raw meat!"

"Wait till Mr. Lo gets his hands on this bunch."

"Tell 'em you're queer, rookie. Get out now, while you still can."

"That's enough," the doctor said. "Or I'll take away your sick slips." He looked over the frostbitten recruits. "Line up. Strip down to your socks and drawers."

The new men did as they were told, while the sick soldiers watched and laughed. The recruits shivered in the drafty building. They edged close to the stove.

Dr. Dudley was a young man with a square jaw and fash-

ionably long sideburns, who had grown cynical and world
weary in his country's service. He came down the line. The
young tough Walsh was the first man. Dudley checked
Walsh's eyes. He tugged at Walsh's teeth. He tested Walsh's
limbs and thumped his chest.

"Hey, Doc," Walsh protested, "they already done this,
when I enlisted."

"Regulations," Dudley told him in a bored voice. "Open
wide." He peered into Walsh's mouth, wincing at the young
man's rancid breath. He examined the frostbite on Walsh's
cheeks and nose. "Wait here," he said.

Dr. Dudley went into his office, closing the door behind
him. He pulled a can of salve from his medicine cabinet,
along with a bottle of whiskey and some quinine powder. He
took a drink of the whiskey, wiping his mouth with the back
of his hand. He hated himself for doing this, but sometimes
his disgust with his job grew so overwhelming . . .

He recorked the bottle and went back outside with the
supplies.

Dr. Dudley put salve on the men's frostbitten extremities,
then taped gauze over them. He mixed the quinine with the
whiskey and gave each man a good dose. "Take this," he
told them. "You'll be good as new by tomorrow."

Dr. Dudley came to Daugherty. The Irishman grinned
awkwardly. He was in pain from his feet, hoping the doctor
wouldn't notice. "Sit on that table," Dudley told him.

With surgical scissors Dudley cut Daugherty's stiff wool
socks and pulled them off. The Irishman winced as the socks
ripped away skin where they had stuck to his feet. Then he
made a more worried face and he swore, "Oh, Jaysus."

His toes were turning black.

Harry's stomach turned at the sight. "How did this happen?" the doctor asked Daugherty.

Daugherty told him how he'd wet his shoes the morning
of the blizzard.

Dudley peered at the toes. He touched them gently. "Feel
that?"

"No, sir," said Daugherty hopefully.

"But there *is* pain?"

"Yessir. But it's sort of inside, like."

Dudley turned the feet over. He sighed and looked up at Daugherty.

Daugherty read the meaning in the doctor's eyes. He gulped. "I—I'm going to lose them, ain't I, Doc?"

"Yes," Dudley said. "Gangrene's set in."

"When will you do it?"

"As soon as possible—today—before the gangrene spreads." Dudley rubbed his tired eyes. "I'm afraid your military career will be a short one." He turned to his orderly. "Schmidt, prepare my instruments, please."

The orderly busied himself, laying out a small saw, sutures, and dressings. Daugherty watched with panicked eyes. "Faith, Doc, will ye give me a drink before ye start?"

"I'll give you as many as you like," Dudley said, handing him the bottle of whiskey. "There's more if you want it. Just be quick. I've got a sick baby to attend to. I can't afford to leave him for long."

Daugherty seemed to take the news better than Harry or Barker. Barker's jowly face was drawn and pale. Harry was shaking. While Daugherty drank, Harry stepped forward. "What'll happen to him, Doctor?"

Dudley was putting on his surgical apron. "We'll keep him here until he recovers, then send him back to Fort Hays with the first escort."

"I mean after that," Harry said.

"He'll get a pension, ten dollars a month."

"That's all?"

Dudley shrugged. "For losing his toes. If he lost his feet, he'd get fifteen."

"But he can't live on ten dollars a month," Harry said. "It's not fair."

Dudley turned to Harry, and for a moment there was sympathy on his cynical face. "Welcome to the Regular Army, son."

Harry went cold inside.

Just then a red-faced giant with enormous side-whiskers stuck his head into the hospital and bellowed, "What d'you mill birds think this is—a tea party? Get them bloody uniforms back on and fall out! *Jaldi! Jaldi!*"

4

With a quick wave to Daugherty, the men got dressed. They grabbed their utility bags and tumbled outside, buttoning their overcoats and forming up.

The beefy, red-faced man faced them. The man's bushy side-whiskers held a healthy dose of gray. In the crook of one arm he carried a short cane carved from some tropical wood. The other hand was tucked behind his back. On the sleeves of his immaculate overcoat were three chevrons with a diamond. His shoes and brass gleamed. Behind him, a corporal and a couple of privates lounged about, watching and grinning.

"I'd hate to be his horse," Hennessy muttered to his friend Mack.

The big sergeant heard the remark. He walked along the line, tucking his chin into his chest thoughtfully. He stopped in front of Hennessy. "We 'ave a comedian amongst us," he said with an English accent. "What's wrong, lad? The music 'alls wasn't 'iring, so you brought your act to the army?"

Hennessy stared ahead. He said nothing.

The sergeant turned. "Corporal Bannon."

A rangy corporal moved away from the other watchers. "Yeah, Top?"

"Bring one of them knapsacks, the ones filled wiv bricks."

Grinning, the corporal laid a bulging infantry knapsack at the sergeant's feet.

To Hennessy, the sergeant said softly, "Put it on, lad." Hennessy did.

"Now, double-time around the parade ground."

"One time, Sergeant?"

"Until you're told to stop."

Hennessy swallowed. He was still exhausted from the long march through the snow. He trotted off, the knapsack weighing him down. The big sergeant turned to the other recruits. "Anyone else 'ave a joke 'e'd like to share?"

No one did.

"Good," said the sergeant. "My name is Townsend. You may call me First Sergeant. Not Mr. Townsend, nor Lieutenant Townsend, nor General Townsend, but First Sergeant Townsend. I'm a soldier. I work for a living. Is that understood?"

The men shuffled and nodded their heads.

"Is it understood?" Townsend shouted.

"Yes," said the men.

Townsend shouted again, "Yes, what?"

"Yes, First Sergeant!" they shouted back.

"That's better," Townsend said. "Welcome to K Company, Fifth Cavalry. The commanding orficer is Captain Bannerman, but I run the company. You will not speak to an orficer unless you are addressed by one. If you wish to address an orficer, you will get my permission first. Is that understood?"

"Yes, First Sergeant!"

"Obey all orders promptly and courteously, keep your weapons and equipment clean, and we'll get along *achchi bat*. Don't, and I'll make yer wish you'd never been born. One more thing. You lads may 'ave noticed a civilian settlement outside this post. That settlement is known as Watsonville—'downtown,' to you. There are recreational facilities there, where you can gamble, drink intoxicating beverages, and catch the clap. You will not go downtown wivout a pass. Are there any questions?"

There were not.

Townsend drew himself up, his massive chest thrust outward. "Squad, atten-tion! Left—face. Forward—march! Left, left. Your left, right, left. Do it right, you bloody clowns, or I'll 'ave yer cleaning latrines wiv ye fingernails."

Behind them, Hennessy was still double-timing around the parade ground—though he was moving more slowly now—

under the watchful eye of Corporal Bannon. As the men marched off, they heard a scream from the direction of the hospital. The ex-grocer Barker whispered to Harry, "That's Daugherty."

Strange, Harry thought. A day before, he, Barker, and Daugherty had been best friends. Suddenly, their lives had been disconnected. Daugherty was faced with one future, Harry and Barker with another. In all likelihood, they would never know what happened to him, or he to them. Harry supposed that was life in the army.

Townsend led the recruits to the Quartermaster's store, one of the post's limestone structures. There, they were issued blankets, pillows, and mattress ticking. They were assigned to platoon barracks, then taken to the stables to fill their mattresses with straw. The straw was not fresh.

They made up their bunks, then were led back to the Quartermaster's, where they drew blue cotton carryall bags. Into the bags went dress jackets and white gloves, new trousers to replace the ones they'd cut up on the march, troop boots, carbine slings, cartridge boxes, cap boxes, sword belts, pistol holsters, ponchos, campaign hats, canteens, tin mess kits, field blankets, leather stocks, and brass shoulder scales. From the armory, next door, they drew sabers, pistols, and carbines.

Under this load they staggered back to the barracks, while Sergeant Townsend left to join the rest of the company, which was forming for evening parade. Off to one side of the parade ground, Hennessy was barely walking now.

Harry, Barker, Walsh, and an Italian named Squillace had been assigned to Sergeant Cronk's platoon. The platoon barracks was a long, narrow building, made of picket logs, with a shingle roof. There was the usual sheet-iron stove in the center of the room. A frame partition at the building's rear served as quarters for the sergeant. There was a double line of bunks, with lockers and shelves for uniforms. There were pegs with equipment hanging on them. The picket logs had been green when put up, and with time they had shrunk and grown warped. The chinking between them had fallen out, and strips of burlap had been nailed over the walls to help keep out the cold. The building smelled of wax and polish, of gun oil and linseed oil, of wet wool and unwashed men. A drum and bugles could be heard outside as the parade began.

There was one carbine in the wooden rack. It belonged to the barrack's lone occupant, who lay in his bunk, wrapped in blankets and looking bored. "Hi," he said, saluting the newcomers with his left hand. He was a pleasant-looking fellow, with an infectious smile. "I'm Tom Campbell, but everybody calls me Hunter. It's a long story why."

"Why ain't you on parade?" the young tough Walsh asked him.

"They won't let me on parade anymore. I embarrass them because I can't do the manual of arms." Hunter held up his stiff right hand. "I got shot in the hand last summer, and I've lost the use of it."

"Shouldn't they discharge you?" Harry said.

"Super Soldier says there's nothing wrong with me. He says I'm faking it."

"Who's Super Soldier?"

"Captain Bannerman, the C.O."

"That's awful," said Barker.

Hunter shrugged. "Typical army bullshit. The doc says I'm faking it, too. What it is, they don't want to give me a pension. If they can keep me here till my enlistment's up, they'll save the government some money."

"What do you do with one hand?" Barker said.

Hunter laughed. "Mostly, I pull barracks guard. Like now."

The newcomers dropped their gear on their bunks. Harry had been assigned to the First Squad, on the left side of the barracks. The other new men were in the Second Squad. They sorted through all the strange equipment and clothing, trying to figure out what to do with it.

Harry picked up his saber. Metal scraped as he slid it from its scabbard. He held it at arm's length and took a cut through the air. Never mind that the sword was made of cheap steel, poorly balanced. This was a cavalryman's weapon. For a minute all of Harry's youthful dreams became real.

There was a blast of frigid air as the door opened and the

rest of the platoon returned from parade. The men saw Harry and they stopped.

"Christ," said one of them, "look at this."

Self-consciously, Harry lowered the sword.

"Hey, rookie," said another. "I hope you don't think you're going to use that pig sticker on Mr. Lo."

"Sure he is," said a third. "We got us a real mad dog here."

Harry felt like an idiot as the men came into the barracks, taking off their dress uniforms. The first one down the aisle, a short, swarthy fellow with dark circles under his eyes, laughed. "Guess what, Jack? The mad dog's your new bunky."

The man who'd called Harry a mad dog made a face. He sauntered down the aisle and sat on the footlocker of the bunk next to Harry's. He was good-looking, slender, and dark-haired. Harry pegged him as a ladies' man. He spoke with a nasal, big-city accent. "I'm Jack Cassaday. I'm your bunky. That means that, in the field, we mess together, share a tent and blankets. We'll march in the same section of fours. In the meantime, I'm supposed to show you the ropes. Can you ride and shoot?"

Harry swallowed. "Not really."

"Well, I'd advise you to learn. If you don't, Mr. Lo will have your balls for breakfast."

"Who's this Mr. Lo everybody keeps talking about?" Harry said.

Jack looked surprised. "You know. 'Lo, the poor Indian.' It's a poem. By that guy Wordsworth, or Longworth . . ."

"Longfellow," volunteered the man with the dark circles under his eyes.

"Yeah, that's the guy. Thanks, Arab."

"Actually, it was Alexander Pope," said a fellow with a neatly trimmed beard.

"The Pope?" said the Arab. "I didn't know the Pope wrote poems."

"Not about Indians, anyway," said Hunter.

"If the Professor says it was the Pope, it must be the Pope," Jack assured them. To Harry, Jack said, "Just watch me, and try to learn. Here, I'll show you how to square away that gear."

"Thanks," Harry said.

"It's my job," Jack told him. "I'm only here in the first place 'cause the judge gave me a choice—this or jail. I'd have taken jail, but this gave me a chance to come west."

Because it was so cold in the barracks, many of the men kept on their overcoats. Some polished boots or brass. Others pulled footlockers around the stove and began playing cards. Bunkies helped the new men with their equipment. The bearded fellow called the Professor read a copy of the *Police Gazette*. No one had yet occupied the bunk on Harry's other side.

"Hey, Skull," said the crippled Hunter, "where's Link? I thought he was supposed to get out of the mill this morning."

"He had a stop to make," answered a man with a guttural foreign accent. Skull's large head was topped with close-cropped blond hair. His grin revealed big, widely spaced teeth and cadaverous cheeks.

As if in answer to Hunter's question, the door opened again and a deep voice said, "Guess who's coming to Fort Pierce, boys? The Hero of Atlanta. General Sherman himself."

"Bullshit," said a corporal. "Why would General Sherman come here?"

"He's touring all the posts in the district."

"They tell you this in the guardhouse?" the corporal asked him.

"Hayes and Gottfried were going on about it while I was there. They're happy as pigs in shit. Which is natural, since they're pigs, and the infantry is definitely shit."

That brought a laugh. The newcomer was older than the other men, most of whom were in their early twenties. He was tall and rawboned, with dark, curly hair. He had a tough, leathery look. On the sleeves of his light blue overcoat were dark patches, where there had once been stripes. He swaggered down the aisle between the bunks. When he came to the empty bunk next to Harry's, he stopped. He glared at Harry.

"What are you doing in Amassee's bunk?" he demanded, and Harry smelled whiskey on his breath.

"What do you mean?" Harry said.

"This bunk belonged to a soldier." The man kicked Harry's gear off the bunk and onto the floor.

Harry sat on the bunk. He didn't know what to do. Everyone was looking at him.

"Oh, oh," cried Skull. "You're messing with the Mad Dog now, Link."

"Pull your sword on him, Mad Dog," yelled someone else.

To Harry, the man called Link said, "Is that what they call you—Mad Dog?"

Harry said nothing.

"Dog Shit would be more like it," Link taunted.

The other men cried out with glee.

Harry wanted to sink into the floor. They were all laughing at him.

Jack spoke up. "Come on, Link. It ain't Mad Dog's fault he got Amassee's bunk. He's got to sleep somewhere."

"Let him sleep on the manure pile," Link said. "I don't want him around me."

"I don't know what you can do about it," Jack told him.

"Shit." Link shook his head in disgust. He went to the far end of the barracks, to join Skull and his friends.

Harry picked up his scattered gear. No one helped him. "Link's upset," Jack told him. "Amassee was his friend. He died last August."

"Indians get him?" Harry said.

"Measles."

Later, after the lights were out and the bugle had blown taps, Harry lay in his bunk, awake. He felt alone and friendless. The army was nothing like he had expected. He wished he had never joined.

Now that he was here, though, he was still determined to make it. He was determined to show his brother Ed, and the rest of his family, that he could be a soldier. He did not think things were going to get better, either, because without knowing how it had happened, he had made an enemy of this fellow Link. And Link seemed like the wrong person to have for an enemy.

5

It was late afternoon when Lieutenant James Starke arrived at company headquarters to present himself to the C.O. He had already reported to Captain Hayes, the infantryman commanding Fort Pierce, and had found him to be a stuffed shirt with a dislike for horse soldiers.

K Company's commander was Neal Bannerman. Starke had served under a Lieutenant Neal Bannerman years ago. It couldn't be the same man, he thought.

The company office was a frame shack with a nailed-down canvas roof. It was furnished with camp chairs and rude tables. A clerk in the first sergeant's office passed Starke through.

Captain Bannerman sat at a crude desk, writing reports, with a leather briefcase beside him. Starke's footsteps faltered as he entered the room, then he recovered and kept on.

It was the same man.

Bannerman looked up. He was handsome, heavy-browed and humorless, with wavy hair combed back from a low forehead, revealing a widow's peak. On Bannerman's shoulder straps were the eagles of a full colonel, his brevet rank. He had been waiting for this new lieutenant, and at first he was glad to see him. Then the pleasure faded and a flicker of recognition crossed his angular face.

Starke stopped in front of the desk and saluted. "James Starke, first lieutenant. Reporting for duty, as ordered, sir."

Bannerman did not return the salute right away. Starke held himself rigid while Bannerman studied him. On Bannerman's face recognition was followed by disbelief, shock, then outrage. Starke had a moustache now, and his curly blond hair was shorter than it had been eight years before, but there was no mistaking the man.

At last Bannerman returned the salute. "At ease, Lieutenant." Starke dropped his hand. He laid his orders on the captain's desk.

Bannerman scanned the orders, trying to get his thoughts together. He looked up again. "May I ask how you became an officer?"

Starke kept his eyes fixed on the far wall as he answered. "My enlistment was up right after the war started, sir. So I went home and joined one of the volunteer regiments. I was the only one in my company who knew anything about the army, so they made me first sergeant. One thing led to another, and I received a commission."

"Brevets?" Bannerman referred to the wartime system of temporary promotions above actual rank.

"Up to full colonel, sir."

Bannerman's jaw muscles worked. To think that this upstart had attained the same rank as he. "Did you serve in that rank?"

"Yes, sir. I commanded a regiment, the Seventh Ohio Cavalry."

"You don't wear your brevet rank." Officers were entitled to wear either their brevet or actual rank. Most, like Bannerman, wore brevet rank and were addressed by that title.

Starke replied matter-of-factly. "I'm not a colonel anymore, sir."

"And how did you get your appointment to the Regular Army?" Bannerman said. "A lot of men have tried for these vacancies. Men with better backgrounds than you. You must have made some influential friends."

"General Sheridan endorsed my application, sir. And General Merritt."

"I see." Bannerman tapped a thumb on his desk. At last he said, "This won't do, you know."

Starke said nothing.

Bannerman went on, "You will, of course, request a transfer."

Starke replied, "Begging your pardon, Captain, but I can't do that. A request like that—so soon after arriving at a new post—could ruin my career. It would make me look like a malcontent, or a troublemaker.''

"That's exactly what you are," Bannerman said, "a troublemaker. I will *not* have an officer under my command who was formerly one of my privates. I will *not* have you regarding myself or my wife as your social equals. Is that clear?''

Quietly, Starke said, "I won't request a transfer, sir."

"I can make life hell for you here."

Starke couldn't hold back a smile. "It'll be no different than what you always did."

Bannerman rose. He took a turn around the small room, hands locked behind his back. "I'll be honest with you, *Mister* Starke." God, but it hurt to put "Mister" in front of Starke's name. "I had a bad war. You'll hear the story anyway, so I may as well tell you. Like you, I resigned my commission and joined the volunteers. But I was stricken with typhoid fever before my regiment saw action. While convalescing, I was appointed to a staff position, in Rolla, Missouri. I performed my duties so well that I was kept on after I grew fit again. Despite my petitions, I was not given an active command. I spent the war shuttling between Rolla and Springfield. I was rewarded for my services, but not the way I might have been. At least half of my West Point classmates became generals. More importantly, they saw combat. My old roommate participated in over a hundred actions. I, on the other hand, never heard a shot fired in anger. Tell me, Starke, in how many actions did you participate?''

Starke shrugged. "Enough, sir. I didn't count them."

"You were fortunate."

"I didn't always think so at the time," Starke joked. Bannerman didn't laugh, and Starke changed the subject. "Might I ask about the military situation here, sir?''

For a moment Bannerman put aside personal animosities. His tone became businesslike. "The regiment was in the field all last summer, taking part in General Hancock's so-called Indian war. After that fiasco, K Company was assigned to Fort Pierce. Our job is to protect traffic on the Smoky Hill route. We provide escorts and patrol between Fort Wallace, in Kansas, and Fort Lyon, in Colorado. It's quiet now, but the Indians will start raiding when the grass comes up in the spring. We'll have our hands full then. Last summer our horses were run off so many times that we were sometimes lucky to mount a corporal's guard.''

Bannerman went on, ''You've fought Indians, Starke, you know what they're like. The red devils profess friendship if we meet them in force. But if our numbers are small, or we appear weak, they attack us. The company is authorized sixty-four men. The arrival of your replacements brings us close to that number for the first time in months. This year I've lost thirteen men—six to cholera, two to measles, one drowned.''

''That's only nine, sir. What about the other four?'' Starke said.

''Deserted.'' Bannerman pronounced the word distastefully. ''Three of them from one squad—Corporal Pickens's.''

''None killed by Indians?''

Bannerman shook his head. ''We had a few wounded, none seriously. One claims to have a crippled hand, but he's pretending. Last year—'sixty-six—we had three killed in action. To tell the truth, we don't usually get close enough to the Indians to fight them. They're a cowardly lot.''

''I seem to recall some of them being quite brave,'' Starke said.

''Then we have different recollections,'' Bannerman said curtly. He drew himself up. ''Now, if you'll excuse me, I have to finish these reports and return to my quarters. My son is ill.''

''Yes, sir. I heard. I hope he'll be all right.''

''Thank you. Dr. Dudley is doing the best he can. He says it's bilious fever. My wife is with the boy, as well. Mr. Conroy will take the company for evening parade. He'll fill you in on our day-to-day operations. You'll find the Regular Army hasn't changed much.''

''I didn't expect it to,'' Starke said.

''You'll likely be invited to Captain Hayes's quarters tonight. Mrs. Hayes likes to make a fuss over new officers. She's used to West Pointers, though. Lord knows what she'll make of you.''

''Yes, sir.''

"There will be no invitation to my quarters. Tonight, or ever."

"I understand, sir."

"I'm glad you do. Very well, then. I'll see you at roll call."

"Yes, sir."

Starke stepped back and saluted. Bannerman returned the salute. Starke did an about-face and marched out of the office.

Bannerman watched Starke go. He watched the broad shoulders, the confident stride. He watched, and he remembered . . .

It had been 1859, at the beginning of October, when the leaves were ablaze with gold and orange and red. Bannerman's company had been stationed at old Fort Kearny, on the Platte River, guarding the Overland Trail. Bannerman had been twenty-five, an officer with a promising future. He had just been made first lieutenant, after the company's previous first lieutenant died from fever, complicated by chronic drunkenness. The captain was on detached service, leaving Bannerman in command of the company.

A band of Brulé Sioux was camped about nine miles from the fort, under a chief called Flat Head. The Indians claimed to be peaceful, but Indians always claimed that. An emigrant train was camped at the fort itself. One of the emigrants, a dour Indiana preacher, had lost a cow several days before. The animal had grown weak on the trail, and the preacher had abandoned it.

When a second emigrant train arrived at the fort, one of its members claimed to have seen an Indian kill a white man's cow, skin it, and eat it. The preacher decided that the cow must have been his. He went to the post commander, demanding compensation for his animal. The C.O. and the Indian Agent thought the preacher a fool, asking compensation for an animal that he'd voluntarily abandoned, but the preacher raised such a stink that the C.O. ordered Bannerman to take a detail to the Sioux camp and look into the matter.

"Just ascertain the facts," the C.O. told Bannerman. "Don't do anything rash."

It was the kind of job Bannerman hungered for. He had his own views on how to treat Indians. He mounted thirty men and took along a six-pound artillery piece. They marched to the Sioux village, where Bannerman lined up his men, facing the camp, with the six-pounder in their center.

Alarmed Indians, including Chief Flat Head, rode out to see what was the matter. Bannerman spoke no Sioux and he'd neglected to bring an interpreter, but some of the Indians understood a bit of English. Bannerman demanded compensation for the dead cow. He further demanded that the chiefs hand over the cow's killer for prosecution. These thieving brutes understood nothing but force. He would teach them not to break the white man's law. He would make sure that it never happened again.

Flat Head and the other chiefs protested. The man who killed the cow had been a Minneconjou, they said. He was not in their camp. They offered to pay ten dollars for the cow, but they could not give up a man who wasn't there.

"I don't believe you," Bannerman told them.

"We speak true," Flat Head swore.

Bannerman pulled out his watch. "You have ten minutes to produce the cow's killer. Then I open fire."

He had the cannon loaded and aimed at the village, where there was great confusion and alarm. Desperate, the Indian chiefs offered to pay more for the dead cow. "Twenty-one dollars," Flat Head said. "It is all the white man's money we have. We will send to the Minneconjou, to see if the animal's killer may be found."

Bannerman looked at his watch. "Six minutes," he told the Indians.

The frightened chiefs wheeled their ponies and galloped away. Bannerman watched the ticking hands of his watch. When exactly ten minutes had passed, he raised his right arm. No one came from the Sioux village, which bustled with people trying to flee.

Bannerman dropped his arm. "Fire!" he told the grinning artillerists.

The cannon boomed. The six-pound shot crashed into an Indian tipi. There was dust, confusion, the screams of women and children and horses.

"Reload," Bannerman told the cannoneers. To his troops, he said, "Volley fire. Ready, aim, fire!"

The men fired their carbines into the village. There were more screams. Horses ran loose. The Indians were abandoning tipis, camp equipment, horses—all that they owned—in their panic to escape.

The cannon boomed again. The cannonball tore into a crowd of fleeing Indians, bowling some of them into a bloody pulp. "Mount!" Bannerman ordered his men. "Prepare to charge."

The soldiers scrambled onto their horses, drawing revolvers or sabers.

Bannerman waved his saber. "Charge!" he cried. "Don't let them get away!"

The thirty soldiers charged into the village. They caught the fleeing Indians from behind, sabering and shooting the laggards, mainly women and children. Bannerman caught an old man with a swing of his saber. The saber stuck in the back of the old man's head, and the hilt was jerked out of Bannerman's hand as the old man fell. Drawing his revolver, and searching for his next victim, Bannerman found himself wondering why the old man's head had not come off. Bannerman had practiced that maneuver with a straw dummy on the training ground a hundred times, and the head had always come off.

Then Bannerman saw what was happening, and he reined in. While the soldiers had been killing women and children, the Indian braves had taken to their horses and surrounded the hollow. They were firing guns and arrows at the soldiers. Bannerman saw one of his blue-jacketed men topple from his horse.

"Trumpeter," Bannerman cried. "Sound the rally."

Before the trumpeter could blow a dozen notes, he went down with an arrow in his throat. Other men and horses were being hit.

"Back to the hill," Bannerman shouted to his men. "We've done enough here."

Bannerman realized that the company had started retreating on its own. He tried to follow, and in the smoke and confusion he and the first sergeant were the last to leave the village. Then Bannerman's horse was hit and Bannerman was thrown to the ground.

Bannerman picked himself up, painfully. His cap was gone. He cocked his revolver and prepared to make a stand, to die like a soldier. Bullets and arrows whizzed around him.

The first sergeant dismounted. "Take my horse, sir," he said, saluting as though they were on the parade ground. "I'll stay."

Bannerman looked at him. The young officer and the aging veteran. It was like a changing of the guard. The old man had a fine sense of duty. Bannerman said, "Very well, Sergeant."

Bannerman took the sergeant's reins. Suddenly there were hoofbeats and a young private galloped up, leading a spare horse. Bannerman didn't know the private's name. He recognized him by his curly blond hair and cheerful, unconcerned disposition, even under fire.

The private reined in. "Here," he shouted. "Get on."

Bannerman and the sergeant exchanged glances. This was not the way the drama was supposed to play out.

"Get on!" the private repeated. It was an order.

Almost sheepishly, Bannerman and the sergeant obeyed. Bannerman led the party out of the hollow, while the private covered them with his revolver, firing at the Indians, who had been closing in.

The three men joined the rest of the company, who were digging in at the top of the hill. The Indians did not attack them. While the braves provided cover, the Indian village pulled up and moved away. The soldiers returned to the fort, carrying their wounded. The dead were picked up later— what was left of them.

Flat Head was later run down on the Powder River and killed by General Connor, but Bannerman never forgave the private, whose name was Starke. Starke had saved the first sergeant's life, but in doing that, he had violated the accepted order of things. More importantly, he had shown up Bannerman in front of the entire company.

Afterward, Bannerman never again felt that he had the respect of his men. He felt that his men—indeed, the entire garrison—were laughing at him behind his back. Fortunately, the war had come along soon after, and Bannerman had left those feelings behind him.

Until now . . .

6

Late that night, Captain Bannerman's son died.

It was just past three A.M. when Dr. Dudley looked up from the bedside. "It's all over," he told the boy's mother. "I'm sorry."

Dudley's cynical manner had disappeared. He could understand men dying, even get used to it—that was the army. But Tommy Bannerman had been a month short of his second birthday. No matter how many times Dudley saw children die out here, he couldn't get used to that. It didn't seem fair.

Helene Bannerman put her hands to her face. She caught her breath. She had known this moment was coming; still, the shock was overwhelming. Something inside her snapped, like cable twisted beyond the limits of its tension. Grief burst from deep within her. Her shrieks shattered the frigid night as she knelt beside her son's bed.

"Tommy! Tommy!" she cried, as if, by her very intensity, she could bring the small form back to life.

Her cries could be heard across the snowy parade ground, by the guards walking their rounds. They could be heard by the Officer of the Day, Lieutenant Gottfried, in the post Adjutant's office. They could be heard by Harry Winston, lying awake in his bunk, and by Jim Starke, in his quarters.

Helene's husband, Neal, was in the little four-room house with her. The wind whistled through chinks in the walls. It fluttered the flames in the fireplace. Captain Hayes's wife, Emily, was there, too. The Bannermans' black maid, Letty, hovered in the background. Neal came up behind his wife. She had loved that boy so much, he thought. He wanted to comfort her, but he did not know how. He was no good at emotional moments, and he was all too aware of his short-coming. He leaned down and pulled his wife away from Tommy's bed. She came reluctantly, still crying her dead son's name.

Neal turned her to him and held her in his arms. "There, there." He stroked the back of her head awkwardly. Her cries were almost hysterical.

"Tommy!"

Neal looked at Mrs. Hayes, who had turned the other way, helping Dr. Dudley with the body. Helene kept crying, and in a gruff voice Neal said, "Control yourself, dear. They can hear you all over the post."

"I don't care," Helene screamed, pulling away from him. "I don't care about them. I want my son back. I want Tommy. It's the army that's taken him from me. If it hadn't been for this place—these horrible conditions—he'd be alive now."

Neal tried to be patient. "He isn't coming back, Helene. You've got to control yourself. There's nothing anyone could do. I told you life at a frontier post wouldn't be easy."

"You never told me it would be like this. No milk, no proper food, no heat in the winter, not even a decent roof over your head when it rains. In the summer there's scorpions, centipedes, snakes, cockroaches so thick on the kitchen floor you think they're a carpet. The wonder is that any of us are still alive."

Neal tried to put his arms around her again. "Please, lower your voice, dear. I feel as badly about Tom's death as you do."

She struggled loose. "No, you don't! Get away from me! You only care about your career. Tommy's death doesn't af-fect your career, so it doesn't affect you."

Neal stiffened. "That's not true, Helene, and I resent you—"

Emily Hayes laid a hand on Neal's arm. "Let me," she said. Emily was forty, but she looked older. There was a generous helping of gray in her tightly pinned hair. Her face was pinched and severe. The intricate network of lines on her leathery skin betrayed the hardships she had suffered as an army wife.

Emily poured a glass of brandy and handed it to Helene. "Take this," she said.

Helene sipped the drink. She was shaking, and some of the brandy slopped over the sides of the glass and onto her hands. Her body was rent with shuddering sighs.

Emily led Helene aside. She said, "My dear, we all sympathize with you. Truly. None more than me. I've buried three of my own children on the frontier."

Helene looked at her with red-rimmed eyes. The Hayeses had a son at West Point, but Helene wasn't aware that there had been other children.

"It's true," Emily said. "Two girls and a boy."

"How . . . how did you live with it?"

"You learn, my dear. You learn. It's part of life in the army."

"But I'm not in the army," Helene protested bitterly.

"Oh, but you are. When you marry a soldier, you join the army as surely as he. Until you accept that fact, you'll never be happy."

"Are you happy?" Helene said.

Emily hesitated. "I'm at peace with myself. I can accept what's happened to me and my family. If I couldn't, I don't know what would become of me. You must do the same, my dear. The Good Man knows what's best for us. If He decides to take one of us from this earth, we must be reconciled, and not cry about it. You are an officer's wife. Like it or not, you must set an example. You've got to be 'army.' "

Helene put down the brandy and turned away. It took all her self-control not to cry out, not to howl with the pain that was tearing her apart.

She saw Letty, her maid, looking at her with teary eyes. Of all the people in the room, Helene felt closest to this black woman right now. Hesitantly, Letty came to where Helene stood. Helene reached out and buried her face on Letty's shoulder, while her husband and Emily Hayes watched, disapproving.

* * *

Tommy Bannerman was buried that afternoon. There was no sense in waiting longer. It was not a garrison, nor even a company, funeral. The child had not been a soldier. There was a small group of mourners.

A sudden thaw had set in, melting the snow and turning the ground behind the fort into a morass. The open grave had filled with muddy water, into which the burial detail lowered the small—the pitifully small—casket.

Helene knelt and laid a handful of dried sunflowers, saved from the previous summer, atop the coffin. Then clumps of mud were shoveled onto her son, onto her hopes and dreams. Onto her life. The mournful wind blew across the prairie.

Helene wanted to fall apart, but she had to stand stiffly while the mourners filed by with condolences. Emily Hayes hugged her and pecked her cheek. The post's officers came next, in their dress uniforms—frock coats, epaulettes, red sashes, white gloves and sabers. Most of them hurried through the formalities, not really knowing what to say, looking happy to get away. This was not a situation that made them feel comfortable. Only the new lieutenant, Mr. Starke, seemed genuinely sensitive to her plight. There was something in his voice—in his eyes—that was different from the others.

"I can't imagine what you must be going through, Mrs. Bannerman," he said, "but you have my deepest sympathy. Please, if there's anything I can do, don't hesitate to ask."

"Thank you," Helene replied. Next to her, Neal stiffened. Neal didn't like Lieutenant Starke, though Helene had no idea why.

First Sergeant Townsend represented the company. He marched up to Helene and stamped to attention, removing his forage cap and snapping it under one arm. The wind blew his thin hair across his head. With his right hand he presented Helene with something. "From the men, ma'am."

It was a tintype of Tommy, mounted in a silver frame. The men must have gotten the photograph from Neal. They must have subscribed the money and purchased the frame in town. On the back of the frame were etched crossed sabers with the company's insignia, "K-5." Below that was an inscription: ALWAYS IN OUR HEARTS.

Helene sniffed. "Th—Thank you," she said.

"Yes, ma'am." Townsend replaced his forage cap and stepped away.

Next came the post sutler, Jordan, and a few other civilians. Last was Letty, who took Helene's hands in her own and squeezed. The two women looked into each other's eyes, then Letty dropped her gaze and moved off.

It was time to go. How Helene made it back to her quarters, she didn't know. Her husband steadied one arm, while, with her other hand, she lifted her skirts out of the glutinous mud.

At last Neal led her through the front door of their quarters. The two of them sat in the cramped parlor, darkening in the late November afternoon. It seemed unnaturally quiet without the cries and laughter of their son. The only sound was the ticking of the mantelpiece clock. Neal looked stiff and uncomfortable, and at last Helene said, "If you have business at the company . . . ?"

"Yes," he said, "there are some things that need attending to. You're sure you don't mind?"

Helene shook her head.

He rose, grateful for the chance to get away. He didn't want to be around his wife and her embarrassing emotions right now. He changed into his garrison uniform and went out, leaving her alone.

Helene sat by herself for a minute, then she rose. To her maid, she said, "Letty, get me a drink."

Letty looked concerned. "It ain't like you to have a drink so early in the day, ma'am."

"It is now," Helene told her.

7

"Formation!"

Harry Winston had been taking a nap after fatigue detail. He sprang from his bunk and raced for the door.

Something caught him by the foot and brought him up short. He slammed head first into the floor. He saw stars. Pain shot through his head.

Around him there was convulsed laughter—with Link Hayward's mocking tones the most prominent—as the rest of the platoon filed out the door.

Harry sat up groggily. Corporal Bannon said, "Formation, Winston. Get your ass outside."

Harry looked at his foot. Somebody had tied his shoelace to the bedpost while he'd been sleeping with his legs dangled over the side of the bunk. He ripped the lace free and staggered out the door, trying to ignore the pain in his head. There was no time to tie the shoe.

The rest of the company was already formed up. Harry fell in beside his bunky, Jack Cassaday. Everybody was snickering at him.

Harry felt his forehead, where a large bump was already rising.

"How's the head?" Jack said.

"I'll be all right," Harry replied. "I guess I don't have to ask whose idea it was to tie my shoelace to the bed."

"*Roko* that bloody larfing," Sergeant Townsend bellowed at the men. "Tie that shoe, Winston, and be quick about it."

Harry bent down and tied the shoe. He was getting used to this. On his first day of mounted drill someone, undoubtedly Link, had shortened his stirrups, with the result that he had not been able to seat his mount properly and had been

38

thrown on his head. The first time Harry had been listed for stable police, Link had told him to report to the first sergeant for a star and truncheon. That had earned Harry a few laps around the parade ground with the brick-filled haversack. The worst trick Link and his friends had played on him was when they'd told him to go downtown and draw the company pork ration from the hog ranch. They'd told him he didn't need a pass. He'd been halted by the guard at the main gate, and when the guard had stopped laughing, he had put Harry under arrest. That had led to more laps around the parade ground with the haversack.

Harry finished with his shoe and stood. Sergeant Townsend looked the company over, while Lieutenants Starke and Conroy watched in the background. Townsend barked, "Company, at—ease!"

The men assumed the position.

Townsend said, "There'll be no company drill today, lads."

"Surprise, surprise," Cassaday muttered.

"We're 'aving work detail instead," Townsend went on. "Squads Three through Six will continue construction on the Orficers Club." Building the club was what all the limestone blocks had been for. "As you know, General Sherman will be visiting this post in a few weeks. Captain 'ayes thinks the post should look more military. Therefore, Squads One and Two will collect rocks from the creek bed. You will white-wash these rocks and line the company street and barracks entrances wiv them. You will also place a circle of them around the flagpole."

There was a muted groan.

"Sergeant Cronk will march you to the Quartermaster's stables to pick up your transport. Company, atten-tion!"

The day was gray and raw. The creek bottom was full of water from melted snow, so the men combed the sides of the creek and the neighboring ravines for rocks of the proper size and weight. When they couldn't find enough, they plucked more from the freezing water. They collected the rocks in wheelbarrows, then deposited them in their wagons. There was a detail from the infantry company gathering rocks, too; and when the sergeants weren't looking, the two details chucked rocks at one another.

Harry's head throbbed from his fall. "This is stupid," he said. "I didn't join the army to pick up rocks. I've only had two days of riding drill since I've been here. I've never even learned how to fire my weapons. If there's an Indian war coming in the spring, why don't they get us ready for it?"

"Welcome to the Government Workshop," said the bearded Professor, whose real name was Miles Woodruff. In civilian life he had been a dentist.

Harry went on, "When we're not doing this, we work on the Officers Club. *We* live in shacks, and all they care about is having a nice warm club for the officers."

One of the squad members laughed. He was a stocky, balding fellow who had joined the army when his business failed. His name was Hudnutt, but everyone called him Numb Nuts. "Listen to him complain. You sound like a twenty-year vet, Mad Dog."

"General Sherman and his staff won't be happy if there's no Officers Club," the swarthy Arab explained to Harry.

When the men had loaded the wagon, they took the rocks back to the barracks. They sat out front, painting the rocks from pots of whitewash. Harry was in a group with Jack, the Professor, Numb Nuts, and a sad-eyed ex-Confederate named Pick Forrester. As Harry set aside a freshly painted rock to dry, Link Hayward strolled by and kicked it into the mud.

Harry rose from his seat in anger. He started to say something, then stopped himself.

"You got a complaint?" Link said with a smirk.

Harry made no reply.

"Huh?" Link said. He pushed Harry's shoulders. "Come on, rookie. What are you going to do about it?"

Harry fumed, humiliated. Then Link noticed Sergeant Cronk looking at them. Link smiled at Harry. He spat on the toe of Harry's shoe and walked away.

Jack Cassaday said, "Link wants you to fight him."

"I enlisted to fight Indians," Harry said, "not my own men. What's he got against me?"

"He doesn't think you've got what it takes to be a soldier."

Just like my brother, Harry thought. "What do you think?" he asked Jack.

Jack shrugged. "I think we'll find out when the time comes."

Harry glanced across the company area to where Link now sat, pretending to work while he yarned with Skull, the crippled soldier Hunter, and some others. "Look at him. He's not doing a thing. Why do Cronk and Bannon let him get away with that?"

Jack said, "Link used to be platoon sergeant. He's the best soldier in the outfit."

"What'd he get busted for?" Harry said.

"Drunkenness, insubordination, fighting—the same things he always gets busted for."

"He's been busted more than once?"

The other men laughed. Numb Nuts said, "Nobody knows how many times. He's been in the army since before the war. He was with this regiment in Texas, back when it was still the Second Cavalry and Robert E. Lee was the colonel."

Pick Forrester, the ex-Confederate, chuckled. "Marse Robert probably busted him, too."

When the first batch of rocks was ready, Harry and Pick loaded them in the barrow and wheeled them out to the center of the parade ground. They began laying them around the flagpole, exactly one foot apart. They measured the distance with a tape. They had just gotten started when they became aware of a commotion at the main guard post. Suddenly the trumpeter sounded Recall from Fatigue.

From the company area Sergeant Cronk shouted, "You heard it! Fall in, in front of the barracks."

Pick and Harry left the barrow and the painted stones. They ran for the barracks and fell in with the rest of the company. Lieutenant Conroy galloped over on his horse. Conroy's youthful face was anxious. To Sergeant Townsend he said, "Captain Bannerman wants the company armed and mounted, Sergeant. Issue ammunition, and fall them in on the parade ground. Don't do anything else until you get the order."

"Might I ask the lieutenant what the problem is, sir?" Townsend said calmly.

"The mounted pickets report a band of Indians setting up camp downstream from here. Their leaders are riding toward the fort."

8

The small party of Indians halted about a half mile from the fort. Four officers rode out to meet them, along with a guidon bearer, the orderly trumpeter, and the post scout, a Harvard-educated squaw man named John Smith. The officers were Captain Bannerman and Lieutenant Starke of the cavalry, along with Captain Hayes and Lieutenant McBride of the infantry. Behind them, out of sight, the remaining lieutenants held the fort's two companies of soldiers, armed and ready for action.

There were eight Indians. One, the leader, carried a scrap of white cloth tied to a feathered coup stick. They all looked to be without weapons.

"What do you make of them?" Captain Hayes asked the buckskinned scout. Hayes was short and pompous, with heavily pomaded black hair and flowing moustache. Both in looks and in temperament, he reminded many people of General McClellan—a comparison that he did little to discourage.

"They're Cheyenne," answered John Smith. "Southern, by their look." Then he drew in his breath. "By God, that's Chief Storm in front, if I'm not mistaken. Yes, and there's Man Above the Clouds, and Crooked Neck, too."

The officers knew those names. "Bad Injuns," said Lieutenant McBride, with a low whistle. McBride was an ascetic teetotaler who spent his spare time working on a translation of Virgil's *Aeneid*.

"As bad as they come," agreed the squaw man, "if they're

of a mind to be. But you see that boy in the back? That's Storm's son, White Wolf. Storm wouldn't have brought his son along if he was planning trouble."

The two sides halted about ten yards apart. White and Indian horses nickered at unfamiliar smells. Their breaths turned to vapor in the chill air. The cavalry guidon snapped in the breeze. Both sides were tense. More than one such meeting had ended with hidden weapons drawn and blood spilled. At a signal from Hayes, the trumpeter was ready to summon the waiting men from the fort.

The five oldest Indians were in front. Three younger ones were to the rear, where they might watch the proceedings but not take part. The Indians' leader was a man of middle age, powerfully built, with a prominent nose. His handsome face showed great force of character. His paint pony was strong and intelligent-looking, like its master. The Indian wore a hair-pipe breastplate and a neck choker of the same material. His deerskin shirt was decorated with fringes and porcupine quills, and worn over red leggings. His long braids were wrapped in otter fur. There was a bear claw in his scalp lock, which meant that at some time he had fought and killed a bear, single-handed. Like most Indians, he had plucked out all his facial hair, including his eyebrows and lashes.

"Which of you is chief of the white soldiers?" he asked, in surprisingly good English.

Hayes stiffened in the saddle. "I am Colonel Warren Sumner Hayes, commander at Fort Pierce." He introduced the other officers, who nodded or saluted.

"I am called Storm," said the Indian. "Formerly war chief of the Kit Fox Soldiers, now leader of the Hair Rope Band of the Cheyenne." He indicated the warriors around him. "This is Bear on the Ridge, Crooked Neck, Red Eagle, and Man Above the Clouds." The four men stared ahead impassively. Behind Storm, his son White Wolf and the two others did their best to hear what was being said, without appearing to do so.

Storm said, "We have come to the white man's fort for protection. The treaty signed on Medicine Lodge Creek between your people and mine says that you must feed us. We will camp here for the winter, then go and live on the new

reservation, south of the river you call Arkansas, as we have
promised to do.''

The officers looked at each other in surprise. They had not
been expecting this. Suspicion was plain in Hayes's voice.
''You and your band have been notorious for not agreeing to
the white man's treaties, Chief Storm. You refused even to
attend the Medicine Lodge conference. Why the change of
heart?''

Storm went on, ''The old way of life, the free way, has
ended for us. We see that clearly now. We must travel the
white man's road. The white man is strong. I do not wish for
my son to live like a hunted animal. I do not wish him to die
in useless war. We have been defeated. We want no more
attacks on our villages, such as the one at Sand Creek, or the
one your General Hancock made upon us at Pawnee Creek.
Wherever we go, the white men shoot at us. The buffalo,
which gives us life, is disappearing. The land itself disap-
pears beneath the white man's iron road and his villages. Our
horses are tired and hungry. There is no place that we are
safe. So we come to you.''

Storm waited for the soldier chief to reply. Storm could
have told the soldiers about the old Cheyenne prophecy that
their people would be destroyed by a race of men with white
skins and hairy faces. But he did not. It had been hard for
him to come here, hard to give up the old life. If he had not
felt that he owed it to his people and, especially, to his son,
he would not have done it. He hoped that their new, settled
life would not be bad. And perhaps it would not. Tradition
said that long ago, in the time before horses, the People had
lived near the great water to the east, in permanent villages,
where they had cultivated the land. Storm could remember a
village of earthen lodges along Porcupine Creek, where his
band had lived part of each year when he was a boy, and
where they had raised corn and tobacco.

At last the soldier chief spoke. ''Where will you make
your camp?''

''On the bottom land, in the big loop of the stream. There
is wood there for our fires. We will disturb no one. We must
have food, though. The hunting has not been good, and our
ponies get little grass because of the early snow.''

"Very well," Hayes reluctantly agreed. "You may camp there. Our peoples will have peace, as the treaty says. Lieutenant McBride is our Quartermaster. He will bring your food."

Storm said, "We will put up our lodges. Then you will come, and we will smoke."

"Er, yes," Hayes said. "I look forward to it."

Storm saluted the officers with his coup stick. He spoke to the other Indians, then they all turned and rode off.

The officers watched them go.

"Well, gentlemen, here's another headache for Christmas," Hayes said. "First Sherman coming, now this. I don't know if we have enough rations to feed our own men this winter, now we're supposed to feed a bunch of savages, as well." He turned. "Mr. McBride."

"Sir?" said McBride.

"You'll take them some of that old salt pork—the casks marked from before the war. Some of that condemned flour, too. Let them have those old Jeff Davis hats, and the surplus blankets. Save us the trouble of burning them."

"Yes, sir," said McBride.

Captain Bannerman spoke up. "Colonel Hayes, my men are mounted and ready. Let us attack the Indians. This would be the perfect time. We couldn't fail to win a glorious victory. You heard Storm—their ponies are weak right now."

"The Indians *are* here under a flag of truce, sir," Lieutenant Starke pointed out.

Bannerman dismissed Starke's protest. "A flag of truce means nothing to them."

"Perhaps not, sir, but it should mean something to us."

Bannerman turned. "I dislike being told my duty by junior officers, especially those who do not know their place. You have been out here before, sir. You should know better than anyone that these redskins will only be peaceful until the grass comes up in the spring. Then their treaty with us will be forgotten, and they'll be off again, killing and raping. And they demand that we feed them in the meantime. It's the height of arrogance, matched only by the government's stupidity for agreeing to it. What will the savages want next? Our horses? They got enough of those earlier this year. You'll no doubt find a number of them in this fellow Storm's village at this very moment, right under our noses, waiting for government grain to feed them.''

Captain Hayes intervened. ''Much as I hate to say it, Colonel Bannerman, Mr. Starke is right about the flag of truce. It might look bad if we attacked now and word of how it happened got out. You remember how the newspapers crucified poor Chivington and his men for what they did at Sand Creek.''

Hayes was also reluctant to order an attack for which Bannerman and his men would get all the credit, but he didn't mention that. Beneath his flowing black moustache, he smiled. ''We'll let Storm and his friends stay. For now. They're bound to make a wrong move eventually. When they do, we'll be ready for them.''

9

On Christmas Day, Fort Pierce was shut down, save for the unfortunate few—like Harry Winston—who had to pull guard duty.

Normally, the men of K Company planned a big jollification for Christmas. This year their celebration had been scaled down. They hadn't been paid in two months, and most of them had no money. There was enough in the company funds to buy nuts, raisins, plum puddings, canned fruits and vegetables from the sutler's. The company's best hunters— Link Hayward and his friend Skull—provided turkeys and deer. This was a welcome change from the diet of beef, bread, and coffee that the men faced day after day. There hadn't been any money left for liquor, until the sergeants contributed several bottles of whiskey for the company punch. The sergeants themselves were having a separate celebration. In the absence of a sergeants' mess, they were at the sutler's—along with the post laundresses.

K Company's mess hall had been decorated with colored paper wreaths and balls. The men had wanted a tree, but there wasn't a pine within two hundred miles. It was bitterly cold outside, with a dusting of snow. The wood-burning stoves did little to warm the mess hall, and most of the men wore their overcoats. Beneath these the veterans wore the tailored white stable jackets that, in K Company, replaced blue jackets for special off-duty occasions. Only veterans were allowed to wear the white jackets.

The men sat around the long mess tables, eating and drinking. There was a low stakes poker game near the stoves. Only a few inveterate gamblers, like Jack Cassaday, had money left for cards.

Army custom decreed that officers spend time with their men on Christmas Day. Captain Bannerman arrived just after noon, with Lieutenant Conroy. The mess hall quieted as they came in. Bannerman and Conroy looked ill at ease, as did the men. Cassaday and the other gamblers hid their cards— regulations forbade gambling on government property.

The two officers carried wheels of cheese, which they placed on the mess table as presents. "Merry Christmas, men," said Bannerman. It was more of a formal statement than a greeting.

For a second no one replied, then Hunter raised a tin cup with his good left hand. "Same to you, sir, I'm sure."

That drew a big laugh, and Bannerman had to bite back an angry reply. He hadn't come here to have his dignity tweaked by a shirker.

"Cup of punch, Captain?" It was Dutch Hartz, a Swiss immigrant who was acting as mess steward. "Lieutenant Conroy?"

"Yes. Thank you," said Bannerman.

Conroy nodded. "Please."

Hartz gave each of them a half cup of the whiskey punch, which had been made with the juices from the canned fruits. The officers sipped the punch, pretending to like it.

"Cold out, sir," remarked the swarthy, dark-eyed Arab.

The Arab's real name was George Jett. He had been an accountant before joining the army.

"Yes," said Bannerman. "It is."

"Very," added Conroy.

Bannerman stole a glance at his watch.

The two officers stayed until they thought a decent interval had passed, about half an hour. By then the company celebration had become muted. There was little conversation. "More punch, sir?" ventured Hartz.

"No, thank you," Bannerman said. He put down his cup and stood.

Conroy followed his example.

Bannerman said, "Well. We'd better be off. Continue your party, men."

"Thank you for coming, sir," said Corporal Bannon.

"You're welcome," Bannerman replied. He raised a hand in awkward farewell. "Merry Christmas."

"Merry Christmas, sir," answered a less than enthusiastic chorus.

"Merry Christmas," repeated Lieutenant Conroy, to the same response.

The two officers left the mess hall. Outside, they stood in the brilliant, cold sunshine, looking relieved.

"Thank God that's over," Bannerman said. "I'm going back to my quarters. I expect you're headed for the Club?" The Officers Club had been completed just in time for the holidays.

"Yes, sir," said Conroy. "We're having quite a feast. Turkey and all the trimmings. Champagne and port by the bucket. Havana cigars." Conroy had an independent source of funds. He had helped pay for much of the feast.

Bannerman was envious. "I'll drop by as soon as I'm able." Christmas at home wasn't the same anymore, without his son Tom. His quarters had become a cavern of gloom. He hated to be there, faced with Helene and her recriminating looks. And Helene was just as happy to be left alone—with her bottle.

The two men began walking across the parade ground, toward Officers Row. "How is Mrs. Bannerman?" said Lieutenant Conroy.

"Getting better all the time," the captain lied.

"Will she be coming to the Club?"

"I doubt it."

"Wish her Happy Christmas for me, then."

"Thank you, Conroy. I will."

K Company's mess hall had grown noisy again. Third and Fourth Platoons were having a biscuit fight, while the others cheered them on. Suddenly the front door opened and Lieutenant Starke appeared. In Starke's mouth was a big cigar; in his arms were eight quarts of whiskey. "Merry Christmas, boys," he shouted.

The men saw the whiskey. "Merry Christmas, sir!" they shouted back.

Starke made his way carefully across the biscuit-strewn floor, depositing his precious burden by the punch bowl.

"Maryland rye," said the crippled Hunter, holding up one of the bottles and reading the label. "This ain't no Injun whiskey. This is the real stuff. Thank you, sir."

Starke winked at him. "Just make sure I get a drink." He hadn't had cash to buy the whiskey, so he'd pledged next month's pay for it at the sutler's. He looked around the room. "Where's the poker game?"

Grinning, Cassaday removed the cards from his white jacket. "Over here, sir."

Starke laughed. "Can't wait to steal my money, eh?" He was in high spirits. This was his first chance to celebrate the holiday. There had been a gala "hop" last night at the Hayes's quarters, but he hadn't been invited. He hadn't expected to be. Old Mrs. Hayes had nearly died when she'd learned he was up from the ranks. ("And him so nice-looking, too," she had lamented.)

Starke sat with the card players. A large group gathered around to watch. Besides Cassaday and Starke at the table, there were Corporal Ware from Third Platoon, Quince the company tailor, "Sad Sam" Hotchkiss, and a Russian named Steroverovka. Nobody could pronounce the Russian's name, so they called him "Starving Mike." Mike claimed to be descended from a long line of czarist army officers. He said he'd left home because of trouble over a woman, and he hoped to win a commission in America. He was sent money from overseas. He smoked cigarettes from an ivory holder.

"Stud or draw?" Starke asked, putting some coins on the table.

"Draw, sir," said Cassaday.

"Deal 'em out."

Dutch Hartz handed Starke some punch. Starke took a drink and pushed his forage cap back on his head. "Christmas in the barracks hasn't changed much. In my day, we played faro instead of poker. That's the only difference I can see." He rubbed his hands together. "It's cold in here. Don't they give you men any heat?"

"Yes, sir," said Link Hayward. "In the summer, they give us all we want." Everybody laughed.

Starke played skillfully, winning more than his share of hands. He drank, smoked his cigar, and yarned about the old days, before the war.

From the group watching the game, Corporal "Slim" Pickens said, "Sir, do you play baseball?"

"A bit," Starke said.

"Maybe you could be on the company team. Corporal Bannon's the captain."

"And star pitcher," Bannon reminded him.

Starke said, "Are officers allowed to join?"

"Yes, sir," said Bannon emphatically. He slugged down a cup of punch. "God, I can't wait to get started again. You should've seen us last season, sir. Regimental champions, we was. We played the other companies when the regiment was camped together at Fort Hays, and we beat 'em all. On Sundays here we play teams from town, or those road mashers from I Company."

Corporal Pickens said, "What position do you play, sir?"

"Most any," Starke said.

Bannon said, "We need a center fielder. We had a fellow named Amassee who played there, but he's gone now."

The card game wore on. The noise level in the mess hall rose, commensurate with the amount of whiskey consumed. Some of the men, led by Dutch Hartz, began singing Christmas songs. Jim Starke felt at home here, in a way he hadn't felt at home in a long time. He didn't belong here anymore, though, and he knew better than to overstay his welcome. He was way ahead in winnings, but he couldn't leave with the men's money. They only made sixteen dollars a month—and Congress was talking about reducing that amount—It would be like stealing from them. So Starke contrived to start losing. When he was in the hole about ten dollars—all he could afford to lose on his own salary—he tossed in his cards.

"That's it for me, boys. You've skinned me." He paused. "Like I said, nothing's changed."

The men around the table laughed. Starke stood and began buttoning his overcoat.

Corporal Pickens said, "Sure you won't stay, sir?"

"I'd like to, but there's other places I have to go." He left the mess hall with a wave of the hand. "Thanks for a good time, boys. Merry Christmas."

"Merry Christmas, Lieutenant," they all shouted back.

Outside, Starke paused. He straightened his overcoat and cap. The winter sun was well down; long shadows crept across the icy parade ground. Starke took a deep breath. He could go to the Officers Club, but why bother? He wasn't wanted there. No one would have anything to do with him.

He took a long walk around the parade ground, to clear his head of the whiskey, then he returned to his quarters.

In the barracks and mess hall the party went on well into the night. Later, when the other men were asleep, a tall figure rose from the gloom of First Platoon's barracks. The figure dressed swiftly and left the building. He sneaked around the parade ground, keeping to the shadows so that he wouldn't be seen. Unwittingly, he passed by one of the guards, who had deserted his post to stand in a cranny of the Quartermaster's store, where he could get out of the frigid wind.

The guard was Harry, who recognized the tall form of Link Hayward as Link stole by. Link kept going, off the post, on his way downtown, where the lights still burned bright.

Though no one was allowed off post, Harry made no effort to stop Link. He was afraid of Link. The last thing he wanted to do was to challenge him or turn him in for arrest. Besides, Harry didn't care. He was angry and feeling sorry for himself. Here it was, Christmas night, and he was walking around a bunch of empty shacks, freezing his ass off, a thousand miles from nowhere. It was all so *stupid*. Chief Storm and the entire Cheyenne nation could attack tonight, Harry told himself, and he wouldn't open his mouth in warning.

Later, after Harry had been relieved and was back in the guardhouse, he told the sad-eyed ex-rebel, Pick Forrester, what he'd seen. He spoke in low tones so that the sergeant of the guard, Cronk, wouldn't hear.

Pick nodded, smoking his corncob pipe. "He goes down there all the time. He's got him a girl at one of the hog ranches, name of Lou. She follers him from post to post. She's got a kid, they say it's Link's."

"Does he ever get caught?"

"All the time. Don't seem to bother him none, though. He does his time in the mill, then goes right on back."

The two men rested on the hard wooden benches which were provided for the guards. Harry wrapped himself in his overcoat, glad of the bit of warmth that the guardhouse provided.

Next to him, Pick knocked out his pipe and laid down. "Good night, Mad Dog. Merry Christmas."

"Merry Christmas, Pick."

10

On Christmas, officers visited their men. On New Year's, tradition called for them to visit each other. It was a day marked by frivolity and high spirits.

It was early afternoon. Jim Starke sat alone in the two-room shack that served as his quarters. Outside he could hear footsteps, laughter, and friendly greetings on Officers Row, but the sounds never paused by his door.

Starke sat on a camp chair. He wore a waist-length blue

jacket with gilt buttons, matching vest, white shirt, and black bow tie—officers were allowed to vary their undress uniform pretty much as they pleased. Starke had bought the outfit in St. Louis earlier that year, right after he'd returned to duty, but he'd had little chance to wear it. Old gunnysacks served as rugs on the floor of his quarters. Overturned crates did duty as chairs. Another crate was used as a sideboard. On it was a bottle of champagne, nestled in a bucket of ice from the stream. There were also bottles of bourbon, rum, and scotch, along with glasses and cigars laid out in a neat row. None of them had been touched.

Starke sat stiffly in the chair, now and then sipping from a glass of scotch. He was reading *Martin Chuzzlewit*, by Dickens. He didn't like it very much—he preferred history to novels—but he kept on with it. He had been barely literate when he joined the army, and had forced himself to read everything he could get his hands on. He thought it was important to educate himself if he were going to be an effective officer.

A rap at his flimsy door startled him. He stood. "Come."

The door opened and Tom Conroy stepped in. Conroy was dressed much like Starke, except that his clothes had cost about five times more, and his jacket was trimmed with black velvet.

Starke was surprised. "Hello, Tom."

"Hello, Jim. Happy New Year."

"The same to you." Starke recovered, remembering his manners. "Care for a drink?"

"Thanks. Whatever you're having will be fine."

Starke grinned. "Let's open this champagne. It cost enough; we might as well get the use out of it."

Starke carefully unwired the champagne's cork. He twisted it out of the bottle with a soft pop. As he poured the fizzy liquid into glasses, Conroy said, "That's an impressive layout, Jim. Doesn't look like anyone else has been here yet."

"They haven't," Starke said. "I'm not expecting anyone. I wasn't expecting you, to be honest."

Conroy didn't understand. "If you're not expecting anyone, why do you have all this stuff set out?"

Starke laughed at himself. "I don't know, really. I guess

I wanted to be prepared if I turned out to be wrong.'' He handed Conroy the glass. ''Cigar?''

''No, thanks,'' the boyish lieutenant said. ''I can't stand the things. They make me go all green in the face.''

''Sit down.'' Starke motioned his visitor into the camp chair. Conroy sat, and Starke rested on one of the overturned crates, which had been tacked with cheap muslin to make it look better.

Conroy looked around, sipping the champagne. He hadn't been in Starke's quarters before. ''I've just come from the Bannermans','' he said. ''Neal—Captain Bannerman— warned me against coming here.''

''He thinks I'm a bad influence,'' Starke said. ''So, why *did* you come?''

''Well, I know the others avoid you because you're a ranker, but still, it's New Year's. I mean, that's cutting it a bit thick, don't you think? I thought officers were supposed to be gentlemen. Real gentlemen aren't snobs.''

Starke poured more champagne. ''Bannerman's taken you under his wing, hasn't he?''

''He's helped me a lot. It can't have been easy for him, either, with all his troubles at home.''

Starke nodded. ''They've been through a lot, especially Mrs. Bannerman.''

Conroy went on. ''This shunning by the other officers— you don't seem to let it bother you.''

''It's the army,'' Starke said philosophically. ''How do you like the army, by the way?''

''All right, so far. They don't let me do much—inspect the guard, be recorder on a board of survey, that sort of thing.''

''Why'd you join?''

''I don't know,'' Conroy said. ''It was just something I fancied. Maybe it's the uniform. It all seemed so glamorous, sort of a grown-up version of *Boy's Own Adventures*. It certainly seemed more fun than the law or banking, and if I eventually take up one of those careers—or even politics— I'll have some useful background.''

''Your father has money, doesn't he?''

''He's an investment banker, in New York. He's got polit- ical connections. That's how I got the commission. Dad wanted to get me into an artillery regiment at the Battery, or one of the posh infantry regiments around Washington.''

"But you chose the cavalry?"

"I figured that if I was going to do it, I should be a real soldier, and the cavalry is where the action is right now."

Starke refilled the glasses. The level in the champagne bottle was going down rapidly. "How long have you been out here?"

"A year in February."

"Seen any action?"

Conroy shrugged. "Hancock's 'war,' if you call that action. Mostly we rode around in circles."

"Well, you keep your head on straight, and you'll do all right when the time comes."

Conroy looked earnest. "Do you think so? I worry about that, you know. I worry if I'll hold up my end. I'm not trained for it like they do at West Point. And then there's you—you've probably seen more action than all the officers at this fort combined."

"There's a first time for all of us," Starke told him. "It's only natural to worry how you'll do. I did."

"Do you think we'll see action this year?"

"I think there will be an Indian war this year. Whether we see action is problematical. Indian fighting is mostly hit and run. You can go for years and never fire a shot in anger. Yet you've got to be ready for it all the time. Just remember something an old sergeant once told me—*use* your head, don't *lose* it. It's even more important for an officer, because the men look to you for an example."

"Captain Bannerman says not to worry about the men. He says that's the sergeants' job." Starke snorted, and Conroy added, "I don't think he knows the names of half the men in the company."

"He never did," Starke said.

"What do you mean by that?"

Starke hesitated. He hadn't wanted to get into this, but he didn't see the harm now. "Captain Bannerman was my platoon officer when I first enlisted, later my company C.O."

Conroy sat back in the chair. "I never knew that."

"It's not something Bannerman likes to talk about."

"Is that why he dislikes you so?"

"You'll have to ask him."

"He wants you out of the company, you know, out of the regiment."

"He wants me out of the army," Starke said.

Conroy finished his glass. He cleared his throat. "Look, I'd better be going. I have other stops to make. Why don't you come with me, Jim? Don't sit here by yourself."

"What good would it do?" Starke said. "Bannerman and Hayes won't let me in. Gottfried and McBride might let me in, but it's not because they want to."

Conroy said, "Well, you're more than welcome at my quarters. I've laid in a supply of Cockburn's port, along with about a ton of tinned cookies and cakes."

"I don't know, Tom. Being seen with me—I don't want to get you on Bannerman's bad list."

"I'm a big boy, I can take care of myself. Come on by" —he looked at his watch— "say at four?"

Starke hesitated again, then he said, "All right."

"Good."

Conroy shook Starke's hand and started for the door. Starke held it open for him.

Conroy turned. "You've heard about the big party Mrs. Hayes is giving for General Sherman, haven't you? Has she invited you?"

Starke laughed without mirth. "Yes, but only because she has to invite all the officers. You watch, I'll be O.D. that day, so that they can keep me out of the way."

Conroy knew that what Starke said was true. He said, "I'll see you at four, then."

"I'll be there." Starke told him.

Starke shut the door. He stood in the middle of the small room, lips pursed. He felt funny accepting Conroy's invitation. It was almost as if he enjoyed not being accepted by the other officers. He knew that was crazy, but he couldn't help it. Maybe it was a way of rebelling, of making himself different. Maybe, deep down, he felt inferior to the others, or maybe he had to show that he could be as arrogant in his way as they were. Now, one of those men wanted to be, if not his friend, at least his equal, and he didn't know how to deal with it.

It had been different in the war. A lot of former enlisted men had become officers in the volunteer regiments. No one had paid attention. But this was the Regular Army, bound by caste and tradition. Starke had crossed an invisible line when he had accepted a Regular commission. Did he have the courage to make a full commitment to that choice? If not, what was he trying to prove?

He didn't know.

He sat back down with his book. Silence descended on his small quarters.

11

On January fourth Captain Hayes summoned his officers to post headquarters.

"Gentlemen," he said, standing behind his desk, "General Sherman is due to arrive tomorrow. He will be here for two days, to inspect the post and the troops. Weather permitting, I have decided to hold a parade in the general's honor, on the evening of the sixth. In addition to the parade, there will be a competition between I and K Companies to determine the soldier who will be the general's special orderly while he is here. Have your representative at guard mount tomorrow, Colonel Bannerman. The Adjutant and the O.D. will be the judges. The winning company gets a week's leave from fatigue duty."

"Yes, sir," Bannerman said.

Hayes looked around the room, trying to hold back a smile. "Questions, gentlemen? If not, you may return to your duties."

The officers left headquarters. Bannerman, along with

Lieutenants Starke and Conroy, walked back to K Company's area. Bannerman smacked his gloves in the palm of his hand. "That bandy-legged little bastard. Did you see the look on his face? This parade is a scheme to make the infantry look good at our expense."

Lieutenant Conroy was naive. "You think so, sir?"

"Of course it is. We've got ten new men; I Company has none. They're bound to look better than us. Mark my word, this is Emily's idea."

"Mrs. Hayes?" Conroy said.

Bannerman nodded. "Hayes has never had an idea that wasn't hers. She'd do anything to gain him preferment. That's why she's having this party for General Sherman. She'd sleep with Sherman if she thought that would get her husband promoted. Though, considering what she looks like, it would more likely get him court-martialed."

Bannerman drew on his gloves. "Well, we'll show them who has the best company at this fort. We'll show them who has the best company in the regiment. Have your men prepared, gentlemen."

Starke said, "What about Hunter, sir?"

"Who?"

"The fellow with the bad hand."

"Damn," Bannerman said. "I'd forgotten about him. I hate to see him get away with that act of his, but we can't have him embarrassing us. Have him report sick that day. I assume you're putting up Hayward for special orderly?" Hayward was one of the few men Bannerman knew, because he'd been before him so much for company punishment, and because he almost always won the company inspection competitions.

"Yes, sir," Starke said. "You agree, Tom?"

"What? Oh, yes," said Conroy.

Bannerman let out his breath. "He doesn't have much of a chance. Hayes stacked the odds there, too. His man McBride is Adjutant, and Gottfried is scheduled for Officer of the Day tomorrow. Hayward will have to have God on his side to win." He paused. "Personally, I'm praying for snow."

* * *

The men of K Company worked late into the night, cleaning and painting their barracks for General Sherman's inspection. After a few hours' sleep, they were up and at it again the next morning.

In the bay next to Harry's, Link Hayward prepared for the special orderly competition. He was assisted by his friend Skull. Skull was a Dane, named Anders, short for Anderssen. Harry didn't know Skull's first name—he didn't know the first names of half the men in the platoon. Skull was a soldier of fortune. He had joined the French Foreign Legion, served in North Africa, then deserted to return home and fight in the Prusso-Danish War. When his country lost, he had come to America. He had joined the Union Army in time to participate in the last campaigns of the Civil War, and when that conflict ended, he had come west as a Regular. He was the only man in the company who could give Link a run for his money in inspection competition.

The two men brushed Link's trousers and high-collared shell jacket. They burnished Link's buttons and shoulder scales. They heel-balled his belt, boots, and cap visor until they shone like glass.

"Better get your hair trimmed," Skull told Link. "Should I get Morton?" Morton was the company barber.

"No," Link said. "He's a butcher." He looked around. "Where's that wop? Hey, Squillace. Cut my hair. You should know how to do it right."

Squillace shook his head. He knew just a few words of English. "No, no, *signore*. I do not—"

Skull brandished a pair of scissors and a straight razor. He pointed from Squillace to Link. "Cuttee hair. Shavee."

"You know," said Link, "like the Barber of Seville."

Squillace squealed, "I no can—"

"Do it," Link said, his voice suddenly threatening.

Reluctantly, Squillace came over. Just because he was Italian, people were always assuming he knew how to cut hair. He said a quick prayer, because he knew that if he did bad work, Link would pound him to jelly.

When Squillace was finished, Link looked up. "How's it look?" he asked Skull.

"Good," said the Dane.

Squillace breathed a sigh of relief.

Link felt his newly shaven cheeks for smoothness. He was satisfied. Without a word of thanks, he stood up. He got dressed. He squared away his forage cap, canting it just the slightest bit to the right, and he put on his overcoat. Outside, a bugle sounded Guard Mount.

"Ready?" Skull asked.

Link nodded. "Mike?" he said.

Starving Mike, the big Russian, came over. He and Skull stood on either side of Link, who put his arms around their shoulders. The two men stooped and picked Link up, making a cradle with their arms. They carried him out of the barracks, down the steps, across the parade ground toward the Adjutant's office, followed by all the off-duty men of the company. This way, Link could not get mud splashed on his shoes or trouser legs.

The trumpet sounded Adjutant's Call. From I Company's barracks a similar procession emerged.

"I's man is Gallagher," Link said. "I knew it would be."

A breeze whipped across the parade ground. The day was bitterly cold. The new guard was already drawn up before the Adjutant's office for inspection, as the two parties for special orderly converged, with the off-duty men at a respectful distance. The carrying parties set the two candidates on the duckboards in front of the Adjutant's office.

Gallagher, a handsome, sandy-haired corporal, grinned at Link. "Look who they sent. The mill bird."

Link said, "Go fuck your mother, Gallagher. Everybody else has."

Gallagher reddened. "You've got a big mouth, boyo."

"Do something about it," Link told him.

For a moment Harry thought that Gallagher and Link were going to fight right there, then one of the infantry sergeants said, "Steady, Paddy. Here comes the Adj."

Harry and the other bystanders backed away as Lieutenant McBride came up for the inspection, along with Lieutenant Gottfried, the Officer of the Day. Link and Gallagher snapped to attention and saluted.

Lieutenant McBride stopped before them. "You men are the candidates for special orderly?"

"Yes, sir," they replied in unison. Both men stood rigid, brass and leather gleaming, capes on their light blue overcoats turned back at precisely the right angle.

"At ease," McBride said. He and Gottfried walked around the two men, studying them. They stared hard at Link, looking for a reason to disqualify him, but they could find none. There was nothing to choose between the candidates.

"Caps off," McBride said.

Both men snapped off their caps and tucked them into their right elbows while McBride examined their haircuts. Lieutenant Gottfried, the O.D., took each cap in turn. He ran a white-gloved finger along each bill, then looked to see if any polish had come off. None had. He returned the caps.

"Gloves off."

Link and Gallagher removed their white gloves. Lieutenant Gottfried examined their hands and nails. They were perfect.

"Now your belts," said Lieutenant McBride.

The two enlisted men removed their belts. McBride examined the polished buckles closely. He took a toothpick and ran it around the insignia stamped on the brass, to see if there was dirt in the corners or indentations. There was none.

"Overcoats."

Off came the coats. Link and Gallagher stood in the freezing cold while the officers examined their jackets.

"Blouses," said McBride, frustrated.

Trying not to shiver, Link and Gallagher unbuttoned their jackets. The lieutenants examined the regulation gray shirts that they wore underneath. Both were spotless, with no marks of darning. Both candidates were still perfect, but Harry thought Gallagher was starting to look nervous.

"Shoes," said Gottfried.

Each man knelt and removed his shoes, although Gallagher hesitated before doing so.

The two men stood on the muddy duckboards in their stocking feet. Then Harry saw why Gallagher had been nervous. Gallagher wore thick civilian socks. Link's socks were thin army issue. The officers looked at each other. With visible irritation, Lieutenant McBride said to Gallagher, "You know that in a competition like this, all articles of clothing must be regulation?''

"Yes, sir," barked Gallagher. Assuming he would have won the competition long before it came to this, he had donned the warmer socks against the cold. Link had difficulty holding back a smirk.

To Hayward, McBride said, "Name?"

The smirk disappeared. "Hayward, sir."

"Very well, Private Hayward, you are selected to be General Sherman's special orderly. K Company wins the competition."

The onlooking cavalrymen cheered. A week without fatigue detail—no latrine cleaning, no wood cutting, water hauling, or garbage burning. Harry found himself cheering with the others. He would never have believed he'd be cheering for Link Hayward. Nearby, the infantrymen swore under their breaths.

Lieutenant McBride continued. "Put on your clothes, Private, and report to Post Headquarters."

"Yes, sir," Link said.

"Corporal Gallagher, you are dismissed."

"Yes, sir," said the infantryman.

Both men saluted, and the officers turned away to inspect the new guard. As the two candidates dressed, Gallagher said, "You were lucky, Hayward."

"I was smart," Link told him. "Have fun cleaning the latrines. Don't get your tongue too dirty."

"I'll get you one day," Gallagher promised.

"I'm scared," Link said. Linc finished buttoning his overcoat, and he turned and winked at the men of K Company. Then he started for headquarters, with just the hint of a swagger in his walk.

From behind the happy cavalrymen came Sergeant Townsend's voice. "What are you lot gawping at? Back to the barracks and get them weapons clean. The *bara-sahib* will be 'ere soon. 'E'll be inspecting you, and woe to the man what buggers up."

12

Mrs. Hayes's party for General Sherman was well under way when Jim Starke arrived at the Officers Club. Mrs. Hayes had been forced to use the club because her own quarters were too small for all the guests. A detail of infantrymen had spent most of the afternoon moving the piano from her house to here.

It was a full dress affair. Officers wore frock coats with black velvet trim, epaulettes, white gloves, and sashes. Starke's saber and the red sash over his right shoulder marked him as Officer of the Day. Though he was on duty, custom required that he make a brief appearance.

Private Hayward, the special orderly, stood at attention just inside the club door, in case he was needed. Starke smiled at the sight. Captain Hayes had been furious when his man had lost the orderly contest.

"My, my. Don't we look knobby?" said Lieutenant Conroy, appearing at Starke's elbow.

"Hello, Tom," Starke said. Conroy held a cup in his hand. "How's the lemonade?" The drink had been made with citric acid crystals. Mrs. Hayes did not drink liquor or allow it to be served at her parties.

Conroy made a pained face. "Captain Thompson"— the commander of Sherman's Seventh Cavalry escort from Fort Wallace—"has a couple bottles of whiskey stashed outside. I'm just on my way out to get this spiked. Want one for yourself?"

"Better not," Starke said. "I'm on duty." He looked around the room. Sawhorses overlaid with planks served as tables. The refreshments were laid out on mismatched bits of china, many of them chipped, the remnants of sets that had been broken in transit to and from a dozen garrisons. Besides the lemonade, there were coffee and tea, pound cake, "apple" pie made from flavored soda crackers, freshly baked bread, and an assortment of Mrs. Hayes's homemade jams, along with the usual raisins, nuts, and candy. An infantry private strolled around the room playing a violin.

Mrs. Hayes was coming and going, talking, refilling glasses. The only other woman present was Helene Bannerman, who sat by herself in one corner, with a glass of lemonade that she did not sip. Now and again one of the officers approached her, but she had little to say, and the officers soon departed in search of more congenial company. If Helene Bannerman had been an actress, Starke thought, she would have played tragic roles. She had that air about her. She had an oval face, framed by a mane of reddish blond hair. Her deep green eyes hinted at high intelligence. Her only flaw was her nose, which was a touch long, giving her a look of aristocratic aloofness.

William Tecumseh Sherman stood at the center of the largest group in the room. He nodded as Starke came over. "Evening, Starke." They said that Sherman never forgot a name.

Starke nodded in return. "Good evening, General."

Sherman returned to his conversation, waving the stump of a cigar as he talked. What remained of his famous red hair was rapidly turning gray. To his audience, he said, "Extermination, gentlemen—that is the solution to the Indian problem. Anything less, and we shall be creating a race of paupers, dependent on the government."

There were murmurs of assent, and Sherman went on. "If the government would give Mr. Lo's management to the army, we could make quick work of him. The Indian Agency protects him, however, so final victory is going to take time. But by the end of this year, I am determined that not a single redskin will remain between the Platte and Arkansas rivers. We must make that country safe for the railroad."

Starke cleared his throat. "Excuse me, sir. But that country is the Indians' chief hunting ground. If we take it away from them, won't we be forcing them to go to war?"

Sherman said, "They'll go to war whether we force them

to or not. War is the only life they know. The sooner we get it over with, the better for all concerned. In the spring, the government will establish a reservation in the Indian Territory, at Fort Cobb. Any savages not settled on that reservation will be considered hostile, and eliminated."

Lieutenant McBride said, "What about the ones who *are* on the reservation, sir?"

Colonel Clifford, one of Sherman's aides, winked. "We'll take care of them later."

Sherman continued, "We expect the Indians to begin raiding in late spring. At the end of May, the Fifth Cavalry will go into camp at Big Creek and await developments. You will be our reaction force, deployed in the direction of the main attacks. The Seventh Cavalry, under General Custer, will be the strike force, to be used in a fashion yet to be determined."

"And the infantry?" said Captain Hayes. He spoke with a sinking heart, because he knew what the answer would be.

"You will guard the forts and supply routes," Sherman told him. It would be a thankless job, with no hope of glory or advancement. Hayes tried to hide his disappointment as the general turned to Bannerman. "Are your men ready for action, Colonel Bannerman?"

"They can't wait, sir," Bannerman said. "They're real Indian killers."

Captain Hayes said, "You know we have our own Indian village now, sir?"

Sherman frowned, chewing on the cigar stub. "Yes. We saw them as we came in. Brazen devils, a perfect example of misplaced government policy." He lowered his gruff voice a notch. "Between ourselves, Colonel, you will await the first opportune time and attack your 'tame' Indians. Deal with them before they can menace settlers or the railroad."

Starke had heard enough. He turned away. "Awfully worried about the railroad, isn't he?" he murmured to Conroy, who had returned with his drink.

"He should be," Conroy whispered, "he's in their pocket. On the boards of half a dozen lines, with blocks of stock to match."

"Leaving us, Colonel Starke?" said the general.

Starke turned back. "Yes, sir. I'm on duty, sir."

Sherman nodded. "Quite right. Good evening, then."

"Good evening, General." Starke bowed to the other officers. He walked over to Emily Hayes. "Mrs. Hayes, my compliments on your party. Thank you for inviting me."

"Thank you for coming," she replied, without a trace of sincerity.

After Starke left, the party grew louder, as more and more of the guests sneaked out for Captain Thompson's whiskey. Captain Hayes stood with his wife, watching General Sherman. The Hero of Atlanta had produced a fresh cigar, and a number of officers were vying to light it for him.

Hayes said, "It's hard to believe we were lieutenants together, isn't it? Back at the old Presidio, in Monterey. They called him 'Cump' Sherman then. I remember when Cump took a detail up to the goldfields, to round up deserters. The deserters just laughed at him, and half the men in his detail ran away themselves. He was helpless to stop them. Now he's the second most powerful man in the army, and if Grant runs for president this year, Sherman will get the top spot."

Emily slipped a supportive arm through her husband's. "It's all luck, dear. Fortune's Wheel. With a little better luck, you might have burned Atlanta, and Cump Sherman might be stationed at Fort Pierce."

Hayes sighed. "I'm forty-two, Emily. If I don't move up the promotion list soon, I never will."

She patted his arm. "I try to help, in my own way."

"I know you do. This party is superb, considering the surroundings."

"Yes," she agreed, "but it seems to be slowing down, don't you think? Excuse me."

She crossed the room to Sherman's coterie. "Enough military talk," she told the men in mock scolding tones. "Lieutenant Conroy, I understand you're quite the piano player."

The young lieutenant smiled. "I play, Mrs. Hayes. I don't know how good I am."

"Perhaps you'll honor us."

The strolling violin stopped as Conroy sat at the piano. He took off his white gloves. He was feeling in a good

mood—he was actually rather drunk—so he struck up a
Strauss waltz while the others gathered around him.

"That's so *pretty*," Emily marveled. She turned. "General, would you think me bold if I asked you to dance?"

Sherman scraped a foot. "I'm afraid you have me confused
with General Sheridan, ma'am. He's the dancer. However,
I'm sure one of these other officers will oblige you."

Immediately, five or six hands were extended. "May I
have the honor?" their owners begged.

Emily picked Sherman's chief aide, Colonel Clifford. The
other officers rushed across the room, asking Helene Bannerman to dance, but she declined politely.

Chairs and tables were scraped aside. Lieutenant Conroy
played a succession of waltzes, polkas, and schottisches.
Impishly, he added "Soapsuds Over the Fence," and "The
Irish Washerwoman." Mrs. Hayes danced with each officer
in turn. Others continued to ask Helene, who continued to
refuse.

Emily was in her glory. One thing she loved about the
army was that even the oldest, plainest women were always
popular. She danced until she could dance no more. It was
the most fun she'd had since the big military ball at Fort
Leavenworth, in '65, to celebrate the end of the war.

"Please," she said at length, holding up her hands. "I
must catch my breath."

Eager officers vied to pour her lemonade. She took a cup
and sat beside Helene Bannerman. "Oh, I'm so over-
*heat*ed," she said, fanning herself with her free hand. "I
fear I'll be lame tomorrow."

Helene stared around the room. There was a distinct un-
steadiness about her, and Emily could guess its cause.

Emily said, "Why aren't you dancing, dear?"

"I don't want to," Helene replied.

"You really should."

"Why?"

"It's expected. A formal occasion like this, all these officers . . ."

"I'm not a dance hall girl. If they want that, they can go
into town."

"I didn't mean *that*," said the older woman. "These men

lead hard lives—gallant, chivalrous lives, for the most part, like knights of old. A lady's companionship is one of the few rewards they receive. Think of your husband, if nothing else. You're no help to him sitting here in a corner.''

"I wasn't aware that he needed help. He can become a general by himself. That seems to be his main interest.''

"Don't you love your husband?''

"Frankly, Mrs. Hayes, that's a personal question.''

"Does that mean you don't?''

"It means I don't answer personal questions. And I resent your asking them.''

Emily's tone became softer, almost wistful. "You two used to be so happy.''

"Before we came here,'' Helene said.

"There are worse places.''

"Please. I don't want to hear how you spent a winter in tents, just now.''

"I realize you're upset about your child, Helene, but you've got to get on with it. We've all had our troubles. This is the army.''

Tears spilled out of Helene's eyes and down her cheeks. "Yes, and you love it, don't you? You love to brag about your dead children and the hardships you've endured. Well, I'm not 'army.' I'd rather have my children alive, thank you. I want a normal life, in a normal house, with a normal family.''

Helene's voice had grown loud. Half the people in the room were staring at her. Stiffly, Emily Hayes said, "I rather think you misunderstand me, my dear. Perhaps if you were to stop drinking—''

"Perhaps if you were to mind your own business,'' Helene snapped. She realized she'd said it too loudly. The room had quieted around her. She composed herself and stood. "If you'll excuse me, I must be going. I'm sure these 'gay cavaliers' can get along without me for the rest of the evening.''

Without making farewells, she got her coat and left the room. Behind her, Neal Bannerman fumed. She had made him look like a fool, right in front of General Sherman. Years from now, when Sherman saw Bannerman's name on the promotion lists, the only thing he would remember about

Bannerman was his wife's behavior. So would the other officers who had been here tonight. Incidents like this could ruin a career.

With Helene gone, the room buzzed with low conversation about what had happened. Emily Hayes and her husband shared a look, secretly pleased.

Outside, Helene drew the coat around her, not buttoning it, even in the freezing cold. She didn't care if she caught pneumonia. She hadn't wanted to come here tonight. She had known what kind of a time she would have. She had known it would be a disaster. Why couldn't Neal have let her—

A figure loomed out of the darkness, startling her. "Oh!" she said.

"I'm sorry," said the figure.

She realized who it was. "Mr. Starke."

Starke bowed. "I was just finishing my midnight rounds. I was on my way back to Post Headquarters. I'm sorry if I frightened you."

"No. No. It's just that I wasn't expecting it. My mind was on other things, I suppose."

"You're leaving the gala?" Starke said.

"Yes," said Helene.

"You're not unwell, I hope?"

"No. I—I just didn't want to stay."

"If you'll permit me, I'll walk you to your quarters."

Helene hesitated, then said, "All right."

13

Starke and Helene walked along Officers Row, toward the Bannermans' quarters. They were alone; everyone else was at the party. The piano could be heard in the background.

Their feet crunched the gravel walk. Starke's saber bits jingled; the weapon thumped rhythmically against his leg. Overhead, the frosty stars gathered in their millions.

Helene said, "You didn't stay long at the party, either."

Starke shook his head. "All that talk about killing Indians. I couldn't stand it. What's being done to them is a tragedy. An entire way of life is being destroyed—an entire people. There must be a better solution to the problem."

He sighed. "The worst part is that it's us—the army—that has to do the dirty work. We put our lives on the line so that other people can get rich. And we get criticized from both ends. The press calls us baby killers and rapists, and if the Indians fight back, we get blamed for not stopping them."

Helene said, "If you feel so strongly, I wonder that you remain in the service."

"I'm a soldier. It's the life I've chosen. I do my duty, even if I don't always like it. I can only hope that I'll get a chance to influence the outcome for the better, in some small way."

She glanced over at him, a quizzical look on her face. "You don't sound like Neal. You see things beyond the confines of that uniform. Have you always wanted to be a soldier?"

"Yes," he said, "ever since I can remember. I never thought about being anything else. If I were a priest, I guess you could say I had a calling."

"Was your father in the military?"

"Dad's a saddler, near Columbus, Ohio. When I was a kid, I used to go into town, to Columbus Barracks. I'd watch the recruits in their new uniforms and pretend that I was one of them."

"You've just joined the regiment. What have you been doing since the war ended?"

"Helping Dad in his shop, and waiting for my Regular commission to come through. I don't know what I'd have done if it hadn't—reenlisted, probably. At one point I went back to school, to college, but I gave that up soon enough—I couldn't stay awake in class."

Helene laughed.

Starke said, "That's the first time I've seen you laugh. I wasn't sure you could do it."

She lowered her head demurely. "There was a time—"

She slipped on a patch of ice. Instinctively, she reached out for Starke's arm. He caught her and stopped her from falling.

"All right?" he said.

"Yes," Helene replied, a bit breathless. She wondered if he knew that she'd been drinking, then wished that she hadn't been. She held on to his arm perhaps a second longer than she had to, then they continued on.

At the Bannermans' quarters they mounted the rickety steps to the porch. The house was dark. The maid, Letty, had her own shack on Soapsuds Row, with the laundresses. There was a lamp on a table, just inside the door. Starke lit it with a sulfur match. He trimmed the wick, and the small room sprang to life with a flickering glow.

Starke stepped back. "Well . . ."

"Would you care for a cup of tea?" Helene said.

"No, thank you. Don't go to any trouble for me."

"It's no trouble," she said. "I'm having one myself." Originally she had planned to finish the bottle of brandy that she opened before going to the party, but now she had changed her mind.

Helene took their coats. Starke got wood for the stove and lit it, while Helene put water in the pot to boil. Next, Starke lit the fireplace. The house was cold, from the wind blowing though the chinks in the wall. Starke looked around at the rough and ready furnishings.

"This is the first time you've been in our quarters," Helene said.

"Yes. Your husband would have apoplexy if he knew I was here."

"It's a shame you and he don't get along."

Starke shrugged.

"And it's all because you were an enlisted man? That's so . . . so silly."

"There's more." Starke told her about the incident years ago, at Fort Kearny. He'd never told the story to anyone. "He holds that against me, for some reason."

"How strange," Helene said. "I suppose I'll never understand the army."

Then the tea was ready. Helene poured Starke's in a china cup and handed it to him. The china had been a wedding present from her parents. Most of the service was broken now.

Starke sipped the hot, sweet tea. "That's good. You've done a nice job fixing this place up."

"You're kind," she said, "but it's really a shack."

"Maybe if this station is made permanent, you'll be able to—"

Helene shook her head. "I'm leaving this summer, going back home, as soon as an escort can be spared."

"Will you be returning?" he said.

"No."

"There's no trouble with your marriage, I hope."

"Our marriage was over long ago. Neal's true love is the army."

"I'm sorry."

"You needn't be. I should have seen it before we were married. But I was young and didn't know better, and it was the beginning of the war. We were all so filled with patriotic zeal in those days. Neal was a dashing soldier on sick leave. He swept me off my feet—or my image of him did. We were married before I really knew what I was doing. Maybe I thought I owed it to my country."

She sipped her tea. "At first, our life together was good. Neal spent most of his time either in Springfield, at my home, or in Rolla. We were hardly ever apart, even with the war. There were endless rounds of visiting, and parties, and hops. I thought it ever so exciting. Then the war ended, and Neal wanted to remain in the army. My father was lieutenant governor of Missouri; he helped Neal obtain a commission in this regiment."

She turned away. "Then we came here, and I began to see the other side of army life. I began to see the other side of my husband, as well. He's obsessed with his career, with promotion. When Tommy was born, I thought that might draw us back together; and for a while, it did—"

Her voice broke. After a second she went on. "You don't realize how hazardous frontier life is for the little ones until they're sick. Early last fall the weather turned cold and it began to rain. The chinking had long since fallen out of these walls. The wind blew the cold and water in. The roof leaked like a downspout. I used to wrap Tommy in blankets and stand over his bed with an umbrella. It looked so funny that I had to laugh, at first. But there was no medicine for him, no proper food. His temperature soared and—''

She broke off. Starke pursed his lips. He put a comforting hand on her shoulder. Then he realized what he was doing and withdrew it.

She turned.

"I'd better be going," he said.

"No. Don't. Not yet. I haven't had anyone to talk to since I came here, except for my maid Letty." She sniffed and wiped the tears from her cheeks, laughing. "Of course, I don't know why you'd want to talk to me, in the condition I'm in."

"That's the second time I've seen you laugh today," Starke said.

She sniffed again. "I must be setting a record."

With a thumb, he wiped a lone tear from beneath her eye.

They stared at each other. He smelled her hair; he smelled the scent she had used. His chest felt tight. He hardly knew what he was saying. "We'll miss you when you leave," he said in a low voice.

"We?" She smiled. "Who? Mrs. Hayes? Her husband?"

"*I'll* miss you."

There was an awkward silence. The room seemed to be spinning around them. Helene looked away. "More tea?" she asked.

Starke's throat was dry. He knew that he should say no. "Yes," he said.

They started for the stove at the same time, she to pour, he to help. They bumped into each other. He felt her warmth, and it sent a tingling sensation through his body.

They faced each other, each starting to apologize. Then they stopped. The room seemed to be closing in on them. Starke felt like he was bursting.

He reached out. She came into his arms as if it were the most natural thing in the world. He gazed deep into her green eyes. He pushed back her reddish blond hair. Then they

kissed. It was a warm, tender kiss, different from anything
Starke had ever known. They clung to each other tightly. Their
kisses grew hungrier, and they were carried away by passions
that they neither wanted to, nor were able to, control.

14

The parade was held on an open stretch of ground north
of the post. A reviewing stand had been erected for General
Sherman, his staff, the civilians of his entourage and guests
from town, as well as Mrs. Hayes and Mrs. Bannerman.

I Company, the infantry, performed first, going through
their evolutions smartly. They finished with fixed bayonets
and a volley of live fire, which elicited polite applause from
the spectators. Then it was K Company's turn. Wearing their
dress uniforms, they marched onto the parade ground in columns of four. Captain Bannerman was on the reviewing stand
with the general, so Lieutenant Starke led the company.

Harry Winston rode his big bay horse, Beau. Beau had
previously been Amassee's horse. He was unruly from lack
of exercise, and Harry did not feel confident with him. Because of fatigue and work details, Harry had spent little time
in riding class—called School of the Trooper by the army.

The company marched past the reviewing stand, and General Sherman took the salute. They moved to bugle calls.
Beau knew the bugle calls better than Harry did, and Harry
trusted him to get them through this ordeal. The plan was to
end up in line, draw sabers, and thrill the audience with a
mock charge, then rally and march once more around the
parade ground.

Harry's platoon was on the far right of the company. As
they began the long wheel into line, a jackrabbit popped up
in front of Beau, startling him. Harry tried to hold the big

bay in, but it was no use. The horse bolted, running flat out across the prairie, with Harry hanging on for dear life.

On the reviewing stand the infantry officers and Sherman's staff were convulsed with laughter at the sight of the lone rider careering away from the parade ground. Sherman turned to Captain Bannerman with a raised eyebrow. "Perhaps they're not *quite* ready for action, eh, Colonel?"

Bannerman was furious and embarrassed. The tops of his ears turned red. "Yes, sir," he muttered.

Helene Bannerman looked from her husband to Jim Starke, who was leading the rest of the company through its paces as though nothing had happened. Next to Helene, Emily Hayes could barely restrain a smile. "Oh, what a *pity*," she said. "But I'm *sure* the general won't hold it against your husband."

Harry pulled on Beau's reins, but the action had no effect on the big horse. Beau thundered across the prairie. The jackrabbit was by now forgotten, and the horse was running for the sheer enjoyment of it. Harry screamed at him. "Stop! Stop, you stupid animal!"

He pulled on the reins until he was arm weary. His butt and thighs hurt from being bounced in the saddle. It was all he could do not to fall off.

"Stop! Damn you, stop!"

Then, for some reason, the horse turned around and began running back toward the fort. Harry continued to pull uselessly on the reins.

The fort grew larger in Harry's eyes. The horse galloped past the cavalry, who were just finishing their final turn around the parade ground. He galloped past the laughing infantry and the crowded reviewing stand. He was headed into the post itself when suddenly the sergeant of the guard jumped out with his hands raised.

The horse came to a sliding, stiff-legged stop. Harry went flying into the air. He saw the astonished face of the sergeant below him. Then the world turned upside down and everything went black.

15

Harry came to. There was a terrific pain in his head and neck. A pungent smell filled his nose.

He was in bed, in the post hospital. Dr. Dudley was rubbing his bare chest with something cold. Alcohol. That accounted for the smell. It was so strong, it made his eyes water. It was probably what had awakened him.

A drop of liquid splashed his forehead. The orderly was standing over him with a canteen, letting water drip onto him. Harry didn't know what that was supposed to accomplish, besides getting the pillow wet.

Inside the hospital, the lamps were lit. It was almost dark outside.

Harry blinked. The action set off a wave of pain in his head, and he groaned. "What happened?" he said.

"Your horse threw you," Dr. Dudley told him. The smell of alcohol on the doctor's breath was almost as strong as the alcohol on Harry's chest. "You landed on your head. We thought you were dead, for a while."

Hunter, the crippled soldier who had gone on sick call for the parade, was standing nearby. He said, "You've been lying here for hours. Lucky for you, you ain't got nothing broke."

Harry tried to sit up. He almost passed out from the pain.

"Lie back down," Dr. Dudley told him. "You're not going anywhere."

Harry closed his eyes. The orderly stopped dripping water on his forehead and laid a cold compress there instead. The smell of the alcohol was overpowering, but, despite it, Harry drifted in and out of sleep. Then he heard the hospital door open. Feet scraped the plank floor.

Harry looked up. Jack Cassaday, Pick Forrester, and the ex-grocer Barker were standing over him. They looked tired, and they were red-faced from exposure to the cold. Barker, especially, was drawn and worn.

Jack said, "How are you, Mad Dog?"

"Alive, I think," Harry said.

Pick said, "That was a heck of a fall you taken."

"I'd rather have watched it than taken it, believe me. Am I in much trouble?"

"Trouble ain't the word for it," Jack said. "After General Sherman left, Super Soldier went off like Fourth of July fireworks. He had us out for four hours of close order drill, without overcoats or gloves. God knows what he's got planned for you."

"We just got back," Barker added. "Lord, it's cold out there."

Pick said, "The boys ain't happy with you, Mad Dog, that's for sure."

"I'm sorry," Harry told them. "It was that horse. I—"

Jack shook him off. "Too late to worry about it now."

Harry sighed. No matter what he did, it turned out wrong. It had been like that as long as he could remember.

Slowly, he sat up in bed.

Dr. Dudley restrained him. "You better—"

"I'm all right," Harry said. He had to get back to the company. He had to show them he was tough. He had to show them he wasn't shirking.

Jack and Pick helped him to his feet. He shook them off. He tried to blink away the pain in his head and neck. "It's not bad," he said. His clothes were on a peg behind his bed. He took two steps toward them and fell on his face, unconscious.

He slept for an entire day. When he woke, he was all right, save for a headache and a raging thirst. He stayed at the hospital until after lunch—hospital food was the best on the post—then Dr. Dudley returned him to duty.

Harry entered the platoon barracks. It was Friday. The men had just come back from the mess hall and were lazing around—talking, laughing, reading—waiting for the next formation.

They quieted as he entered. He walked down the aisle to his bunk. He felt all eyes on him. He tried to ignore them.

He got to his bunk. Link was up at the other end of the barracks, with Skull and his cronies.

"Hi," Harry said to Jack Cassaday.

"Mad Dog," Jack acknowledged. Something was wrong with Jack; Harry wondered what it was.

Harry started to unbutton his dress jacket, then noticed a lump under his tightly drawn blankets. He pulled the blankets aside. On the top sheet were two pieces of salt pork and a hardtack biscuit.

He looked at Jack. "What's this?"

Jack wouldn't meet Harry's eyes. "It's a sign," he said. "From the others. It means they don't want you here anymore. It means they want you to desert."

16

Harry looked across the barracks. Link Hayward was grinning smugly at him.

Harry picked up the pork and hardtack. He crossed the aisle and threw the food in Link's face. Link's eyes opened wide in surprise, but before he could do anything, Harry punched him as hard as he could on the jaw. Link was knocked backward, over Skull's bunk and onto the floor.

Harry scrambled over the bunk after him. As Link got up, Harry swung wildly, so angry and frustrated that he couldn't see. He hit Link with a left and a right, knocking him down again.

"You son of a bitch," Harry said.

Link lay on the floor, looking up.

Harry stood over him, breathing hard, fists clenched. "Get up! Get up!" he shouted.

Link smiled. He reached behind him, picked up a heavy troop boot and threw it.

Harry ducked. The boot struck him a glancing blow on the side of the head. As it did, Link launched himself off the floor. He barreled into Harry and the two of them reeled across the aisle. They crashed off a bunk on the other side and fell to the floor.

Harry pushed Link off and stood. He heard the men around him yelling, their excited faces a blur. Link came at him, and he responded with another flurry of blows, one of which caught Link on the jaw and sent him to his knees. Link tried to grab Harry's leg, but Harry skipped out of the way.

Link got up, working his jaw. Both men circled in the center of the barracks, fists up. The first flush of Harry's anger had worn off. He was more sober now, more aware of what he had gotten himself into.

Link feinted, then moved in and aimed a kick at Harry's groin. Harry wasn't expecting the maneuver, but he jumped back just in time. It threw him off balance, and Link was able to catch his arms and wrestle him down. Link swung a knee at Harry's face, but it missed and caught him in the ear. Then they were on their knees, with Harry underneath. Link pummeled Harry's kidneys. Harry grabbed Link behind the thighs and bowled him over. He felt his shirt and shell jacket rip up the back. Link gripped him around the head, and Harry butted him in the nose, making it bleed.

They scuffled on their knees. Harry got Link's head down and banged it again and again on the rough plank floor. Link reached around, grabbed Harry's ear and tried to rip it off. "Ow!" Harry yelled, pulling away.

Both men got up again. Link wiped blood from his nose onto his jacket sleeve. His forehead was scraped raw and trickling blood, as well. There was a welt on one cheek, below his eye. His pants were ripped out at both knees. Harry's shirt and jacket were in tatters. He could feel his ear swelling, and he was covered with cuts and scrapes. The yelling in the barracks was very loud.

Link unclasped the leather belt from around his waist. He

wrapped the belt around his right fist, letting the metal buckle dangle. He smiled grimly.

"Come on, Link," Jack Cassaday protested.

"You'll kill him," complained Dutch Hartz.

Link paid no attention. He swung the heavy belt buckle loosely as he and Harry circled in the center of the barracks.

Link feinted with the belt. Harry backed away. Link came after him, slashing at Harry with an overhand motion. Harry dodged the blow. Link swung the belt again. Harry blocked it. The metal clasp caught Harry's left forearm, ripping it open. Harry yelled with pain. Blood flowed down his arm and hand. Link swung the belt again, gashing Harry's arm in another spot.

"Stop it, Link," said the Professor.

Link swung again. Harry caught the blow on his mangled forearm. He twisted the arm, wrapping the belt around it, trying to pull the belt from Link's hand. Link bulled forward behind the blow, kneeing Harry in the groin and knocking him over. Harry's side hit the sharp corner of a footlocker as he fell.

Harry lay on his back, momentarily helpless, the breath knocked out of him. There was bile in his throat; tears filled his eyes. Link straddled him. Showing his teeth, wolflike, Link drew back the belt and prepared to finish the job.

" 'Ere you—'ayward! *Roko* that!"

It was First Sergeant Townsend. He pushed through the crowd of men, tossing them aside like rag dolls. "What the 'ell is going on 'ere? Break it up! *Jaldi!* On your feet, you two."

Reluctantly, Link dropped the belt. He looked hard at Harry, then he got to his feet, giving Harry's face a shove as he did. Harry rose more slowly. His groin and ribs hurt; blood covered his throbbing forearm. He saw that blood was running from Link's nose again, and that made him glad.

Townsend tucked his wooden stick under his right arm; his left arm was behind his back. "What's this about, then?" he demanded.

Neither man answered. Harry had a difficult time standing at attention.

Townsend nodded, chin tucked into his chest. "Right, you

know the company rules against fighting. You *ought* to know 'em, 'ayward, you bloody well break 'em enough. Where's Sergeant Cronk?''

Hunter said, ''He's still at the mess hall, Top.''

Townsend looked around. ''Corporal Bannon. Why didn't you break this up?''

Bannon stepped forward, hemming and hawing. ''Dunno, Top. It all happened so fast—''

''Take a detail and escort these two to the guard'ouse,'' Townsend told him. ''Then get back 'ere for fatigue. And don't stop at the sutler's on your way.''

''Right, Top,'' said the star baseball player.

To Link and Harry, Townsend said, ''You two can cool off in the mill till the C.O.'s ready for you.'' He turned and bellowed. ''The rest of you bloody clowns clean up this barracks. Then fall in for fatigue.''

Jack Cassaday made a quick bandage for Harry's arm, then Bannon and four men marched the prisoners to the guardhouse.

Gallagher of I Company was corporal of the guard. He grinned when he saw Link. ''Well, well. Look who it is. Welcome home.''

''Fuck you, Gallagher,'' Link said.

Gallagher grabbed a musket and drove the butt into Link's kidney, making him woof, propelling him into the confinement area. Rough hands shoved Harry after Link. Harry half fell down a short flight of steps and into the cell.

''You two stay quiet, or I'll have you out shoveling mule shit,'' Gallagher told them. He closed the wooden door and barred it.

Link and Harry found themselves in a sunken room, about twenty-five feet square. There was a barred window near the ceiling, for ventilation. In two of the corners were tiny partitioned cells, where the most recalcitrant prisoners were confined. It was damp and freezing. There was no flooring, no heat, no furniture. The lower walls were rock; the portions above ground level were made from blocks of sod. Prisoners were only allowed out once a day, and consequently the earthen floor was wet and thick with human waste, tobacco juice, and every kind of trash. It reeked of urine, excrement, and stale vomit. Harry gagged on the stench. It was bad enough now, he thought. What must it be like after payday, when half the garrison might be under arrest and jammed in here? Link Hayward spent half his life in these guardrooms, yet he didn't seem to mind. How did he do it?

Link pulled a penknife from his pocket. He slipped into one of the solitary confinement cells. Harry heard scraping. A minute later Link stood in the cell doorway with a bottle of whiskey. He tilted the bottle and drank.

Harry couldn't hide his amazement. "Where did you get that?"

Link grinned. "That's my business." The truth was, Link had helped build the guardhouse—he had volunteered for the job. He had hidden bottles behind the sod bricks in the solitary rooms, where he spent much of his time, for just such occurrences.

Link was going to offer Harry a drink. Harry could see it in his eyes, and he was ready to accept. He hated himself for wanting the approbation of a man like Link, for wanting to be his friend; but it would mean that he was finally accepted in the company, and he wanted that more than anything. At the last moment, however, Link decided against it. He took another pull from the bottle, then returned the whiskey to its hiding place in the punishment cell.

Harry was dismayed. What more did he have to do to prove himself?

Link reemerged. The floor was too wet to sit on, and he didn't anticipate being here long, so he turned away from Harry and leaned against the whitewashed wall, lost in his own thoughts.

Link Hayward's real name was David, though no one had called him that since he was a boy in Illinois. His home State had been frontier country in those days, and David's family were farmers. David hated farming. He hated work of any kind. His only talent was for getting in trouble. He early on acquired a reputation with the constable for fighting and drunkenness. When he was eighteen, he stabbed a fellow with a knife and ran away. Not knowing what else to do, he joined the army.

He was underage, but they took him anyway. David liked the army; it was the first place he had felt at home. At first the boys called him Blackie, because of his hair. Then, after the rise to prominence of Abraham Lincoln, he was dubbed Link, because, like Lincoln, he was so tall. His second enlistment ended just after the Civil War, and he took a discharge. He drove a freight wagon for a while, but he didn't like civilian life, so he reenlisted in his old regiment. When the recruiting officer suggested that, because of his height, Link would be more suited to the infantry than the cavalry, Link suggested throwing the recruiting officer out a second-story window. Link had twice been nominated for the Medal of Honor, once during the war and once on the frontier. Both times he'd been turned down. "Lack of verifiable corroboration" was the official reason, but the real reason was his character. Link didn't care.

The jailhouse door opened again. Link and Harry turned and saw a florid face and graying dundreary whiskers. "All right, you two," Sergeant Townsend said. "Captain Bannerman will see you now."

17

Townsend and two guards marched Harry and Link into the C.O.'s office.

Captain Bannerman was behind his desk. He looked up as the men halted before him. Harry's shell jacket and shirt were ripped up the back. His ribs were sore; his stomach hurt; and the bandage on his left arm was red with blood. His head had started to ache again. Link's left eye was swollen. His forehead was bruised and crusted with dried blood.

There was blood on his nose and on the sleeve of his jacket. Both men's trousers were torn; their shoes were scuffed.

Townsend saluted. ''Prisoners reporting, as ordered, sir.''

Link snapped to attention and saluted, as though he were on the parade ground. Harry followed as best he could. Waves of pain rocked him.

Bannerman returned their salute. Link and Harry dropped their arms but remained at attention.

Bannerman said, ''You men violated standing orders against fighting. What do you have to say for yourselves? Hayward?''

Link stared straight ahead. ''Nothing, sir.''

''Winston?''

''N-Nothing, sir,'' Harry replied.

Bannerman leaned back in the chair. He steepled his fingers, looking down his long nose at the two men. ''Mmm.'' He was tired of seeing Hayward in here all the time, and he wanted to punish Winston because of the runaway horse. He sat forward again. ''You two are guilty of neglect of duty. You're to be fined fifteen dollars each. In addition, you will each be bucked and gagged for four hours. Kneeling.

Sergeant Townsend cleared his throat. ''Kneeling, sir?'' The usual procedure was for the man to be seated during punishment.

''You heard what I said,'', Bannerman told him. ''Sentence to be carried out immediately, dressed as is.''

''Temperature's dropping, sir. Looks like snow again.''

''When I need a weather report, Sergeant, I'll ask for one. You heard the sentence. Now, see that it's carried out.''

Townsend stiffened. ''Yes, sir.'' He saluted. ''Prisoners, about—face. By the left, forward—march.''

Townsend and the guard detail marched Harry and Link to the company drill area, behind the barracks. ''Detail—'alt.''

''No overcoats, Top?'' Link protested. ''It's freezing.''

''You 'eard the Cap'n,'' Townsend said.

The northwest wind was raw and biting. There was no protection from it. Rags were stuffed in the prisoners' mouths and tied behind their heads. ''Tightly, there,'' said Townsend.

Harry's rag tasted of dirt. It made breathing difficult.

''Kneel,'' Townsend ordered.

Link and Harry knelt. "Tie their ankles," Townsend told the guards. With lengths of rope, the guards bound each prisoner's ankles together.

"Put your wrists together and slip 'em below your arses," Townsend said.

Harry had to bend double to perform the maneuver. At a sign, the guard tied his wrists.

"Now, tie the wrists to the ankles."

A short length of rope connected the wrists to the ankles. Both men were bent over. They had to raise their heads to see anything. "We'll be back for you in four hours," Townsend told them. He marched the guard detail off, leaving Harry and Link alone.

Four hours, Harry thought. It would be after dark when Townsend returned. The temperature was dropping. The cold seeped up from the ground, through Harry's knees. The wind blew over him, damp with the promise of snow, its icy fingers searching through the rip in his shirt. His back stiffened from being bent over. The only way to alleviate the pain was to raise his head, but after a few minutes that made his neck hurt and he lowered it again. The awkward kneeling position put pressure on his ankles and the tops of his feet, pressure that turned to pain. Harry flexed his fingers, to keep the blood moving through them, to keep from losing the feeling in them. The least effort was accompanied by labored breathing, because of the gag in his mouth. Next to Harry, Link was quiet, now and then raising his head to ease the pain in his back.

There was no sensation of time passing. Occasionally, Harry heard boots crunch gravel, as someone walked by, but he soon became lost in his private war against pain. His lower back burned; so did his feet and ankles. The cold penetrated his every pore. He shivered violently. The spittle on the rag in his mouth was turning to ice. There were tears in his eyes from the wind.

He stayed on his knees until his back and feet screamed with pain, so much pain that he momentarily forgot the cold. At last he toppled over, onto his right side. For a moment his back and feet knew relief. Then he became aware of a new problem. The entire weight of his body was on his right forearm. It felt like the bone was being crushed; the circulation to his lower arm was cut off. His hand and forearm started to lose what little feeling remained to them. Harry thought about frostbite, and gangrene. He remembered what had happened to Daugherty. He shifted his arms as best he could with his wrists and ankles tied together. He got himself to a position where there was a bit of circulation to his lower arm, but that made his back hurt again. It was hard to breathe with the gag, and he had to fight to keep from panicking.

When he could take the pain in his arm no longer, he rolled onto his back. For a few minutes he was more comfortable, but he couldn't stretch the length of his back. His shoulders were in the air. There was pain in them and his back, as well as in the backs of his thighs. The ropes cut more deeply into his wrists and ankles in this position. With his ripped jacket and shirt, his back was protected from the icy ground only by his undershirt. The cold stabbed into his spine. His cap had fallen off, and his head was cold, too. He was shivering so badly that he was practically bouncing on the ground. Despite his efforts, he lost all feeling in his hands and feet.

He thought about trying to get back on his knees but decided it would be too hard. He didn't have the strength. The bitter cold seemed to have bled the strength out of him. He fell back onto his side and lay there, arm hurting, cheek pressed against the frozen ground.

He had to pee, from all the coffee he'd drunk at the hospital. He'd been holding it for hours, but he could hold it no more. He let go, feeling the hot liquid pour down his frozen thigh and through his trousers, warming them. He cried with humiliation and degradation, and the tears froze to his cheeks.

Now the snow began to fall, borne on the ripping wind. Harry's breathing was labored. For the first time, he began to think that he might not live through this. He grew scared. He lost all thoughts about anything but survival. The pain was beyond imagining. He would have screamed, but the gag made that impossible. It was funny, he thought. He had joined the army worried about Indians, but he was going to be killed by his own men, by the military system itself.

The snow fell more heavily, covering Harry with a thin layer of white. He was wet and cold. He'd long ago lost touch with his extremities. Then a strange thing happened. The pain went away. Harry felt a pleasant warmth seeping through him, and he wondered how that could be. However it was, he didn't care. It was a relief. It was wonderful. He closed his eyes and enjoyed it. He could sleep. He could sleep in his cocoon of snow until it was time to go home. It was dark, but he didn't know if that was because his eyes were closed or because it was night. He didn't care about that, either. He wanted to laugh. He didn't care about anything. He would just close his eyes and sleep. . . .

Cold air poured into his mouth, into his lungs. His gag was gone. He sputtered and opened his eyes, and he felt crusted snow fall off them.

"Untie those bonds," a voice ordered. It was Lieutenant Starke. Starke's blond moustache swam into focus through the falling snow.

"Excuse me, sir," protested another voice—Sergeant Townsend's—"but the Cap'n says 'e's supposed to stay 'ere for—"

"This man's freezing to death, Top," said Starke. "I'll take responsibility for letting him go." Townsend had told Starke about the punishment at evening retreat, and the lieutenant had come to investigate.

Whoever was untying Harry's ropes was having difficulty with the frozen knots.

"Just cut them," Starke snapped. He pulled a sheath knife, knelt, and with some difficulty sawed the frozen ropes himself.

Through ice-laden lashes Harry made out Barker and Pick Forrester, along with Starke and Townsend. With the ropes cut, Barker and Pick eased Harry's frozen limbs into a semblance of a natural position.

"Careful," Starke told them. "Not so fast. All right, now rub some life back into them."

Vigorously, the two men rubbed Harry's arms and legs. Feeling started to return to them. The feeling was pain. Harry's hands were beet red from the cold and snow.

"Can you stand, son?" Sergeant Townsend asked.

"I—I think so." Harry was so cold, he could barely talk.

Barker and Pick gently lifted him to his feet. They held him up. Somebody set his forage cap back on his head.

Link. Harry had forgotten all about Link.

He looked. Link was on his knees, bent over, though whether he'd remained in that position the whole time, Harry had no idea. The snow was falling so heavily as to fill in any impression Link's body might have made in it had he been lying down.

Lieutenant Starke motioned to Pick. "Cut Hayward loose, too."

The ex-rebel removed the rag from Link's mouth.

"Sir?" said Link, looking up. His voice was constricted from cold and pain. "I'll finish my sentence, if it's all the same to you, sir."

Starke looked at Hayward, considering. He had no doubt that Hayward could handle the nearly one hour remaining on his sentence. Hayward was used to it. But if he let Winston up and let Hayward stay, it would give Hayward something to hold over the younger man.

"No," Starke said, "you're done for the day. And if you try something smart, like sitting out here by yourself for the next hour, to show off, I'll give you a month in the mill on bread and water. Understood?"

"Understood, sir," said Link.

"Cut his ropes, Forrester."

Pick did as he was told. Slowly, painfully, Link hauled himself up. Snow dropped in clumps from his uniform. Harry was able to move his arms and legs a bit now. He was thankful to be alive.

Starke said, "You two men get back to the barracks and warm up. If you're lucky, there'll still be food in the mess hall. Winston, see Doc Dudley and have that arm stitched."

Link and Harry saluted as best they could. While Starke headed through the snow for the C.O.'s office, Link and Harry started for the barracks, with Barker and Pick helping Harry.

Halfway there, Link turned back to Harry and smirked. "I knew you wouldn't make it," he said. "You ain't no soldier. Not now, not ever."

Part II

SPRING

18

Corporal Sam Pickens of the second squad, called "Slim" by the men, dug at his lower jaw with a clasp knife. Grimacing, he pried out a rotten tooth. He looked at the tooth, then tossed it on the mess hall floor and spat a wad of blood after it.

Across the table the bearded Professor was disgusted. "I told you to let me pull that. I used to do that sort of thing for a living."

"And you were a quack," Pickens told him.

"I wasn't a quack, I was a drunk. I'm sober now. That's why I joined the army."

"Well, I don't trust a man what don't drink," Slim said stubbornly.

"Let Doc Dudley pull it, then," the Professor told him.

"I trust him even less than I trust you. Plenty of other fellas got their teeth falling out. Work on them."

Above them, the mess hall's shingle roof reverberated to the drumming of rain. It had been raining for three days. The roof leaked, and rain dripped everywhere.

"It's this damn scurvy," said Hunter. Like Slim and many of the others, Hunter's face was mottled with black spots. With his good hand he ate his lunch of slumgullion—a stew made from salt pork, beans, and dessicated vegetables. "I'd like to get my discharge and get the hell out of here."

"I'd be happy just to get dry," muttered George Jett, the Arab.

The young tough, Walsh, made a face as he ate his slum. "This shit is awful. When will some rations get through?"

"Not till the weather changes," Jack Cassaday told him. Between the snow and, now, rain, it had been months since a supply train had reached Fort Pierce. The men had been living on field rations for the last three weeks.

With his knife, Link Hayward scraped mold off a piece of hardtack. He banged the ancient cracker on the table. He waited for the weevils to crawl out, then he soaked the biscuit in his slum, to soften it. "We wouldn't be so low on rations if we didn't have to feed them Injuns."

"That's Uncle Sam for you," said Numb Nuts Hudnutt, the former businessman. "Starve our boys in blue, but feed Mr. Lo, whatever you do."

"Stop complaining," said Corporal Bannon. "That last batch of bacon we took to the Cheyenne village was full of mice and worms. It was so old, the fat had turned yellow and fallen off the lean. We wouldn't have eaten it, anyway."

"Bullshit, we wouldn't," Hunter said. "What makes you think this stuff was any better before the cook boiled it off?"

Skull agreed. "It's different for the Indians," he told Bannon. "They eat mice. Probably worms, too."

Link said, "They probably thought it was a treat."

Numb Nuts added, "It might be different if Super Soldier had let Link and Skull go on that hunting trip, like they wanted."

From down the table, Sergeant Cronk said, "Super Soldier was worried there would be trouble with the Injuns while they were gone."

"He was worried they'd desert, is what he was," said Slim Pickens.

"Come on," Hunter told them. "Link ain't going to desert."

"Skull, either," said Starving Mike, the Russian. "Who else would want those two but the army?"

Harry Winston had been quiet through the conversation. Any remark he made was usually greeted with derision by Link and his friends. Now, he looked across the table. "Hey, Pick. Are you all right?"

The ex-rebel leaned over his bowl of slum. He looked pallid and unwell. Perspiration glistened on his lugubrious face. "I *am* a bit used up," he admitted. "It's this rain, I reckon."

"What did the doc say when you went on sick call this morning?" Harry asked.

"He give me quinine and whiskey, same's he does ever'-body. Tolt me to go back to the company."

At that moment a large black beetle, perhaps dislodged from the ceiling by the rain, dropped onto the table, landing next to Jack Cassaday's soup bowl. Jack flicked the beetle across the table, into Squillace's lap. The Italian jumped and brushed the bug onto the floor.

Jack said, "I can't eat any more of this shit. Let's get out of here, Mad Dog." He stood, slipping his hardtack cracker into his pocket.

Jack and Harry returned to the barracks, where Harry saw Jack put the hardtack in his footlocker. It was not the first time that Harry had seen him save part of his meal, which was strange, considering how hungry they all were. Not long after, formation was called, and the company fell out. They wore rubberized ponchos and cap covers against the rain. They'd already been told that they would have extra duty this afternoon.

First Squad was assigned to pull weeds around the buildings on Officers Row. Led by Corporal Bannon, they slopped and splashed their way across the parade ground, which had become a quagmire. Despite the rain, it was a warm day. Harry felt like he was being steamed alive beneath his airtight poncho.

"Officers," swore Link, at the front of the column. "Let 'em pull their own weeds. They're all worthless."

"What about Starky?" said Corporal Bannon.

"That's different. He's one of us, isn't he? He's a soldier."

The Professor said, "I hate going to Officers Row. I'm always afraid I'm going to run into Mrs. Bannerman and have to say something."

"At least she's good-looking," said Numb Nuts. "You *could* run into Old Iron Pants." That was the men's name for Mrs. Hayes.

"I'd rather run into her than be married to her," said Link.

"I don't know," said the Professor. "At least that way you'd be married to the real post commander—or is it 'commandress'?"

"As long as it isn't 'undress,' " Link said. "That's one woman you want wearing as many clothes as possible."

Jack Cassaday walked beside Harry. "Snow's melting in the mountains," he observed. "The Montana gold mines will be opening."

"What's that got to do with us?" Harry said.

Jack kept his voice low. "I'm going there."

"How? You're not due for a discharge." Then Harry realized. "You're not . . . you're not deserting?"

"Shh, keep your voice down," Jack said.

"When are you going?" said Harry.

"As soon as I can."

"So that's why you've been saving food."

Jack nodded. "I got grain for my horse, too."

"Why? I mean, why are you doing it?"

" 'Cause I hate the fucking army, why do you think?"

"You're going to be a miner?"

Jack gave Harry a look. "Do I look stupid? Mining's hard work. I'm going to play cards for a living."

Harry glanced around. No one was listening. The others were still making jokes about Mrs. Hayes. "What if you get caught?"

"They'll shave my head and stick me in the mill for a while. When they let me out, I'll skip again. I sure ain't staying here. Look, Mad Dog—why don't you come with me?"

Harry missed a step. "Me?"

"Yeah. You don't like the army any more than I do. Probably less. I got food enough for two. I'll teach you to play cards, if you want. You can make good money when we get to Montana."

Harry wasn't prepared for this. He would have done almost anything to get out of the army. But deserting—that was a big step. That was a crime.

"What do you say?" Jack asked him.

Harry shook his head. "No, I guess not."

"Scared?" Jack said.

Harry answered truthfully. "Yes."

Jack shrugged. "Suit yours—"

There was a gagging sound behind them. Jack and Harry

turned, along with the rest of the squad. Pick Forrester was on his knees in the mud, vomiting.

"Pick!" The men ran over to him.

Pick fell to the ground, writhing and vomiting uncontrollably. The veins stood out blue on his face and forehead.

Cassaday stepped back. "Jesus."

"What is it?" Harry said.

Cassaday looked terrified. "He's got cholera."

Harry and some of the others visited Pick in the hospital that evening. Many of the men were afraid to go near him, for fear they'd catch the disease. Two infantrymen who had also come down ill had died before supper.

Pick lay in the hospital cot. In just a few hours the cholera had turned him into a mockery of his former self. He was wan and drawn, so weak as to be on the verge of unconsciousness. The orderly hadn't cleaned him, and the stench around him was nauseating. Dutch Hartz, his bunky, said, "How are you feeling, Pick?"

Pick shook his head. "Poorly." He was quiet for a moment, collecting his strength, then he said, "Mad Dog, I want you to have my knife. Dutch, you take everything else."

"All right," said the Swiss, nodding.

Then Pick was sick again, and the men left him, for what they knew was the last time. The sloshed through the mud, back to the barracks. Inside, Dutch went into Pick's footlocker. He pulled out a bowie knife in a fringed sheath and he handed it to Harry. "Here."

Harry pulled out the wicked-looking blade. It was razor sharp, its surface polished to a mirrorlike quality. "Why did he give it to me?"

"I don't know," Dutch said. "He liked you, I guess. Poor fellow. He was from Georgia, you know. He lost everything—his home and family—to your General Sherman during the war. He had nothing to go back to, so he joined the Regulars."

The Professor said, "That's how he got the name Pick—that knife."

Harry looked at him.

The Professor explained. "His real name is Ralph. But he

carried that big Arkansas toothpick in the field, and every-body got to calling him the Terrible Toothpick. Later, it got shortened to Pick.''

Harry stared at the bowie knife. Pick was one of the few men in the company who had accepted him, and now Pick was gone. Harry looked over at Jack Cassaday. Soon Jack would be gone, as well.

Harry felt more alone than ever.

19

Pick Forrester and the two infantrymen were buried the next day. Their funeral was made gloomier by the rain. Pick's coffin was drawn on a caisson, followed by his horse, with Pick's boots reversed in the stirrups. K Company's two trum-peters played the death march. Captain Bannerman read the funeral service, an honor guard fired three volleys, and the company marched back to barracks, to ponder who might be next.

Several more men fell sick, but there were no more deaths. As suddenly as the cholera had come, it departed. Prevailing wisdom held that it had been brought by a dispatch rider from Fort Wallace, the fort's only visitor since General Sherman's party had left.

There were other ailments to go around, though—fever, and ague, or ''the shakes.'' With the incessant rain, the men couldn't get their uniforms dry, and they developed painful eczema. Everyone was weak from scurvy.

''We need fresh vegetables for this scurvy,'' said Barker, the grocer. ''You should have a garden here.''

''No shit,'' said Hunter caustically.

Numb Nuts explained. ''We had a vegetable garden last summer, but grasshoppers ate the crops.''

There was no food to be purchased in town. Because of the weather and the impassable roads, supplies were short there, as well. So the suffering went on.

At the beginning of April the rain stopped. On Easter Sunday, after inspection and parade, the men were given off-post privileges.

Most of the men put on their white jackets and went downtown. A few, like Jack Cassaday and Starving Mike, the Russian aristocrat, had money to spend. Link Hayward went to see his girl. The rest just went for a change of scenery. Harry wasn't interested. He was glad to get away from them all. He lay on his bunk, reading a back issue of *Police Gazette*—to which the company subscribed.

Barker came down the aisle. "Hey, Harry. You want to go to the Indian village?"

Harry looked up. "Are we allowed to?"

"Yeah. The Captain told Cronk it's all right."

Harry sat up. He was curious to see real Indians, to see the men he'd joined up to fight. Maybe they'd even see Storm, the scourge of the plains, the chief they said would never surrender.

"Is it safe?" Harry said.

"It should be," Barker replied. "We're at peace with them."

"All right, I'll go," said Harry, swinging off his bunk. "Can we get a mounted pass?"

"No. We have to walk. The captain's afraid Lo would steal our horses."

The two men got ready and set off, wearing undress uniforms. It was a mild day and they didn't take their overcoats. They followed the stream. It was about seven miles to the Indian village. The path was little more than wagon ruts in the mud, and they kept to the side, where the footing-was better.

Barker might say this excursion was safe, but Harry wasn't sure. He was more than a little bit scared, but filled with anticipation, as well, at seeing the ferocious Cheyenne warriors decked out in their paint and feathers, brandishing their weapons.

The two men were overtaken by a party of civilians in

wagons. They were gamblers and whores, laughing and passing bottles, showing teeth rotten from scurvy.

Harry and Barker waved them down. "How 'bout a ride?" Harry cried.

The wagons drove by, splashing the two soldiers with mud. "Dream on, brother," called the laughing civvies.

"See you on payday," yelled one of the whores.

At last they saw the great circle camp of the Cheyennes. Smoke curled from the tipis. In the distance the pony herd grazed.

The two soldiers smelled the village long before they entered it. It was a musty smell, of smoke and old buffalo. Scrawny, wolflike dogs ran back and forth, barking at their arrival.

Harry and Barker entered the circle of lodges through the opening in the eastern end. They wandered around, admiring the painted decorations on the tipis. They watched the women cure hides and cook what little food they had in iron kettles. They watched children wrestling and playing games. They watched the men seasoning wood for bows and arrows. Most of the Cheyenne men and boys wore cast-off bits of army uniforms. Some had taken the black Jeff Davis hats and cut out the crowns, wearing only the brims. Others had cut the crotch and seat from the sky blue trousers, the better to wear with breechclouts. Black boot tops and been turned into moccasins. In addition to hornpipe breastplates and necklaces, they wore army shirts and jackets, some with sleeves, some without, as it pleased them. Some of the women carried umbrellas, though it was not raining. Some were dressed in cheap calico and gingham. Others wore the traditional ornamented deerskin dresses.

The Cheyenne women were small. The men were smooth-limbed and lithe. They wore their black hair lank and long. Some had broad flat faces, while others looked more like Mexicans, and some had features that could only have come with an infusion of white blood. All were emaciated from lack of food. Many showed the effects of disease.

Harry was surprised. "They don't look scary," he said.

Barker agreed, "They look worse than us, if that's possible."

There were a few other soldiers in the village, some wearing the white jackets of K Company. The civilians who had passed Harry and Barker earlier kept in a tight group around their wagons. The whores twirled parasols. The gamblers laughed and taunted the Indians with their public drinking. They seemed to find the Indians contemptuous, amusing.

Harry and Barker were approached by men and women trying to sell them deerskin shirts, pottery, arrows, and ornamented knives.

"Food," the Indians begged. "You have food? How 'bout whiskey? Whiskey, me like."

A flat-faced girl blocked their path, standing in what she hoped the white soldiers would find an attractive pose. "You like?" she said, indicating herself. "You got whiskey, you have."

Harry and Barker excused themselves and walked around her. A horde of starving children followed the two soldiers, begging for food. One boy couldn't keep up with the rest. The boy had a pleasant, smiling face, but he was skinny as a stick, and his limbs were weak and rubbery, floppy like a rag doll's. Though he followed well behind his stronger fellows, he never gave up. He squealed with pleasure in his pursuit of the white soldiers. Harry knew enough about Indians to wonder why they had let one who was this weak live at birth. Maybe they thought he possessed strong medicine.

Harry stopped. He and Barker had brought some hardtack and salt pork to eat on their way back to the fort. Harry took out his rations. He waded back through the crowd of grasping hands and he gave the food to the floppy boy. The boy cried excitedly. He turned and held up the gifts with a big smile, showing them to someone in the crowd, his parents most likely. He said something to Harry in Cheyenne.

"Sure," Harry replied. Then he added, "You're welcome." He wished he had more to give.

Inspired by Harry's example, Barker handed his rations to a chubby-cheeked girl, who clutched them tightly to her chest and waddled away to eat.

Harry and Barker walked on. Someone touched Harry's shoulder. He turned to find a Cheyenne of about seventeen, tall and open-faced. There was a streak of yellow paint down the boy's left cheek. In the boy's hand was a new pair of moccasins, fringed and ornamented with porcupine quills. He pushed them toward Harry.

"No," said Harry, shaking his head. "I can't buy. No money. No food."

The boy said something in Cheyenne. He pushed the moccasins forward with more insistence.

"No," Harry repeated, "I can't—"

"It's a gift," Barker told Harry, "for what you did for that kid. He must be the kid's brother, or something."

To the young Indian, Harry said, "I don't want anything for that. It was only pork and angle cake."

The Indian was more insistent, speaking again in his own tongue.

Barker said, "I think you'll insult him if you don't take them."

Harry hesitated. He felt guilty, but he had no choice. He accepted the moccasins. "Thank you," he told the teenager.

"Thank you," the tall boy repeated slowly, nodding.

On impulse, Harry held out his hand. The young Indian stared. "Take it," Harry told him.

Awkwardly, the Cheyenne took Harry's hand. Harry pumped.

"Friends," Harry said, pointing back and forth with his free hand. "You, me. Friends."

The Indian brightened. "Friends." He repeated the word as if he liked its sound. "Friends." Then, shyly, he stepped back. He turned and, beaming with pride, went to join the floppy boy, who was happily gnawing the salt pork.

"I feel bad," Harry said. "These moccasins are beautiful. They're worth a lot more than a handful of army field rations."

Barker was philosophic. "Maybe to him they weren't."

The two men came to a large tipi, decorated with paintings of horses and buffalo. The owner's shield was out front, on a wooden tripod.

"Look at this," Harry said, awed.

The shield's deerskin cover was painted red. In the shield's center was a group of eagle feathers. On each side of the feathers were pairs of bear claws. Below the eagle feathers was a row of owl feathers, below them a row of feathers from a sandhill crane, then more eagle feathers, the attached rows reaching halfway to the ground.

"That's something, isn't it?" Harry said.

"I wonder who it belongs to?" said Barker.

"Somebody important. I wouldn't doubt if it isn't Chief Storm hims—"

"Hey, look over here," Barker said.

Harry turned. Barker indicated a pole in front of another lodge. The two men moved closer. Hanging from the pole were little hoops, with tufts of dried, shriveled material stretched across them. The tufts were different colors, many of them faded—black, brown, gray, pale yellow.

"Jesus," Barker said, realizing. "They're scalps."

Harry's stomach turned. Then he saw something that made his stomach turn still more. "Look," he said.

He pointed to a glossy black scalp with gobbets of bloody flesh still adhering to its underside.

"That one's fresh," Harry said.

The two soldiers looked around. The village, so friendly and peaceful minutes before, had suddenly taken on a sinister aspect.

"What the hell is going on here?" Barker said.

"I don't know," Harry said, "but we better get back to the fort and tell the Sarge."

20

Sergeant Josef Cronk's real last name was Cronkewicz. He had shortened it when he'd joined the army. He came from western Pennsylvania, where his father, his brothers, and all his male relatives dug the coal that fueled the growing industrial might of the United States.

Josef had hated that world. When the Civil War had come,

he left, and he had never looked back. Life in the army was hard, but never as bad as life in the mines. Josef had seen men die from an accumulation of coal dust in the lungs. He had seen men killed in cave-ins, men blown up by gunpowder improperly placed for blasting, men killed by accidents so routine that they were barely noticed, save by the families of the victims. He had seen strong men grow old beyond their years, in grimy towns where even the rain fell black.

Josef was not a man of great intellectual attainments, but he was hardworking and ambitious. He wanted to become K Company's first sergeant after Townsend retired, which was bound to happen before long, as old as Townsend was. Josef knew that many, if not most civilians despised the Regular Army, but he intended to give his life to it. It was an honorable profession, a step up from what he had known. Someday he would marry and have children, and his children would move up yet another step on the ladder of success.

When Privates Winston and Barker came to Josef with their story about the scalp, he questioned them carefully about what they had seen. He then took them to Sergeant Townsend, who took them to Captain Bannerman, who took them to Captain Hayes, the post commander.

When Hayes had heard the story, Bannerman said, "Let me mount my company and take them to the Indian village, Colonel. I know how to deal with these people. I've done it before."

But Captain Hayes was loath to give Bannerman a chance at glory while he sat twiddling his own thumbs here at the fort. "No," he said, "we'll make their chief and head men come here and explain themselves."

"Do you think they'll do it?" Bannerman said.

"If they know what's good for them, they will."

Hayes sent the Harvard-educated squaw man, John Smith, to summon Storm to Fort Pierce. A chief like Storm was unused to being summoned, but he swallowed his pride and went. There would be many new things to get used to if he was to live in the white man's world.

Man Above the Clouds and Crooked Neck accompanied Storm, along with two younger men. With the unpredictability of the prairie, the mild spring weather had turned gray and cold. The Indians huddled in blankets as they rode. The wind rattled the branches of the budding trees along the stream. Occasional crows overhead made the sky look even more desolate than it was.

At the fort, the Indians were met by Lieutenant Conroy, the O.D., and taken to post headquarters. The off-duty personnel and civilians stopped what they were doing to watch. Mrs. Hayes and Helene Bannerman looked on from the porches of their quarters. Unknown to the Indians, Captain Hayes had his infantry company armed and hidden behind their barracks, with bayonets fixed, in case they were needed.

Storm was ushered into post headquarters. At the last moment Man Above the Clouds and Crooked Neck remained outside with the younger men, unwilling to enter the white man's wooden lodge.

Storm walked inside proudly. Captain Hayes waited for him, seated behind his desk with his hands clasped. Hayes was flanked by Captain Bannerman and Lieutenants Starke and McBride. Two infantrymen, with bayoneted rifles, stood guard on either side of the door. For all his bold exterior, Storm felt ill at ease. He was used to being in a real lodge. He was used to passing the pipe and mulling over formal speeches. He knew that, with the possible exceptions of Smith the scout and the yellow-haired lieutenant, he was not among friends here.

There was a chair, but Captain Hayes did not invite Storm to sit. "I'll get to the point, Chief. I've had a report of fresh white scalps in your village."

Storm looked at the white men, one at a time. "These stories are lies," he said. With the blanket wrapped around him and one shoulder bare, Storm reminded Jim Starke of pictures he'd seen in his history books, of noble Romans declaiming in the Senate.

Hayes's dark eyes flared. He said, "I believe my men to be reliable, sir. They have seen the scalps themselves." He turned to Harry Winston and Barker, who stood at parade rest by the wall. "Is that right?"

"It was just the one scalp, sir," said Harry, as the two men came to attention. "That was all we saw."

Storm said, "There is a new scalp in my village, but it belonged to a Crow, not a white man."

Both Hayes and Bannerman looked skeptical. Bannerman said, "Where would your people find Crows around here? They live to the north."

Storm said, "The scalp was taken by Walks at Night. His cousin was killed in battle with the Crow, and Walks at Night swore revenge against the Crow who did it. He saw in a dream that he should kill this Crow in the winter. There is no grass for the horses, so Walks at Night journeyed on foot to the land of the Crows. He endured cold and hunger. He crossed the water you call . . ." He forgot the word.

"The Platte," John Smith suggested.

"Yes. Platte." As a young man, Storm had learned the white man's language from the trappers and traders at Bent's Fort on the Arkansas River. He had decided that he needed to be able to talk to this new race of men. He had been afraid that they were not going to go away. He went on with his story. "Walks at Night found the village that he sought. He lay hidden outside, until he learned where his enemy was. When night came, he went into the village and killed the man. He took the man's hair, then he returned to his own people, running many risks, because the Crows were looking for him. It was a great deed. I would be proud to claim it as my own."

Starke said, "I believe him, sir. There's been no reports of white people being killed."

Hayes retorted, "That's because there's been no communications, because of the weather."

John Smith, the scout, said, "I believe him, too, Colonel. I saw that scalp when I was at the village, and it looked like an Injun's."

The room fell silent. Hayes tapped a pencil on his desk. This was not what he wanted to hear. He had hoped that Storm's story would give him an excuse to have Storm arrested, or—better yet—shot. He turned to the two enlisted men who had started all this. "This scalp that you saw, what did it look like?"

Winston and Barker looked at each other, unsettled. They

were not used to being addressed by an officer. "Don't know, sir," said Barker. "It was black."

Starke said, "Like an Indian's?"

"Yes, sir. I guess so, sir."

Hayes was unconvinced. "White men have black hair, too," he said. He considered what to do, tugging his big moustache.

He reached a decision. He stood. "Chief, you've been a bad Indian." He spoke as if he were addressing a child. Behind him, Jim Starke rolled his eyes at the captain's choice of words.

Hayes went on, "I cannot overlook this behavior. You agreed to keep the peace, and keep the peace you must. You must not attack your white brothers, or your red brothers. You and your people must be punished for what they have done. You must, and you will, learn the difference between right and wrong. Only then will you understand what it means to give your word."

Storm faced him, silent.

Hayes said, "I'm going to withhold one-half of your rations this month, Storm. If more scalps are seen in your village, more food will be taken away. You must be good Indians. You must learn to do as the White Father says."

Storm revealed no emotion. He might not have understood English, for all that it showed. After a minute he said, "I go now." Before Hayes could reply, the Cheyenne chief turned and left the building.

Angrily, Starke approached Captain Hayes. "You know that by withholding those rations, you're condemning some of those people to death, Captain—women and children."

"They've brought it on themselves," Hayes snapped. He didn't like Starke, and the man irritated him even further because he never addressed him by his brevet rank of colonel. "I'm not convinced that scalp is Crow. Even if it is, they're bound to have white scalps somewhere." He looked Starke in the eye. "And I'll counsel you to watch your tone with your superiors."

Not at all chastened, Starke stepped back.

Hayes walked out onto the porch, to watch the Indians depart. Bannerman joined him. In a low voice, so that the others couldn't hear, Bannerman urged, "Let me march out there and finish them. You remember what General Sherman said. Surely this is enough provocation."

Hayes watched the Indians through narrowed eyes. Without looking at Bannerman, he said, "I can't give that order, Colonel. There's the chance your man Starke or Smith might send in a formal protest. Our grounds *are* a bit shaky, you know. Given the pro-Indian state of affairs in Washington right now, an inquest might ruin both our careers."

Hayes went on, "We've cut the Indians' food. With luck, that will force them to show their hand." He smiled. "This is another nail in their coffin."

Bannerman was less sanguine. You old woman, he thought. He was convinced that Hayes lacked the guts to deal with the Cheyennes. All Hayes's talk about attacking them was just that—talk. The only way the Cheyenne issue would be settled was if Bannerman did it himself. Nothing would ever be done while Hayes was in command at Fort Pierce.

Outside post headquarters Storm said to his friends, "We leave." He swung onto his horse, and the five Cheyennes rode out of the fort. All of the white men's eyes were on them. Storm could feel their stares, but he did not look. He held his head high, but inside he was troubled.

He knew the white soldier chiefs wanted an excuse to attack his people. He remembered Sand Creek, and how the whites had behaved just before they attacked there. He knew the white soldiers did not believe him about the scalp. They did not trust him.

He would have to make them trust him, he decided. He would have to find a way to prove his friendship.

21

At the end of April, Emily Hayes gave a birthday party for her husband. All the post's officers were invited, even Jim Starke—the party was in the Hayes's quarters, and Starke guessed that Emily wanted to make the little house seem as crowded as possible. She'd had the house decorated by men from her husband's company, with the walls freshly painted and garlands of wildflowers placed in tasteful locations. The company cooks had prepared the food.

Emily wore her best dress, a prewar affair of lavender silk. The men wore undress uniforms. Helene Bannerman was in black. She had not recovered from her son's death. She was rarely seen outside her quarters these days. Her eyes were clear, though; she hadn't been drinking.

Emily Hayes was a tower of forced gaiety. "Before you cavalrymen leave for the field, we should organize a buffalo hunt," she suggested. "It would be such fun." She turned to Helene. "Have you ever shot buffalo, dear?"

"No," Helene replied. "I've never shot anything."

"Such a *thrill*, I assure you. I've done it many times, of course."

"Of course," Helene said.

Neal Bannerman was enthusiastic about the idea. "It would be good for you," he told his wife. "Fresh air, all that."

Emily said, "And afterward we can feast on the tongues and humps. They're *so* delicious."

"Perhaps we could give the rest of the meat to the men," Starke suggested. "It's been a while since they've had anything but salt pork."

"Why, yes. Of course. What a wonderful idea," Emily

said frostily. She changed the subject. "Lieutenant Conroy, would you grace us with your piano playing?"

Conroy bowed. "Delighted, ma'am."

He sat at the piano and began a sprightly rendition of the "Radetsky March." Mrs. Hayes liked to dance with the junior officers. Only Starke and Gottfried were available. She would have died before dancing with Starke, so she chose Gottfried. Of all the officers on the post, young Gottfried was the least keen on dancing. He especially wasn't keen on dancing with Mrs. Hayes; but she was the wife of his company commander, and if he knew what was good for him, he would dance and act as though he loved every second of it. So he did.

Neal Bannerman found himself standing beside the guest of honor. Warren Sumner Hayes was not as happy as might have been expected. He was forty-three today. Another year gone by, and he was no further along the road to general—or even to major. For once, Bannerman felt sorry for the diminutive infantryman. He knew how Hayes felt.

Hayes said, "We need a war, Bannerman. A real war, with England or France. England would be my choice. They've got the bigger empire. Presents us more opportunities. Where's the glory in fighting a bunch of cowardly savages?"

Bannerman laughed to himself as he lit a cigar. Hayes was a paper pusher. What good would he be in a war? Bannerman couldn't resist a dig. "Speaking of that, sir. When are we going to deal with our own bunch of savages?"

"In good time."

"The grass will soon be high enough to support their ponies, you know."

"I assure you, they won't be allowed to move south," Hayes said. "Not without a significant reduction in population."

Bannerman puffed the cigar. He wished he were rid of this cautious foot slogger. Bannerman knew that if he were commanding the fort, the incident with the scalp would have been enough. He'd have done more than deprive the Cheyennes of a few boxes of hardtack. He would have attacked them, and damn the consequences. He couldn't wait for summer, so he could get into the field, away from the stultifying atmosphere of Fort Pierce.

With Conroy at the piano, Jim Starke found himself with no one to talk to. He shifted from foot to foot, smoking a cigar, trying not to look bored. He saw Helene Bannerman by the punch bowl.

He hesitated, then he put down the cigar and moved toward the punch. "Good evening, Mrs. Bannerman."

Helene looked up. Coolly, she said, "Mr. Starke. Good evening."

Their eyes met, and Starke's heart almost fell out of his chest. The two of them had not talked since that evening in her quarters. They had agreed it must be that way. It would have been impossible to conduct an affair at a military post, especially one as small as Fort Pierce, and keep it secret. Everyone would have known. The scandal would have ruined both Helene's reputation and Starke's career. More importantly, as they had both realized, such an affair would have been morally wrong. Helene was a married woman.

"How are you this evening?" Helene said, with stilted politeness.

"Fine, ma'am. And you?"

"As well as can be expected."

Memories flooded over Starke. Memories of her pale body, the taste of her lips, the feel of her silky skin against his. He wondered what she thought of that night. He wondered what she thought of him. She acted as though it had never happened.

"May I pour you some punch?" he said.

"Yes. Thank you."

He poured punch for both of them. It was lemonade. They sipped it awkwardly.

"The punch is good," Starke said.

Helene arched an eyebrow. "You don't really mean that, do you?"

Starke laughed in spite of himself. In a low voice he said, "As a matter of fact, I've made better concoctions from week-old puddles of rainwater."

Suddenly there it was—her smile—like a glimpse of hidden treasure. She said, "The Hayeses must drink lemonade till it comes out their ears. No wonder she's so sour."

They grinned at each other. Across the room, Emily Hayes, dancing, observed them with shrewish eyes.

Helene became reserved and somber once again. "Shall you hunt the buffalo, Mr. Starke?"

Starke felt his pulse quicken. "Yes, I believe I may. And you?"

She was about to reply when there came the crackle of gunshots.

The music stopped. Everyone turned. The men began moving toward the door.

"What is it?" said Hayes.

"Don't know," Bannerman said. "Sounds like it came from the stables."

"Indians stealing the horses?"

"That's my guess."

The door was flung open. Cool night air poured into the stuffy house. Outside, there were shouts and the sound of running feet, as the guards moved in the direction of the gunfire.

The men came out onto the porch. Mrs. Hayes was right behind them. The O.D. hurried up, crossing the parade ground. It was the ascetic translator of Latin, McBride, saber clanking, the red sash over his shoulder.

"What is it?" Captain Hayes demanded.

"Deserter, sir," said McBride, slightly out of breath. "One of the K's. He stole a horse and rode out. The guards fired at him."

"Did they hit him?"

"Don't know, sir." McBride hastened back to join the guards.

Just behind McBride came Sergeant Townsend, who had the ability to move fast without seeming to hurry. Despite the late hour, and the fact that he'd been off duty, every button of his jacket was fastened, his forage cap squared away, and his cane tucked under his arm. He came to attention in front of Bannerman and saluted.

Bannerman said, "Who was it, Sergeant?"

"Cassaday, sir."

Bannerman shook his head. "Don't know the fellow."

Townsend spoke patiently. "Dark 'air, sir, medium 'eight, comes from New York. Always playing cards. You remember 'im from the campaign last summer, sir."

"Oh, yes. I think I do know who you mean."

"Yes, sir. Orders, sir?"

Bannerman was tight-lipped, aware of the infantry officers and Mrs. Hayes staring at him, aware of their smug superiority. He recalled the ridicule he'd endured for having so many deserters last summer, and he was determined not to have a repeat of it this year. "I'll have no more desertions in my command, Sergeant. Assemble a detail of ten men, with Sergeant McDermott in charge. Have them ready to ride at first light. Full marching order, rations for ten days. I'll lead them myself."

"Very well, sir." Sergeant Townsend saluted briskly, did an about-face, and set off toward the company area.

Smiling, Mrs. Hayes shepherded her guests off the porch and back into the house. "The excitement's over," she said. "Please, continue the party."

22

Jack Cassaday stumbled along the rough ground. The ground looked flat as a flapjack, until you tried to walk it, then it became a pain in the ass. Jack was not used to so much walking in his heavy troop boots, and his feet were killing him.

Jack carried his seven-shot Spencer carbine; he'd thrown away his heavy leather carbine sling. His blanket was rolled over his shoulder, infantry style. His horse had died late yesterday. A lucky shot from the guards at the fort had wounded it. Jack had gotten as much mileage out of the

animal as he could before it gave out on him. The nearest
settlement was Julesburg, on the South Platte. That was
where he had originally planned to exchange horses. He
would have to buy a horse now, along with some civilian
clothes. That would probably take most of his money. First,
he had to get to Julesburg. It was going to be a hard walk.
He reckoned he was somewhere near the South Fork of the
Republican right now.

Pausing on a low ridgeline, he sat on a rock, pulled out
some of his hardtack, and munched it. God, but he'd be glad
to see the end of this stuff. He didn't know what they ate in
the mining camps, but it had to be better than salt pork and
angle cake.

From this spot he could see a long way. What a country—
empty as an officer's head. In the distance, he thought he
could make out the breaks of the Republican.

Then something on his back trail caught his eye. Move-
ment. He squinted.

"Shit," he said.

It was a small column of riders. They were soldiers; he
could tell by the way they rode. They must be coming after
him.

He looked around. There was nowhere to hide. And there
were too many soldiers for him to shoot it out.

"Shit," he said again.

If it hadn't been for that damn horse getting hit, he would
have made it. His mistake had been stealing the animal from
the stables, letting the guards have a shot at him. Damn those
foot sloggers, he'd never figured they'd fire on him. Next
time, he'd do it another way.

Glumly, he stayed on the rock and awaited the inevitable.
All the deserters who had gotten away last summer, and he
had to be the one to get captured . . . He wondered how long
he'd get in the guardhouse for this. He hated that damned
mill. Maybe if he bribed Link, he could get him to reveal
where he'd hidden some of those bottles—everybody knew
Link had booze in there. Or maybe he could get somebody
to sneak him booze when he was released for the daily shit
detail around the post. If he was going to be in the mill, he
might as well be drunk.

* * *

Jack was twenty-three. He'd never known his father; he'd heard he was in prison. His mother was a lazy slut who'd taken little interest in him. He'd been raised by his grandmother, which meant that he'd more or less raised himself. He'd been in trouble on and off since he was a kid—fighting, stealing, rolling drunks for money to stake himself in card games. His ambition was to be a big-time gambler like Mike Collins, a legendary figure in the saloons of Hell's Kitchen.

Then he and some friends had been caught robbing a warehouse full of imported furs. Jack was the only member of the gang who had chosen the army over jail. He'd figured that the army would provide him transportation close to the western mines, and those mines were a place where he could practice his trade and maybe get rich in the process. Then he could return to New York in style.

Jack had hated the army from the first day. It had been summer when he'd joined K Company in the field, too late in the year to desert. He'd needed to learn how to ride and take care of his horse before he tried anything like that. He thought of Mad Dog Winston and his horse, which had bolted during General Sherman's parade.

A year ago Jack hadn't been much different from Mad Dog. The big difference was, he hadn't had as much trouble with the veterans, especially Link. He didn't know why Link had such a burr up his ass about Mad Dog. Link was a funny guy. If he didn't like you, he didn't like you, and that was it. Jack decided it must be because Mad Dog had replaced Amassee. Amassee had been an old campaigner. He and Link had served together in Texas, in the prewar days. There weren't many left from that time, and Link had been upset when Amassee died.

Jack sighed. He could make out his pursuers clearly now. They were coming on fast; they could tell from his prints that he was close by. That Injun-loving scout, Smith, was in the lead. Behind Smith was a detail of ten men, along with an officer and an NCO. It looked like Super Soldier himself in command. He must be big time, Jack thought, for the C.O. to come after him.

The NCO was Sergeant McDermott. Jack swore. Mc-Dermott was the meanest sergeant in the company, if not the regiment. Talk had it that Bannerman wanted him to be first sergeant when Townsend retired. The ride back was going to be rough. McDermott would see to that.

A quarter mile off, the soldiers stopped. They must have seen him, sitting on the ridgeline, forlornly munching the hardtack. They must know he couldn't be a threat to them, one man against thirteen. Why didn't they just come and take him?

The detail dismounted. Horse holders led the mounts to the rear. The rest of the men spread out, carbines drawn.

"Oh, for Christ's sake," Jack said out loud. Trust Super Soldier to make a big production out of this. "Typical army bullshit."

The men spread around Jack's position in a rough circle. Jack shook his head at the stupidity of it. Then he had a thought. What if they expected him to make a stand? What if they started shooting? Exposed like this, he was an easy target.

He moved down and along the ridgeline to a cluster of boulders where he had cover.

When the soldiers had completed their circle, they halted. Now what? Jack wondered.

Two of the figures detached themselves from the circle and started forward. It was Super Soldier and that bastard McDermott. Bannerman had his pistol drawn; McDermott carried his carbine at the ready. Bannerman said something to the sergeant, then the two men spread out.

Jack sighed and waited. He drank as much water as he could from his canteen. McDermott probably wouldn't let him have any water after he was captured. McDermott was that way.

When Bannerman and McDermott were about thirty yards off, Jack cried, "I give up. All right?"

"Show yourself," Bannerman ordered.

Jack stood, hands above his head.

"Get rid of the carbine."

Slowly, Jack reached down. He took the carbine and tossed it a little ways from him.

Bannerman and McDermott advanced until they were right in front of him.

In a low voice McDermott said, "Take out your pistol, troop."

Jack unsnapped his holster flap. He drew his pistol. "You didn't have to go to all this trouble, sir. I swear, I would never shoot at—"

Bannerman and McDermott opened fire. The first bullet gouged a hole in Jack's sternum and lodged in his spine. The second hit him in the left eye, passed through his brain, and blew out the back of his skull. The third shattered a rib and broke into pieces, shredding a lung. The fourth smashed through Jack's lower jaw, knocking out four teeth, and was deflected upward, lodging behind his nose.

Jack fell onto his back, the pistol in his hand. His remaining eye stared sightlessly.

Bannerman and McDermott stood over the dead man. Bannerman said, "We attempted to disarm him. He drew his pistol on us and we were forced to fire." They had discussed their story while walking forward, but Bannerman wanted to make sure McDermott remembered it.

"Yes, sir," said McDermott.

"He deserted under wartime conditions. As far as I'm concerned, he got what was coming to him."

"Yes, sir."

"Do you drink, McDermott?"

"A bit, sir. Now and again."

"When we get back to the fort, you'll find five gallons of whiskey in your name at the sutler's, charged to my account."

"Thank you, sir."

Five gallons of whiskey, Bannerman thought. The price of a man's silence. The price of a man's life.

McDermott said, "Do we bury him here, sir?"

"No. We'll wrap him in a blanket and take him back to the fort. Let him be an example to anyone else who might want to run for it."

23

The men of K Company were engaged in dismounted drill when Captain Bannerman and his detail returned. Bannerman led his men through the main gate and around the parade ground in columns of twos. Sergeant McDermott came last, leading the supply mule. Slung across the mule's back was something wrapped in bloodstained gray army blankets. Boots protruded from beneath the blankets.

On the parade ground there were muttered curses and oaths from men as they went through the manual of arms. "That bastard Bannerman," whispered the Arab, glancing sideways at the returning detail.

"Jack must've put up a fight," said Numb Nuts, behind him.

"Not Jack," said Dutch Hartz. "He was not so stupid."

There was a note of panic in young Walsh's voice. "They murdered him, that's what they done."

"Enough o' that," barked Sergeant Townsend, never missing a beat of his cadence. "Eyes front. Keep your minds on what you're doing. Right shoulder—arms!"

Harry went limp inside. His stomach turned. That lump under those blankets had been his bunky, Jack. Harry despised a system that could do this to a man, yet he was trapped by that same system. The worst part was, he had joined that system of his own free will.

Bannerman's detail was dismissed. As they led their horses to the stables, the rest of the company was ordered to form up in the company area.

The men came to attention, and Captain Bannerman addressed them. The mule with Jack's body was behind him. Bannerman's uniform was dusty and sweat-stained. His face was streaked with trail grime. "We have brought back the body of a coward and a deserter," he told the sullen men. "Let his end be a lesson to those who might choose to run." He indicated the shapeless form. "This man has forfeited any claim to a military funeral. The army has no more use for him. Anyone who wants him can have him. Otherwise, I'll have him burned, with the rest of the trash."

Bannerman turned and walked away. Sergeant Townsend said, "Company—dis-miss!"

Jack's friends took charge of his body. Hunter, the one-handed cripple, was near tears with grief and anger. "God-damn son of a bitch army. There was no need for this. No need. They didn't have to kill him."

"Jack was a big boy," said Link Hayward. "He knew the chance he was taking. Nobody held a gun to his head and made him desert."

"Yeah," Hunter said. "It was after they caught him that they held the gun to his head."

About half the company accompanied Jack's body off the post. Sergeant Townsend gave them permission; he would have gone with them, but he had business with the C.O. They buried Jack on the open prairie. The Professor carved Jack's name on a hastily made headboard. "Anybody know Jack's birthday, or how old he was?" the Professor asked.

Corporal Bannon said, "He was born in 'forty-four. That's what he put on his records, anyway. I seen 'em once, in the company office."

From the fort came a great whooping and shouting.

The men turned. "Now what?" said the Arab.

"Maybe Super Soldier's got cholera," Link suggested.

"We should be so lucky," Skull said.

Dutch Hartz, the most religious man in the company, said a few words over Jack's grave. The men filled in the dirt and started back to the fort, where the whooping and hollering went on unabated. Harry stayed at Jack's grave for a minute, then followed the others.

As they reentered the post, Link stopped a passing infantryman. "What's going on?"

"We're getting paid!" the foot slogger cried. "The news

just come over the telegraph from Wallace! The paymaster will be here tomorrow.''

The men from K Company let out their own whoops of joy. For most, it would be their first pay in seven months. In the excitement, Jack Cassaday was forgotten.

The paymaster arrived on Friday. Payday was Saturday. The men spent Saturday morning getting ready for inspection. Uniforms were brushed, brass polished, belts and shoes heel-balled until they shone. The men went to the bathhouse by platoons. There, they turned in their old, lice-ridden underwear to be burned and drew a new issue.

In line in front of Harry, Link Hayward pulled off his undershirt. Harry winced involuntarily. Link's back was a mass of old scars.

Behind Harry, Walsh's eyes bulged. "Jesus, Link. What happened to your back?''

Link acted nonchalant. "That's from the old days, before the war, when they still allowed flogging in the army. You had to be tough to be a soldier then. There weren't any pansies around, like Mad Dog.''

Harry didn't rise to the bait. He'd gotten used to it.

Link went on, "Hey, Skull—tell him what they used to do to you in the Legion.''

Skull gave his big-toothed grin. "The sergeants, they used to tie us across the gun carriages and beat us with sticks. A refinement of the bastinado.'' He and Link laughed, as if they had considered such treatment great fun.

The men bathed and dressed. At precisely noon they lined up for pay.

The pay table had been set up in front of Company H.Q. The paymaster and Captain Bannerman sat behind it, with the pay chest. Armed guards flanked them. Lieutenant Starke and Sergeant Townsend stood to the side. One by one the men presented themselves. Those who passed inspection were paid; those who didn't were sent back to barracks to try again.

When it was Harry's turn, he marched up, snapped to attention, and saluted. "Winston, Henry J. Private, 23507. Reporting for pay, sir.''

Captain Bannerman looked him over, pursing his lips. "Your shoes are dirty, Winston. Go back and polish them."

Harry tried not to let his disappointment show. He had polished the shoes for half an hour. "Yes, sir." He dropped his salute, wheeled, and returned to the barracks.

Inside, those who had been paid got ready to go into town. The veterans were putting on their white jackets. The stable jackets had been issued to the regiment for evaluation, against possible army-wide issue. The men of K Company had purchased extras with their own money, then had them altered by Quince, the company tailor, adding brass buttons, until they were tight-fitting and quite smart.

The men who'd been sent back were lounging around, or working on their deficiencies. Harry got his cleaning kit from his footlocker. Nearby, the Professor lay on his bunk reading the new *Police Gazette*. "What did they get you for?" the Professor asked Harry.

"Shoes," said Harry. "What about you?"

"Brass."

"They got me for dirt under the fingernails," complained Barker, walking in. He held out his hands. "Look, there's no dirt. I cleaned them."

To the Professor, Harry said, "So why aren't you working on your brass?"

The bearded Professor smiled benignly. "There's nothing wrong with my brass—or your shoes. It's just typical army bullshit. They're playing with your mind."

"Why?" Harry asked.

The Professor shrugged. "They don't have anything better to do, I guess. It's supposed to make us better soldiers. Just sit here and wait till everybody else has been paid, then go back."

Harry said, "What if the captain sends me back again?"

"He won't. He got paid today, too. He's got other things to do besides wait all day for you to get your shoes shined right."

Harry took the Professor's advice and waited. When the pay line was gone, he gave his shoes a perfunctory swipe with his polishing cloth, then drifted back to the pay table with the Professor and the others, forming a new line. When Harry's turn came, he presented himself once again.

Captain Bannerman said, "Let's see those shoes, Winston."

Bannerman glanced at Harry's shoes. Harry held his breath.

Then the captain nodded. "That's better. You should have done it right the first time." He examined Harry's pay sheet. "That's six months, at sixteen dollars a month; plus eight days in November, at fifty-three and a third cents a day. That comes to one hundred dollars and twenty-six cents. Less stoppage of fifteen dollars' fine, and it comes to eighty-five dollars and twenty-six cents."

The paymaster counted out the money. "Sign here."

Harry signed and took the money. It looked like a fortune, after so long without. He saluted and stepped out of line. The sutler was waiting for him, to collect what he'd been pledged on credit. So were the company tailor, the barber, and the laundresses. When they were finished, Harry had seventy-six dollars and fifty-one cents. With that, he was better off than a lot of the men.

He started back to the barracks. Barker was right behind him. "Come on, Harry," he said. "Let's go downtown."

24

Watsonville. "Downtown." Sodom and Gomorrah on the Smoky Hill River.

Harry crossed the bridge into town with Barker, the Italian Squillace, and Dutch Hartz. Watsonville was a community of shacks and painted tents, with tin chimneys sticking through the tops. It meandered along a couple of winding streets, and consisted of cheap saloons and whorehouses, a

few restaurants, a dry goods store, and some tumbledown
residences. The streets were rutted, muddy, and full of garbage. On this Saturday afternoon, the town was dotted with
little knots of soldiers, come to spend their pay.

"What'll we do first?" Harry asked.

"Let's get a drink," Dutch said.

"There's the Professor," said Barker, sighting the bearded
ex-dentist across the street. "Come on, Professor, join us."

They all went to a saloon called Burke's. Harry felt ex-
pansive. He was glad to get away from the fort, and he wished
he never had to go back. "I'll get the first round," he said
as they entered.

"Nothing for me," said the Professor. "I've learned my
lesson. Once I start, I can't stop. Anyway, I'm saving my
money for when I get out—I only have ninety-eight more
days, you know. I'll just watch you boys make fools of yourselves. I'll be with you in spirit, though."

They bellied up to the bar. "Four whiskeys," Harry told
the barman.

The barman, a seedy fellow, poured the drinks. "That's a
buck," he said.

Harry laid out a dollar bill. The barman held out his hand
for more. Harry gave him a look.

"Greenbacks are discounted here," the barman explained. "They're only worth eighty-five cents on the dollar.
You want them drinks, you owe me fifteen more cents."

"What kind of bullshit is this?" said ex-grocer Barker,
with unusual boldness.

The barman said, "You don't like it, drink somewhere
else, soldier boy. See if you can do any better."

Harry and Barker looked to the veteran Dutch Hartz, who
nodded. "He's right, unfortunately."

Harry laid out another bill and got his change, making a
big show of counting it.

Barker was still angry. "I don't believe it. This is the thanks
we get for defending you people."

The barman laughed derisively. "You ain't defending me,
pal. You're defending the Kansas Pacific Railroad. They want
to steal land from the Indians, and you're here to do it for
them."

The men had their drinks, then went to another place for more. Then it was on to a restaurant, for a meal and yet more drinks. Harry wasn't used to hard liquor. He'd only had it a few times at home, and never to excess. He felt light-headed. It was fun. Everything seemed to be happening in slow motion. He felt like his feet were no longer touching the ground.

The meals were brought, the first civilian food the men had had in months. They dug in eagerly. At the next table a man from Fourth Platoon yelled "Onions!" and buried his face on his plate, lapping up the fried onions like a dog.

After the food and more drinks, the five men sat around the table, laughing and talking about how they'd come to join the army.

Squillace said, very seriously, "I join because I want to learn the English. I want to be a—how you call it—an *avvocato*, a lawyer. So far, all I learn to say is 'goddamn' and 'son of a bitch.' "

Dutch Hartz lit his pipe. "When I came to this country, I didn't know English, either. So I get off the boat, and a man comes up and talks to me, and I sign some papers. I'm happy—I think they're giving me the free land that I heard so much about at home. Instead, I'm in the army."

The whole table roared at that.

After another drink, Dutch said, "Let's go to the Tiger Club."

"What's that?" Barker said.

"You'll see."

The Professor left them before they went to the club. "I've got some errands to run, then it's back to the fort for me. You boys enjoy yourselves."

By now it was dark. The town was noisy. Music played. Somewhere a pistol went off, but no one paid much attention. From the outside, the Tiger Club was just a big saloon. In the front window was a sign that said, SOLDIERS WELCOME. Harry and the others went in. There was a front-room bar and a back room, called "My Lady's Bower," from whence came piano music and the sound of men yelling and cheering. The bar was crowded with soldiers and civilians employed at the fort. People came and went from the back room.

"We'll have a few drinks out here," Dutch said. "They cost twice as much in back."

By the time they went to the back room, Harry was slurring his speech and his gait was unsteady. Things drifted in and out of focus.

It cost them a dollar each to get into My Lady's Bower. It was darker in there, with only a few lanterns on the walls. A piano pounded. Men were whistling and cheering. As Harry's eyes adjusted to the dim light, he saw a bar that ran the far length of the room. Atop the bar a woman was dancing, to the catcalls and cheers of the packed crowd. The woman was naked. Men pushed forward to see her better. Bouncers, holding shillelaghs, sat on the edge of the bar to keep the men off. When a drunken infantryman tried to touch the woman, the nearest bouncer rapped his hand smartly with the shillelagh.

The room was hot and sweaty. It was smoky. The men's faces were flushed with excitement. Uniform jackets were unbuttoned from the heat. The white jackets of K Company mixed with the blue of the infantry and the cloth or buckskin of the civilians. Gaudily dressed whores circulated through the crowd.

Harry stared at the dancing girl in fascination. He had never seen a naked woman. She must be one of the whores, he thought. She was about twenty-two, skinny, with thin lips and a pinched face. She did not dance very well. The men loved her, though, especially when she made enticing gestures to them. They threw money on the bar for her. Next to Harry, Barker stood with his mouth open. Squillace squeezed behind them in the crowd, beaming. "I love this country," he said. Dutch Hartz was next to Squillace. Dutch had been here before, and he regarded the spectacle with detached amusement.

Harry saw Link Hayward in the front row. With Link were Skull, Starving Mike, Hunter, and Corporal Pickens. On Link's arm was a frowzy blonde. Harry wondered if that was Link's girl, Lou, the one Pick Forrester had mentioned, the one who followed Link from post to post.

Somebody touched Harry's shoulder. He turned to find a girl of about fifteen. Her plain face was heavily made-up, to make her look older. She wore a cheap, off-the-shoulder dress.

"Hi," she said. "I'm Judy. You're cute—what's your name?"

"Harry," Harry replied awkwardly.

"Do you like me?"

"What? I—I guess so."

"Do you want to go with me?"

"Go where?"

She looked put-upon. "Upstairs. Do you want to fuck me?"

Harry felt himself blushing. He'd never heard such language from a girl before.

"Come on," she said. "Twenty-five dollars."

Harry felt no attraction to her. She was just a child. He shook his head.

"Twenty," she said, above the noise of the crowd.

Harry said, "No, I don't—"

She grabbed his arm. She stood on tiptoe and stuck her tongue in his ear, breathing hotly. "Come on, Harry. Fifteen dollars. That's as low as the boss'll let me go."

"Really, I don't want to."

"Afraid of me?" she said.

"No. No, of course not. Why should I be afraid of you?"

A smile broadened her painted lips. "You've never been laid before, have you?"

"Huh? Sure I have," Harry lied. "Not a lot, maybe. But I have."

"No, you haven't. You're a cherry." She reached down and grabbed his penis. "Come on, I'll fix—"

He backed away in horror. "Jesus, would you stop that?"

He bumped into another soldier, who shoved him away. He turned back to the girl, but by then she had wearied of the chase and gone after more cooperative game. Barker and the others were laughing at him.

Harry kept drinking. Drinks were fifty cents in here, and the whiskey was watered down, but Harry didn't care. He poured the liquor down his throat.

The first dancing girl left the bar, and another climbed up. She was a big, red-haired farm girl. She started dancing, clumping around with exaggerated pelvic thrusts, taking off her clothes piece by piece, while the drunken soldiers roared their approval. Harry was not excited by the sight. He had not been excited by the first girl, or by the young whore. He wondered if there was something wrong with him.

In the crush, Harry became separated from his friends. He was close to the front of the bar now, near Link and his gang. He saw the frowzy blonde hand Link a bunch of sepia-toned *cartes de visite*, small souvenir photographs. Link and his friends passed the pictures around, chuckling and making lewd remarks. Harry peered over Link's shoulder. They were photographs of bare-breasted Cheyenne girls. They must have been taken at the gallery in town. Link's blonde laughed and made remarks along with the men.

On the bar, the big redhead was naked now. She bent down, twirling her heavy breasts in unison, first to the right, then to the left. Men yelled and cheered and pounded the tables. The first girl had gotten dressed and was going upstairs with an infantry sergeant.

There was a sudden undercurrent of muttering. Heads turned. Somebody had entered the back room. It was Gallagher, the corporal from I Company, with some of his buddies.

Gallagher and his friends shouldered their way to the bar. Harry was one of those who got pushed aside. Gallagher's friends were not a nice-looking bunch.

Gallagher sidled up next to Link's girl. "Hello, Lou. Free tonight?"

"I'm never *free*," replied the blonde. "And tonight I ain't available, neither."

Gallagher was not put off. "Another night, then. I've waited for you plenty of times before."

Anger flashed across Link's face, but he controlled himself.

Gallagher and his friends surrounded Link. The room grew tense. Infantry and cavalry began drawing apart, taking each other's measures. Above them, the naked girl danced on, oblivious. The piano pounded louder. Harry was so drunk that he had a hard time standing. He wondered where his friends had gone.

Gallagher moved closer to Link, forcing the girl Lou to step aside. Link leaned against the bar, drinking, seeming to pay no attention.

Gallagher ground a fist into his palm and smiled. "Now, boyo. What was that you said about me mother?"

Link put down his drink. He was apologetic, conciliatory. "I said, she's a wonderful lady. Heart of gold." He paused. "Plus, she's a great fuck."

Gallagher's eyes widened with surprise. Before he could do anything, Link drove his fist into the point of his nose, knocking him backward.

Link raised his fist to strike again, but somebody swung a chair and hit Link in the head, sending him to the floor. Skull kicked the man in the testicles. The infantryman dropped the chair and fell to the floor beside Link, clutching his groin in silent agony.

Instantly, the room became a battlefield. White-jacketed K's fought the blue-coated infantry and some of the civilians. There was shouting and cursing, the breaking of glass. Bottles and furniture flew. The head bouncer stood on the bar and shouted for order. Someone pulled him off, and he disappeared in a sea of fists.

Atop the bar the naked redhead screamed and scrambled to pick up the money that had been thrown at her, at the same time dodging hands that tried to pull her into the crowd and Lord only knew what fate. She picked up her clothes and scurried off the far end of the bar, leaping an outstretched arm, her fat buttocks bouncing. The rest of the bouncers flailed away with their shillelaghs, to no effect.

Harry looked around, dazed with drink. Men gouged at each other with broken bottles. They fought with belts, chairs, and pocket knives. Somebody took a swing at Harry and missed. He seemed to be leading a charmed life. A flying bottle hit the Arab in the face, breaking his nose. Harry saw Skull pick up an infantryman and slam him onto a wooden table, cracking the tabletop. The infantryman slid to the floor, unconscious. With his good hand, Hunter was hurling bottles as fast as he could. Starving Mike had somebody down and was kicking him in the ribs. Corporal Pickens stared at a knife wound in his right arm. Then somebody punched him in the jaw and laid him out.

Harry had to help. He moved into the fray. Somebody grabbed his arm, hard. It was Link, just getting up. Link's white jacket was covered with blood from a cut in the side of his head. He said, "Mind your own business. We don't want your help. You're not a K." He shoved Harry back out of the fight.

Gallagher was up now, too, facing Link. Gallagher pulled something from his pocket and slipped it onto his fist. Brass knuckles. He grinned. Link pushed his girl away. "Get out of here, Lok." The girl covered her head against the flying glass and made her way from the fight.

Gallagher came on, fist cocked. He swung. Link ducked and countered with a blow to the stomach that staggered Gallagher backward. Link tried to follow up, but Gallagher stopped him with a chopping blow to the jaw with the brass knuckles. Link's knees buckled. He shook off the pain. Gallagher swung again. Link tried to back away, but there were too many people around him, and the blow caught him on top of the head. His eyes went briefly white. He swayed. Gallagher swung again. Link blocked the blow with his forearm, but he yelped as the brass knuckles bit into the bone. Bleeding, Link lowered his head and waded through another punch. He caught Gallagher around the waist and bulled him to the floor, using his superior weight.

Gallagher tried to get up, but Link head-butted him. Gallagher's forehead split open. Blood ran into his eyes, blinding him. A punch from Link knocked Gallagher onto his back. Link leaped on him, smashing his recumbent form with his fists.

A shotgun boomed.

"Break it up, men! Break it up!" It was Lieutenant McBride, the O.D., wading through the crowd. He was followed by the town marshal and his deputies. The marshal was a long-haired gunman, and the deputies looked more like highwaymen than anything else. The marshal had fired the shotgun.

"Break it up!" McBride yelled again. "That's an order!"

Angrily, Link stood. He grabbed McBride by the collar

and the seat of the pants. He ran the lieutenant across the
room and threw him through the saloon's flimsy wall, into
the alley beyond, while the men from K Company howled
with glee. Then the marshal's shotgun butt cracked the back
of Link's skull. Link took a couple wobbly steps and collapsed to the floor.

The shotgun boomed again. The marshal, the deputies,
and guards from the fort moved in to break up the riot, ar-
resting the participants.

Without really knowing how he did it, Harry slipped away.
He was so drunk, he was not in control of himself. One
moment he was in the middle of a madhouse; the next, he
was outside in the cold night air. There was a full bottle of
whiskey in his hand. He must have stolen it from the bar or
from one of the tables, but he did not remember doing it.

He took a drink, burning with humiliation and hatred. He
hated Link; he hated the army. He hated the stupidity on his
part that had gotten him here. He couldn't take five years of
this. He had to get out.

Harry wandered the streets and alleys of Watsonville. He
looked for Barker and the others, but he didn't know where
they had gone. His head hurt, he was dizzy, and his stomach
was rolling. He stumbled and fell in the muck. After sitting
there stupidly for a minute, he pushed himself to his feet and
had another drink.

The next thing Harry knew, he was back at the fort. He
had no idea how he'd done it. He didn't remember going
through the gate, or passing the guards, or anything. Maybe
he'd sneaked in the back way. His bottle was almost empty.
Just looking at it made him feel sick. He tossed it away. He
wanted to go to bed.

He went into the barracks and wandered down the aisle,
bouncing off bunks. His head was spinning. In front of him,
Walsh's bunk had been curtained off with blankets. A man
was standing in front of the curtain. His gray shirt was hanging out of his unbuttoned trousers. Harry didn't know the
man; he was probably one of Walsh's friends from another
platoon. Harry wondered where Walsh was. Other men were
standing around in various stages of undress, drinking and
joking with one another.

The first man stopped Harry. In a comradely voice he said, "Hey, you want to get laid?"

"Huh?" Harry said.

"Go on, man. We got us a little Cheyenne bitched in there. We drunked her up and sneaked her in. Go ahead. She's doing it with everybody"

Harry stared at the curtain. He remembered the young whore in the bar. He remembered the burning shame. He was twenty-one, and he'd never been with a woman. Here it was for the taking, behind that curtain. It would be so easy.

"You sure it's all right?" he said.

"Sure, I'm sure. Go ahead."

Harry's heart was pounding.

"All right," he said. "Thanks."

He pulled open the curtain and went in.

It was dark inside the cubicle. Harry could barely see. The girl lay on the bunk. Harry smelled whiskey and something else—the same musty smell he'd noticed at the Cheyenne village that day. The girl made no noise.

Harry was unsure what to do. "Hi," he said.

There was no answer.

This was not the way he had pictured his first romantic encounter. He lay on the bunk beside the girl. Her face was a blur in the darkness. Harry started to kiss her.

"No," she begged. "No."

Her voice was plaintive, pitiful. She rolled her head from side to side, crying. "No," she said again. It was probably the only word of English she knew.

A wave of revulsion came over Harry. He pushed himself away from her.

The girl kept crying. "No. Please, no."

Harry stood. He stumbled back outside, trying to escape the sound of that voice.

The soldier was still there. He was surprised. "You done already?"

"Huh? What? No, I changed my mind."

"Why, man? She's really good."

"Yeah, I'm sure she is. I'm—I'm just not interested."

He wished he could do something to help the girl, but he was too drunk. Around him there were faces, looking at him like he was crazy. He stumbled down the aisle to his bunk. His head was whirling. His stomach turned. All he wanted was to sleep.

He got to the bunk and threw himself across it.

He landed on a uniform jacket. It couldn't be his jacket, because he was wearing his. It must be someone else's. Looking more closely, he realized that this was not his bunk.

He was in the wrong barracks.

Harry panicked. Where was he? How was he going to get back to his own barracks?

He got up and staggered back out. Men stared at him. No wonder Walsh hadn't been where he was supposed to be. The soldier by the curtain had probably thought he was somebody's buddy.

He went back outside. The cold night air chilled his sweating face. Nothing looked familiar. The stars above him were spinning, and he could not make them stop. He had no idea where he was. He started crying. He just wanted to sleep. Suddenly his stomach heaved and he was sick all down the front of his uniform. The blood drained from his head. Hot flashes surged over him. He sank to his knees in a helpless stupor. He felt so awful, so sorry for himself.

He forced himself to get up again. His legs were as weak and unsteady as a newborn colt's. He stumbled around, peering at the building he had just come from. It was an infantry barracks. He was in I Company's area. He headed toward his own company, or where he hoped to find it. He moved from building to building, holding on for support.

He heard distant shouts and laughter, from the sutler's. He was sick again. Tears ran from his eyes and mixed with the vomit on his chin.

At last he came to his own building. He crawled up the steps on his hands and knees. It took all his strength to pull himself up and go inside. He weaved down the aisle, knocking into bunks, bruising his shins. He heard someone snoring.

Then there was a bunk in front of him. It was his own. He collapsed across it and fell into a dead sleep.

25

First Sergeant Edgar Townsend was scared. He was scared of the future.

A week ago he had been called into Captain Bannerman's office. Bannerman had been looking through Townsend's service records. The captain had said, "I see your time expires in a few months, Top."

"Yes, sir," Townsend replied.

"You putting in reenlistment papers?"

"I 'ad 'oped to, sir."

Bannerman looked at the file again. "How old are you now, Top—forty-seven?"

"Yes, sir," said Townsend. Actually, he was fifty-five.

Bannerman chewed on the end of his ever-present cigar. Without conviction he said, "This is hard for me to do, Top, but I won't be able to approve your reenlistment. I'm afraid the time has come for you to retire, to make room for younger men."

There it was. Just like that. Townsend said nothing. It was useless to argue—he knew that Bannerman wanted his own man in the First Sergeant's job—and he had too much pride to beg, especially before an officer like Bannerman. He had known this day would come eventually. He'd been lucky to hang on as long as he had. Soldiering was a young man's game.

Bannerman went on, "You won't be getting a pension. I'm sorry, of course, but we can't credit your time with the British Army."

"I was aware of that when I joined up, sir. I do receive a small amount from 'er Majesty."

Bannerman had seemed relieved. "There you are, then.

You're all set. Very well, Sergeant. That's all. You've been a credit to the company—to the entire regiment.''

"Thank you, sir.'' Townsend had saluted and left.

Now Townsend sat behind his desk in the company office. He was supposed to be rearranging his duty rosters. Half the company was in the guardhouse because of that brawl at the Tiger Club. He had barely enough men to fill out his extra duty assignments, plus he was supposed to find men to help the Supply wallah inventory equipment for the field—the regimental camp at Big Creek was in three weeks. If that wasn't enough, Lieutenant McBride of I Company was raising hell. He wanted Link Hayward court-martialed, sentenced to hard labor—boiled in oil, if it could be arranged—for throwing him through the wall of the saloon.

Try as he would, Townsend couldn't keep his mind on his work. He kept daydreaming. He found himself doing that more and more lately, reliving his youth, looking back instead of looking ahead. He supposed it was a sign of growing old. Or of fear . . .

Edgar Townsend was the son of a Hampshire parson. He had been a wild, rebellious youth. The life of a country parsonage had not been for him. He had run away when he was twelve and apprenticed himself to a wandering horse trader. Later, he'd been a prize fighter and wrestler, traveling the circuit of county fairs. At seventeen he'd taken the old King's shilling and joined His Majesty's Eighth Regiment of Foot. Eventually he'd been posted out to India.

India. The very name triggered memories. Of searing heat and drenching monsoons. Of sights and sounds and smells. Of women. One woman Townsend would never forget—a dancing girl in Delhi named Hosainee. Even now the thought of Hosainee made him squirm. She had been lithe and beautiful, mysterious and perfumed and skilled in the ways of love, a world apart from those painted cows in Watsonville. If ever he had been in love, it had been with Hosainee.

Then had come the Mutiny. That had been eleven years ago. Hosainee had disappeared during the siege of Delhi— killed by the Pandies because she'd associated with the British, perhaps, or killed by the British because she was a wog.

Or simply gone back to her village. Townsend had never found out.

Townsend had fought all through the mutiny. He'd been reckoned old even then—not up to the rigors of campaigning, they'd said. He'd showed them, though. Afterward, sickened by the horrors he'd witnessed, and by the loss of Hosainee, he had taken his discharge. He'd come to the States just in time for the Civil War.

Now, a lifetime of soldiering was about to end. Townsend was a relic, gray-bearded and bald, he who had once been handsome enough to turn the ladies' heads. What was there for him after this?

He could return to India. He could be a plantation overseer. Then he remembered the bad parts about India—the heat, the fever. He had no wish to go through that again. He'd been lucky to live through it the first time.

He could open a public house near a military post. Spend his days pouring drinks and slinging the bat with the lads. But he had no money for a pub. The little bit he got from England was of no account, and in thirty-eight years of soldiering, he'd not saved more than a few dollars.

What, then? He was too old to start any sort of career. Like as not, he'd end up like many another hero, wearing his ribbons and standing outside Hyde Park, begging for charity. No, he thought, he couldn't even do that. He didn't have the money to get back to Hyde Park, and beggars weren't likely to last long in the American West, where charity was an unknown concept.

He sighed. He'd suffered wounds, disease, and unspeakable privations; and he had nothing to show for it. But the truth was, if he had to do it all over, he wouldn't change a thing. He'd had some grand times.

There had been that Christmas in Aligarh, when he and Driscoll and Tilden had . . .

A knock on the door roused him from his reverie.

He looked up. "Come," he said.

The door opened. It was Private Winston. Winston had just come off punishment. This was the Monday after payday. Winston had been dirty at roll call this morning—

apparently he'd been sick all day Sunday. Along with Walsh, who'd also been delinquent, Winston had spent the morning carrying a heavy log around the parade ground. The lad looked all in. Townsend remembered some of his own payday hangovers, and he laughed to himself.

"Yes, Winston. What is it?"

With difficulty, Winston held himself at attention. "I'd like permission to speak to the captain, First Sergeant."

"What do you want to speak to 'im about?"

Winston hesitated. "I want a transfer, First Sergeant. Out of the company—out of the regiment, if possible."

Townsend tucked his chin into his chest. He assumed his thoughtful air. "I see. And why do you want this transfer?"

"It's a personal matter, First Sergeant."

Townsend stared at him.

After a second, Winston went on, "I—I can't get along with the other men, First Sergeant. I've tried, but I can't."

Townsend nodded. "This 'as something to do with Private 'ayward, 'asn't it?"

"I'd rather not say, First Sergeant."

"That's all right. I know it does." Townsend remembered when he had been a young soldier, thrown in with the wolves. It had been rougher for him in one way, because, unlike the American Army, so many of the British Army were long-serving hard cases; easier in another way, because he'd been a hard case himself. To Winston, he said, "Permission to see the Captain refused."

"But—"

"You'll get no sympathy from me, laddie. You're a man. You're old enough to make your own decisions, old enough to live wiv them. You signed on to be a soldier, and that's what we're going to make of you."

Winston was silent, but his frustration and anger showed.

Townsend went on, "Running away from your troubles won't do you no good. There's a Link 'ayward in every company. You've got to face up to 'im."

"I have faced up to him, First Sergeant. I even fought with him, but it didn't help. Link won't accept me, and in K Company that means the company won't accept me. Link and his friends push ahead of me in the mess hall line. They rip up my bunk and footlocker before inspection. They've kept me on punishment since I've been here. I can't take any more.''

"You'd be surprised what you can take, lad. It might also surprise you to know that I believe you can make a soldier. But you've got to give yourself a chance." Townsend could see that Winston didn't believe him. He added, "By the way, was you involved in that scrap at the Tiger Club Saturday night?''

Winston's jaw tightened, as if at a bad memory. "I was at the Tiger Club, but I wasn't in the fight.''

"Mm. Sounds like a grand dust-up. Sorry I missed it.'' Townsend cleared his throat. "Very well, Winston. Dismiss. Return to your duties.''

Winston started to protest.

Townsend's voice hardened. "That's all, Winston.''

The young soldier bit back his words. "Yes, First Sergeant.''

Harry wheeled and left the company office. Tears welled in his eyes. He couldn't help it. Sergeant Townsend was wrong. His brother Ed and Link were right. He didn't have what it took to be a soldier. Not now, not ever. In this, as in everything else, he was a failure.

Four and a half more years of K Company would drive him mad, or kill him. If they wouldn't transfer him, he would get out. He only knew one way out, and he was determined to take it.

He was going to desert.

26

Harry began to store up hardtack and salt pork, just as Jack Cassaday had done. There were only three weeks until the company marched out, so he had to work fast.

He knew the dangers he faced. He knew that Jack's fate could be his own if he were caught. But he didn't care. He'd rather be dead than spend any more time in the army.

His plan was to desert while he was at the grazing area, on herd guard—a detail he drew at least once a week. Nobody would shoot at him that way. He would stampede the horse herd behind him, to spread confusion and delay pursuit. He would go right before the company marched for Big Spring, when he hoped they would be too busy to send men after him.

With the few dollars left from his pay, he bought some civilian clothes in Watsonville. Unlike Jack, he would head east, hoping to lose himself in the thriving Kansas rail towns. There, he would sell his weapons, saddle, and government-issue horse. Then he would drift south, to Texas. He would stay there a few years, until the heat had blown over, then return home to Pennsylvania.

He wondered about the reaction of his parents and his brother Ed when they found out that he'd deserted. It didn't matter. His mind was made up. He counted the days until he knew blessed freedom again, even if as a fugitive.

In the meantime, the company was getting ready for the campaign. Wagons were repaired. Horses and pack mules were reshod. Weapons and equipment were inspected, and defective items repaired or replaced. Sabers and other surplus stores were boxed and turned in.

In the midst of all this preparation and bustle, Hunter re-

ceived his discharge. After the riot at the Tiger Club, Dr.
Dudley was finally persuaded that Hunter had lost the use of
his right hand. He petitioned to have Hunter let go. Captain
Bannerman was tired of fighting it, and he agreed.

Hunter was mustered out. He said his good-byes and left
the barracks for the last time.

A few minutes later the men heard Hunter's voice. "Hey!
Boys!"

The men crowded out onto the barracks porch. Hunter
stood on the parade ground. "Watch this," he cried.

He held up his right hand, the crippled one, and began
flexing the fingers. There was no evidence of pain or difficulty. He tossed his forage cap into the air with the hand. He
picked up his carryall with it and twirled it around, laughing
like a madman.

"Ha! Ha!" he cried. "Fuck the armyyy!"

On the porch the men were laughing and whistling. "Way
to go!" they cried. "Good job!"

Sergeant Townsend came up, stick tucked beneath his arm.
He took it all in stride. "I knew that lad was swinging the
lead," he said.

In front of Post H.Q., Captain Bannerman did a slow burn.
Captain Hayes had been called down the line, to Fort Riley,
to serve on a board of court-martial, leaving Bannerman in
temporary command at Fort Pierce. Bannerman turned to
the duty orderly. "Orderly, my compliments to the sergeant
of the guard. Have him escort that 'civilian' off the post."

"Yes, sir," said the orderly.

With Hunter's departure, Barker—who had been Hunter's
bunky—obtained permission to switch platoons and become
Harry's new bunky. Barker had changed since he'd joined
up. Months of hard work and carrying the punishment log
had turned his pudgy frame to muscle. His once prominent
jowls had disappeared.

As Barker stowed his gear, he was excited. "Harry, guess
what? I got a letter from Susan in today's mail. She wants to
get back together, Harry. She says it's her fault we broke up,
and she's sorry. She says she's going to wait for me. Isn't that
great?"

"Yeah," said Harry, "it is. I'm glad for you. I know how much you wanted to stay with her. At least the army's done somebody some good."

Emily Hayes saw her husband's absence as no reason to cancel her buffalo hunt. It would be the last social event before the cavalry left for the summer—possibly the last social event with the officers of K Company for a long while, for who knew where they would be stationed next winter?

The enlisted men of K Company were needed for the hunt, as well, to load the picnic lunches, to scout for buffalo, then to drive the herd toward the hunters. . . .

The buffalo herd thundered across the prairie. There were thousands of the shaggy beasts, large and small. The hunters rode on the buffaloes' left flank, heads low on their horse's necks, each hunter picking out an animal and looking for a shot. Both men and women wore scarves knotted around their heads, to decrease the wind resistance. The ladies rode astride; their riding dresses had been slit up the middle, then sewn together to form rough pants. Each rider carried a carbine and a revolver. Now and then a shot rang out. Above the roar of hoofs a faint cry of triumph could be heard as one of the huge animals fell.

Emily Hayes was an old hand at buffalo hunting. She'd ridden on her first hunt twenty years before, when the great herds had stretched as far as the eye could see. She loved the sport. It gave her a chance to show that she could ride and shoot as well as any man.

This was Helene Bannerman's first hunt. She was here for the thrill of the chase. Shooting animals was not in her blood. She carried weapons, but she had no intention of using them.

The stream of buffalo flowed across the plains, over and down the rolling hills. The chase was spread out over a good mile when Helene's horse went lame. She pulled away from the hunt, unnoticed in the noise and dust and confusion. The buffalo and the hunters disappeared, leaving Helene alone in a little valley.

The heavy drumming of hoofs receded into the distance. The thick dust settled around Helene and her horse, a white-

stockinged sorrel mare. She suspected the animal had caught
a stone in its hoof. She propped up the bad leg and found that
she had been right. She couldn't work out the stone with her
fingers, and she had no knife. She walked the animal along
slowly, searching for a sharp twig with which to dig it out.

On the hillside above her were hoofbeats. She looked up
to see Jim Starke riding down to her. Starke wore a blue
flannel shirt and buckskin trousers. The red bandanna tied
around his head and the blond moustache gave him the look
of a pirate.

He drew up and dismounted. "Are you all right? I saw
you pull your horse out of line."

"Yes," Helene said. "She has a stone in her hoof."

"Here. Let me see."

Starke handed her his horse's reins. He took her mount's
foreleg. He pulled his sheath knife and dug out the offending
stone.

"There," he said, as the horse tested its leg gingerly.
"She'll be all right." He went on, "You're lucky she didn't
break her leg. Lose your horse out here, and you could be in
real danger. You're a long way from the fort. You could get
lost, run out of water. You could even run into hostile Indians."

As he handed her back the horse's reins, their fingers
touched. They looked away from each other shyly.

After a second, Starke turned back. "How have you
been?" he said. He felt awkward. It was as if he were meeting her for the first time, as if that night in her quarters had
never happened.

"Fine, I suppose," she said. "And you?"

"Well enough. Will you . . . will you still be leaving for
the East soon?"

Her full lips narrowed. "There's a government supply train
scheduled to come through from Colorado next month. I'll
be going with them."

"Looking forward to it?"

"In some ways, yes. In others . . ." Her voice trailed off
and she gave him a pointed look.

They were silent for a moment, then Starke said, "It seems
funny being like this. Alone."

"I know."

"There's so much I've wanted to say to you, since—since that night. I'd started to think I'd never meet you like this again."

"I thought we decided it's for the best if we don't meet like this," she said.

"I know what we decided, but is that really the way you want it to be?"

She lowered her eyes and shook her head.

"I—I've never spoken like this to a woman before," Starke admitted. "It's hard for me to put this into words. But I felt guilty about what happened between us. I felt like I'd taken advantage of you, like I'd caught you at a bad time."

"You did catch me at a bad time, but you didn't take advantage. I was attracted to you from the first moment I saw you." Helene stepped back, blushing. "God, here I go, sounding like some kind of loose woman. But I'm not, really. You must believe that."

"I do," Starke said. "I was attracted to you, too. I never wanted that night we shared to end. Just like I don't want this moment to end."

"I don't want it to end, either. You know, I see you every day, on the parade ground and the Row. I want to speak to you, to be able to say something besides 'Good morning, Mr. Starke,' or 'Good afternoon, Mr. Starke.' It's tearing me up."

"How do you think I've felt? There hasn't been a day—there hasn't been an hour—that I haven't thought about you." Starke paused. "I love you, Helene. I know it's crazy, and I've tried not to, but it's no use. I love you."

"I love you, too," she whispered. "If it's crazy, then we're crazy together."

Starke took her hand. "You could get a divorce. I could leave the army. We could—"

"You can't leave the army," Helene said. "You're a soldier. You're not cut out to be anything else."

"But you're not cut out to be a soldier's wife."

"I know. Oh, God, Jim, what future is there for us?"

"No future," he said. "Only now."

He pulled her to him and kissed her. She responded, hungrily. Their bodies molded together. He pulled off her bandanna and ran his fingers through her thick, reddish-blond hair.

Starke's horse whinnied.

Starke whirled, reaching for his pistol. His first thought was of Indians as he looked up.

Silhouetted against the bright blue sky, a lone rider sat at the crest of the hill.

It was Emily Hayes.

Helene let out a low groan.

Slowly, Emily's horse picked its way down the hill. Starke and Helene drew apart, wordless.

Emily closed up. She did not dismount. Her leathery face crinkled as she smiled down at Starke and Helene. "I've suspected there was something between you two for a while now. And I was right."

Starke said, "Mrs. Bannerman was not to blame. It was my—"

"I have eyes, sir. I know exactly what it was—an assignation between illicit lovers." She peered down her nose at Helene. "Adulteress."

Helene reddened with anger. "All right, *dear*. You've said your piece. Now why don't you—"

"No, I've not said my piece, not by a long shot. There is no place in the army for people like you. Either of you." To Starke, she said, "You, sir, will submit your resignation. Your military career is at an end."

Starke stood like stone.

Helene looked at him, worried. To Emily, she said, "And if he doesn't?"

"If he doesn't, I'll spread the word of what I've seen here. Your lover's career will be over in any event. The other officers will drive him out. This way, Mr. Starke, you can go with honor. You can avoid scandal and the damage that will be done to this 'lady's' name."

"Jim, don't," Helene said. "I don't care about my name. I'm leaving here in any case. Don't let this dried-up prune of a woman ruin your—"

Starke looked at Helene. "She's right. My career is ruined. It was ruined the first time I laid eyes on you."

Starke turned back to Emily. He felt hollow inside, empty. His voice seemed to be coming from the bottom of a deep well. "Very well, Mrs. Hayes. Captain Bannerman will have my resignation within the week."

Emily regarded him with a look of triumph. "I knew I'd get you. A jumped-up ranker like you has no business pretending to be an officer. If you wish to stay in the army, change your name and enlist in another regiment as a private. Go back to the barracks where you belong." She turned to Helene. "And you. You should be ashamed of yourself. Do your marriage vows mean nothing to you? Does the honor of being an officer's wife mean nothing? No. To a trollop like you, I should think they wouldn't."

Helene moved forward angrily, but Starke held her back. "She isn't worth it," he murmured.

Emily laughed, more of a bark than a laugh. "Feel free to continue whatever it was you were doing," she said.

She turned and spurred her horse back up the hill, leaving Starke and Helene alone.

27

Chief Storm had finally found a way to prove his friendship to the whites.

He had thought long and hard about what to do. He had taken council with the men of his camp. One of them had heard about two white women being held captive by the Kiowas, and it had been decided that Storm would try to purchase these women and give them to the whites as a peace offering.

So Storm and Man Above the Clouds had traveled south, to the winter camps of the Kiowas. The women had cost them much—many horses and some of the new rifles which the whites had given the Cheyenne for hunting—but they had been worth the price.

Now, Storm and his son, White Wolf, were taking the two women to Fort Pierce. The women had been captives for three years. Both had been abused, which should make the whites all the more happy to get them back.

White Wolf said, "Do you think the whites will give us presents for these women?"

"Perhaps," Storm replied. "My wish is that they leave us in peace until it is time to travel south, to the new reservation."

"They have been peaceful so far," White Wolf said. "They have been giving us beef, now that their roads are open once more."

"Yes. But they are reluctant to do it. I see it in their eyes. I hear it in their voices. The whites do not like us. They would like to attack us. Do not forget that your mother and grandparents died at Sand Creek. You and I were wounded there, and it was only by good fortune that we escaped."

"I remember," White Wolf said somberly. "I still dream about that night."

"I do, also," his father said. "That is why we must make certain that night is not repeated."

Tensions between Storm's people and the whites had been growing. A week ago, while Storm had been with the Kiowas, a Cheyenne girl named Winter Moon had been found in a ditch beside the road to the fort. She had been naked, bruised, and battered, near death from exposure and consumption of whiskey. Many of the white soldiers had lain with her, bringing shame to her family and anger to her people. When her father had complained to the soldiers, their new leader, Banner-man, had said the affair was not his business.

Storm looked over at his son. White Wolf was fifteen, willowy like his mother had been, and handsome. Man Above the Clouds had been supposed to accompany Storm to the fort, but he had grown leery. Storm had thought it would be well for his son to do an adult's work. White Wolf had worn his best deerskin shirt for the occasion. His braids were wrapped in otter fur, like his father's.

Storm sighed. The world was going to be much different for this boy. Two summers before, White Wolf had ridden in his first buffalo hunt. This year he would have gone on his first war party. He would have received a new name on his return. But now his people were pledged to follow the white man's road. There were to be no more war parties, not even against the Pawnees, the Crows, or the Snakes. In Storm's lifetime there would probably be no more buffalo hunts. Already the great beasts grew scarce. That was the price to be paid for peace. It was a heavy price, but Storm knew that the only choices for his people were peace on the white man's terms or extermination.

At the main entrance to the fort Storm and his party were halted by the guard, a pimply-faced infantry private. The private looked at the two women and blanched.

The women wore Indian blankets and dresses. The older one, the one with dark hair, might have been mistaken for an Indian. The one with yellow hair, dirty as it was, never would. The dark-haired one was twenty-five, but she could have been forty. She was covered with ulcerated sores. There was gray in her hair, and she was hunched, with an unfocused look in her eyes. She stared at the unfamiliar surroundings, grinning and babbling incoherently. The yellow-haired one might once have been pretty, but her nose had been burned off to the bone, the result of Kiowa women repeatedly awakening her by holding a burning brand to her nose. Her face was puffed from beatings, and several of her teeth had been knocked out. Her eyes were dead. She had not uttered a word since Storm had first seen her. She was twenty.

The private stammered. "Um, wait," he said to Storm. "Wait right here. You speak English? Understand, 'wait'?"

Storm smiled at the boy and nodded. He and White Wolf shared a look of amusement. The private turned and bellowed, "S-Sergeant of the guard!"

The sergeant pounded up, and immediately sent for the Officer of the Day, Lieutenant Gottfried. Young Gottfried saw the two women. He fought down the urge to be sick. To Storm he said, "I'd better take you to the post commander, sir."

Gottfried led the little group across the parade ground.

Off-duty soldiers and civilians stopped to watch. There was muttering and pointing.

As they reached Post Headquarters, Gottfried ran ahead. He shoved his head in the door, forgetting military formality. "Captain Bannerman, you better come out here, sir."

After a second Bannerman emerged from the frame building, buttoning his jacket and adjusting his forage cap irritably. "Yes, what is it, Gottfried?"

He stopped when he saw Storm and White Wolf.

Storm swung off his pony, handing his bridle to White Wolf. "Greetings, Banner-man."

Bannerman replied without warmth, "Hello, Storm. What brings you . . ."

His voice trailed off as he realized that the two women in Indian robes behind Storm were white, and he saw their condition. Revulsion crossed his face, then outrage. In a quiet voice he said to Gottfried, "Send for Mrs. Bannerman and Mrs. Hayes, to take care of them."

"Yes, sir." Gottfried started off.

"Who are you?" Bannerman asked the women. He approached them, then drew back, because of the smell. "What are your names?"

The dark-haired woman, the one with the sores, cackled senselessly. The yellow-haired one remained mute.

Storm said, "I have brought you these women as a gift of friendship."

Bannerman rounded on the Cheyenne chief. The captain's heavy lips were bloodless and compressed in rage. His eyes were wide. "Friendship!" Spittle flew out of his mouth. "How many more 'friends' like this do you have in your village?"

"They do not come from my village," Storm said. "I—"

"The devil they don't! What are you doing with them, then?"

Lieutenant Starke and the scout, Smith, had come up. They exchanged glances, and Starke said, "Sir, perhaps we should listen to—"

"Listen?" Bannerman said. "To this savage? Don't you

have eyes, mister? Can't you see what they've done to these women?''

Storm tried to remain calm. This was not going the way it was supposed to. The whites were supposed to be happy. "You do not understand, Banner-man. I journeyed to the land of the Kiowas for these women. I purchased—''

"Oh, I understand," Bannerman said. His chest rose and fell with anger. "I understand everything. These women have been in your village all along. All winter you've been drawing government rations and laughing at us, while you raped and mutilated these poor creatures. Now that you're getting ready to leave, you expect some kind of reward for them.''

Storm's pride was injured. He drew himself up. "If that is what you believe, Banner-man, we have no more to say. I will go.''

"The devil you will," Bannerman told him. "You're going to stand trial. You can say your piece before a federal judge. Mr. Gottfried!''

Starke stepped forward, worried. "Sir—''

"Be quiet, sir!" Bannerman thundered. He turned to the O.D., who had returned with the wives. "Mr. Gottfried, these savages are under arrest. Place them in irons and confine them in the guardhouse, until we get to the bottom of this.''

"Yes, sir," said Gottfried. He turned. "Sergeant.''

"You cannot do this," Storm protested. "The treaty—''

"Damn the treaty," Bannerman said. "Sergeant, do your duty.''

The sergeant of the guard moved forward. He reached for Storm's arm. "Come on, you heathen bastard.''

"No!" Storm cried. He grabbed the sergeant's arm and swung him into the other guards, knocking them off balance. He turned and vaulted onto his horse, taking the bridle from White Wolf. "Ride!" he cried to his son.

The two Indians turned their ponies and raced them across the parade ground. Behind them Bannerman yelled to the guards, "Fire! Open fire, you fools!''

There was the crash of rifles. Bullets hummed past the fleeing Indians. They rode for the main gate, past the flagpole. All around them was shouting, rifles firing.

Then White Wolf reeled in his wicker saddle, shot in the side. Storm reached over to steady his wounded son. As he did, half of the boy's face disappeared in an explosion of blood. White Wolf slumped onto the neck of his horse. Storm gathered the boy's bridle. He must try to save the body. But the body bounced off the galloping horse and fell to the ground. There was no chance to retrieve it. Bullets buzzed around Storm like angry bees. He quirted his pony toward the main gate of the fort.

At the gate the corporal of the guard, Gallagher, ran up with his rifle leveled. Storm's horse was startled by the action and bucked in the air. As it did, Gallagher fired. The bullet grazed Storm's forehead. Quirting his horse furiously, Storm urged the reluctant animal forward. The horse's chest crashed into Gallagher, knocking him down. The horse jumped over the fallen soldier, kicking him in the head with its hind hoofs. Then horse and rider were out the gate.

Storm raced across the flat ground. The soldiers' fire diminished behind him. About a mile from the fort he halted. Looking back, he saw the soldiers' pony herd being driven to the fort in haste. A bugle sounded.

White Wolf's body was back there. The boy was not even to have a proper burial. The grief and bitterness that Storm felt were beyond expression, and he knew that time would not erase them. His son, the pride of his life, was dead. His entire family was dead, killed by white men. The white man could only answer friendship with death.

There could be no friendship with the whites now. There could be no peace. With the blood of his dead son still wet on his arm, Storm swore vengeance against his killers. He dedicated what remained of his life to fighting them. He would show them what death was. But first he must save his people.

He turned his horse and rode toward his camp. The white soldiers would be after him soon. There was not much time.

28

In front of Post Headquarters shreds of powder smoke hung on the breeze. Captain Bannerman stood with the fort's other officers and the two white captives, who were still on their Indian ponies. By the main gate, four men carried the unconscious Gallagher to the hospital. Blood trickled from the corporal's left ear.

On the parade ground the white-gloved sergeant of the guard examined White Wolf's body. He stood and called to Bannerman, "This one's dead, sir."

Bannerman nodded acknowledgment. "Good," he said. "One less future warrior for us to worry about—though he might have made a useful hostage."

"What should we do with the body?" the sergeant asked.

"Dig a hole somewhere and drop it in," Bannerman told him. He turned to Lieutenant Starke. "I'll have Boots and Saddles sounded, Mr. Starke. The company will take the field in one-half hour. Light marching order. One hundred rounds of ammunition per carbine, twenty-four per pistol."

Starke spoke earnestly. "Sir, let me go out and talk to Storm by myself. I'll take the boy's body back to him. If you go with the company, it's war for certain."

Bannerman smiled. "Why, yes, I suppose it is." He'd finally gotten Hayes out of his way. He wasn't going to miss this chance. He would punish the Indians for what they had done to these white women—for what they'd done to countless other innocent settlers. He would show them the power of the United States Government.

To Starke, he said, "That's an order, Lieutenant. If you won't carry it out, I'll find someone who will."

Starke stiffened. "Yes, sir." He saluted and hurried to the company area, calling for the trumpeter.

As Starke left, Mrs. Hayes and Mrs. Bannerman helped the captive white women from their horses, assisted by Dr. Dudley and Helene's maid, Letty. "Lookit what them devils done to these poor womens," Letty said.

"Let's get them to the hospital," said Dr. Dudley, who looked unusually sober.

The dark-haired captive was reluctant to get off her horse. She screeched and fought Emily's attempts to help her. "Come along, dear," said Emily in a soothing voice. She had seen this sort of thing before, more times than she cared to remember. "You're among friends now." The dark-haired woman continued to resist. Dr. Dudley grabbed her waist, and he and Emily wrestled her to the ground.

The blond captive was mute and unresisting as Helene and Letty lowered her from the pony. Helene tried hard not to look at the woman's burned-off stump of a nose. She tried to ignore the woman's musty stench.

Captain Bannerman turned to the infantry officers. "Mr. McBride."

"Sir?" said McBride, who commanded I Company in Captain Hayes's absence.

"Send for Pennington, the teamster. Load your infantry into his supply wagons. Follow behind us as fast as you can. If we're in action when you arrive—and I expect we will be—use your own discretion about where and how to join in."

"Yes, sir." McBride saluted and called his first sergeant. "Sergeant O'Brien!"

The cavalry bugle sounded Boots and Saddles. The infantry drum rolled. The men of K Company worked feverishly in their barracks, assembling their field gear. Next they marched to the magazine, where they drew ammunition, loaded their weapons, and had them checked by the sergeants. Then it was on to the stables, to saddle and bridle their horses. As the bugle sounded Assembly, they led their mounts out, heavy carbines banging their thighs at the end of their slings.

They formed up in two lines, each man standing to the left

of his horse, in the company area. The First Sergeant called the roll and inspected the men and animals.

Captain Bannerman rode up, along with Starke and Lieutenant Conroy. There were pistols in the officers' belts and carbines in scabbards across their saddle pommels.

Sergeant Townsend saluted. "All present, sir."

"Very well, First Sergeant. Mount the troop."

"Yes, sir." Townsend did an about-face. "Company, prepare to—mount!"

The men turned to their horses. They placed their left feet in the stirrups, their left hands on the saddle pommels with the reins, their right hands on the cantles.

"Mount!"

The men swung into their saddles.

Bannerman said, "Right by fours, Sergeant. Lead them out."

Townsend said, "Count by fours. Guide right by fours. Company, forward—march!"

The men swung into line of fours. They marched around the parade ground and out the main gate, where Bannerman pumped twice with his fist. "At the canter . . ."

"At the canter!" repeated Townsend.

"March."

"March!"

The company clattered down the trail toward the Cheyenne camp. Captain Bannerman and the scout John Smith were in the lead, followed by Lieutenants Starke and Conroy, then the trumpeter and the guidon bearer. Behind them came Sergeant Townsend and the rest of the troops.

Harry Winston rode in a group of four with his new bunky, Barker, Link Hayward, and Numb Nuts Hudnutt.

"Close up," Sergeant Cronk told them, above the noise of horses and equipment.

Harry's stomach was tight at the prospect of action. The weight of the ammunition on his belt felt strange. He had yet to fire his Spencer seven-shot carbine or his .44 pistol, though he had practiced loading them.

Link said, "What's wrong, Mad Dog? You look a little green. Or is it yellow?"

"Leave him alone," Cronk ordered.

As the trail grew less well traveled, the company assumed columns of twos. "Close up, men," the sergeants cried. "Keep your intervals."

They crossed the seven miles to the Cheyenne camp more quickly than many of them would have liked. Old hands loosened pistols in holsters and carbines in saddle sockets. The scout Smith was sent on ahead.

Soon they sighted the bend in the stream where the Cheyennes had camped. As they did, Captain Bannerman raised a hand and the trumpeter sounded Halt.

The Cheyenne village was gone. Wisps of smoke from old campfires were all to show where it had been.

"They packed up and moved," Barker said, disbelieving.

Harry sighed with relief. "They've run for it."

Behind them Link sounded bored. "What did you think, you lunkhead—they was going to stick around and wait for us to jump 'em?"

Skull chuckled. "They got scared, because they knew we had Mad Dog with us."

Captain Bannerman and the trumpeter trotted ahead, with Starke and Sergeant Townsend. Young Conroy remained with the company. Far to the rear there was a dull rumble and a cloud of dust, as the wagon-borne infantry came on.

The scout Smith galloped back from the campsite. He reined in next to Bannerman. "They headed west, Captain. Along the line of the Smoky Hill."

"All of them?" Bannerman said.

"For now. My guess is, they'll split up. The village and enough braves to guard it will go one way, while the rest of the bucks go raiding. They'll meet later at some prearranged site."

Bannerman thought about it. "We won't catch them, not today," he said. "They can outrun us. There's three or four horses for each one of them." He turned to Starke and Townsend. "Take thirty minutes here to rest the horses. Then we'll return to the fort. Prepare the company to leave on campaign tomorrow."

Starke said, "Sir, we're not supposed to be at Big Spring for two weeks. We're not ready to—"

"I know that. With luck, we'll eliminate Storm and his

band of savages before we join the rest of the regiment. Top, can you have your men ready to go by Reveille? Full marching order?''

Townsend scratched his bushy side-whiskers. ''I expect, sir. If they work all night.''

''See that it's done. Tell Pennington we'll be taking the wagons and pack mules both.''

''Yes, sir,'' Townsend said. He rode back to the company, along with the trumpeter and the scout, Smith.

As Bannerman started back to the formation, Starke spurred his horse forward and wheeled it in front of Bannerman's, forcing the captain to rein in.

No one else was in earshot. Starke curbed his horse, livid with anger. ''I hope you're happy, Captain. You just started an Indian war.''

Bannerman's heavy brows knit. ''I've had about as much of your insolence as I care to take, Mr. Starke. Consider yourself under arrest. Confine yourself to your quarters.''

''You can't keep me off this campaign,'' Starke told him.

''Watch me.''

''What if something happens to you? Do you want Conroy running the company?''

Bannerman considered. He was soldier enough to know that an inexperienced officer like Conroy could bring disaster, even with a sergeant like Townsend to help him. Such a disaster could reflect on Bannerman's own record. ''Very well. You may come with us. Your arrest will take effect when we come out of the field.'' He paused. ''By the way, there's talk that you're resigning your commission.''

Emily Hayes wasted no time spreading the word, Starke thought. He said, ''I wouldn't know about that, sir.''

''Well, don't let me stand in your way, if that's your plan. Frankly, I think it's past time you realized you don't belong as an officer.''

Starke ignored the insult. In formal tones he said, ''Any more orders, sir?''

''No orders. Carry on.''

Starke saluted and rode off.

29

The men of K Company worked through the night. They started at the transport lines. There were rations and ammunition to be packed on the supply wagons, along with axes and spades and extra horseshoes, tents and ground sheets and cooking equipment.

As they worked they were joined by a familiar figure.

"Hunter!" said Sergeant Cronk. "What are you doing here?"

Hunter took a place loading the wagons. He was wearing his uniform. "I'm back in the army," he said.

"What!" cried Slim Pickens. "After all you went through to get out?"

"Why?" said the Professor.

Hunter shrugged. "I got drunk and lost all my discharge money at cards. I didn't have nowhere else to go. I asked Super Soldier, and he said he'd tear up my discharge. He said it would be like none of it ever happened."

That set off a round of hoots and derisive comments.

"Hunter, you fucking moron," the Arab cried.

Numb Nuts said, "You're even stupider than you look."

"Anyway," Hunter said, "I heard about that chief's kid, and you fools leaving for the campaign. I guess I couldn't stand to see you go without me. I mean, how are you going to beat Mr. Lo if I ain't with you?"

"Easy," Starving Mike said.

"What are you going to do?" Link added. "Make Lo laugh himself to death?"

The Arab said, "Why didn't they give *me* that discharge? I'd have known what to do with it."

Down the line came Sergeant Townsend. "Let's 'ave less

153

talk and more work there. The poor benighted sod 'as seen the error of 'is ways, is all.''

"Right!'' several of the men hooted together.

Harry Winston worked with the rest, but his mind was not on what he was doing. All he could think about was how his plans to desert had been ruined. His only chance to leave the company now would be from the field, and with the Cheyennes on the warpath, that could be too dangerous.

What was he going to do?

Lieutenant Starke came by. With Sergeant Townsend at his side, he addressed the company. "Now that Hunter has made his miraculous recovery, we need a barracks guard while we're gone, to watch our things and make sure they're sent on to the next post, if we're transferred. Any volunteers?''

Several hands went up. Barracks guard was the best duty in the army. You were on your own, with minimal supervision. Before Starke could pick someone, Link Hayward spoke. "Take Mad Dog, sir. He won't be no use to us in the field.''

Starke looked first at Link, then at Harry. For a moment Harry's heart leaped. If he was barracks guard, he'd be able to desert anytime he wanted. Then he saw the smirk on Link's face, and resentment boiled inside him.

"Not me, sir. I'm going with the company.''

The words popped out, surprising Harry. It was as though someone else was speaking. He knew he was passing up a perfect opportunity, but he didn't care. He still intended to desert, but first he had something to prove to Link Hayward—and to himself.

To Starke, Sergeant Townsend said, " 'Ow 'bout Colter, sir? Third Platoon. 'E's nearly time-expired, and 'e's got two kids at 'ome.''

Starke nodded. "Very well. Detail him.''

At Post Headquarters Neal Bannerman had a lot of work to do. He would probably be here most of the night, but he didn't mind. He felt more at home here than he did in his quarters. Helene had stopped drinking, but she was still cold to him. He had his pride. After being rebuffed so many times, he had given up trying.

He leafed through the stack of papers and folders on his desk. There were orders to be drafted, reports to be made, other reports to be read and endorsed—so much administrative work to be done before the company could take the field. The door to his office was open. There was a rap and Dr. Dudley entered.

Bannerman put down his pen. "Good evening, Doctor. What brings you here?"

Dudley said, "We've found out who those women are. Your wife got that young one to talk—the blonde."

"The one with the burned-off nose?"

Dudley nodded grimly, then went on. "They're Texans. The blonde's name is Martha Lockhart; the dark-haired one is Cynthia Perryman. They were in a party traveling west, looking for ranch land, when the Kiowas attacked them. Martha had just gotten married. Her husband was nineteen. The Kiowas tortured him, then burned him alive and forced her to watch. The older girl was married, too, had a child. Martha doesn't know for sure, but she thinks that all the rest of their party were killed."

"And how are the ladies—physically, I mean?" Bannerman said.

"In some ways, better than you'd expect. Martha has a hard time talking—she hasn't used much English in the last three years. She and Cynthia were in the same camp, but the Kiowas wouldn't let them see each other much. There's no sign of disease on either of them. We got 'em cleaned up—got rid of the fleas and lice, scrubbed out the buffalo dung that Indians grease their hair with. We burned their Indian clothes and gave them new ones, from your wife and Mrs. Hayes. I put some salve on Mrs. Perryman's sores. She's quieted down some, but she's still got that queer look in her eye—like she expects the Kiowas to come back for her any minute. Mrs. Lockhart . . . well, she'll never look right again, poor thing. It's a shame, she seems quite intelligent."

Bannerman steepled his fingers. "Good work, Doctor. We'll try and locate their families, someone who can take them in. Sounds like a job for Mrs. Hayes.'' His tone indicated dismissal.

Dr. Dudley took a step forward. ''You miss the point, Colonel. Their story means that Chief Storm was telling the truth. He did ransom those women from the Kiowas, to bring them to us. There's no need for war.''

Bannerman smiled indulgently. ''It's too late now, I'm afraid. We've killed Storm's son. He's going to want revenge. The war is on, whether we like it or not.''

''I think some of us like it a little too much,'' Dudley suggested.

Bannerman's smile faded. His voice turned cold. ''Anything else, Doctor?''

''No, sir. Nothing else.''

''You may return to your duties.''

Dudley saluted stiffly and left. When he returned to the hospital, he went to his office and closed the door. He pulled out his bottle and began to drink.

At Headquarters Bannerman lit a cigar and went back to work, signing orders for Lieutenant McBride to take command of the fort until Captain Hayes's return. Bannerman thought of the rescued captives, and of how Storm and his brat had fled in a hail of gunfire, and he smiled to himself. The only excitement they were ever likely to have at Fort Pierce, and that fool Hayes had missed it.

The night wore on. It began to rain. It was a steady rain, drumming on shingle roofs, rippling musically in the puddles on the parade ground. Jim Starke thought the sound relaxing as he packed his field kit. Rain dripped through the holes in his roof. The drops plunked into pans and quart bottles scattered strategically around the floor of his small quarters.

Starke gathered some of the magazines to which the company officers subscribed—*London Punch, Galaxy, Blackwood's*—and he stuffed them in his saddlebags. They might come in handy while the regiment was in camp. He was folding his spare flannel shirt when there was a knock and his door opened.

He turned. Helene Bannerman stepped in, shutting the door behind her.

Starke put down the shirt. "Helene."

She shook the raindrops from her reddish hair.

He crossed the room and took her shoulders. "Helene, you must be mad to come here."

"Mad, or in love," she said. "I couldn't let you leave without seeing you."

They embraced and kissed, and Starke said, "But what if someone saw you . . . ?"

"I don't care. I don't care who sees. I don't care who knows."

"Helene," he breathed, "I'll miss you so much."

She beat his chest weakly with her fist. "I know. I know."

"There's so much I want to say to you. So much I—"

She put a finger to his lips. "There's no time for words, darling."

They stared into each other's eyes for a moment, then Starke lifted her and carried her to his bed.

In the next quarters down the row, Lieutenant Tom Conroy was vomiting into a bucket. He was worried about how he'd do if there was fighting. He was full of fear and self-doubt, and he wondered if he'd done the right thing by becoming a soldier.

He stumbled out his front door, raising his face to the sky. His forehead was blazing hot, and the rain cooled it. The water trickled down his face and into the neck of his shirt. It felt good, refreshing. Gradually his weak knees steadied. He went back into his quarters to finish packing. Then a new wave of nausea swept over him, and he ran for the bucket, to be sick again.

When they were done with the transport, the men of K Company returned to their barracks, where the work went on by lamplight. The veterans were enthusiastic at the prospect of leaving.

"You'll like the field," the Professor assured Harry. "There's less bullshit than here at the post."

The men made up their blanket rolls and field kits. Weapons were given a final cleaning. Some, like Harry and Barker, wrote hasty letters to families and loved ones. Others went to the sutler's, to buy molasses, vinegar, sugar, and salt to add to their field rations. Still others slipped off for a last round of beer or whiskey. Link Hayward sneaked into town to see his girl.

When their field equipment was ready, the men packed and labeled their footlockers. They rolled up their bedding and turned it in. They cleaned the barracks and had it inspected for the last time. Harry was exhausted. He would have given anything for a few hours' sleep, but that was not going to happen.

Dawn came, gray with rain. Reveille sounded across the soggy parade ground. The men went to roll call, then to breakfast.

"Last meal in the mess hall, kiddies," Link cried from the middle of the line. "After this, you cook your own weevils."

The men bolted their food, then hurried back to the barracks to finish their last bits of packing.

Boots and Saddles sounded. The men tied their blanket rolls. They buckled on their belts, checked their ammunition and cap boxes, closed the flaps on their revolver holsters. They eased their leather carbine slings over their shoulders and clipped their carbines onto them.

"Let's go," Sergeant Cronk shouted. "Fall out."

The men grabbed their gear and left the barracks.

Cronk marched his platoon to the stables. Quickly, the men groomed their horses, watered and fed them. The animals were saddled and bridled. Overcoats and blankets were tied onto the saddles, along with lariats, canteens, nose bags, and saddlebags.

Assembly sounded. Sergeant Townsend moved down the line, resplendent in polished leather and a white cork helmet that he'd gotten God-only-knew-where. "Move it, lads. *Jaldi. Jaldi.*"

The men formed up and led their horses to the company area. Noise and cursing from the transport lines told where Pennington and his teamsters were getting the wagons and mules together.

* * *

Jim Starke led his horse from the stables. The brim of his worn campaign hat was tipped down against the rain. He wore a faded blue jacket and red bandanna over a checked flannel shirt. Fringed gauntlets and trousers reinforced with buckskin, tucked into troop boots, completed his outfit. At his waist were two pistols in open holsters and a knife in a fringed sheath.

Suddenly, Emily Hayes appeared in his path, standing beneath an umbrella.

"Morning, ma'am," Starke said, touching his hat brim.

Emily wasted no time on formality. "You promised me you were quitting the army," she said.

Starke gave her an easy grin. "My week's not up yet." Before she could say anything, he added, "I'll quit, all right, but not till I help get these men through this campaign, and no rumor or slander that you can spread is going to change that."

She stared at him, her brows furrowed in an angry vee.

Starke pushed his horse by her. "Now, if you'll excuse me, ma'am, I've got a war to fight."

The men mounted and formed for inspection. They wore jackets in every shade of blue—from new and dark, to faded almost gray. Some wore old-style shell jackets, with the stiff collars cut down for comfort. Almost all wore red or yellow bandannas around their necks. Some had their own pistols or knives, in addition to the ones they had been issued. A few wore forage caps, some with bandannas hung from the back as sun shields; but most had wide-brimmed hats that they'd purchased at the sutler's or in town, with crowns and brims creased and dented at the wearer's whim. Harry Winston wore the black Jeff Davis hat that he'd been issued when he arrived at the fort.

The officers rode up. Captain Bannerman wore a black campaign hat. A white silk bandanna was tucked neatly into the collar of his jacket. The trumpeter followed Bannerman as he rode down the company line, inspecting men and horses.

The rain was heavier now. Harry's new hat was already waterlogged. A drop of water trickled down his temple and cheek. He heard the men near him snicker. He looked sidelong and realized that they were snickering at him. Another drop of water ran down the side of his face. He wiped it away. He looked at his hand; it was black from where the hat's cheap dye had run.

Captain Bannerman saw the black dye smeared across Winston's face. He considered saying something, then thought better of it. He'd grown to expect this sort of thing from Winston.

Bannerman returned to the front of the formation. He cried, "Company—guide right by fours. Forward—march!"

The company marched off. The wagons and pack mules fell in behind them. Everyone at the post was there to see them off. As they passed Officers Row, Neal Bannerman pulled away from the column. Helene was standing in the rain, in front of their quarters. Bannerman dismounted and kissed her good-bye. It was a formal kiss, without love. As he turned from her and remounted, her eyes searched out Jim Starke's. The lovers' gaze held for a moment, then Starke was past.

Lieutenant McBride, the acting commandant, stood with a color guard at the main gate. There was no band, but an Irishman from I Company with a tin penny whistle tootled "The Girl I Left Behind Me." The color guard took Captain Bannerman's salute, and K Company marched out of Fort Pierce.

PART III
THE FIELD

30

Rumble of hoofs. Jingle of bits. Creak of leather. Rattle of canteens and tin mess cups. Cavalry company on the march.

"Keep your intervals," the sergeants ordered.

K Company was a day out of Fort Pierce. It was hot. The men had taken off their blue wool jackets. Some, like Harry Winston, wore the gray shirts they'd been issued; but most wore red or checked flannel shirts that they'd purchased in town—they could have bought blue shirts, but that would have looked too "army."

They were on the trail of Chief Storm's Cheyennes. As the scout John Smith had predicted, the Indians had split up. The village—the travois, packhorses, women and children—had crossed the South Fork of the Smoky Hill and headed southeast, for the new Indian Agency at Fort Cobb. The main party of braves had continued west. The company had followed the braves, both to try and stop them from raiding and because the regimental rendezvous at Big Spring lay in that direction.

At the rear of the company, between the soldiers and the trailing wagon train, walked Link Hayward, carrying his saddle and eating dust. It was field punishment, for being drunk on the march. He had sneaked a bottle of whiskey into his horse's nose bag and covered it with grain. He'd been discovered by Sergeant McDermott, at whom he'd promptly thrown the empty bottle.

Harry looked back. Link was a strange fellow, he thought. He remembered when the company had pulled out of Fort Pierce. They had marched through Watsonville. Link's girl, Lou, had been among the quiet crowd gathered in the rain to see them off. She'd had a tawdry-looking little girl of about four with her. The pair of them had lifted their hands to Link as he rode by. Link had grinned and doffed his campaign hat to them.

Now, the column neared Hobson's Ranch, a way house where stagecoaches changed horses and passengers bought meals. The company would take their noon halt there.

In the distance, vultures swooped. Something was dead up there. Then a shot echoed across the flat plains. More vultures rose into the sky, flapping their long wings. Against the endless horizon they could see the scout Smith, who had been sent forward. Smith circled his arm twice, then pointed down, a sign that he had found something.

At the head of the column Captain Bannerman raised his hand. "Company! At the canter—march!"

The company clattered ahead, leaving Link to follow with the wagons.

As the men drew near, they saw the ranch. The house, outbuildings, and corrals had been burned to the ground. A few large pieces of wood still smoldered. The stock was gone.

"Shit," Hunter muttered.

The company rode into the ranch yard. Pale forms, already swelling in the heat, dotted the ruins. The ground and buildings were sprinkled with broken arrows. The good arrows had been taken by the Indians, to be reused. Blood splashes here and there suggested that the Cheyennes had also suffered casualties.

Captain Bannerman halted the column. "Post your guards, Mr. Starke. Have the horse holders water the animals and take them out to graze. Form a burial detail. Everyone else is to police up this mess."

While one detail dug graves, another gathered the bodies and pieces of bodies. The Hobson family and their hired hands had been fearfully mutilated, even the children. A baby had been brained, then nailed to the trunk of a cottonwood tree. Harry Winston was violently ill at the sight, and he was not the only one.

* * *

Skull, the Arab, Starving Mike, Hunter, and Squillace searched what was left of the building that had served as bar, restaurant, and hotel. Two of the hired men had made a stand there, and the ground was littered with shell casings from somebody's Henry repeater. The soldiers wore bandannas over their faces against the smell.

Squillace stayed in the main building. The rest of the men seemed more interested in poking through the storage shed out back. "Here are the bodies," Squillace said, puzzled.

"Who cares?" Hunter said.

"They're not going anywhere," the Arab added.

"I've found it!" Skull cried.

The other men gathered around him.

The ex-Legionnaire had come upon two barrels. The barrels lay beneath collapsed rafters, in the charred ruins of the shed. Skull tapped them. They were full. "Whiskey," he crowed in his guttural voice. "How did the Indians miss this?"

"Maybe they didn't miss it," the Arab said. The Arab looked less like an accountant than ever. Beneath his red bandanna his nose was out of kilter where it had been broken in the fight at the Tiger Club. Before going into the field, he'd had his head shaved, save for a small, bushy strip down the center, in the manner of a Pawnee roach. He said, "Maybe their chief wouldn't let them drink."

"It's a hell of a chief who can keep Injuns from drinking whiskey," Hunter observed.

Mike, the Russian, said, "Whiskey, always whiskey. Why don't we find vodka, for a change?"

Skull motioned with a bony hand. "Squealer"—that was what they called Squillace—"go get our canteens."

The young Italian protested. "But I do not drink the—"

"We do," Skull told him. "Now, get the canteens." Skull kissed one of the rough barrels. "Look at it, *mes amis*. Look at it. We are dead and gone to heaven."

From behind them came Sergeant Cronk's gravelly voice. "That's right, Skull—look at it. But God help you if you drink it."

The soldiers turned.

"Aw, Sarge," said the Arab.

Hunter said, "You know us, Sarge. We wouldn't drink, not in the field."

"Well, maybe just one drop," Skull suggested. "What do you say, Sergeant? One drop will hurt nothing. Who is going to know?"

"I am," Cronk told them. He turned. "Squillace, instead of canteens, you fetch an axe from them wagons. Then you bust up these barrels. Destroy this stuff. The rest of you— get busy with them bodies!"

As the men went back to work, Hunter shook his head sadly. "Typical army bullshit," he said.

Jim Starke searched the remains of the Hobson house, kicking through the ashes. The family's personal possessions were scattered over the yard. Furniture and glass had been smashed. There were torn photographs, bits of clothing, and broken kitchen utensils.

Starke was not surprised by what the Cheyennes had done to the Hobsons. That was the way Indians made war. A society that produced a "hero" like William Tecumseh Sherman could scarcely afford to criticize the brutality of another.

Starke came upon a large book, lying open on its face. It was the Hobsons' family Bible. He picked it up, brushing it off with his gauntleted fingers. He looked in front. Like many families, the Hobsons had kept a record of births and deaths there. As Starke read, a frown crossed his face.

He took the Bible and crossed the yard to where Captain Bannerman stood with his orderly and the trumpeter. In the background the wagon train came up in a cloud of dust and cursing teamsters.

Starke stopped in front of the captain. "Sir, how many bodies did we find?"

Bannerman chewed on a cold cigar. "Nine."

"Four children, right?"

"That's right. Why?"

Starke showed him the Bible. "According to this, there should have been five children."

The two men looked at one another.

"Top!" Bannerman called.

Sergeant Townsend came up. "Sir?" Even in the field,

Townsend managed to keep his white cork helmet immaculately pipe-clayed. His boots and leather were spit-polished, in contrast to those of the men, who took perverse pride in letting their uniforms get sloppy.

"There's a body missing," Bannerman told him, "a child. Have a detail search the area."

"Yes, sir," Townsend said.

Bannerman and Starke went to where the men were digging graves. From the Bible entries and the bodies that had been found, they worked out who the missing child must be. "This one," Starke said, tapping the page. "Rebecca. Born 1860—she'd be seven."

Just then Sergeant Townsend came back. "The lads've looked all over, sir. They can't find noffink."

"Very well, Sergeant," Bannerman said.

Starke said, "We must assume the Cheyennes have taken her." He remembered the condition of the two white women who had been released from captivity at Fort Pierce, and he said, "At that age, they won't mistreat her too much. They'll raise her as one of their own. Still . . ."

"Still, we must try and get her back," Bannerman said.

"Yes, sir." For once Starke and Bannerman seemed to agree on something.

Bannerman turned to the scout. "How far behind the savages are we, Mr. Smith?"

"Near eighteen hours, Captain. They've gained on us since we left the fort."

Bannerman paced back and forth, thinking. He had been looking for an excuse to avoid joining the regiment and go off on his own, chasing Indians. He stopped. "Orderly, my compliments to Mr. Pennington. Have him report to me." He pulled a notebook and pencil from his jacket and began to write. "Sergeant Townsend, detail your best galloper. Have him ride to Big Spring. Tell him to travel by night and hide during the day. Have him tell General Carr we're trailing a band of hostiles that have kidnapped a white girl, and we intend to follow that trail wherever it leads. Have him give the general this note."

"Yes, sir," Townsend said. He turned away as Pennington came up.

To the teamster, Bannerman said, "Mr. Pennington, we're cutting loose from our wagons. From here on, we go with pack mules only. We will take no tents, no mess chests. Our bedding will be the ground and the blankets we carry on our horses. The men will cook with the utensils in their packs. I'm sending the wagons on to Big Spring to join the regiment. You're welcome to go with them, if you want."

The sweat-stained teamster chewed his tobacco thoughtfully, then spit. "I reckon I'll go with you, Cap'n. Somebody's got to look after them mules."

"Good," Bannerman said. "Load the mules with ammunition and ten days' rations for the animals—five days' rations for the men. Leave everything else with the wagons."

To Starke, Bannerman said, "As of now, the men are on half rations. We'll take our noon break here. We march in one hour."

"Yes, sir. What about Hayward, sir? He's on punishment. Is he still supposed to walk?"

Bannerman bit back an oath. "Tell him to get on his horse. He can finish his punishment later."

31

The scout John Smith rode up to the South Fork of the Smoky Hill, following the Cheyennes' trail. He saw where Storm and his braves had watered their horses, then crossed. He dismounted and examined the tracks along the sandy bank.

John Smith—that was not his real name—had left Harvard in '59. He had taken a degree in literature, but he had not been ready to settle down. He had joined the gold rush to Pikes Peak, in Colorado. On the way, he'd fallen ill, and the members of his emigrant train had been forced to leave him at a roadside ranch. He had recovered, but he'd lacked the money to continue his journey. So he had taken a job with the rancher, trading with the Indians. He had grown to like Indian life; he liked it better than that of the whites. He'd taken an Indian wife and gone to live with a band of Southern Cheyennes. He'd fathered two children by his wife, whose name was Little Creek Woman, and the Indians had seemed to accept him as one of their own. Then had come the Sand Creek massacre of '64. Feelings had run strong against all whites, and Little Creek Woman had brought Smith word that the Indians planned to kill him. She'd brought him a horse and helped him escape the camp. Smith had not seen his wife or children since. Their band had not been present at the conference on Medicine Lodge Creek. Finding them was his only goal, but until he could, he worked for the government. He sometimes felt guilty about scouting against those whom he considered his own people, but he had to make a living.

There was a rumble and clatter as the company came up. Smith stood and waited.

The troops halted. The company's three officers trotted toward Smith, along with the trumpeter.

Smith waved a buckskinned arm across the stream. "They've crossed the river, Captain. They've got the Hobson girl, all right. Here's her prints."

The officers dismounted, while the trumpeter held their horses. The officers squatted beside Smith and examined a set of small footprints in the muddy sand. The prints were narrow, and they'd been made by someone wearing shoes, not moccasins.

Captain Bannerman stood and looked across the river. "That savage Storm, or whatever he calls himself, is going to join his village and head for the agency at Fort Cobb. He'll lay up there, eating government beef and planning his next raid. He'll be safe if he gets to the agency. He'll be protected by the government. We won't be able to touch him."

Lieutenant Starke said, "We won't be able to get the Hobson girl back, either. I don't know why, but Indian Agents pretend the Indians don't take white prisoners. They won't help us recover them. I remember that from when I was out here before. If we lose her now, it may be years before we get her back—if ever. If they sell her to another band, or to Comancheros, we may never find where she's gone."

Bannerman nodded grimly. He didn't seem as interested in the girl as he did in punishing the Cheyennes. He said, "We'll water the horses and rest them here. Then we move out. It's forced marches from now on, Mr. Starke, and the devil take those who fall behind."

The company crossed the river and marched on.

Riding at the head of the column, Jim Starke looked back. During the war, a thousand men had marched to Starke's orders, guidons flapping and bugles playing. And that thousand had been but a drop in a mighty river of men that flowed along, irresistible, clogging roads and stripping the countryside as they passed, like a species of ravenous insects. Now Starke was followed by sixty men and a small pack train. They looked insignificant, lost on the vast ocean of prairie.

Starke had loved the war. God help him, he had loved it. He knew something that terrible could never be right, but he'd never felt so alive as he had during those years.

This would be his last campaign. When this was over, he would resign—forced to it by Emily Hayes and by his love for another man's wife. What then? He didn't know.

And Helene Bannerman? She might already have started back east, for home. He might never see her again. He might have lost the only two things in his life that had any importance for him.

But that was for later. Right now, he was still a soldier.

The day wore on. The heat worsened. The short prairie spring had vanished, and summer had come with furnacelike intensity. The men carried their day's ration of salt pork in their two-piece mess kits. The intense heat made the pork melt, until the grease ran out of the mess kits and down the sides of their saddles.

That evening, they camped beside Ladder Creek. The men were tired and hungry from the day's march. Their melted pork had worms, and the hardtack had bugs, but they ate it without caring.

Before dawn they pulled out again. "Close up, men," the sergeants said. "Keep your intervals."

"We're gaining on them," the scout Smith told Bannerman, when he rejoined them at the noon halt.

"Can we catch them before they get to Fort Cobb?" Bannerman asked.

Smith looked doubtful. "I don't know, Captain. It'll be hard."

"We can't give up," Starke said.

"Who said anything about giving up?" Bannerman told him. "Prepare to mount."

That night they made a dry camp. Most of what water was left they gave to their horses. The next day they were on the trail again before dawn. The sun rose in a brassy sky, promising more heat than the men were likely to want. The hours dragged by. The heat intensified, until it lay on the column like a weight. At mid-morning they watered their horses and refilled canteens in the Arkansas River, then they pushed on.

The landscape was horizon-to-horizon flat, broken here and there by dry watercourses, by bluffs and steep ravines. They passed a prairie dog village, and the curious rodents stopped what they were doing to watch the soldiers go by. From time to time the men dismounted and walked, to rest their horses.

"I'm damned if I see the point in all this," the dark-eyed Arab said as they trudged along. He was still mad at not being able to drink the whiskey they'd found at the Hobson ranch. "What's going to happen if we catch old Lo? I mean, there must be a hundred of them at least."

"Numbers ain't everything," Hunter said. "You sound like an accountant."

"I *am* an accountant. We'll get our scalps lifted."

"No, we won't," Slim Pickens said. "We got Super Soldier. He eats a hundred Injuns for breakfast."

"All the same," the Arab said, "I'd as soon go slower and keep my hair."

"What about that little girl?" Starving Mike asked.

"What about her? If we get close, the Cheyennes will kill her. You know that."

"Christ," Skull said, "you're fun to be around, Arab. If that's true, there's no sense in us being here at all."

"That's the first intelligent thing you've said today," the Arab told him.

"It puts me one up on you, asshole."

Behind them Link said, "Shut up, you jugheads, and look over there."

They followed Link's gaze. In the distance, off to the right, puffs of smoke rose in the air from a high bluff. At the head of the column the officers had seen the smoke, too.

"What's it mean?" said Numb Nuts Hudnutt.

"It means the Cheyennes have seen us," Link said. "They know we're after them."

32

All the rest of that day, smoke puffs dotted the horizon. The men grew tense.

"We're going to get hit tonight," Sergeant Cronk predicted.

The company camped on the North Fork of the Cimarron. The men were assigned defensive positions in case of attack. The horses and mules were grazed, then fed, watered, and picketed on a line made of strung lariats. As a further precaution, the animals were cross-hobbled.

Harry Winston's platoon had guard. Harry was set to go on at midnight. There was a fluttery feeling in his stomach as he cooked his evening meal.

Each group of four messed at one fire. They roasted green coffee beans in the skillets they'd bought at the sutler's—the frying pans the army issued were useless. When the beans were done, the men wrapped them in their bandannas and crushed them with their pistol butts. Then they mixed the beans with boiling water in their mess cups. The hardtack was too hard to eat, so the men soaked it in water first. Numb Nuts broiled his salt pork on a stick before eating it. Link dipped his pork in vinegar and ate it raw. Harry and Barker fried their salt pork, then crumbled their hardtack and fried it in the pork grease. They mixed the pork and biscuit and sprinkled it with brown sugar, then ate.

Harry was starting to look like an old campaigner. His black Jeff Davis hat had turned out to have more sizing than wool. The hat was already faded from rain, and the sizing had washed out, leaving the brim limp, like a dishrag. Harry's shirtsleeves were rolled up, revealing two long scars on his left arm, where he'd been cut by Link Hayward's belt buckle during their fight.

Darkness fell. The trumpeter played Taps. The men turned in, jackets on, weapons by their sides. In the starry distance fire arrows rose and fell, signaling no one knew what. Coyotes howled across the vast prairie.

"Hear that coyote?" Link said. "That one, right there? That's a Cheyenne. He's telling his friends where we are and how many of us there are."

"Will they attack?" his bunky, Numb Nuts, asked.

Link wrapped his blanket around himself. He pulled his hat over his eyes, seemingly unconcerned. "Who knows?"

Harry couldn't sleep. He was too scared. He expected the Indians to come down on them at any minute. He snuggled under the doubled blankets that he shared with Barker.

"You asleep?" he asked Barker after a while.

"No," Barker said.

"Scared?"

"What do you think?" Barker said. Then he added, "Harry, if anything happens to me, you'll—you'll let Susan know, won't you?"

"Sure," Harry said. Then he added, "Actually, I'm more worried about something happening to me."

Harry lay there, unblinking. Time passed. The coyotes howled; the distant fire arrows rose and fell. Link left for his turn at guard. Harry hoped that his own turn would not come. He hoped that something—anything—would happen first. He grew more and more scared.

Then Cronk, the sergeant of the guard, was shaking his shoulder. "Wake up, Winston. Guard."

Harry got up. He put on his boots and overcoat. He buckled on his pistol and took his carbine. He and the other relief guards formed up, were inspected by Cronk, then followed the sergeant on his rounds.

Cronk dropped off the new guards and picked up the old ones. Harry had Post Four, on the eastern end of the camp, with the river to the right. Harry had seen the post earlier. It was a good firing position, located in a break of a shallow ravine that ran down to the stream. The relief approached quietly.

Suddenly, from quite near, came a whispered challenge. "Who goes there?"

Cronk answered with the password. "K Company."

Link emerged from the darkness a few steps away. He lowered his carbine.

"Why weren't you in the position?" Cronk asked him.

"I didn't want to be," Link replied.

Cronk shook his head at Link's answer. "See anything?"

"No."

Cronk showed Harry to the position. He kept his voice at a whisper. "Keep down. Don't skylight yourself. Don't move around. Remember, the password is 'K Company.' If you challenge somebody, and they don't give it to you, shoot 'em up."

"R-Right," Harry said.

As the relief left, Link stooped and said to Harry, "Don't fall asleep, stupid."

"Go to hell," Harry told him.

Then Cronk and the guards were gone. Harry was alone. The night sounds were all around. The howling of the coyotes, the wind in the trees down by the river, the rustle of the tall grass—they were all suddenly much more threatening than they had been. Harry shivered, and not from the cold.

He leaned against the side of the break. His eyes tried to pierce the darkness. There was a sliver of moon, but he couldn't see much. There was no sense of time passing. Minutes seemed like hours. An hour seemed like forever. Harry prayed for this to be over. He felt alone and vulnerable. He wished the rest of the company was around him. He wouldn't be so scared then. He'd never thought he would miss those men.

There was a noise, different from the others. Was someone out there? Harry's eyes strained into the darkness until he thought they would pop out of his head. There—had he seen something move? He rested his sweating thumb on the hammer of his Spencer carbine. His finger curled around the trigger. He hunkered lower in his firing position, trying to make himself invisible. He hoped whoever it was hadn't seen him—if, indeed, there was anyone there. Should he issue a challenge? Better wait. He would feel like a fool if he ended up challenging the empty night.

Harry stared. The dimly seen object became first an Indian, then a deer, then a tree. Harry rubbed his eyes and looked off to one side, trying to view the object from the corner of his eye, to see if that was any better. It wasn't.

After a while the object seemed to go away. Harry wasn't sure if it had been there in the first place. He relaxed a bit.

There was a noise to his left.

Harry turned, wide-eyed.

The noise sounded again. Footsteps. Someone was coming toward him. Harry made out a shadow in the darkness. He raised his carbine to fire.

"Who—" His voice broke. "Who's there?"

"K Company." It was Lieutenant Starke.

"Ad—Advance," Harry said.

Starke slid into the ravine. "All quiet?" he whispered, looking into the night.

Harry said, "I thought I saw something before. I guess it was nothing."

Starke nodded. It was funny, Harry thought. When you stood next to Starke, you realized that he seemed taller than he actually was.

Starke's whisper lapsed into a conversational tone, but he kept studying the terrain outside the guard post. "How are you making out, Winston?"

"All right, I guess, sir."

"Adjusting better to the army?"

"No, sir. Not really."

Harry hesitated. Then, without really knowing why, he told Starke about his plans to desert, and how he'd changed them at the last minute. He felt like he was talking to a big brother—an idealized big brother, not his own brother, Ed.

When he was finished, Starke said, "And how do you feel now?"

Harry told the truth. He didn't think Starke would mind. "I still intend to desert, sir. When we get back to the fort."

Starke was silent for a moment. Then he said, "A man's word should be good for something, Winston. You gave your word to be a soldier, and if you desert, I think you'll be selling both your oath and yourself short. I won't tell you what to do, though. Think it over, then do what you believe is right."

"Yes, sir," Harry said.

"Now, I'd better finish my rounds. You keep alert here."

"Yes, sir."

Starke patted Harry's shoulder, then he climbed out of the break and disappeared into the darkness, walking in a crouch so as not to expose himself.

Right after that, Sergeant Cronk brought Harry's relief. It was Corporal Bannon. Bannon settled into Harry's post with a veteran's practiced ease. He seemed unworried about what might happen.

Harry returned to his blankets, sweating with relief, even through the nighttime chill. He lay beside Barker and fell asleep instantly.

He was awakened by a shot. It had come from a Spencer carbine. There was another shot, and a flash in the darkness, farther up the line. That was followed by a sudden thunder of hooves, wild yelling, the clanging of bells. More shots.

"On your feet!" It was Lieutenant Starke. "They're after the horses! Ones and twos to your defensive positions. Threes and fours to the horse lines. Hold those horses!"

Men grabbed their weapons. Half of them raced to their assigned defensive posts, cocking carbines on the way. The rest ran to the picket line of plunging, neighing horses, to keep them from being run off.

There was a scattering of gunfire all around the perimeter. Harry hurried to the picket line, where he held his own horse and Barker's. Out of the darkness came the Indians, waving blankets, yelling, ringing bells. They brought a cloud of dust with them, choking the men, obscuring vision. The gunfire picked up. The Indians went right by the horse lines, yelling and screaming, shooting guns and arrows. But the picket ropes and cross-hobbles held. The horses did not run off.

As suddenly as the Indians had come, they were gone. The drumming of their horses receded into the distance.

"Everybody all right?" Sergeant Townsend cried. "Guard posts—report!"

The posts called in. All except Post Four—Harry's station.

"Post Four!" Townsend yelled.

Townsend ran into the darkness. Lieutenant Starke and Sergeant Cronk ran with him. Harry and some others followed. Harry was drawn to the spot. He pictured Bannon wounded—or even dead, and scalped. A few minutes earlier, Harry thought, and it could have been him.

The little group neared the guard post. "Bannon?" Cronk called. "Where the hell are you?"

There was no answer. There was no one at the post. The ground was dug up, though. There were signs of a struggle.

"Bannon!"

Townsend rested a big hand on Cronk's shoulder. " 'E's gone, lad. The Cheyennes 'as grabbed 'im."

33

They found Bannon the next afternoon.

The Cheyennes had staked him out on the trail, naked. They had crammed gunpowder into his mouth, then exploded it, destroying his tongue and vocal cords so that he couldn't scream. They had built fires on each of his limbs.

The last fire, the one that had killed him, had been built over his heart. He had not been scalped.

"Why didn't they take his hair?" asked Captain Bannerman.

"Sign of respect," Lieutenant Starke told him. "Means he died well."

Bannerman nodded grimly. "Wrap him in blankets and bury him."

Harry's squad got the job. Lieutenant Conroy was in charge. Even after days on the trail, Conroy stood out from the men. His wool jacket was deep blue and beautifully cut. So were his sky-blue trousers, unlike the men's trousers, which were invariably too baggy or too small. Conroy's gray felt hat was still blocked, not dented and shapeless. The supple leather of his troop boots glowed with black dye, even through the dust. The men's issue boots were more like cardboard.

Conroy averted his eyes from Bannon's body. He tried not to let the men see how his knees were shaking. He was afraid the men wouldn't respect him, afraid he'd be a failure as an officer. First the Hobsons, he thought, now this. Please, God, please don't let this happen to me. If I have to die, please let it be quick.

The shovels had been left with the wagons. Harry and some others had to dig Bannon's grave with their knives. Harry would have been sick at the sight of the body if he hadn't already seen what the Indians had done to the Hobsons.

He couldn't get over what had happened to Bannon, the fact that that had almost happened to him. That "thing" he had seen in the darkness when he was on guard duty—it really had been an Indian. If Lieutenant Starke hadn't come along . . .

Harry's stomach crawled. How would he have borne up if he had been captured? He couldn't imagine the agonies that Bannon must have gone through.

Link Hayward and Numb Nuts cut Bannon's body from its stakes. "Looks like the team needs a new pitcher," said Hunter, who was standing nearby. "Mick's going to have trouble throwing the high, hard one after this."

Harry threw down his knife. "Do you have to joke about it? Do you think what happened to him is funny?"

"It's funnier than it would have been if it had happened to me," Hunter said.

Numb Nuts said, "Just think, Mad Dog, a half hour earlier and this would have been you."

"Too bad it wasn't," Link said. "At least Bannon could pitch."

Harry stood angrily. "This man was your friend. Don't you feel anything about him except that he could play baseball?"

Link's eyes narrowed. He spoke through clenched teeth. "What we feel or don't feel don't make a damn to you, rookie. There'll be a time for payback, but it ain't right now. Now shut your yap and get back to work."

Off to one side Captain Bannerman and Lieutenant Starke talked to Smith, the scout.

"Will they hit us again?" Bannerman said.

"I doubt it," Smith replied. "They don't think we can catch them. This last attack was done more to strike out and hurt us. If they'd run off our horses and gotten us afoot, they might have tried to finish us off. But I think now they'll be content to go to the agency."

Bannerman walked off a step, then turned around. "Well, if they think we're going to give up, they're in for a surprise. I want Storm dead, gentlemen. He's as famous as Red Cloud, as famous as Roman Nose. Putting an end to his career of rape and murder will be—if you'll pardon the metaphor—a feather in our caps." He did not mention that eliminating Storm would almost certainly put him in line for the regiment's next majority.

Starke said, "What about the Hobson girl?"

"What about her? We'll get her back if we can. If we can't, that's too bad. It's all the other Hobson girls Storm might cause that I'm thinking about. Or don't you want to see that red devil stopped?"

"Right now, I'm more interested in the girl."

Bannerman gave a small smile. "Scared, mister?"

Starke looked him in the eye. "I'm always scared, Captain."

Bannerman gave him a disgusted look and walked away.

As they watched him go, Starke said to the scout, "Tell the truth, Mr. Smith, I feel sorry for Storm. Even after what he did to Bannon, even after what he did to the Hobsons. Storm didn't want this war. He was driven to it. He's as much a victim as anyone else."

"Maybe we're all victims," Smith suggested.

Starke nodded. "Maybe we are, at that."

They buried Bannon. The captain said a few words from the Bible, then the company moved out. They marched over Bannon's grave, obliterating all traces of it, so that the Indians wouldn't find it later and dig it up.

The company pressed on, over an endless expanse of brown, sagebrush-covered plain. The summer sun burned down. This far west, despite a wet winter and spring, there was water only in the major watercourses. The men had to conserve, saving most of what they had for the horses. The heat seemed to suck all moisture out of them, until they felt shriveled, like prunes. The dust turned men, clothing, and animals a uniform yellow. The men's eyes were blinking holes of brightness in the caked adobe formed by dust and sweat on their faces.

Sergeant Townsend's pipe-clayed white helmet stood out like a beacon. "Close up, there," he told the men. "Keep them intervals. This is noffink. I been on marches what made this look like a stroll in 'yde Park."

Townsend watched the column go by. As he turned after them, his shoulders sagged. So did his face, where pain was etched in every wrinkle. His back hurt. He looked around, to make sure no one saw. He felt every one of his fifty-five years. He was too old for this sort of thing; he was finally forced to admit it. It was only pride—and lack of an alternative—that kept him going.

" 'Ere, you! Squillace! Close up, there."

The pursuit went on for a week. The company followed the Cheyenne trail south and east, across the North Canadian River, Kiowa Creek, Wolf Creek. They were in the Indian Territory now. Twice they made dry camps. The first time they were able to dig for water. The second time they were not. Each night a few stragglers came in behind the rest. Harry took pride that he wasn't one of them—his big horse Beau had large reserves of strength.

The horses' shoes began to wear out. Some of the animals had bleeding feet. Their riders made moccasins for the horses from the hide of an old buffalo that the teamster Pennington carried for just that purpose. One man's horse broke its foreleg and had to be shot. The animal was cut up, and the meat cooked for the evening meal. The man—Hennessy, who had come to Fort Pierce with Harry—was mounted on one of the mules.

Food ran low. The men were reduced to quarter rations— three hardtack biscuits a day, and a bite of salt pork, until the pork ran out. The horses were down to a half ration of grain, and the mules seemed to be kept going only by Pennington's seemingly inexhaustible supply of curses. As the mules used up their loads of grain, the loads were redistributed and the spare animals were shot. Bearded scarecrows swarmed over them, butchering them. Some of the men didn't even bother to cook the meat, but ate it raw.

"The lieutenant said we'd get to like mule meat," recalled Barker, as he gnawed at a hastily cooked steak. The meat was charred on the outside, partly raw inside.

Slim Pickens agreed. "Least it ain't got worms, like that sowbelly they give us."

On the seventh day of the pursuit, the company camped along the South Canadian River. An hour before sunset the scout Smith rode in. He saw to his horse, then joined the officers, who were sitting by their campfire, eating supper. Bannerman and Conroy had supplies of tinned meats, vegetables, and fruits that they'd purchased in town for the campaign. Starke ate mule meat and hardtack, like the men.

Starke handed Smith a cup of coffee. Smith took a drink, then said, "They've caught up to their village. They're traveling together now."

Bannerman said, "How far behind are we?"

"Half a day, maybe, with two to go. The day after tomorrow they'll reach Fort Cobb."

Lieutenant Conroy said, "We can't make up half a day in forty-eight hours, can we?"

"We'd need a miracle," Starke admitted.

"We'll keep going," Bannerman told them. "I'll follow Storm to the front door of the agency building, if I have to. One mistake, and he'll become what General Sherman calls a 'good Indian.' "

Smith sipped his coffee. "They're not watching their back trail anymore. They must think they're safe from pursuit."

Starke said, "Indians always think they're safe from pursuit. Don't know why."

"Because they're savages, that's why," Bannerman said. "They have simple minds. That's why they never beat us in battle."

Starke looked over at him. "Never?"

Bannerman gave him a dark stare. "That was a long time ago, Lieutenant. And anyway, I wouldn't call it a defeat. *They* ran. *We* remained in possession of the field."

Starke smiled. "Whatever you say, sir."

The next day came in with strong southerly winds. The sky was dark, the air sultry. An hour after the company broke camp, the skies opened up.

"Keep them moving, Top," Bannerman shouted above the rain. He turned to Starke. "This may be our miracle, Mr. Starke. If Storm doesn't think we're behind him, he may wait this out in camp. If he does that, we can catch him."

The men rode on, heads bent into the driving rain. The sandy plains turned to mud. Dry ravines and arroyos became gushing torrents. The men slid their mounts down muddy banks and waded them across. Horses struggled for footing in the mud. Sometimes the banks crumbled, and men and horses fell. Sometimes they were nearly swept away by the force of the water.

"Keep going, men," Lieutenant Starke cried. "Keep going. It's not far now."

The men were weak from hunger and dysentery. With the rain, many suffered from chills, as well. They slumped in their saddles, barely able to stay awake. Harry had never known such exhaustion. It was hard to keep his red-rimmed eyes open, even with the rain beating into them. The rain soaked his ill-made clothing; it turned his hat into a flannel mop. The cheap stitching in the seams of his McClellan saddle split open, revealing the wooden tree underneath.

Barker fell asleep and rolled off his horse, into the mud. No one laughed at the sight. They were too tired. Harry held Barker's horse while he remounted. Barker nodded thanks. He didn't have the strength to speak. He had trouble keeping his eyes in focus.

Late in the afternoon, the rain stopped. At the evening halt, the men climbed off their horses. There was no dry wood for fires. That meant no coffee, and cold food.

Harry ground his teeth on his last piece of damp hardtack. "Thought you told me I'd like the field," he said to the Professor.

Across from him, Link Hayward said, "Aw, Mad Dog ain't havin' a good time. Poor baby. You should've been barracks guard when you had the chance, Mad Dog."

Harry said, "Crawl back under your rock, Hayward."

Link mocked him. "Turned into a real tough guy, ain't you, Mad Dog? You think you're so tough, we can always finish what we started in the barracks."

Harry threw down his hardtack and stood. "That's fine with me."

Link stood, too. The two men started for each other. "Hey," Hunter said suddenly, "here comes Smith."

"Yeah," the Professor added, "and it looks like something's up."

Link and Harry stopped. Everyone turned to watch the bearded scout ride in. Even at this distance he looked animated.

Smith reined in his horse in front of the officers. "I found Storm's village," he said. "They're camped on the Washita, not ten miles from here."

34

The company remounted in the fading light. Guided by Smith, they rode toward the Washita. Overhead, the clouds had cleared. The quarter moon provided faint illumination.

They halted about three miles from the Cheyenne camp, downwind, so that the Indian dogs and horses wouldn't pick up their scent.

While Smith and the officers went ahead, the men dismounted and loosened their saddle cinches. The men shivered in the breeze; their uniforms were still wet from the rain. Many, like Harry, sat in the mud, exhausted. They looped their horse's reins around their wrists, put their heads down and fell asleep. Others, like Townsend, Cronk, and McDermott, stayed awake. They had to.

The three officers followed Smith through the darkness. At last the scout motioned them to stop. They tethered their horses to a scrub oak and crept through the mud to the edge of the bluff.

Below them, the winding river sparkled in the faint moonlight. The dark spots in the middle were islands. Across the stream was the Cheyenne circle camp. Fires twinkled in front of the tipis; the Indians must have found dry wood. The faint tinkle of the pony herd's bell mare could be heard from farther downstream.

Captain Bannerman could scarcely contain his glee. "We've done it, gentlemen. We've got them. What's wrong, Mr. Smith?"

The buckskinned scout looked worried. "Don't know, Captain. I've got a bad feeling about this. I think there's more than just Storm's bunch down there."

"Did you see any more?"

"Didn't have time to look," Smith said.

Bannerman shrugged off the scout's hunch. "It makes no difference how many there are. The more, the better. We attack at dawn."

Lieutenant Starke said, "You're not going down to reconnoiter?"

"Why? We couldn't see much in the dark, and there's too much chance of being discovered."

"What about the Hobson girl?" Starke said.

Bannerman wished Starke would stop raising the subject. "You have an idea to save her?"

"Yes, sir. Instead of attacking the village, I'd like to run off the pony herd."

"What good would that do? You know as well as I do, Indians sleep with their favorite horses tied in front of their tipis."

"Yes, sir. But if we have the rest of their horses—and there's a lot of them—they might be willing to trade the girl to get them back. Horses are like money to Indians."

Bannerman said, "If we do that, we'll lose the element of surprise. We'll have to parley. Storm and his village will be able to get safely to the agency."

"Yes, sir," Starke admitted.

Bannerman considered briefly. "No," he said. "We attack."

Starke said, "Sir—"

"If you're worried about getting hurt, you can remain with the pack train," Bannerman told him.

Starke bit back a retort. Conroy and Smith looked at him. Conroy saw both sides of the question, but he found himself siding with Starke. Smith agreed with Starke, too, but he was just a hired guide. It was not his job to tell the military how to run their operations.

Starke went on. "At least let me sneak into the camp before the attack. Let me see if I can locate the girl and bring her out when the fighting starts."

Bannerman shook his head. "It's too dangerous. You could give us away."

"If we attack, they'll kill her," Starke persisted.

"We have to take that chance. We have to balance the loss

of one life against the number of white lives that we'll be saving in the long run.''

Bannerman continued, addressing the group. "Mr. Smith, you will find us a place to descend into the valley. We will bring the company to meet you. We'll keep the present order of march; that means Fourth Platoon in the lead. We'll cross the river and attack in line.''

Bannerman motioned toward the distant camp, drawing an invisible diagram in the air. "Fourth Platoon, on the right, will go around the village and run off the Indians' horse herd. Third Platoon, on the left, will also go around and form a blocking force downstream, cutting off the Indians from retreat. First and Second Platoons will go straight in. When Fourth Platoon has secured the horses, as many men as can be spared will join the blocking force. Mr. Conroy, you will command the blocking force. Don't let any of the red devils get away.''

"No, sir—I mean, yes, sir,'' Conroy said.

"Questions, gentlemen?''

"What about women and children?'' Conroy said. "Do we let them through, or try to capture them?''

"You shoot them,'' Bannerman said. "All savages are to be considered hostile. God knows, they don't spare our women and children.''

Conroy let out a long breath. Smith went stone-faced. Conroy looked at Starke, who gave him a helpless shrug.

"What about the pack train?'' Starke asked Bannerman.

"Mr. Pennington and his mules will remain on the bluffs until the action is terminated. Distribute ammunition before the attack, as much as the men can carry.''

Bannerman looked around. "Any further questions? Very well, gentlemen, let us rejoin the company. And good luck.''

"Good luck, sir,'' Conroy mumbled in reply.

Starke and Smith said nothing. Starke stared toward the distant village, as if his eyes could somehow penetrate the darkness and show him where the Hobson girl was being held.

The party crept away from the bluff. While Smith remained to search for a way down, the three officers mounted their horses and rode back to the company.

* * *

Bannerman briefed the sergeants. "Have the men tie down anything that might make noise," he concluded. "They'll wear no overcoats, and there's to be no talking."

The teamster Pennington broke open the ammunition boxes from the packs. The men marched back by squads for issue. They took carbine ammunition, pistol ammunition, and percussion caps. They crammed them in the boxes on their belts, in their pockets, in their saddlebags. They then drew rations for the coming day—three hardtack biscuits each.

The men returned to their lines. It was a warm night, but their teeth chattered because of their wet clothing. They bit back coughs and sneezes. They sniffled. They grabbed last bites of hardtack, last drinks of water. Some watered their horses from their hats. Saddle cinches were tightened. Pistols, carbines, and knives were checked and rechecked. Rattling mess equipment was muffled inside blanket rolls.

At last all was ready. There was nothing to do but wait. Harry hefted Pick Forrester's bowie knife. He tried to picture himself stabbing somebody with it, but he couldn't. This entire situation seemed unreal. He swallowed. His throat was dry, but he wasn't thirsty. Nearby, Barker fingered one of Susan's letters. Dutch Hartz prayed silently. Link Hayward's brow darkened as he prepared himself for what was to come.

Sergeant Townsend's white helmet bobbed in the faint moonlight as he made his way down the line, checking men and equipment. For Townsend the prospect of battle came as a relief. All his self-doubts were washed away. The routine built up in thirty-eight years of soldiering took over. He felt comfortable, normal.

"Winston, 'ow are you, then?"

"A bit scared, First Sergeant."

"That's natural. We're all a bit scared. Keep your 'ead tomorrow, and you'll be *achchi bat*. Barker, what about you? Ready?"

"I—I think so, First Sergeant."

Then a whispered command was passed down the column. "This is it. Form up."

Those who were sitting heaved themselves to their feet.

They formed a double line. Men flapped their arms for warmth; they stretched frozen joints.

"Forward. Move out."

They walked their mounts toward the river. The only sound was the muted clop of hoofs in the mud. The fatigue and exhaustion of the last week seemed to drop away. Men and animals were tense with excitement.

At the head of the column, Captain Bannerman couldn't wait to get started. He could already see the newspaper headlines. He could feel the adulation, the glow of being a hero. This was why he had become a soldier. He was on the verge of fulfilling his destiny.

Behind him, Jim Starke thought about Helene Bannerman. He wondered what she was doing right now, and if she missed him. Then he looked back at the men. The newspapers called them the scum of the earth, and maybe some of them were, but for the most part they were just a bunch of frightened kids. They'd be all right, though. Starke had confidence in them.

Next to Starke, Tom Conroy fought down the growing unease in his stomach. He prayed that he would acquit himself well.

Smith met them, chewing a piece of jerky. The scout had been thinking about his Indian wife and his children. He wondered whether they were still alive, or whether some other guide had led soldiers to their camp to kill them, as he was doing now for K Company.

Smith led the column to the descent he had found from the bluffs. The men walked their horses down, single file. The grade was relatively easy. Partway down, somebody's horse kicked loose a large rock. The rock bounded down the decline, cracking off other rocks on its way.

There was the barking of a distant dog. Everyone stopped. They held their breaths. At last the dog quieted. The night was still again. By hand signal the order was passed to move on.

The men reached the bottom of the grade. They were about two miles from the Indian village. At the river, they quietly watered their horses and filled canteens. Then they formed column of twos. They mounted and crossed the river. The cold water, swollen by the rain, rose to their waists.

They reached the opposite bank and moved downstream. The sky had the faint glow of false dawn.

The men rode in silence. Harry found his breath shortening. He felt the hair on the back of his neck stand up. Then, ahead, there was a deeper darkness. Conical tipis were outlined against the fading stars.

The column guided right, away from the river.

"Halt," came the hand signal.

"Left into line."

The men formed a single line, facing the darkened village. The officers, trumpeter, and guidon were in front. Sergeant Townsend was on the line's extreme right. The other sergeants were in front of their platoons.

Men's hearts beat faster. They pulled down the chin straps on their forage caps. They jammed campaign hats on their heads.

"Draw pistols," came the order. "Advance."

The line moved forward. They'd practiced the maneuver a hundred times, but this time it was for real.

They advanced at a walk. Behind them gray streaks of dawn lit the sky. The village was less than a mile away now.

Ahead, dogs started barking. Horses whinnied.

"At a trot."

They spurred their horses. The animals were getting so excited, it was hard to hold them in. The men were excited, too, sweating even in the dawn chill. The noise of the company was a growing rumble in the stillness.

More dogs were barking. Alarmed voices cried out.

In front of the line Bannerman turned to Fearless Freddie, the trumpeter. "Trumpeter. Sound the Charge."

35

The high, thin notes of the Charge split the dawn stillness.

The men raised a cheer. They sank spurs to their horses' flanks. The line surged forward. Link and the other veterans screamed the unofficial war cry of K Company— ''Fuck the army!''

They dashed toward the Cheyenne village, which was growing more visible in the gray light. They saw figures moving in the village. From one of the figures came a flash, a gunshot.

In the lead, Bannerman waved them on. He knew it was silly, but he wished he had his saber. He felt undressed without it.

The trumpet continued to blow. The line of men came on. The ground trembled beneath them. The stronger mounts moved into the lead as the men raced to be first into the village.

Harry clung to the neck of his big bay, Beau, trying not to roll off as the horse pounded across the uneven ground. Harry's cheap hat blew off. Suddenly he heard a cry of warning.

Directly across the company's path was a brush-filled ravine. The ravine was too wide to jump. The soldiers pulled up their charging horses in confusion, trying not to tumble in. Harry tugged Beau's reins as hard as he could. It was only luck that he did not somersault over the horse's head again and break his neck.

The cavalry horses reared and balked at going farther. Across the ravine more figures could be seen running in the village. More shots were directed at the soldiers. Beyond the village the pony herd was moving.

''Find a way through,'' Bannerman yelled at the milling men. ''Don't stop.''

Bannerman urged his horse down the slope of the ravine. Lieutenant Starke did the same, in another spot. So did white-helmeted Sergeant Townsend. Then others. They crossed the ravine and climbed the other side. The rest of the men followed.

"Hurry!" Bannerman cried. "Charge! Charge!"

Without waiting to re-form, the men continued their attack. All semblance of order was gone. They were a mounted mob now—screaming, shouting, lusting for blood.

There were more shots, and then the soldiers swept into the village. Before them were old men hobbling on sticks, women pulling shawls over their heads, screaming children, young boys fighting back with play arrows. The soldiers shot them, they trampled them with their horses. They knocked over tipis and set them on fire. Screams of the dead and dying shrilled in their ears.

Bannerman yelled, "Keep going, boys! Don't let them get organized!"

Link Hayward thundered along at the front of the attack, picking his targets coolly. When he'd exhausted the six rounds in his service revolver, he drew his own pistol and began using that on the fleeing Indians.

Jim Starke paid no attention to the fighting. Bullets buzzed past him. Figures ran by in the smoke and dust. He rode around and through the circle of tipis, looking for the Hobson girl. He hoped that she would have made a break when the troops attacked. Either that, or the Indians would drag her outside before killing her, giving him a chance at rescue.

Harry Winston likewise paid no attention to the fighting, but for a different reason. He had all he could do to control his horse. A figure loomed out of the smoke on his right. Man or woman? The figure fired a bow. The arrow grazed Harry's cheek. Harry rode on by. His pistol was in his hand but he was afraid to take the hand off the reins long enough to use it.

The village was a mass of smoke and dust and confusion. There were shouting men, neighing horses, shrieking women and children. Gunshots.

Men became disoriented. Barker got turned around and rode the wrong way. He blundered into Starving Mike, who shot at him as he came out of the dust, thinking he was a Cheyenne. The bullet clipped the ear of Barker's horse. Barker wheeled off as Starving Mike screamed obscenities at him in Russian.

"Forward, men! Forward!" Captain Bannerman cried. The trumpet continued to sound the Charge.

Sergeant McDermott led what he had been able to regroup of Fourth Platoon around the right flank of the village, but he missed capturing the pony herd. The break in the attack caused by the ravine had given the Indians time to get their horses to safety. McDermott took his men back to join the blocking force. Suddenly bullets began flying around them.

"Cease firing!" Lieutenant Conroy's voice came out of the smoke and dust. "It's Fourth Platoon."

McDermott rode forward and joined Conroy. "We missed the horses, sir."

"Too late to worry about it," Conroy told him. "Get your men into line."

Fourth Platoon joined the Third. The blocking party ranged from the river to the bluffs. They shot anyone attempting to escape the boiling confusion of the village. When they had used up the ammunition in their pistols, they drew their carbines and fired them. The majority of their targets were old people, women, and children.

"Most of the warriors must have escaped with the pony herd, sir," McDermott shouted to Conroy above the noise.

Conroy nodded.

In the village, Jim Starke despaired of finding the Hobson girl alive. Back and forth he rode, heedless of the bullets and arrows that flew around him. Then, through the smoke, he caught a distant glimpse of blond hair. He saw a figure in a tattered dress, running toward the river.

Starke spurred his horse out of the village and after the girl. He bore down on her, but another soldier was ahead of him—Dorfman, from Second Platoon. Dorfman aimed his carbine at the fleeing girl.

Starke rammed his horse into the other soldier's. Dorfman's carbine fired into the air. His horse went down, screaming, and Dorfman rolled from the saddle.

"She's white, you fool!" Starke yelled at the fallen trooper, and then he was past.

"Rebecca!" he called after the girl. "Rebecca! Becky!"

The girl didn't stop. She ran for the trees and undergrowth along the river.

"Becky!"

The girl stumbled and fell. She looked back at Starke in wide-eyed terror.

Starke threw himself from his horse. "Becky!"

He knelt by the girl and took her shoulders. She tried to run, to break away, like a frightened animal.

"It's all right, Becky," Starke said. He held her close, stroking her head.

The girl suddenly realized that this man was a friend. Her tense little body relaxed. Starke picked her up, speaking gently. "Come on, Becky. We're going for a ride." He placed her on his saddle, then swung up behind her.

Ahead, he heard Bannerman's voice, urging the men on. The fighting in the village was nearly over. Only a few scattered shots sounded around him. The battle was moving on down the valley, in the direction that the fleeing Indians and the pony herd had taken. Starke followed the sounds, rejoining the bulk of the company as they re-formed and prepared to push on. Some of the men were taking quick drinks of water. Others reloaded pistols and carbines.

Starke stopped the first man he came to. "Tudor!"

The young soldier looked at Becky Hobson, wide-eyed, as if he couldn't believe what he was seeing. "You found her, sir!"

"Yes," Starke said. He transferred the girl to Tudor's saddle. "Hold on to her. Stay close to me."

"Yes, sir," Tudor said, seating the Hobson girl in front of him.

The girl was frightened again. She looked longingly at Starke, who said, "It's all right, Becky. We won't let them get you back."

Tudor added, "Don't worry, sweetheart. You're safe with me."

Bannerman ranged in front of the company. "Forward, boys! They're getting away!"

The company galloped away from the village, downstream after the fleeing Indians. The ground here had been cut up by the hooves of the grazing pony herd, and the going was slow. Then the footing firmed, and the yelling troopers plunged ahead with renewed speed.

Around the bend in the river they charged. Then they stopped, involuntarily.

Ahead of them was another, larger Indian village.

36

The second village had been alerted. Its inhabitants could be seen running away. A few warriors sat their horses in front, firing long shots at the soldiers.

Bannerman laughed, to cover his surprise at finding more Indians. He cried, "The more the merrier, boys. Dress your lines. Form by platoons. Trumpeter—the Charge, if you please."

Fearless Freddie raised the bugle to his lips. Again the Charge rang out. Again the soldiers spurred forward. They were not as loud this time. Their throats were dry from breathing smoke and from the yelling they had done already.

More Indians appeared in front of the village, to shoot at the soldiers, to defy them. But when the soldiers drew close, the Indians broke and ran.

The company hit the second village. First and Second Platoons took it straight on. Third and Fourth took the flanks, then scoured the edges of the bluffs and the river. As before, the soldiers swept through, shooting anyone they saw, burning tipis, killing horses. Most of the Indians had left this village by now, and resistance was light.

There was shooting along the riverbank, too, where Third Platoon rooted out some Indians who had attempted to hide.

The river was too deep to wade here, and a number of the Indians tried to swim across. The soldiers fired at them. Bullets splashed around the swimmers. Some sank under the water; others faltered in their strokes and were swept downstream.

John Smith was riding with Bannerman. As the company charged through the second village, Smith recognized the markings on the lodges. These were Hill People, Little Creek Woman's band. These were the people with whom he had lived for over four years.

Smith slowed and let the soldiers go past him. He rode around the camp circle, searching for the lodge of his wife's parents—that was where Little Creek Woman and the children would be, if they were here. Around him were gunshots, the shouts of troopers, the crackle of flames, the screams of wounded men, women, and animals.

Smith saw the lodge of his father-in-law, Two Moons. He recognized the pictographs painted on the buffalo hide. He galloped over, ignoring soldiers who rode past.

He jumped from his horse in front of the lodge and his racing heart almost stopped.

A woman's body lay in front facedown.

Smith turned the body over, scarcely daring to look. Part of the woman's face had been shot away. It was not Little Creek Woman.

Smith let out his breath with relief, then pushed aside the lodge flap and went in. Inside, the lodge was deserted, as if in haste. Blankets and articles of clothing were scattered about. The fire still smoldered. Smith started back out, then stopped. He bent down and picked something up.

It was a rag doll, painted with the face of a woman, wearing a buckskin dress. The doll was much stained and worn by weather and time.

Smith recognized the doll. He had made it for his daughter, Calling Dove, five years before.

His family was here, then, or they had been just minutes ago.

Smith stuffed the doll in his buckskin shirt. He strode out of the tipi. He wanted to call their names, but he knew it was

useless. They were out of his hearing, somewhere past that
line of charging soldiers. Smith prayed—to both white gods
and red—that they wouldn't be killed.

And if they were killed, it would be partly his fault. He
had led the soldiers here. How could he have gotten himself
into a situation like this? Damn this war. Damn all war.

He was frantic to find his family. Yet he could not. He
could not leave the protection of the troops he had brought
to kill them.

He mounted his horse and rejoined Bannerman. If he
stayed in the front of the attack, maybe he would get to them
first, before . . .

But he did not want to think about that.

The company emerged from the second village in pursuit
of the fleeing Indians. Men and horses, weakened by the long
march on short rations, were getting tired. Harry Winston
was exhausted from holding in his horse. His arms shook
from the effort. He had yet to fire a shot. He just wanted this
to be over.

As the men proceeded down the valley, they saw a large
dust cloud, made by hundreds of ponies—the parched, sandy
soil had already dried enough from yesterday's rain to raise
dust. Cheyenne warriors rode in and out of this dust, firing
their rifles at the oncoming soldiers.

Captain Bannerman slowed. It looked like all the Indians
in Hell were in front of him. The rest of the men slowed
behind him. The company's momentum died and the charge
came to a halt. The troops milled under the ineffective, rag-
ged fire of the distant Indians.

Starke closed on Bannerman. "Keep going, sir. We're
outnumbered. Indians generally run if attacked, but if we
stop, they'll be on us for certain."

"You're mad," Bannerman said. He waved his pistol toward the dust cloud. "If we go any further, we'll be swallowed in a sea of the red devils."

"Not if we attack right now," Starke insisted.

Smith joined in, much as he hated to say anything that
might help the troops kill more Indians. "He's right, Captain. That dust, it's just Cheyenne boys riding back and forth,

leading the spare horses. They're trying to make you think there's more of them than there are. They're trying to cover the retreat of the villages. Stop here, and you're likely to be attacked yourself.''

Bannerman hesitated.

Starke's voice dripped with sarcasm. "I thought you said K Company could lick any number of Indians we found.''

"So we shall,'' said Bannerman, getting his nerve back. "But I've got a better idea. If they want to attack us, let them. We'll give them a taste of volley fire. Mr. Starke, dismount the company.''

"Sir—''

"That's an order, Lieutenant.''

"Yes, sir.'' Starke turned. "Company—dismount! Horse holders to the rear! Form a skirmish line!''

Storm had been fortunate to escape the attack on his village. No one had dreamed that the white soldiers could still be following them, and with the bad weather, there had been no guards out. Had it not been for the ravine into which the whites almost tumbled, he and his band might have been destroyed.

As it was, many had died. But most of the warriors had escaped, along with their horses. Storm had saved his war bonnet, his weapons, and, most importantly, his medicine, given to him by his uncle, Man Who Goes in the Middle. The medicine had been prepared from ground bitterroot, along with special herbs that Storm's uncle had added. The medicine was worn in a pouch around Storm's neck in battle, and, if its laws were obeyed, it protected him from injury.

Storm's people and the Hill People retreated in confusion down the valley. The boys were sent out to raise a dust screen, for protection.

After a short ride, the Indians stopped. Among the warriors, there was disagreement about what to do. Some wanted to flee to the Indian Agency for protection. Others wanted to scatter and lose themselves in the vast countryside. Still others wanted to wait and see what happened.

Storm had a different idea.

"Let us go and fight with the soldiers,'' he told the assembled warriors. "I am going, in any case." He looked at his oldest friend, Man Above the Clouds. "Will you join me, brother?"

Man Above the Clouds' forearms were grotesquely scarred, where strips of skin had been removed over the years in ritual sacrifice. He grinned. "*Ai-ee*. Yes, brother. It is a good day to join the spirits of our ancestors."

Storm's word was not binding on his own people, much less on the Hill People, but his example was a powerful one. He was one of the most famous war chiefs the tribe had produced. Before the other warriors could make a decision, there was a lull in the firing.

"The soldiers are getting off their horses!" came the cry.

That decided it. Everyone regarded this as a good omen. Everyone was curious to see why the soldiers had stopped. Soon all the Cheyennes were singing their war songs, as they made ready for battle.

Helped by the surviving women, Storm mixed his war paint. He painted his upper body and his arms down to the elbows black, the mark of the Kit Fox Soldiers. The top half of his face was painted red, the bottom half yellow. With blue earth he painted zigzag lines down the front of his white horse's legs, symbolizing lightning. The animal's tail was tied up.

He tied his medicine pouch around his neck. He took a bit of the medicine in his mouth, and he blew on each of his horse's hoofs in turn, to bring the animal speed and good footing. Then he donned his long war bonnet. The bonnet was made of eagle feathers, and between each pair of feathers was a lead bullet. The bonnet's brow was decorated with beads and the skin of a swallow. Lastly, Storm uncased his red shield with its rows of eagle feathers and owl feathers and sandhill crane feathers. He lifted the shield in the directions of the rising sun, the sky, and the setting sun. This would make the sun enter the shield; then, when the shield was turned toward the enemy, the sun would go out of it again, blinding them.

Man Above the Clouds wore a single eagle feather in his hair. His upper body was painted black, like Storm's. There

were enormous black circles painted around his eyes, along
with two more circles on his cheeks.

The old friends grinned at each other. "We will have tales
to tell of this day," Man Above the Clouds said.

Then Storm raised his new Lancaster rifle, given to him
by the whites, and he yelled his war cry. The two warriors
rode off to battle, followed in rapid order by the rest of the
Cheyennes.

37

The soldiers dismounted. One man in each group of four
had been designated as a horse holder. Each dismounted man
snapped the links attached to the left side of his horse's bridle
into the halter ring of the horse on his left. The holders led
the coupled mounts to the rear.

Barker was holder for Harry's group. He licked his lips as
the men joined their horses, then gave him the reins of the
first one. Dave Tudor switched with the holder of his group,
so that he could continue to take care of the Hobson girl.

"Hurry up!" the sergeants shouted. "Get on line!"

The men formed a skirmish line five yards apart. With the
loss of the horse holders, the effective strength of the company was forty-five, not nearly enough to cover the area between the river and the bluffs.

"Extend your intervals three yards," Bannerman ordered.

That was still nowhere near enough to cover so much
ground, plus the men were now so far from each other that
they felt unsupported.

The officers and guidon bearer stood behind the firing line,
along with the trumpeter and John Smith. The officers had
carbines; Smith, a Henry repeater. Bannerman tried to look
confident. Starke was grim. Conroy swallowed nervously.

Smith couldn't keep his mind on the battle. All he could think about was his family, running for their lives somewhere behind that dust cloud.

"Here they come!" Sergeant Cronk shouted.

A line of Indians came yipping out of the dust, brandishing bows and lances and rifles.

"Volley fire!" Bannerman cried. "Ready. Take aim. Fire!"

The Spencer carbines crashed. Smoke swirled around the line. One Indian toppled from his horse, but the soldiers didn't have time to see more, as each jacked another shell into the breech of his weapon. Behind the firing line the horse holders watched the fight nervously, fists tightening on the reins of their charges.

"Ready. Aim. Fire!"

"Fire!"

Volley after volley crashed out. The Indians attacked singly, or in small groups. Some rode along the line of soldiers, at long range, trying to make the soldiers waste ammunition. Others rode closer, firing at the soldiers from beneath their horse's necks. Some fired rifles; others launched arrows high in the air.

"Ready. Fire!"

This was the first time Harry had fired his carbine. He pointed the weapon in the direction of the Indians and pulled the trigger. He tried to aim, but the Indians were zigzagging and going too fast. With all the smoke, it was hard to see.

"Fire!"

Harry fired again. Bullets kicked up dirt near him. Arrows stuck in the ground, or came in at an angle and bounced harmlessly away. Down the line somebody yelled and grabbed at an arrow in his thigh. It was the company's first casualty.

"Fire!"

Through the smoke, Harry saw an Indian reel on his horse. The Indian slumped over the animal's neck, and it galloped away from the firing.

"Alternate men reload," Sergeant Townsend cried.

"Fire!"

Harry snapped open his ammunition box. With fumbling

fingers he took out shells and inserted them in the loading tube in the butt of his carbine. He dropped one of the shells on the ground. The hell with it. Another volley blasted out. Harry's throat burned from the acrid powder smoke. His eyes stung. He could see nothing of the battle but the little space in front of him. He did not know if the soldiers were winning or losing. He concentrated on firing his carbine, on keeping it loaded.

Behind the line, the officers squeezed off carbine shots at the charging Indians. The scout Smith wasn't firing; he seemed preoccupied.

More and more Indians entered the fight. Their attacks were becoming continuous.

"Independent fire," Captain Bannerman cried. "Fire at will!"

The men loaded and fired. Their faces were blackened and smeared by sweat and powder smoke. Sergeant Townsend walked coolly behind the line. "Don't waste ammunition, lads. Sight your targets. Squeeze off them rounds. Don't jerk that thing, Squillace, it's not your dick."

While the Indians darted in and out, keeping the soldiers occupied all along the line, a small group dashed around the right flank, aiming for the horses. Starke had ordered the platoon sergeants to post their best shots on the flanks. Most of the Indians were picked off, but some got through. They attacked the horse holders, who fired pistols at them. Frightened horses reared. Indians crashed to the ground or swayed in their wicker saddles and rode off. The horses had been saved—this time.

Another trooper went down, screaming with pain, his shoulder shattered by a bullet. The men were too hotly pressed to carry him to the rear. Another Indian fell, bouncing hard on the earth.

"You got him, Link!" Numb Nuts yelled.

"No shit," Link said.

More Indians rode to the battle. There were not enough soldiers to hold them back. The worried men looked over their shoulders at the officers.

"Eyes front!" Sergeant Cronk yelled.

"Ammunition!" men cried. "We're running out!"

Townsend yelled, "Alternate men, back to your 'orses for ammunition."

Men ran to their horses and got ammunition from their saddlebags. They hurried back to the firing line, while the next group went for ammunition. Large numbers of Indians were gathering on both flanks for another run at the horses.

By the guidon, Lieutenant Conroy observed, "If this goes on another few minutes, we're going to be surrounded."

Starke grinned at Bannerman. "Just like old times—eh, Captain?"

Bannerman said nothing. His earlier confidence seemed to be fading.

Starke went on. "We've got to withdraw, Captain." He peered through the powder smoke and dust. "Those bluffs across the river would make the best defensive position."

Conroy gulped. "We'd have to ride right through the Indians, Jim."

"It's our only chance," Starke insisted. "We either move now, or we get buried right here."

It went against Bannerman's grain to withdraw in the face of savages. He wondered if Starke was trying to trick him, to make him look bad. He said, "What do you think, Mr. Smith?"

Smith didn't hear. He recognized many of the warriors who were attacking them. He was sure that they recognized him, as well. He had lived with these men. He had hunted with them. He had gone on the warpath with them against the Crees and Pawnees. . . .

"Mr. Smith?" Bannerman repeated.

Smith turned. At that moment a slug from a .50 Sharps carbine blew off the top of his head. Bannerman's face was splattered with blood and brains, with bits of bone and hair.

Bannerman was stunned. The bloody mess dripped down his face. Smith's body fell at his feet, and Bannerman stepped away from it with a little cry. He had only been in action once, and he had never experienced anything like this.

Behind them one of the horses was hit. The holder cut the plunging animal loose from the others with a knife.

Starke said, "Captain?"

Bannerman tried to wipe his face clean, but he only succeeded in spreading gore down the front of his uniform.

"Captain? What are your orders?" Starke said.

Bullets and arrows flew around them. Another man went down, wounded. Bannerman stared through his bloody mask.

"Captain, we have to get out," Starke insisted. "Permission to withdraw to the bluffs?"

At last Bannerman croaked, "Very well. Withdraw to the—"

Starke didn't wait to hear the end. He turned. "Sergeant Townsend! Mount the troop. We're pulling out."

38

"Horse holders forward!" Sergeant Townsend cried.

The horse holders brought their mounts just behind the firing line.

Lieutenant Starke turned to Conroy. "Tom, you take 'em. I'll give you covering fire. Get to the river. Third Platoon will cover the crossing. First Platoon will cover the withdrawal up the bluffs."

Conroy said, "What about the Captain?"

They looked at Bannerman, who was still dazed, with Smith's blood and brains dripping down his face and the front of his jacket. Starke said, "He's no good to anybody right now." To Townsend, he said, "Top, get me Sergeant Cronk, along with Hayward, Anders, Childress, Logan, and Tasslemeyer. Have them mount up and join me. Make sure their weapons have full loads."

"Yes, sir," Townsend said. "Permission to join you, sir?"

"Denied. You help Lieutenant Conroy here."

"Yes, sir." Townsend went down the line, calling for the men Starke wanted.

The little party mounted and formed on Starke. Around them the gunfire went on. The air was pierced by the screams of Indians, by the curses of soldiers, by the neighing of wounded and frightened horses.

"We're going to cover the retreat," Starke told his men. "Spread out and move forward fifty yards." He turned to Conroy. "All right, Tom. Good luck."

The two officers shook hands, then Starke rode out with his men. They formed a mounted skirmish line, firing at the Indians, who reacted with surprise, wondering what the white soldiers were up to.

Conroy turned to the rest of the company. "Prepare to mount!" The sergeants repeated the call down the line.

The men rose. They clipped carbines to their slings; they took the reins of their horses. Some of the horses, like Harry's mount, Beau, were frightened and dancing around, and the men had a hard time bringing them under control.

"Mount!" Conroy cried.

The men climbed into their saddles; they slipped carbines in their sockets. The wounded men were helped on board, and their buddies mounted after. Townsend took Captain Bannerman's arm. "Come on, then, sir. Time to go." He helped Bannerman onto his horse, then followed.

Harry's big horse, Beau, was still dancing around, and it pulled Harry away from the line. It wouldn't let Harry mount. In the dust and confusion, no one noticed. Most of the men were too scared to worry about anything but themselves.

"Be still!" Harry cried. "Be still, damn you!"

Conroy waved a hand. "Left by twos. At a gallop. Forward!"

The company rode off. The skirmishers covered them. Harry was still struggling with his horse. "Wait!" he cried to the retreating soldiers, but no one heard. Beau gave a sudden sideways lunge and broke free. Harry grabbed at the animal's bridle, missed, and fell on his knees in the dirt. Beau galloped away, following the company.

Harry looked around. The company was gone. The skirmishers covered them with carbine fire, then they, too, departed.

Harry was alone, with several hundred Cheyennes closing in on him.

There were hoofbeats to Harry's rear. He whirled, raising his carbine.

It was Link Hayward. Link pulled up his horse in a cloud of dust. He slid his left foot from the stirrup and held out a hand.

"K Company doesn't leave men behind," he told Harry. "Not even you."

Harry took the proffered hand. He put his foot in the stirrup and swung onto the horse behind Link, grabbing Link's waist. Link sank his spurs into the horse's flanks and they started after the others.

Behind them the Indians came on.

The company raced for the river. Conroy was in the lead. Bannerman was at his side. Bannerman had lost his hat, and his face and uniform were a mess. It seemed as if he only half comprehended what was happening. White-helmeted Sergeant Townsend rode along the line, attempting to keep the company in some kind of formation.

When the Indians realized that the soldiers were retreating, they attacked. A large group blocked the company's path. Conroy appeared to lose his fear, or maybe he drew inspiration from necessity. He waved his pistol, yelling, "Charge, men! Don't stop for anything!"

He rode straight at the Indians, leveling his pistol and firing into their midst. The men were right behind him, firing and cheering. Several Indians fell from their horses. The rest dropped back and let the soldiers through. Many were scared by Bannerman's appearance. They thought him some kind of apparition.

The Indians came on again. They hung on the flanks and rear of the retreating soldiers. There was a running fight to the river. Conroy found himself leading the men along an old buffalo track; he prayed that it led to a ford. The soldiers fired pistols. The Indians shot rifles, pistols, bows. The Indians tried to shoot the big cavalry horses. Many of the horses had arrows sticking in them. Men were hit and fell.

One of the wounded men—Princeton, whose shoulder had

been smashed—couldn't hold on any longer. He slipped from his horse. Two Cheyennes swooped down on him. One of them lassoed him with a rope and galloped off, dragging the screaming trooper along the ground.

Hennessy, who was riding the mule, fell behind. He got cut off and surrounded by a party of painted, feathered braves. Terrified, Hennessy stuck his pistol in his mouth. He pulled the trigger. His head snapped back and his body fell off the mule, to the ground.

Link and Harry were last. Harry's bottom bounced painfully on the horse's rear. He prayed that he didn't lose his grip on Link's waist and fall off. There were Indians all around. Link and Harry passed Slim Pickens, whose horse had gone down and rolled onto his leg, trapping him. Pickens was firing his carbine. He waved to Link and Harry as they rode by. "Adios, boys," he cried. Harry looked back and saw a swarm of Indians descend on Pickens.

A painted Cheyenne closed on Harry and Link. The Indian shouted something at them. He reached over and grabbed Harry's arm, trying to drag him from the horse. The Indian's grip was strong. Harry felt his own grip on Link's waist loosen. Then Link pointed his pistol at the Indian and fired. The Indian let go of Harry, slumped over his horse's neck, and dropped behind, disappearing into the cloud of dust.

The company reached the riverbank. Conroy wheeled about. "Third Platoon! Covering fire!"

Captain Bannerman did not halt. He jumped his horse off the six-foot drop, into the river. Some of the Third Platoon listened to Conroy and stopped to provide covering fire. Some didn't, and followed Bannerman into the water. The rest of the company came up to the bank. The men jumped their horses into the water, splashing. Some hesitated and were pushed off by the press of men and horses crowding behind. The riverbank was softened from yesterday's rain, and the weight of men and horses collapsed it, making the descent easier.

The river wasn't deep right here. The men half rode, half swam their horses across. The Indians went into the water as well, up- and downstream. Guns blasted, arrows flew. Men and horses were shot. They fell and floated away. One trooper—"Sad Sam" Hotchkiss—strayed from the formation. An Indian leaped from his horse, knocking Hotchkiss into the river. The Indian held the struggling soldier's head underwater.

Barker was halfway across when an Indian with his face painted blue closed in on him. The Indian carried a war axe. With a squeal of fear, Barker pointed his pistol and pulled the trigger. *Click.* He cocked the weapon and pulled the trigger again. *Click.* It was empty. He threw the pistol at the Indian. The heavy weapon hit the Indian in the face, breaking his nose. The Indian straightened in his war saddle and closed on Barker again. Face contorted with rage and blood, the Indian swung his war axe. Barker raised a hand to ward off the blow. The axe blade caught him between the fingers. It sliced through his hand all the way to the wrist.

Blood spurted. Barker screamed with pain. He swooned in the saddle. The Indian jerked loose his axe. He started to swing it again, but Dutch Hartz shot him in the chest. The Indian toppled backward into the water. Dutch grabbed Barker's bridle and led Barker's horse across the stream.

The first men across the river found a steep bank. They had to jump their horses almost straight up to get to the top. Only the animals' fear enabled them to make the leap. Other men dismounted and walked their horses up. Still others rode up- and downstream to look for easier exit spots.

"First Platoon! Covering fire!" shouted Sergeant Townsend. Hunter, Walsh, and Squillace turned their horses and opened fire on the Indians. Squillace ran out of bullets and tried to reload, even as a bullet killed his horse. Starving Mike and the Arab joined them. Their horses were stuck full of arrows, like pincushions.

"Up the bluffs, men!" cried Townsend, as the rest of the company crossed. Captain Bannerman hadn't waited. He spurred his horse up a steep ravine to the top. Men followed him.

Lieutenant Conroy and the Third Platoon crossed with Starke and his six-man covering party. Link and Hayward were behind them. Bodies of Indians and soldiers floated in the river. Horses screamed. The gunfire was continuous.

Link's big horse galloped through the shallows in a spray of water. Harry saw the steep bank. We'll never make it, he thought. As the horse threw itself at the bank. Harry slid off the back and held onto the animal's tail, climbing up. At the top he got back on. He and Link joined the mad rush up the bluffs.

Two deep ravines ran down the bluffs at this point, creating a promontory. Some of the men rode up the ravines. Others scaled the bluff itself. Some rode or ran in blind panic. Others were orderly, turning and firing their weapons at the pursuing Indians. Men fell and rolled down the hill. The Professor was hit by an arrow in the back of the thigh. He fell from his horse, propped himself up with his carbine and kept going on foot. Squillace was on foot, too. He was caught from behind by two Indians, who dragged him back down the bluff, screaming, a prisoner.

The last men up the bluff drew covering fire from the men already on top. Sergeant Townsend's white helmet could be seen moving about, organizing a defense. Harry and Link were the last ones up, just behind Lieutenant Starke. At the top they slid off Link's horse. There was no time for anything else, because the Indians came boiling over the bluff right behind them.

There was a confused swirl of hand-to-hand fighting. The Indians attacked with lances, bows, guns. The dismounted soldiers, many of whom were out of ammunition, fought back with anything they had. They pulled Indians off their horses. They stabbed at them with knives. They choked them with their bare hands.

The cavalry horses were led to a shallow depression in the center of the bluff, and the holders returned to the fight. The teamster Pennington arrived, riding his mule. He had cut the rest of the pack train loose.

Dave Tudor remained with the horses, holding Becky Hobson close. "Don't let them take me again," she whimpered, looking up at him.

"I won't," Tudor said. He fingered his revolver, which had one bullet in its chamber. "I won't."

Captain Bannerman stood near Tudor, incapable of action. Several more men, who were too badly hurt or too scared to fight, were also gathered by the horses. Panicked, some of them tried to hide among the animals.

The fighting raged all around the bluff. Men went down, from arrows, bullets, or with their brains clubbed out. Horses reared, trampling the wounded.

Fearless Freddie, the trumpeter, caught a lance through his jaw and fell screaming. The Indian who had thrown it leaped from his horse, only to have his head crushed by a rock wielded by another trooper. Barker rolled on the ground, holding his injured hand and moaning. Dutch Hartz stood over him, covering him with his carbine, trying frantically to reload. The Professor propped himself on his wounded leg, firing his pistol. He was shot in the right shoulder and fell. He switched the pistol to his good hand and kept firing until the chamber was empty.

Harry fired his carbine into the charging Indians. When the carbine was empty, he threw it down and drew his pistol, but the pistol was empty, too. At that moment an Indian rode at him with a feathered lance. Instinct took over. Harry sidestepped, grabbed the lance by the shaft and fell backward. The Indian came off his horse and landed in the dust near him. Both men jumped to their feet. The Indian drew a knife and lunged at Harry, who grabbed the attacker's wrist. The two men grappled and fell to the ground, rolling around, grunting, straining. Then somebody grabbed the Indian by his long hair and pulled him up. It was Skull. He stuck his pistol to the Indian's temple and fired. He let the body fall back to the dirt and continued on.

Sergeant Townsend was out of ammunition. He swung his carbine at an oncoming Indian. The red-hot barrel caught the Indian across the stomach and knocked him off his horse. Townsend smashed in the Indian's head with the carbine's metal butt plate.

In the depression, an Indian ran up behind Tudor, while Bannerman stared helplessly. The Indian fired a pistol. The ball hit young Tudor in the back, shattering his spine. Becky Hobson screamed. The Indian grabbed for the girl, but before he got hold of her, somebody shot at him and he fled.

Then, suddenly, the Indians were retreating down the bluff.
The exhausted soldiers watched them go. A few fired after
them. Most were too tired to do anything. Many slumped to
the ground, overcome by weariness.

Lieutenant Starke roused them. ''There's no time to waste,
men. Dig in!''

39

The bluff was in chaos. The men were scattered about, in
disorder. There were dead and wounded everywhere, plus
horses that had wandered loose from the dip. There were
ravines on two sides of the bluff, and a steep drop on the
third. The fourth side was open to the prairie. The Cheyennes
were all around. They opened scattered rifle and arrow fire
at the soldiers.

''Straighten this line,'' Lieutenant Starke ordered, taking
command in the face of Captain Bannerman's inability to
function. He walked around the bluff, with Sergeant Townsend at his side. A bullet plucked at Starke's sleeve but he
paid it no attention. There was a gash across the front of
Townsend's white helmet.

''First Platoon, regroup and take the open side, of the
bluff,'' Starke said.

''Oh, thanks,'' swore Hunter under his breath. ''That's
the most likely spot for an attack.''

Starke went on, ''Second Platoon, take the east side. Third
Platoon, the west. Fourth, cover the drop.'' The Fourth,
McDermott's platoon, had been hit hardest on the retreat.
Starke gave them the easiest spot.

''You 'eard the Lieutenant,'' Townsend bellowed at the
men. *''Jaldi, jaldi!''*

The tired men shuffled to their places, urged on by the

sergeants and Lieutenant Conroy. The Indian fire picked up. A soldier—Dorfman—spun and fell, flopping on the ground in pain.

"Sergeants, take the roll," Townsend ordered. "Assign firing positions."

"What about the wounded?" Lieutenant Conroy asked Starke.

"They'll have to wait," Starke told him. "The Indians could attack again at any minute."

First Platoon took up their positions. They began to return the Indian fire. Harry Winston was just now realizing how hot it had gotten. He looked at the sun. It couldn't be more than eight or nine o'clock. That shocked him. It seemed as if they had been fighting all day. He had started the morning wet from the rain; he had dried off and was now soaked again, this time with sweat. There was a crust of dried blood on his cheek, where he'd been grazed by the arrow.

"Dig in, men!" Sergeant Cronk cried. "Dig in!"

The men shucked their heavy carbine slings and their blue wool coats. They dug in with knives, tin cups, forks, their bare hands. They took cover behind clumps of brush. They unsaddled their horses and piled the saddles in front of them as improvised breastworks, along with their blankets and overcoats. They took the canteens from their saddles and drank deeply.

"Not too much," Cronk cautioned. "That water may have to last you a long time."

The Indian fire grew heavier. The Indians had plenty of guns and ammunition, thanks to the government distribution of last fall and what they'd captured from the pack mules.

Link Hayward ducked as a bullet struck close to him. He fired back and said, "I wish Amassee was here, don't you, Skull?"

"*Absolent,*" said the ex-Legionnaire. "I wish he was here and I wasn't."

In the center of the bluff Townsend received the roll call from the other sergeants. He reported to Lieutenant Starke. "Thirty-one effectives, sir. Counting orficers."

"Very well," Starke said.

"Could be worse," Townsend ventured.

"Yes, and it could be a hell of a lot better," Starke said.

Conroy stood next to Starke. He swallowed his fear, trying to ignore the bullets and arrows the way Starke did, trying to ignore the screams of wounded men and horses. To Starke, he said, "There's so many Indians. If they pushed it, they could overrun us."

Starke nodded. "That's not the way Indians fight, thank God."

"Do we have a chance?" Conroy asked.

"Just one that I can see. That our galloper got through to the regiment, and Major Carr's bringing them after us."

"And if he isn't?"

"Then I hope you've made out a will," Starke said. He turned to Townsend. "Top, have the men redistribute their ammunition, by platoons."

"Yes, sir."

Under the watchful eyes of the platoon sergeants, the men counted their ammunition and redistributed it—along with that of the dead and wounded—until every man had an equal amount. Considering how much they had crammed into their pockets and saddlebags last night, there was not much left. The seven-shot Spencer carbines consumed bullets at a fearsome rate. Harry had seventy-five rounds of carbine ammunition, and twenty-three for his pistol.

Heads down behind their flimsy entrenchments, the men reloaded as the Indian fire beat around them.

"These repeaters really saved our asses," said Hunter, pushing shells into his Spencer's butt-end loading tube.

Numb Nuts said, "You're not going to believe this, but I read that the army wants to replace them with single-shots."

"Bullshit," Hunter said. "Why would they do that? If we'd had single-shots, we'd have been wiped out by now."

Link finished reloading. He placed a shell into the carbine's breech, giving him eight to fire. "What do you care, you dumb shit? You didn't have to be here in the first place."

"I'm here because I'm a patriot," Hunter said.

They all laughed at that.

Starke and Townsend went to the dip in the center of the bluff. Townsend found two malingerers hiding among the wounded, pretending to be hurt. He grabbed their collars and booted them in the rear. ''There's noffink wrong wiv you, Armstrong. Back to your platoon, or I'll shoot you meself. You, too, Ruddick.''

Starke saw the civilian teamster. ''Mr. Pennington, get your rifle and take a place on line with the First Platoon.''

Pennington spit tobacco. ''I didn't sign on to be no soldier boy, Lieutenant. You want me to fight, it's gonna cost the government an extry dollar a day.''

Starke laughed. ''All right. You draw up the papers and I'll sign them.''

K Company's guidon had been set up in the center of the bluff. Captain Bannerman sat beside it, still looking dazed and unfocused. He rose as Starke approached. The Scout Smith's dried blood and brains were mixed with dirt and sweat on Bannerman's face. He said, ''It's all over, Mr. Starke. There will be no fuss, no panic. We must die like soldiers.''

Starke said, ''If it's all the same to you, sir, I'm not quite finished living yet.''

''But we have no chance. No chance.''

''We'll see about that,'' said Starke, and he moved on. Nearby, a horse shuddered from the impact of a bullet and fell. Starke paid no attention. The danger excited him. It made him feel alive. This was what he had been made for. As much as he hated to see men die, this—the battlefield—was where he belonged. His mind worked on that paradox, even as bullets and arrows sought him out.

''Get down, sir,'' shouted one of the men. ''You'll be hit.''

Starke laughed. ''I'm helping Mr. Lo waste ammunition.''

Townsend was beside him again. ''Bluff's secure, sir. Ammunition's redistributed.''

''Very well. See to the dead and wounded.''

''Sir.''

Men were detailed to take the wounded to the dip in the bluff, near the horses. They laid the wounded in rows, moaning, screaming with pain, their blood draining into the center of the dip and mingling there. The dead were laid in another row. Stewart, a trooper from Third Platoon, looked after the hurt men as best he could, though he had no medical training. The Professor, who was a dentist—as close to a doctor as the company had—might have done that job, but he was one of the wounded.

Braving the Indian fire, Harry searched the bluff for Barker. Dutch had told him that Barker was wounded. Then Harry saw him. He saw Barker's hand, mangled by the Cheyenne war axe, and his stomach turned.

"Oh, Jesus," he said.

Harry knelt by his bunky. Barker was holding his wrist and crying. Tears cut channels through the caked dust and sweat and powder smoke on his cheeks. He said, "It hurts, Harry. It hurts."

"I know," Harry said.

He helped Barker up and assisted him to the dip. Stewart put a hasty tourniquet around Barker's wrist, and he improvised a bandage from somebody's dirty shirt. "Sorry I don't have a clean one," he said. He wrapped the bandage around Barker's hand. The bandage quickly turned red. Harry got Barker's canteen from his horse. As he did, he stopped. His own runaway horse, Beau, stood placidly among the cavalry mounts.

"You bastard," Harry said. He drew his pistol. He cocked it and pointed it at the big bay. Then he lowered it. There was no sense wasting a bullet on such a worthless beast. He kicked the horse's buttock as hard as he could, then took the canteen back to Barker.

Barker lay next to the Professor. Harry handed his bunky the canteen, after first unscrewing the cap for him. "I've got to get back," Harry said.

Barker nodded. Beneath the grime, his face was pale and drawn. "Thanks, Mad Dog," he whispered. It was the first time he'd ever called Harry by his nickname.

Harry patted him on the shoulder and left. With his good hand, Barker raised the canteen to his lips.

Becky Hobson sat with her hands around her knees. She had seen horror piled upon horror the last ten days, and the sights no longer registered on her face. Her eyes were dead. Jim Starke sat beside her, putting an arm around her shoulder. She looked over. She remembered the man who had saved her at the village. Dave, the man whose horse she had ridden during the retreat, was still alive, though not for long. She did not like to think about him.

Starke said, "You all right?"

Becky sniffed and nodded.

Starke smoothed the dirty hair from her eyes. His fingers worked through the tangles. "You were lucky to get away from the Indians, you know. How did you do it?"

Becky fought back tears. "I was . . . I was asleep. I heard the music—you know, the bugle—and then shooting, and yelling. I got out of my blanket. I guess the Indians forgot me for a minute. They were all yelling and running around. Except for one . . . one old woman. She grabbed me. But I bit her arm, then I ran out of the tipi. They were yelling at me, telling me to come back, I guess, but I didn't listen. I ran for the woods. I thought, I can hide there. Then you came, and . . ." Her voice trailed off.

Starke hugged her. Spunky thing, he thought. He would have liked her to help give water to the wounded, but he didn't want her to see any more. She'd been through enough. He stood her up and walked her over to Captain Bannerman. "You sit with the Captain for a while."

To Bannerman, he said, "If you don't mind, sir." Then he returned to the battle.

First Platoon's dead and wounded had been seen to. Those of the Indian dead who hadn't been removed by their tribesmen were scalped and pitched off the bluff. The Indian wounded were killed, then similarly disposed of. Skull hooked a bloody scalp to his belt, grinning.

Link found a wounded Indian. The Indian was about twenty. His face was painted with wavy yellow lines. He had been shot in the ribs, but his lungs had not been punctured; there was no bloody froth at his lips.

Link bared his teeth in a wolfish grin. The young Indian looked up at him, wide-eyed.

Link knelt and held his hands over the Indian's wounded ribs. "Where does it hurt?" he asked innocently. He pressed down hard. "There?"

The Indian gasped with pain, trying not to cry out.

Link shifted his hands, and he pressed down again. "How about there?"

The Indian's feet kicked out. He made little animal noises.

"Won't talk, eh?" said Link. "Maybe your hair's too long."

Link drew his knife. With one hand he pulled the Indian's hair. With the other he jabbed the knife beneath the Indian's scalp and began cutting.

The wounded Indian squirmed. He grit his teeth to keep from crying out. He struggled harder, trying to get away, in obvious agony. Link punched him twice in the jaw to keep him still.

Link sliced a rough circle around the top of the young Indian's head. He threw down the knife, grabbed hold of the Indian's hair and pulled.

The scalp gave. The Indian arched his back in pain. Link pulled harder, neck muscles straining. Suddenly the scalp came off, with a sound like ripping fabric. The Indian jumped several inches off the ground. He rolled around, biting through his tongue to keep from crying out. His head and face ran with blood.

Link held up the scalp with a laugh. Then he took the Indian by the arms. He dragged the Indian to the edge of the bluff and threw him off.

The Indian fell down the steep bluff, bouncing off rocks and brush. Now he could hold himself no longer. He screamed in agony. Halfway down the bluff, he came to a stop. He lay there, crying piteously. Other Indians ran to help him as the soldiers fired at them.

Link looked down at the Indians and shouted, "That's for Mick Bannon, you motherfuckers!"

Link swaggered back to his spot on the line, contemptuous of the bullets that zipped around him . He lay in his scrape. He took the bloody scalp and tied it to the barrel of his carbine.

Some of the old-timers thought that what Link had done was great. Skull and Hunter hooted with laughter. Pennington spit tobacco juice. "Hell, boy, you cut hair better'n the redskins."

Walsh—the tough guy—looked like he was going to throw up.

Harry just stared.

Link looked at him. "Something the matter?" he snarled.

"Nope," Harry said. "Nothing at all. I never had it so good."

40

The bluff to the west of K Company's position was higher than the one on which the soldiers were trapped. This enabled the Indians there to fire down and from behind on all but Third Platoon, who were facing them.

There was nowhere to hide from the Indian bullets and arrows, so the men dug deeper. They were tired from a week of pursuit, from little food and sleep. They had been awake most of last night. It seemed they were moving in slow motion as they deepened their scrapes.

The heat grew worse. It was going to be the hottest day of the year. The sun was like a ball of molten fire, suspended above them. There was not a cloud in the sky to give them shade. The men had cursed the chill rain yesterday. Today, they would have been glad to see it.

The teamster Pennington spit tobacco. "Them Injuns must be some riled to be fightin' thisaway. Hit and run, that's their usual style."

"We've got to get out of here," Walsh said. "I can't take much more."

"Oh, stop your bellyaching," Link told him. "You're getting paid for it, ain't you?"

"I ain't getting paid enough. I'll tell you that."

Link snorted. "You ain't even earned your sixteen a month yet."

The sun's rays blasted Harry Winston's unprotected face. He wished he hadn't lost his hat. He could feel his nose and cheeks burning—it was almost like they were frying. As he lay in his scrape, he reached into his saddlebag. He had drawn his day's ration of three hardtack biscuits this morning—had it only been this morning?—and now he pulled one out. He tried to eat it, but he couldn't. It was too hard. He was too tired to break it up, and there was no water in which to soak it.

He got his canteen and swished it. There was a swallow left. Should he drink it now, or wait? What difference did it make? There wasn't enough to quench his thirst, and he wasn't going to get any more. There was no rain in the offing, and he didn't know when—or if—they would get off the bluff. He decided to save the water, as a test of his willpower.

He could have avoided all this, he thought. He could have stayed at Fort Pierce, as barracks guard. He could have deserted by now, and been a free man.

In a way, he had made a mistake by coming with the company. Nobody in their right mind would wish themselves in a situation like this—except maybe Link Hayward, and Link wasn't in his right mind. But in another way, he had no regrets about coming. He was almost glad that he was here. He suddenly felt close to these men, in a sense that he'd never felt close to anyone before. It was something he couldn't explain, even to himself. He'd experienced more in one day than most men experienced in a lifetime.

Now, if only he could live through it.

Beyond First Platoon's line the Indians had taken cover behind brush and rocks and folds in the earth. They fired rifles. They sent arrows high in the air, to fall on the soldiers' positions. Behind them was the main body of mounted Indians, who sat their horses in little groups, waiting to trade places with their tribesmen up front and take some shots at the white soldiers. It was like a game to them.

The soldiers returned the fire. "Make sure you have a target," Sergeant Cronk told them. "Don't waste ammunition. There ain't no more when this is gone."

"Hey," said the Arab, who had the best eyes in the company, "see that Injun back there, on the white horse—painted black, with the big war bonnet and the red shield? That's Storm. I remember him from the fort."

Harry looked. With a shock, he recognized the red shield and its trailing rows of feathers. It was the shield that he and Barker had seen on Easter Sunday in the Cheyenne village.

Sergeant Cronk spoke to Pennington. "Why don't you try a shot at him, Pop?"

Pennington carried a Smith & Wesson .44 hunting rifle, with a longer range than the cavalry carbines. "I ain't your pop," he said irritably. "Hell, I can do it longer and with more women than you soldier boys ever could."

Hunter laughed. "The only thing you ever did it with was a shavetail mule."

Pennington swore. He lined up the shot, drew his breath, and fired.

A heartbeat later Storm looked around, startled, as if something had just passed close to him.

"Damn," said Pennington, looking surprised. "Glare from the sun got in my eyes. Must have throwed off the shot."

Before Pennington could line up another shot, Storm turned his white horse and jogged out of range.

"Shit!" Skull said suddenly.

"You called?" Hunter replied, without looking.

Skull said, "I'm hit, you idiot."

They turned. There was an arrow sticking out of the big Dane's side. He'd been hit from behind, from the western bluff.

Link said, "Well, that's a hell of a thing. How are you going to fight with an arrow in your ass?"

"It's not in my ass, it's in my hip. Shut up and get it out."

Link held Skull down, and Hunter pulled out the arrow. The shaft came out, but the head worked itself loose, and it stayed in Skull's side.

Link flipped Hunter his knife. "You'll have to cut it out."

Hunter dug into the wound, as gently as he could. Skull grimaced. "Jesus, be careful. You were right when you told them you couldn't use your hands."

"Shut up," Hunter said. "It's too bad this thing didn't hit you in the head. It probably would have bounced off."

Then the arrowhead came out—popped out, really. Pennington plugged the wound with some well-chewed tobacco.

Link and Numb Nuts helped Skull to the dip, where he was placed with the rest of the wounded, not far from Becky Hobson.

The day wore on. The sun seemed to get even hotter. It was like a living thing, beating down. It took the men's breath away. It sucked the life from them. It baked them into a stupor as they lay in their scrapes, pinned down by the Indian fire. They were crusted with dirt and sweat. Their blue trousers and flannel shirts had all turned the color of brown earth, until it was nearly impossible to tell one man from another.

In the dip more and more of the horses were hit. They fell, dead or wounded. Others reared in pain and ran loose across the bluff. There was not enough ammunition to waste on wounded animals, so their owners had to put them out of their misery with knives.

The heat, the exhaustion, and the acrid powder smoke that the men breathed exacerbated their thirst. Most of the canteens were empty, or nearly so. Those men with water left in their canteens took them wherever they went on the bluff, so that they wouldn't be stolen before they returned.

"Ten dollars for a cup of water," Walsh implored. "Come on, ten dollars. Fifteen, for Christ's sake. I'll give it to you on payday. Somebody give me some water."

"Dream on," the Arab mumbled.

In the dip, the wounded cried out for water, as well. The rest of the men tried to put those cries from their minds as they watched the sun crawl across the sky. The heat rose in shimmering waves from the earth, obscuring the distant Indians, making them look unreal, like ghosts, or figments of the imagination.

After a while the fire from beyond the lines slackened. Some of the men rested, dulled by the heat. They lay in their scrapes, heads against their saddles. Dutch Hartz read from a pocket Bible. Starving Mike, the Russian, smoked cigarettes from his fancy holder. Some of the others smoked pipes, or simply chewed on the stems.

Mike finished his cigarette. With his long fingers he rolled another and placed it in the ivory holder. He drew a sulfur match from a box. He sat up to strike the match on his boot sole. Then he lay back against his saddle. The match burned in one hand. The cigarette and holder were in the other. There was a vacant look in his eyes.

Mike's bunky, the Arab, smelled burning flesh. "Hey!" He looked over and saw the match burning Mike's finger. He knocked it away. "What the hell are—"

He looked closer. There was a hole in Mike's chest. Blood was starting to leak from it.

"Holy shit. Mike's been hit. He's dead."

Everyone looked. "I told him smoking those things would ruin his health, Link said."

The Arab closed the dead man's eyes. He and Hunter carried Mike's body to join the others in the center of the bluff. As they lifted Mike's body, his hat fell off. Harry took the hat and put it on. It was made of good felt. The shade of its wide brim brought welcome relief to his eyes and sunburned face. All he really knew about Starving Mike was that Mike had always insisted on wearing one of the old shell jackets in the field. He'd said it reminded him of being in the hussars.

By the company guidon, Captain Bannerman sipped the last of his water. He felt better now. He began to think about living again, about surviving. He watched Lieutenant Starke stride from position to position on the bluff, exhorting the men, cheering their spirits. It was amazing how much energy Starke had, he thought, though he didn't see why Starke spent so much time talking to the men. But then, with a ranker like Starke, he guessed that was to be expected.

Starke came by the guidon, carrying a tin cup. Bannerman stood. "Any more water?" he asked his lieutenant.

A bullet zipped by. Bannerman ducked; Starke paid it no attention. Starke said, "I've given instructions that all water is to be saved for the wounded."

"You might have checked with me first," Bannerman said.

"Yes, sir. I might have."

"You have a cup. What are you drinking?"

"Blood from one of the dead horses. Care for some?"

Bannerman cleared his throat. "No. No, thank you." He went on, "What is the situation?"

"We're still alive, sir. That's about all we can ask for right now."

Nearby, Skull was propped up on some blankets, with seven-year-old Becky Hobson by his side. Skull had gotten rid of the scalp in his belt. Wincing from his wounded hip, he carved a piece of wood he'd gotten from Lord knew where while Becky watched, fascinated.

"What kind of animal is *that*?" Becky said as the carving took shape.

"A camel. You see them in Africa, where I was with the French. You see this big hump? That's where the camel stores his water so he can cross the desert."

He finished the model and handed it to her. "Here. It's yours."

The model was amazingly realistic. Becky looked at it with delight. For a moment she forgot the noise and the suffering around her.

Like Starke, Sergeant Townsend walked around the bluff, impervious to bullets and arrows, defying them to hit him as he talked to the men.

"Come on, lads. This is noffink. I recollect the Great Mutiny. Four bloody months we sat on Delhi Ridge. 'Eat like the 'arse end of 'ell. 'Arf of us down wiv cholera, the other 'arf wiv fever. Little water and less food. Before us the city, an' inside it fifty thousand Pandies, firing great bloody cannons and screaming for our 'ides. Be'ind us, a country in flames, an' no relief in sight. Then along comes ole Johnny Nicholson, an' 'e says, 'Right lads. We've got 'em where we want 'em. Let's attack.' "

A young soldier said, "What happened then, Sarge?"

"Me regiment got massacred, of course, and Johnny Nick, 'e caught 'is death of lead. But we took Delhi. 'Twas a great day."

At that moment a downward-arcing arrow struck Townsend just under the cheekbone, knocking out several of his teeth and penetrating his throat. He gave a strangled scream and grabbed at it, blood pouring from his mouth. As he did, a bullet hit him in the stomach. He stumbled and fell heavily, turning his head to keep from driving the arrow deeper. His white helmet bounced off and rolled away.

Lieutenant Conroy got to him first, then Sergeant Cronk. The two of them picked Townsend up, staggering under the weight, and carried him to the dip.

Cronk said, "Sit him upright, sir. So he don't choke on his own blood."

They balanced the sergeant against some saddles and coats. Private Stewart looked at his latest patient. "There's nothing to be done about that bullet in the gut," he said.

"Try to get the arrow out," Conroy told him.

Stewart was exhausted from working on the wounded. His hands were wet with blood and sweat. He grasped the feathered shaft protruding from Townsend's face. He pulled.

The sergeant screamed through his blood-filled mouth.

"I'll bet it's barbed," said Lieutenant Starke, who had hurried over. "Pull it out, and you'll tear his throat apart. It'll have to be cut out."

"Fucking red bastards," muttered Stewart. "I'm no surgeon. I should be on the line, fighting. Not here. I'm not cut out for this."

Bracing himself, Stewart broke the arrow shaft where it protruded from Townsend's cheek. The big sergeant groaned. Sweat poured down his whiskered face, mixing with the grime there. His chest rose and fell heavily. Gingerly, Stewart opened the sergeant's mouth. He thought maybe he could get at the arrowhead that way. But it was no use. He couldn't even see for all the blood and broken teeth.

"I can't do it, sir," he told Starke. "He needs a real doctor." Townsend was gut-shot, so he'd likely die anyway, but neither man mentioned that.

"All right," Starke said. He patted Townsend's shoulder. "You'll be all right, Top."

Townsend nodded. "Yes, sir," he mumbled thickly. His long dundreary whiskers were stained with blood.

Starke stood. "Cronk, you're temporary First Sergeant."

"Yes, sir," said Cronk.

Over in Fourth Platoon, Sergeant McDermott heard those words with anger. The job should have been his. That was all right, he thought. Captain Bannerman would be better soon. He would put things right.

Starke went on? "Private Hayward!"

"Sir?" cried Hayward from his position.

"You're temporary sergeant of First Platoon."

"Yes, sir."

Link's friends laughed. "What's your first order, Link?" the Arab said.

"Everybody gets a three-day pass," Link said. "Effective immediately.

Cronk yelled, "Sir! The Injuns are up to something."

Starke sprinted to First Platoon's lines. Out on the prairie, the Indians had built a large fire. Other Indians had gathered bundles of brush and were riding forward, dropping the bundles in a rough line and riding away again. One of the Indians was hit, but he stayed on his horse.

"They're going to fire the brush," Starke said.

Even as he spoke, Indians lit grass torches from the fire. They rode up and tossed the torches onto the dried brush. The brush began to smoke. Soon a wall of flame spread across the prairie. What there was of a breeze blew the smoke toward the bluff.

"They'll attack behind the smoke," Starke warned. "Be ready."

The smoke bore down on the men in billowing white waves. It filled their dry throats. They started choking, coughing. It burned their eyes until it hurt to open them.

Gunfire from the surrounding bluffs redoubled. Somebody screamed in agony. The soldiers heard yelling. The drumming of horses' hoofs shook the ground.

"Fire!" Starke shouted. "Pour it on, boys. If they get in here again, we'll be overrun!"

Lieutenant Conroy ran across the bluff to Fourth Platoon. "Sergeant McDermott, pull every second man out of your line and send them to First Platoon." Conroy couldn't weaken the line anywhere else. He couldn't be sure that the other Indians wouldn't attack out of the ravines.

"Yes, sir," McDermott said.

Harry Winston fired blindly. The smoke was suffocating. For a moment Harry couldn't breathe. He fought down panic.

He reloaded his carbine and fired again. Ghostly arrows hummed out of the smoke. All around was the crash of weapons, the yelling of men. Now and then the smoke parted and Harry glimpsed painted Indians, like wraiths, advancing toward him on horseback.

Somebody yelled, "I can't see!" It was Walsh. He tried to run.

Cronk grabbed his arm and turned him around. "Get back there."

"I can't see, I tell you!" Walsh screamed. "I can't see!"

Cronk pointed his carbine in Walsh's face. "You see this? If you don't get back there, it's going to go off between your fucking eyes."

Walsh stumbled back to the firing line.

Harry was standing now, like the rest of the men, carried away with excitement, heedless of the better target he presented. Like the rest of the men, he found himself screaming meaningless obscenities as he levered shells into the breech of his Spencer and fired.

The carbine overheated and jammed. Harry threw it down and drew his pistol. He saw a painted face, shot at it. It disappeared.

Then, as if by a miracle, the breeze shifted. The smoke began to shred and blow away to the east. Indians appeared, as if conjured up from nothingness. Suddenly they were in plain view, with the closest not ten yards away.

The soldiers had targets now, and the repeating rifles did their work. Indians began falling. Harry saw Storm directly in front of him, his face painted red and yellow; he saw the red shield and feathered war bonnet. Storm aimed his rifle at Harry. Harry's bowels went cold as the Indian fired. He expected to die, but the bullet missed. Then Storm and the other Indians were riding away, back across the prairie, unwilling to sustain the losses it would take to get into the soldiers' position. The soldiers fired after them.

"Hold your fire, men," Lieutenant Starke shouted. "They're out of range."

The men got control of themselves. Some slumped to the ground, exhausted. Others, like Link, were wild-eyed, open-mouthed, frenzied with the lust of battle.

Harry looked at the smoke-blacked faces around him, broken by only the whites of eyes and by pink tongues. He was reminded of the Christy Minstrels, when his father had taken him to see them in Philadelphia. He couldn't help laughing at the sight.

"What the hell's so funny?" Numb Nuts said.

"You wouldn't understand," Harry told him.

Hunter said, "I'm glad somebody is having a good time here."

Then the patter of bullets in the dirt around them reminded them to take cover once more.

The battle went on.

41

There was no time for Harry to let his jammed carbine cool. He broke it down, using his jacket as a glove to protect his hands from the hot metal. He cleaned the weapon thoroughly and oiled it, until it worked again. He hurried, praying that the Cheyennes would not renew their attack until he was finished.

All across the bluff men were doing the same thing. Some tried to urinate on their carbine barrels to cool them, but they did not have enough water left in their bodies to make urine.

Hunter rammed an oily patch down the barrel of his weapon. "Hey, Link. What's the difference between the rifles the government gives us and the ones the government gives the Indians?"

"The Indians get the ones that work," Link replied.

Nearby, the Arab said, "Wait a minute, Hunter. A little while ago you were going on about how great these seven-shots are."

"That was then, this is now," Hunter told him. "Time marches on, my son."

By the greatest good fortune, the Indians did not attack again. They were content to snipe at the men on the bluff, to let the sun and lack of water do their work for them.

By now there was hardly a man in the company without at least a minor wound. Many of the injuries were haphazardly bandaged. Harry discovered that he had a nicked shoulder. He didn't even remember getting it. He took his dirty, sweat-stiffened bandanna and stuffed it between his shirt and the wound to stop the bleeding.

Suddenly Walsh screamed, "I can't take this! I can't take any more!" He jumped up from his scrape and started to run. Sergeant Cronk tackled him, and the two men went down in a cloud of dust. Walsh thrashed around. "I can't take it!" he cried tearfully. Cronk and Link Hayward tied Walsh up and carried him to lay with the wounded.

The other men watched Walsh without expression. They were tired, thirsty, dizzy from the heat. They lay in their scrapes as bullets and arrows fell around them. Their mouths were too dry to smoke their pipes anymore. Their tongues had swollen, making it hard to talk. Their lips cracked and bled. The teamster Pennington couldn't even make enough saliva to chew his tobacco.

Some of the men removed their shirts and sucked sweat from them. Link took his knife, opened a vein in his wrist, and drank the blood from it.

In the center of the bluff most of the horses were dead now. Then Beau, Harry's horse, was hit.

"Winston," Cronk said. "Your mount's down. Better finish him off."

"I'll help you, Mad Dog," the Arab said. "Bring your canteen cup."

The two men crossed to the dip, heads bent to avoid the bullets. Beau lay on his side, kicking weakly. The horse had been hit in three different places. The last shot, in the chest, was the one that had put him down.

Harry drew the bowie knife that Pick Forrester had given him. While the Arab held Beau's head, Harry straddled the big bay's neck. He had thought about killing the horse more than once over the last six months, but now that the time had actually come, he felt sorry for the beast.

The Arab looked up. "Do it, Mad Dog."

Harry swallowed. He did as he'd seen others do that day. He plunged the knife into the horse's neck. The animal reared with pain.

"Cut!" the Arab shouted. He twisted the horse's head, holding it tight.

Harry sawed through the muscles, tendons, and arteries of the animal's neck. Blood spurted. The horse's thrashings grew weaker, then stopped altogether.

Men appeared from seemingly nowhere. They pushed Harry aside and filled canteen cups with the blood that drained from the dead animal's neck. They drank the blood greedily.

The Arab tapped Harry's shoulder. "Over here."

The Arab took his knife and punched open the dead horse's stomach. As the stomach juices drained out, he filled Harry's cup with them.

He handed the cup to Harry. "Drink this."

Harry looked at the brownish liquid, swimming with bits of who knew what. Thirst was driving him crazy. The Arab drank his own cup down without flinching.

Harry held his breath. He took a drink and swallowed.

He pitched forward. The vile, bitter liquid twisted his guts and made him gag.

"Keep it down," the Arab urged.

When Harry looked up again, the Arab took his cup. "It's better than nothing," he told Harry. "Want some more?"

"Why not?" Harry gasped.

He took another cup of the nauseating liquid and drank. When he was done gagging, he said, "You've got brains, Arab. What are you doing in the army?"

The Arab took off his campaign hat and scratched his roached hair. "I don't know, really. I hated being an accountant. All those numbers. I went out with some friends one night. I got drunk, and the next thing I knew, I was in the army. I don't even remember signing up."

* * *

When the two men had finished drinking, the Arab returned to the platoon. Harry stopped with the wounded, to
see Barker and the Professor. The Professor was sleeping,
but Barker was awake.

Barker's injured hand was swollen. The blood-soaked bandage was filthy and crawling with flies. Barker's lips were
cracked and blackened with dried blood, and his canteen lay
by his side, empty. Harry gave his bunky the last swallows
from his own canteen, the swallows he had been saving as
an act of willpower.

Barker drank with difficulty, because of his swollen tongue.
He looked over. "Shoot me, Harry. Go on, kill me."

Harry said, "What? You can't be—"

"Please. I want to die. I can't stand this pain. Please,
Harry, kill me."

"Shut up!" Harry told him. "What about Susan? You
can't leave her. You have to get back to her."

Barker said nothing. He looked glum, as though he'd given
up hope.

Harry rooted through his bunky's jacket, which lay next
to him. He found Susan's last letter. "Here," he said, "hold
this. It'll make you think of her. Hold it, I said."

Barker took the wrinkled letter with his good hand. He
was crying now.

Harry's voice softened. "Don't give up." He patted Barker's shoulder. "Hang on. We'll get out of this. You'll see."

Barker sighed. "Do you really believe that?"

"I promise you," Harry said. He stood. "I've got to get
back. I'll see you later."

Sergeant Townsend sat not far from Barker, gasping his life
away. The bullet in his gut was boring a red-hot hole in him. It
was hard for him to breathe, with the arrowhead and part of the
arrow's shaft lodged in the back of his mouth. His lower jaw,
side-whiskers, and the front of his shirt were covered with blood.
The sun had dried a lot of the blood, turning it into a blackened,
crusty mess, but fresh blood continued to dribble over it.

Private Stewart held Townsend's canteen under his chin.
"Drink, Sarge?" He knew you shouldn't give water to a gut-
shot man, but he didn't think it would make any difference
in this case.

Townsend smiled wanly. It hurt to smile because of the arrowhead. "No, son. You give the rest of my *pani* to the young lass. She needs it more than me."

By late afternoon there was no more water on the bluff. The cries of the wounded grew louder.

From the opposite bluffs and the ravines, the Indians taunted the soldiers. "White man—you want water?"

The Indians held up skins full of water and poured it over their heads. They poured water onto the ground, laughing.

"White man—we come for you. Soon."

Link Hayward picked off one of the Indians with a good shot. The Indian fell and his companions scattered.

"You won't be coming for nobody, asshole!" Link yelled at the fallen man.

The smell that hung over the bluff curdled the men's stomachs. They breathed through their mouths to lessen its impact. Corpses of men and animals swelled in the heat. Flies swarmed over them, feasting in the open wounds, which soon teamed with maggots. Several species of beetles crawled in and out of the bodies, as well, along with columns of red and black ants. Vultures circled overhead. Now and then stray bullets plowed into the swollen bodies, puncturing them, splattering rotten flesh and juices over the wounded or anyone who happened to be nearby. The Indians hooted with laughter at that.

Little Becky Hobson was helping Stewart now. She walked along the lines of wounded, fanning away the flies with a hat. She tried not to look at the ghastly wounds, and she occupied her mind by remembering Bible stories that her mother had taught her. When she came by her friend Private Anders—Skull, to the other soldiers—she had a special smile for him.

"Merci, cherie," he said as she fanned him.

Barker died just before sundown. He died in agony, his bloated tongue half out of his mouth, his back arched in pain, the flies making his bloody bandage look like it was alive.

Harry was with him at the end, crying, cradling Barker's head in his arms. Barker lost consciousness about a half hour before his death, and he never regained it. His good hand still clutched the letter from his wife.

Next to Barker lay the Professor, now awake. When it was all over, Harry took the letter from his bunky's hand. He smoothed out the wrinkles, sniffling. "She's waiting for him. She thinks he's coming back to her."

"That's war," the Professor said. "Maybe he's the lucky one. His suffering is over. The rest of us have a while to go."

There was no beautiful sunset that evening, the kind that inspired poets and painters to come west. Instead, the sky turned from blue to a brassy yellow. Then it faded, and suddenly it was dark.

The men were grateful to see the sun go. They were all sunburned from the day on the bluff. They had headaches and spots before their eyes from the glare. Under cover of darkness they were able to move freely about the bluff, though the Indians continued sniping blindly at them.

After the guard was set, Link and the others from First Platoon cut up a dead horse and ate its flesh raw. It was too dangerous to light a fire, even if there had been fuel. Harry chewed on the raw horse meat. The meat had ripened in the heat, but that didn't bother him. The blood and juices revitalized him.

Off to themselves, Lieutenants Starke and Conroy ate hardtack that had been soaked in horse blood to soften it. Conroy had tinned peaches in his saddlebags, but he'd given them to Becky Hobson and the wounded men. Around the bluff, flashes winked in the darkness as shots were fired into their positions.

"Can we sneak a man through, to ride for help?" Conroy asked.

Starke shook his head. "There's too many Indians. He'd never make it, even if we still have a horse in decent shape—which I doubt."

Footsteps sounded behind them. Captain Bannerman approached, chewing some tinned ham. In a low voice he said, "What do you think our chances are?"

"Slim and none," Starke told him.

"Do you think the Indians will return to the attack tomorrow?"

"Wouldn't you?" Starke said. "One more good push, and we're done for."

Bannerman agreed. "All right," he said. "We'll make a break for it tonight."

The other two officers looked at him.

Bannerman went on. "The three of us and maybe a few of the men—as many horses as we have left. We'll break through the Indian lines and ride north, try and link up with the regiment."

Conroy said, "What about the wounded, sir? What about the rest of the men?"

"We'll have to leave them."

Starke and Conroy exchanged glances.

Starke said, "I'll not be a party to that, sir."

"Nor I, sir," Conroy said. "And neither will any of the men. We'll order them not to go, if we must."

Bannerman was shocked at Conroy's act of rebellion. "You forget, mister. *I* give the orders here."

"Not that one, you don't," Starke told him.

"I could have both of you brought up on charges of mutiny," Bannerman pointed out.

"Somehow I don't think you'll try that, sir," Starke said.

"What do you propose, then? That we stay here and die?"

"If we must."

"You always were a fool, Starke."

Starke said, "You can leave, if you want, sir."

"By myself?"

Starke shrugged.

Bannerman was afraid to go by himself, but he couldn't admit that.

They were interrupted by the distant pounding of drums. Reddish light tinted the night sky to the east. It reflected off the three officers' faces. They looked off the bluff, with the rest of the men.

Downstream, along the riverbank, the Cheyennes had lit bonfires. Their war drums were beating. Shadowy figures moved back and forth in front of the fires, dancing. There was singing, as well, as the Indians celebrated the day's triumph.

Then there was another sound. Screams. Human screams.

Screams of indescribable pain. They sent a shiver up each man's backbone.

Sergeant Cronk came up beside Starke. "That'll be Private Squillace, sir," he said quietly.

Starke nodded.

"Poor Squealer," Dutch Hartz muttered.

"He's really living up to his nickname, ain't he?" added Hunter.

"He wants to be a lawyer," Link said. "Let him take 'em to court."

The screams continued. Knowing the Indians, Starke guessed they would go on most of the night. They were accompanied by the drums and singing, by the howling of Indians on the opposite bluffs and on the prairie, who let the soldiers know they were still surrounded. All this in addition to the tormented ravings of Walsh and the wounded men on the bluff.

The red light of the fires was reflected in the winding Washita below, giving it the look of a river in hell. Cronk said, "All that water, sir. So close, yet so far, as they say."

Starke nodded. He said, "First Sergeant, call the men together, with the exception of the guards. I wish to address them." He turned to Bannerman. Sarcastically, he said, "With your permission, sir."

Bannerman cleared his throat. "Go ahead. Say what you wish."

The men—what was left of them—gathered in the center of the bluff, around Starke. An occasional bullet whined overhead.

Starke said, "Men, I'll be plain. The company won't last the night without water, no matter what Mr. Lo has planned for us tomorrow. I need two volunteers to take canteens and go down to the river and fill them."

Before anyone could reply, Starke held up a restraining hand. He'd have gone for the water himself, but he was in de facto command, and his duty was to remain on the bluff. He said, "The odds are, you won't come back. Those ravines are crawling with Indians. If you're caught, you can expect death, at best. At worst . . ." He didn't have to elaborate. They could hear Squillace's screams for themselves.

"Now, who'll go?"

Link Hayward stepped forward. Starke had expected that.
Hayward's buddy Skull would have been the other logical
choice, but Skull was hurt.

Conroy said, "Jim, can I—"

"No, Tom. I need you here. In case I'm hit."

Then another man stepped forward. It was Harry Winston.

Harry had surprised himself yet again. And, again, he was
not entirely certain why. He felt compelled to help his comrades, compelled to do his part. He had learned something
that day. He had learned that when the chips are down, men
do not fight for glory or adventure. They do not fight for love
of country or the honor of the regiment. They fight for themselves and for the men around them. Plus, he'd seen Link
volunteer, and that was like a personal challenge to him.

Lieutenant Starke was nearly as surprised as Harry had
been. "You're sure?" he said.

"Yes, sir," Harry replied. "I'm sure."

Starke glanced at Link, who made a gesture of reluctant
acceptance.

Starke said, "Very well. Get yourselves ready. You leave in
ten minutes. The rest of the company, return to your positions."

As Harry started away, Link stopped him. "Just don't get
in my way," he warned.

"Don't *you* get in mine," Harry replied.

42

Link and Harry collected canteens from all over the bluff.
They would carry a dozen each. That wouldn't provide much
water, but it was all they could reasonably handle. They
would sling the canteens over their shoulders, a half-dozen

to a side. With pigs of rope, they bound the canteen straps together, just above the caps, so that the canteens wouldn't thump together and alert the Indians to their presence.

Each man carried a knife. Harry had one pistol; Link had two. They took off their hats. They would have blackened their faces, but dirt and powder smoke had already done that. Their shirts and trousers were the color of mud; they would blend in with the dirt of the bluff.

To the east the Cheyenne fires lit the sky. The dancing and singing went on. Squillace's screams had stopped. The soldiers hoped that he was dead.

Link and Harry decided to go out through Second Platoon's line. The bluff wasn't as steep there; it would be an easier descent, and they wouldn't make as much noise. Captain Bannerman watched their preparations from a distance, as if he thought this was a waste of time.

Lieutenants Starke and Conroy and Sergeant Cronk came over to the two men. "Ready?" Starke said.

Link and Harry fixed the canteens over their shoulders. "Yes, sir."

"Very well." Starke held out his hand. "Good luck to you."

"Good luck," added Conroy and Cronk, and most of the men who were standing nearby.

Link and Harry shook Starke's hand. "Thank you, sir," they each said.

Link said, "All right, Mad Dog. Let's do it. Try not to make too much noise."

"If I do, you'll be the first to know," Harry told him.

They approached the edge of the bluff on their hands and knees, so that they wouldn't be skylighted against the horizon, dark though it was.

They slipped over and started down.

The sides of the bluff were rocky and stunted with brush. Link and Harry moved as quietly as possible. The quarter moon was some help, but not much. Harry had a hard time seeing Link, who was only a few feet away.

They moved downward on their butts and the sides of their legs, searching for footholds, trying not to make noise. They came to a flat bench and wriggled across it on their stomachs.

Then Link put out a hand, stopping Harry.

Harry hardly dared to breathe, for fear he would be too loud. He made out Link's hand, pointing.

Off to the right were two shadows, deeper than the night sky. One of the shadows moved—or was he dreaming? Harry wondered.

No, it had moved.

The shadows were Indians.

The two Indians whispered among themselves. They were no more than ten feet away. They sounded young. There were probably a lot of younger warriors out here, keeping watch on the white soldiers while the older men celebrated.

One of the Indians stood and fitted an arrow to his bow. He let the arrow fly, over the top of the bluff. There was a surprised oath from the bluff top. The two Indians laughed in low tones.

Link tapped Harry's shoulder. They took advantage of the Indians' distraction and crawled on.

They continued down the side of the bluff again. Harry struggled to keep up with Link. Then he stopped, his heart racing.

Where *was* Link?

He strained to see in the darkness, but didn't spot Link. Nor did he hear him. Had Link stopped again?

"Link!" he hissed.

No answer.

Harry went prickly all over. He moved a few more feet.

"Link!"

Still nothing. Way off to the left a rifle banged, as an Indian fired at the bluff.

Harry's hands and feet turned cold. He was alone.

Had Link left him on purpose? No, not even Link would do that. As much as he hated Link, the veteran's presence had been reassuring. Harry was scared, real scared. God knew how many Indians were around. He thought about giving up and going back, but he couldn't do that. He had volunteered to get water, and he had to go through with it. He owed it to the other men. They were counting on him. He couldn't let them down.

He was nearly paralyzed by fear, but he forced himself to keep going. He was hot and thirsty, and his swollen tongue partly cut off his breath. He itched from flea and louse bites, but none of that mattered. His senses had come alive in a way he could not have believed possible. Several times he stopped when he heard Indians moving on the bluff to either side of him. Even if he got the canteens filled, he thought, how the hell was he going to make it back to the top?

He kept to the side of the bluff, angling toward the river. The easiest way would have been to go straight down until he hit the ravine bottom, then follow that, but the ravine bottom was where he would be most likely to encounter Indians.

In the distance, Squillace started screaming again. Harry missed a step, then firmed himself and kept on. Squillace had either recovered consciousness or the Indians had brought him to. Harry tried not to listen to his terrible cries. He tried not to imagine what the Indians were doing to Squillace.

He took his time, testing footholds and handholds. He wondered if his brother Ed had to go through anything like this during the war. His brother, the great hero. It would be pretty funny to find out that Ed had really been a clerk or something.

Harry had lost his concentration. He knocked loose some rocks. They rattled down the bluff, hitting against others. To Harry, it sounded like an avalanche. He stopped, holding his breath. It seemed that the Indians must have heard. But no one came to investigate. Maybe the scattered gunfire had drowned out the noise. After a moment Harry went on.

At last he reached the bottom of the bluff, sliding down in a little shower of stones. He crouched in the weeds and brush, listening, his eyes quartering the darkness.

He half expected to find Link here, but he heard and saw nothing. He smelled the river in front of him. The water was like an intoxicant, drawing him on. He resisted its lure. He had to take his time. He filled his lungs with fresh air. The smell of death and corruption from the hilltop was mercifully faint down here.

He started across the open ground for the river, which was partially screened by cottonwoods. He moved in a crouch, pausing every few steps to see if he was observed. He reached the tree line then moved through the trees carefully, trying not to step on fallen branches.

A few yards more and he had reached the water. His first impulse was to plunge in headlong and drink, but he fought it down. His duty was to the men on the bluff, not to himself. He must think of them first. Carefully, he unslung the canteens from each shoulder. He unscrewed the metal caps and pushed the canteens underwater. The water was surprisingly cold. While the canteens filled, Harry lay beside the stream and scooped water into his mouth. He'd never imagined plain water could taste so good. He drank more. Then more.

Remembering himself, he lifted the canteens from the water. He shook them, then put them back in again, to get rid of any air bubbles and make sure they were filled to the top. Then he screwed the canteen caps back on.

When he was done, he paused for another drink. He put his head to the water this time. His stomach had shrunk so badly, it couldn't hold as much as he'd like. He wished he had a hump to store it, like those camels Skull was always talking about.

He would have stayed and drank longer, but he had to get the canteens back to the men up top. Every minute he remained here increased the chance that he'd be caught and his mission would be a failure. He rose to leave, looking all around, listening intently. He looped the canteens over his shoulders and he started back for the bluff.

He crossed the open space as he had before, then he heard a muffled cry of surprise. It came from around a rocky outcrop to his right, and it was followed by the sounds of struggle.

Harry stopped. The struggle was violent. There were grunts, then curses in English.

It must be Link.

Harry hesitated. Should he help Link? Should he risk losing the water? Should he risk his life for a man he hated? The scuffle continued. There was noisy thrashing in the bushes. The racket would soon attract more Indians.

"Shit," Harry muttered. He drew his bowie knife and ran toward the fight.

He rounded the outcrop in the darkness. Before him were

struggling shadows, dimly perceived. He heard Link curse
again. There were two Indians, and they had Link by the
arms. Harry ran at the Indian on Link's left. He put a shoulder into the Indian and sent him reeling. The Indian came
back at him. Harry slashed blindly with the knife. The blade
hit something hard, and the Indian screamed and staggered
away. Link and the other Indian were scrabbling in the dirt.
Harry jumped on the Indian's back, stabbing with the knife.
The Indian yelled and let go of Link.

A third Indian rushed out of the darkness. There was a
flash and a shot from Link's pistol, and the attacker toppled
backward.

"That's done it," Link said, getting up. "Come on, Mad
Dog. Let's get the hell out of here."

The two of them sprinted for the bluff. All around them
were guttural shouts and the sounds of moccasined feet.

They ran up the steep grade. Harry's heart was pumping
hard. The heavy canteens thumped against his ribs. His thighs
and calves burned. Awkwardly, he put the knife back in his
belt and drew his pistol.

He heard shots. A bullet whined off rock. Other bullets
buzzed near his head. There was a shadowy figure to his left.
He fired his pistol at it, but didn't know if he hit the figure
or not.

Harry's early momentum carried him a good distance, then
he began to falter. Footsteps pounded behind him, and he
pushed himself harder, propelled by fear. Beside him, Link
turned and fired over his shoulder.

In places the grade was so steep that the two men had to
use their hands for support. God, how far was it to the top?
Harry wondered. He slipped, slid partway back down, and
scrambled to his feet again. As he did, a hand grabbed his
ankle from behind. With a cry of fear, Harry tried to kick
the hand loose. Link fired his pistol. There was a stifled
scream, and the grip on Harry's ankle dropped away.

Not far above them, Harry heard Lieutenant Starke shouting. Carbine flashes winked along the bluff top, followed by
the sound of firing.

"Keep low!" Link told him.

Harry bent down, scrambling up the hill. He was on his

last reserves of energy. Bullets hummed over his head. The soldiers were firing high, trying to scare the Indians off.

Then the two men reached the top of the bluff. Anxious hands reached out and pulled them over.

Harry and Link lay on their backs, chests heaving, faces on fire from exertion. Harry was shaking. The fear was still in him, even though he was safe for the moment.

"Did you get the canteens?" someone asked.

"Yes," Harry wheezed.

There was a cheer. Familiar voices congratulated them— the Arab, Hunter, Cronk, Numb Nuts. Even Captain Bannerman was there.

Lieutenant Starke knelt beside them. He put a hand on Harry's shoulder. "Good work, men. When we heard the shots down there, we thought you were goners."

Harry's breath became more regular. He and Link sat up. They took the canteens from their shoulders and gave them to Starke for distribution.

"Is there anything I can get you?" Starke asked them.

Link said, "I'm kind of thirsty, sir. You wouldn't have any whiskey, would you?"

43

The water was given out under Lieutenant Starke's supervision. The wounded men and seven-year-old Becky Hobson drank first, then the rest. Twenty-four quarts wasn't much. Each man got a few swallows. The rest of the precious liquid had to be saved for the following day. There was none to be spared for the few horses that were still alive.

The bluff was abuzz with Harry's and Link's exploit. As Harry settled back in his scrape, he chewed a rapidly spoiling cut of raw horse meat. Nearby, Link was reloading his pistol and joking with his friends.

Harry said, "What happened to you down there? How did we get separated?"

Link turned a baleful eye on him. "How do I know? It was you that couldn't keep up."

Few of the men slept that night. The gunfire and the cries of the wounded kept them awake, as did pangs of hunger and thirst. Toward morning Squillace's distant screams died out with one long, terrible moan. The men looked at each other. Dutch Hartz crossed himself.

Dawn came, red and ominous. It was already hot. As soon as the Indians opposite the company could see, they began sniping. They crept much closer to the soldiers than they had been the day before. Corporal Ware, of Third Platoon, took a bullet between the shoulders while he was relieving himself. Some of the men thought that was funny.

The sun climbed into the sky. The men lay in their scrapes, which they had deepened overnight. Now and then one of them popped up to take a shot at their tormentors. Before them lay another day of searing heat and thirst, of flies and the ungodly stench of death. Even worse, great swarms of buffalo gnats had risen from the stream. The gnats got in the men's throats, in their eyes and noses. They bit bare skin while the weary soldiers tried to swat them away. High above the bluff vultures circled in anticipation.

"God, it's hot," said the stocky ex-businessman, Numb Nuts. "When's the Lieutenant going to let us have more water?"

"When he's ready," Skull replied. "Starky knows what he's doing." Skull had rejoined the platoon, despite the wound in his side, because he wanted to be with them at the end.

Next to Skull, the Arab said, "What day is this, anyway?"

"Sunday," Dutch Hartz said.

"Shh," Hunter cautioned. "Don't let Super Soldier hear that. He'll want to have an inspection."

The Arab swore. "Christ, that's the last thing I feel like doing—shining boots and polishing bullets."

"I'll clue you," Link said. "There ain't a whole hell of a lot of bullets left to polish."

Hunter rose and snapped a shot toward the Indians on the prairie. He was answered by the zing of bullets. He paused for a look around before resuming his place in the scrape. "There's a lot of them in the ravines," he said. "I think they're going to rush us before long."

"Bye-bye us," Link murmured.

The Arab laid his head against his bullet-scarred saddle and sighed. "I'm not ready for it all to end. I've got goals to accomplish."

"Like what?" Hunter said.

"Well, for one thing, I always wanted to get my name in the papers."

"You will," Hunter assured him. "It'll say: 'Among the dead, otherwise unidentified because of wounds.' We'll all be in there."

"Ah, well. I feel better, then. Except that George Jett's not my real name."

"No shit?" Hunter said. "I never knew that. What is your name?"

The Arab winked at him. "Bad luck to tell."

Edgar Townsend was back in Hampshire. He was not sure how it had happened, but he was glad to be there. The country hadn't changed much in the years he'd been away. There were the same rolling hills, the same dusty lanes between the hedgerows. The sky was blue; the birds were singing. Townsend walked along with a youthful step. His red army jacket stood out against the bright green countryside. He was on his way to the parsonage. He wondered if he'd get in trouble for having been away so long. Like as not, he'd receive one of his father's interminable sermons on duty.

Townsend saw a woman coming up the lane, from the other direction. She was strangely dressed for this part of the world, with a thin bodice, pajama trousers, and pointed slippers. She wore bangled jewelry and a veil across the lower half of her face. Painted lips smiled behind the veil; painted eyes beckoned above it. Even at this distance, Townsend smelled patchouli.

" 'Osainee," he said in surprise. " 'Osainee, it's you. All this way you've come. You do love me, then. Ah, let's 'ave a *dekko* at yer, darlin'. More beautiful than ever, you are. Come to me, lass. Come to me, and we'll never be parted again. Lord 'ow I missed you."

He began running to where she stood with open arms. Running . . .

Stewart closed the old sergeant's eyes. "He's dead."

K Company's three officers were gathered around. Starke, who was kneeling beside Townsend, hung his head.

"Poor fellow," Lieutenant Conroy said.

Starke rose. "He's happier this way, I think. He died like a soldier."

Captain Bannerman looked on without emotion. They were making too much of an old man, he thought. Townsend had stayed on past his time. Everyone had known it except Townsend. He had only himself to blame for the end he'd come to.

Starke sighed. "Let's put him with the others."

Starke and Conroy carried the sergeant's body across the dip. They laid it in the ever-lengthening row of bodies and covered it with a gray army blanket, like the others. Booted feet stuck out beneath some of the blankets. Dark stains showed through others.

Starke saluted the old soldier. So did Conroy, though Conroy felt guilty about it. He did not think he had earned the right to salute a man like Townsend. He had not proved himself as a soldier. He was afraid that Jim Starke would think him presumptuous.

The two officers walked away from the dip. Suddenly, Conroy's legs went rubbery and he almost fell. "Damn," he said.

Starke turned. Blood trickled out of Conroy's neck and down what had once been his white shirt. Conroy steadied himself, then went rubbery again, grabbing Starke's shoulder to keep from falling.

"I'm hit," he said.

Starke took the young lieutenant's weight. He walked him

back to where Stewart was tending the wounded. "Here's another case for you," he said.

Starke and Stewart helped Conroy lay down. Conroy grabbed Starke's arm. "I'm sorry, Jim. I didn't want to . . ."

"It's all right," Starke told him. "It's not like you shot yourself. You've done a good job. Now, just rest easy."

"But I want to help."

"If you really want to help, say some prayers. That's about all that can save us now."

Becky Hobson sat not far from Conroy. Her blond hair was dirty and in disarray. Her Indian dress was torn and smeared with the blood of the wounded men to whom she'd served water. She played with her wooden camel and a doll that her friend Private Anders had fashioned for her out of old shirts and jackets. She had been so happy to be saved from the Indians. Now she was sure that the Indians were going to get her back. She wondered if they would punish her for running away. She was sure they would—especially that old woman, who had beaten her several times already. She wondered if she would ever be saved again. It would have been better if she had died with the rest of her family, she thought.

Tears ran down her cheeks.

By noon it was a hundred degrees on the bluff. More of the heat-swollen bodies of men and horses were burst by gunshots, releasing their noxious gases. The sickly-sweet smell of death made breathing difficult. Some of the men tied bandannas over their faces to try and lessen the smell. The water in the canteens—so hard come by—was already low.

Casualties mounted. Dutch Hartz was hit in the bicep, but he stayed on the line. More of the wounded died, their claw-like hands frozen in agony, reaching for water that wasn't there.

Increasing numbers of Indians filtered into the ravine beneath Third Platoon's line. That part of the bluff was studded with large, broken rocks, which afforded perfect cover. The closest Indians were no more than twenty yards away.

Starke lay on his stomach, watching the buildup. Sergeant

Cronk joined him. Cronk's deep voice was affected by thirst and weariness. "They're getting ready to rush us, sir."

"Yes," Starke said.

"I'm surprised they're coming in here, sir, instead of across First Platoon's line, on horseback."

Starke said, "I guess they figure they can get closer this way. Take less casualties."

The two men backed away from the edge of the bluff. The bullets and arrows that fell around them had long since become part of the background, and they went unnoticed.

Starke said, "We're going to beat them to the punch, Sergeant. We're going to make a charge. Maybe we can disrupt them that way. It's better than sitting here, waiting to be killed. How many effectives do you have?"

"Seventeen, sir, at last count."

"All right, get me twelve of them. Loaded weapons. The rest will hold the perimeter, along with the wounded. Be quick, there's not much time."

"Yes, sir."

"Mr. Pennington's to go, as well," Starke added.

Cronk grinned at him. "That'll probably cost the government another dollar, sir."

"Tell him to draw up the papers."

Starke, who had retained possession of the canteens, went to where Bannerman sat, by the guidon. He told the Captain what he had planned. "If it's all right with you, sir?"

Bannerman looked up in resignation. His mood had swung wildly again. He had given up any hope of surviving. "What difference does it make? We're all dead men. This is just false heroics, like everything else you've done."

"But we have your permission?"

"Yes, yes. Go ahead. Do whatever you want."

"Thank you, sir. I appreciate your support." Starke shook the canteens and handed them to Bannerman by their straps. "Would you keep these, sir? If I'm hit, you'll have to give out the water ration."

Bannerman took the canteens, and a strange look came into his eyes. "Why, yes. I'll do that. I'll be happy to."

Starke gave him a quizzical glance, but it was too late to change anything now. He hurried away.

44

Cronk assembled his party just behind Third Platoon's line. Harry, Link, Hunter, the Arab, and Numb Nuts were there from First Platoon, along with Pennington, Sergeant Mc-Dermott, and some other men. Skull and Dutch Hartz had been left to hold First Platoon's section of the line.

Lieutenant Starke squatted before them. He said, "No speeches, men. It's do or die. The Cheyennes are ready to rush us. We're going to charge them first. It's our only chance. Are your weapons loaded?"

The men nodded. Harry was nervous, but no longer scared. Whatever was coming, it couldn't be worse than last night. Besides, they were all going to die here. He had re-signed himself to that. So had the others.

The men moved up, into the rocks of Third Platoon's line. Starke took off his hat, revealing his sweaty blond hair. His blue eyes seemed to come alive as they surveyed his little command.

"Ready?" he said. He paused. "Let's go!"

The soldiers poured out of the rocks, running downhill, yelling and cheering. "Fuck the army!" They burst upon the startled Cheyennes with guns blazing.

Surprised, the Indians jumped up and ran back down the hill. The soldiers chased them, rooting out more as they went on. "Come on," Starke cried. "Keep going."

The Indians were scared and confused by the charge. The soldiers shot them. They clubbed them with carbines. They grappled with them on the ground, stabbing with knives, choking, gouging. Cronk moved downhill, firing his carbine steadily. Link's lips were drawn back in a mad grin. Numb Nuts went down, screaming, his right kneecap blown apart by a pistol ball.

"Keep going," Starke cried. "Keep the pressure on!"

The rocky hillside turned into a melee. Private Kelly, one of the soldiers from Fourth Platoon, had been a friend of Jack Cassaday's. He was part of the detail that had chased Cassaday. He had seen Cassaday murdered, and he'd waited a long time to get revenge. Taking advantage of the confusion, he shot Sergeant McDermott in the back. McDermott threw up his arms and fell forward.

Harry Winston fired his carbine until it was out of ammunition. There was no time to reload. He swung the carbine like a club, hitting a Cheyenne across the temple. The Indian went down, but the rifle stock was shattered. Harry threw it away. He drew his bowie knife and hurled himself on another Indian. They rolled on the ground, then the Indian pushed Harry off and ran away. Harry followed him over a rocky outcrop and found himself in a kind of den, surrounded by boulders. He paused. As he did, a tall young Indian came over the rocks from the other direction, carrying a bow.

The Indian saw Harry. He dropped his bow and pulled a war axe from his belt. The two men prepared to leap upon one another, then they stopped.

The bottom half of the young Indian's face was painted black, save for the streak of yellow down his left cheek. Harry recognized him. It was the teenager who had given Harry the moccasins at the Cheyenne village, the floppy-limbed boy's older brother.

The young Indian had recognized Harry, as well. The two of them stared at each other. Then, tentatively, the Indian said, "Friends?" It was the word Harry had taught him.

Harry battled the blood lust, the mad desire to kill, that had taken hold of him. He tried to become human again. Suddenly, all the fighting and killing seemed stupid. Harry's hand sweated on the knife's grip. Dry-throated, he said, "Friends."

The young Indian smiled. Slowly, he moved backward. He reached the rocks, then climbed out of the den. His eyes met Harry's for a second, then he was gone. Harry caught his breath, then he climbed out the other side. He saw soldiers farther down the hill. He stumbled along to join them.

The soldiers were still charging, driving all before them.

Starke emptied his carbine. He tossed it away and fought with pistol and knife. Link fired pistols with both hands. Cronk stood calmly amidst the confusion, reloading his Spencer carbine. The Arab was shot in the chest with an old musket. He staggered and fell on his back. Pennington was hit in his right arm, but he transferred his pistol to his other hand and kept fighting. When his pistol ran out of bullets, he ran back up the hill and took the Arab's.

The Indians tried to rally. They were led by a big warrior with grotesquely scarred forearms. The upper part of his body was painted black, and there were black circles around his eyes and on his cheeks. He carried a stone war club. He swung the club and crushed Kelly's skull. Kelly sank to the ground, blood and brains oozing from his wound. As he did, Starke stepped forward and shot the big Cheyenne in the head. The loss of their leader broke the Indians' rally. They wavered and fled down the bluff.

The soldiers chased them a few steps, then stopped, exhausted and out of ammunition. "This is far enough," Starke told them. Any farther and the Indians might, be able to regroup and cut them off from the bluff top. They were being fired on from the bluff across the ravine, though they hardly noticed as they watched the fleeing Indians. Hunter yelped as a bullet smashed his right hand.

"That's stopped them for the moment," Starke said. "Come on, let's get back. We'll bring the dead and wounded with us."

They retrieved their casualties. Pennington held his bloody arm. "This is a lot of grief for one damn dollar," he complained to Starke. "You make sure I don't get no greenback, neither." He tried to spit, but his mouth was too dry.

The Arab had crawled into the shade of a mesquite bush. His hat had come off, revealing his roached Indian haircut. His face had taken on a chalky pallor beneath its layers of powder smoke and grime. Some of the men knelt beside him.

"How are you?" Cronk asked.

The Arab grinned. "Typical army bullshit," he said.

Hunter said, "Your name, Arab. What's your real name?"

The Arab smiled faintly. He started to say something, then

his breath escaped in a long, shuddering sigh, and he was dead.

The men half carried, half dragged the dead up the bluff—the Arab, McDermott, Kelly. As tired as they were, it took all their energy. Harry's carbine was broken, so he took the Arab's. Link and Hunter helped Numb Nuts hop up the slope on his good leg. Bloody splinters of bone stuck out of Numb Nuts's smashed knee. Blood trickled down his chin, where he'd bitten through his lip in pain.

"Shit," he cried. "Goddamn. Shit. Oh, goddamn."

"Say something original, will you?" Link told him, straining under his bunky's weight.

At the top of the bluff the men lay down their burdens of dead and wounded. Then they fell themselves, exhausted, all except Starke, who went to Captain Bannerman, by the guidon.

"I'll have the canteens, sir," he told Bannerman.

Bannerman handed him the canteens. Starke felt their weight. He looked at the Captain. "You've been into these, haven't you?" He felt the canteens again. "You have been. Christ, while those men were down there risking their necks, you were up here drinking their water."

Bannerman looked guilty.

"You worthless bastard," Starke said.

Bannerman stood. "Watch what you say," he warned.

"Why?" Starke asked. "What are you going to do? Court-martial me? Challenge me to a duel? Nothing would give me more pleasure."

Bannerman said nothing.

Looking Bannerman in the eye, Starke added, "Come near this water again, and I'll put a bullet in you."

Starke took the canteens back to the men who had been with him. "One swallow each," he said. "Two for the wounded."

Some of the men groaned at the meager ration. "It's all that's left," Starke said harshly. "And don't take all day with it." He didn't tell them what had happened to the water while they were gone. They would probably have killed Bannerman, and the last thing the company needed right now was a mutiny.

The men drank, trying to make their swallows last. Harry felt faint. The water was just enough to turn the dust inside his mouth to mud.

When the last man had drunk, Cronk said to Starke, "What about you, sir?"

"None for me," Starke replied, with a supreme effort of will. "I'm not thirsty."

The men laughed weakly at that, and Starke added, "Get the casualties situated, then get back to your posts."

Harry and Sergeant Cronk carried the Arab's body to the dip in the center of the bluff, where they laid it with the others. They were joined by Link and Hunter, who had left Numb Nuts with the wounded.

"Poor Arab," Harry said. "Somewhere, he's got family or friends—somebody—who cares about him. They'll never know what happened to him. The army never knows who to notify."

Hunter said, "I guess, in the end, K Company became his family."

"He was a good man," Cronk averred. "Come on, back to your posts. Hunter, are you going to get that hand looked at?"

"By Stewart?" Hunter said. "Hell, I can fix it better than he can."

The men returned to their positions. The little scrapes seemed like home by now. Each was surrounded by a mixture of trash, personal effects, shell casings, and cartridge wrappers. The men settled in under the blazing sun and waited for the end. Water, food, ammunition—they were all gone.

Hunter cut a strip from his shirt and wrapped it around his wounded hand. "Christ, they'll be able to walk in here this time. The only thing we can do is throw rocks at them, and we're too tired for that."

"Where the hell is Bannon when we really need him?" Link said. "He was always hitting somebody in the head."

Cronk and Starke surveyed the perimeter, which was held

by a handful of men and all the wounded, like Skull and Lieutenant Conroy, who could still use a weapon.

"That was a nice bit of work just now, sir," Cronk said, referring to the charge.

Starke nodded. "We bought ourselves a little time. We earned the right to live an hour or two longer."

Out beyond First Platoon's line rode Chief Storm, with his war bonnet and feathered red shield. A growing number of mounted warriors gathered around him. They began singing.

"Not long now," Starke said. The men loaded their few remaining shells in their weapons. Starke wished they'd had some entrenching tools. They could have dug a trench across the narrow part of the bluff, to stop a mounted charge, or at least slow it up. First Platoon's improvised breastwork of saddles and blankets would be useless against horses.

Neal Bannerman watched the Indians singing, too. He did not want to die, but he could accept death. The press would make him a hero. Schoolchildren would learn about him. People all across the country would know his name. He would go into the history books. That was no bad thing.

The singing grew louder. Starke crossed the bluff to Private Stewart. In a low voice he said, "When they break through, kill all the wounded, then yourself."

"Yes, sir," Stewart replied. With a sideways glance he added, "What about the little girl, sir?"

Starke turned. Becky Hobson was looking at them. She knew what they were talking about. Starke drew a deep breath. "Let her go. At least she'll have a chance that way."

"Yes, sir."

Starke started back. Becky's look made him stop. "They're coming, aren't they?" she said in a small voice.

Starke knelt beside her. "Yes, Becky. They are."

She looked away.

Starke put a hand on her shoulder. "I've got to go, Becky. Good-bye."

"Good-bye," she said. Then she added, "Sir?"

"Call me Jim."

"Thank you, Jim. For what you did for me."

Starke nodded. "I'm sorry it didn't work out. Keep your chin up, though. You'll be all right in the end."

He kissed her forehead and hurried back to First Platoon.

Most of the Indians seemed to have left the ravines and opposite bluffs. They had come together on the prairie, still singing. All at once the singing stopped.

"This is it," Link said. He thumbed back the hammer of his carbine.

Those who were able, stood. The wounded lay in their scrapes, sighting along their weapons. The dust on the prairie was blowing in a big cloud, obscuring vision, as were the heat waves.

"Wait a minute," Link said. "What are they doing?"

"It looks like they're riding away," Skull replied in disbelief.

Hunter said, "They are—they're leaving."

The men lowered their carbines, dumbfounded. The Indians were indeed riding away, headed downstream.

Lying on the ground, Tom Conroy looked up at Starke. "Is it a trick?"

"I don't know," Starke replied. "I don't think so."

Below the bluff, in the valley, they saw more Indians, also riding downstream.

Sergeant Cronk said, "But why, sir? They had us dead."

Starke looked north, shading his eyes against the sun. "There can only be one reason. The regiment must be coming. We got ourselves a miracle, Sergeant. We're saved."

As the Indians departed, their dust settled, revealing Storm alone on the prairie. The Cheyenne chief waved his rifle high in the air, toward the soldiers, as if in salute.

On the bluff, Starke touched his hat brim in acknowledgment.

Then Storm rode off, following the others.

45

To the northwest a long plume of dust became visible. Through Lieutenant Starke's field glasses, the dust resolved itself into a column of soldiers.

"It's the regiment, all right," Starke said, lowering the glasses.

There was no cheering, no jumping up and down. The men stood in stunned silence, dirty, smoke-blackened, their clothing in tatters.

Harry Winston couldn't believe it. He had been convinced he was going to die here. This was an unlooked-for reprieve. It was like being reborn.

Nearby, Link Hayward snorted. "About time those jack-offs turned up."

Only one person on the bluff showed any animation. Still holding her doll and wooden camel, little Becky Hobson ran to Jim Starke, who picked her up and hugged her. She kissed him, and when he put her down, she ran to kiss Skull, being careful because of Skull's wounded side. Becky was crying with happiness, and Skull patted her head. "You brought us luck, *cherie*. Yes, you did."

While the men were waiting to be relieved, they took the few surviving horses down to the stream to be watered and set out to graze. Some of the horses were wounded and they had to be put down—after having lived through so much. More than one man cried at the sight.

Everyone who could walk descended the bluff. Nobody said much. On the way down, they passed the bodies of Indians that their tribesmen had not been able to recover. They passed dead cavalry horses from the previous day's retreat. They passed broken and abandoned rifles, pistols, bows, bits of uniforms and equipment. Here and there arrows were embedded in the earth.

At the foot of the bluff the men drank slowly and deeply. They filled canteens for the wounded. The teamster Pennington was there, an improvised bandage around his right arm. When he had finished drinking, he bit off a big chew from a plug of tobacco and sighed with satisfaction.

Back at the top the men gave canteens full of water to the wounded. Walsh, the self-styled tough guy, was untied by Sergeant Cronk. Walsh had calmed down. He drank from his canteen gratefully, though he still seemed jumpy and unsure of where he was. Link Hayward walked by and kicked his backside.

"Shirker," Link said.

Miles Woodruff, the Professor, drank until the water spilled out of his mouth and down his unkempt beard. He was in surprisingly good shape for what he'd endured. The arrow had been pushed through his leg, and his wounded shoulder was bandaged. "We made it, didn't we?" he chortled as he took another drink. "Damn, it looks like I'm going to live to get out of this man's army, after all."

"How long you got?" Hunter asked. He had brought him the canteen.

"Seventy-two days."

"You sure?"

"I never lose count," said the Professor. "When I get home to Indiana, I'm going back into the dental trade. Any of you boys come visit me, I'll pull a tooth for free—whether you need it or not." He laughed uproariously.

The men began to realize how hungry they were. Link and Hunter built a fire and started cutting steaks off one of the more recently killed horses. Harry smashed his last hardtack biscuit with his pistol butt. He soaked the crumbs in water and ate them.

As Harry ate, Lieutenant Starke came by. Harry stood, but Starke motioned him back down. They were out of earshot of the other men, and Starke smiled. "You still intend to desert, Winston?"

Harry hadn't thought about it. He chewed the soggy hardtack, frowning. "I don't know, sir. I may." Then he grinned. "Then again, I may not."

Starke grinned in return and walked off. Starke had changed his mind about what he would do. He was not going to resign his commission. He was not going to give up Helene Bannerman, either. He would marry her, if she'd have him; and if marrying the wife of another officer ruined his career, so be it. He wouldn't be the first man to spend thirty years as a lieutenant. If they forced him out, he'd join a foreign army—if Helene would go with him.

Always it came back to Helene. How could he reconcile his love of the service with Helene's longing for a settled life? He didn't know, but he had to try. He had to make it work.

And if it didn't work? If he had to choose between them? He'd worry about that when he came to it.

Storm, chief of the Hair Rope band of the Cheyenne, rode his painted white horse downstream, following the tracks of his retreating warriors.

He removed his war bonnet and hung it from his wicker saddle, letting the breeze cool his sweating hair. He was satisfied. The white soldiers had surprised his camp, and that had been bad, but his people had fought the soldiers well. The soldiers had fought well, also. Storm respected them for it. Many on both sides had died, among them Storm's oldest friend, Man Above the Clouds, killed by the white leader. If help had not come for the white soldiers, they would have been killed to a man.

Storm could never fully punish the white men for the wrongs they had inflicted upon him and his people—for the death of his son, White Wolf; for the shame brought upon the maiden Winter Moon; for all the deaths from starvation last winter, when the whites had cut the food ration; and, before that, for the wrongs done to his people at Sand Creek and a hundred other places. He could never fully punish them, but on this raid he had made a start.

The women and children of Storm's village would have reached the Fort Cobb reservation by now. The men would be there tonight. These new soldiers would not be able to catch them. At the reservation his people would be safe. The soldiers would not be allowed to attack them there. Such a way of making war seemed strange, but the white men had many strange rules.

Storm would see his people safely onto the reservation. He would see them started on their new lives. Then he would give up his position as chief. He would leave his band and ride north. There were Cheyennes in that region who were still at war with the whites, and he would join them. And when the Northern Cheyenne surrendered, as they were one day bound to do, Storm would go on fighting alone.

It would be a good fight.

The regiment came up, a long column of dust-covered soldiers, followed by an equally long supply train. The regiment halted on the prairie. The Commanding Officer and his staff rode toward the bluff, with a ten-man escort.

The men of K Company pulled aside their barricade of saddles and blankets. They saw the looks on the newcomers' faces as the new men were confronted with the sights and stench of the bluff.

Captain Bannerman was chewing on a cold cigar. The dried blood and brains of the scout Smith were still on his face and uniform, mixed with a layer of dirt and powder smoke. He took out the cigar, walked up to the C.O. and saluted with a flourish. He said, "I see our messenger got through, sir."

Major (Brevet Major General) Eugene A. Carr was a stiff-backed veteran with a heavily waxed cavalry moustache. He took in Bannerman's condition and said, "Yes. We picked up your trail at that burned-out ranch. We've been coming like Billy-be-damned ever since."

Major Lundquist, the regimental Adjutant, added, "From the look of things, we got here just in time."

"Yes, sir," Bannerman said.

Major Carr turned to the orderly galloper. "Orderly, my compliments to Dr. Haskell. He and his assistant are to come forward immediately. I fear they've a deal of work before them."

"Yes, sir." The orderly saluted and galloped back to the column.

The Major and the Adjutant dismounted, slapping dust from their uniforms, while Bannerman gave them a brief account, highly favorable to himself, of the fight. Lieutenant Starke listened, expressionless. He did not contradict what his commanding officer said. He was not that kind of man.

When Bannerman was done, Major Carr nodded sagely. "Good work, Bannerman. Excellent work. In fact, I'm going to recommend that you get the Medal of Honor for what you've done here."

Bannerman cleared his throat. "Why, thank you, General."

Lieutenant Starke interrupted. "Excuse me, sir. What about medals for the two men who went off the bluff for water last night? None of us would be here if it wasn't for them."

"What?" Carr said. "Hm. Yes. Yes, I'll give it some thought. Write it up."

"Yes, sir."

Becky Hobson had come up beside Starke. Major Carr knelt before her. He put a hand on her shoulder. "And you must be the little girl that these men came here to save."

Becky nodded shyly.

"Her name's Becky Hobson," Starke said as she sheltered against his leg.

Carr said, "And a very pretty little girl you are, too. You remind me of my own daughters when they were your age. Well, Becky, we're going to take you to a big fort, called Fort Riley. You'll stay there with one of the officers' families. There will be lots of girls and boys for you to play with, until we can locate some of your relatives to take you. Do you think you'll like that?"

Becky nodded again.

Carr smoothed her tangled hair. "Good. Good." He patted her shoulder once more and stood. To Bannerman, he said, "Your company is unfit for further service, Colonel Bannerman. I'm sending you back to Fort Pierce. Those who can ride will be given mules. The rest will travel in supply wagons. You'll refit at Pierce and receive replacements."

"Yes, sir," Bannerman said.

Carr turned. "Major Lundquist, if you'll make the arrangements?"

"Yes, sir," the Adjutant said.

Carr went on, still addressing the Adjutant. "B Company is to police this bluff. D will bury the dead."

Starke interrupted again. "Beg your pardon, sir. K Company will bury its own dead."

Carr cast a cold eye on this impertinent lieutenant. He saw that Starke was not about to back down. Perhaps he appreciated Starke's motives. "Very well," he agreed. To Lundquist, he said, "D Company will remain with the regiment, in that case. The horses and mules are to be watered at the river. As soon as that is done, the regiment will pursue the Cheyennes."

Bannerman said, "I doubt you'll catch them before Fort Cobb, General. Not with the lead they have."

Carr sighed. "I know. Still, we must make the effort."

The men of B Company policed the bluff. They picked up shell casings, abandoned articles of clothing and equipment, and trash of all kinds. They made a bonfire and burned the dead horses. They cut scalps from the dead Indians for souvenirs, then rolled the Indians' bodies into the ravine, to provide food for the vultures. In the background the rest of the regiment, having watered their animals, rumbled southeast in pursuit of the Cheyennes.

As they worked, the men grumbled. "We didn't make this mess. Why the hell do we have to clean it up?"

Some of K Company's survivors dug a common grave, with shovels borrowed from the supply wagons. Other K's collected the bodies of their comrades from the bluff and from the valley. When the grave was ready, the bodies were rolled in, one on top of the other—Townsend, Starving Mike, Barker, the Arab, Slim Pickens—all of them. Those who had been recently killed went in with flopping limbs. Those who had been dead awhile were bloated grotesquely, and several of their stomachs burst as they fell into the grave. The bodies from the valley had been severely mutilated. Squillace could never have been identified if the men hadn't known who he was from where he was found. The funeral party wore bandannas across their mouths and noses, to avoid choking on the gut-turning stench of death. Above them was a pall of smoke from the burning horses.

When the last body had been toppled into the grave, Captain Bannerman prepared to say a few words.

"Sir?"

Bannerman turned.

It was Link Hayward. He said, "We'd prefer Lieutenant Starke to do this, sir."

Bannerman stared at Link for a moment. Hayward was incorrigibly insubordinate, but this was not the time to make an example of him.

"As you please," Bannerman said. He nodded to Starke, who stepped forward.

Dr. Haskell had set up a dressing station in the center of the bluff. Wagons were being prepared to carry the wounded. Haskell went down the line of casualties, examining men like Skull and the Professor, giving instructions for their disposition.

He came to Numb Nuts Hudnutt, who lay on a blanket, a tourniquet above his shattered knee. The doctor, a nononsense sort who had learned his trade at the Wilderness and Spottsylvania Court House, took one look at the knee and said to his assistant, "This man's leg has to come off right now. It can't wait. Prepare my surgical equipment."

A group of Numb Nuts's comrades had gathered around him. Numb Nuts joked with them nervously. "Fifteen dollars a month and a free wooden leg—I'll be in the pink. You boys wait. This time next year, I'll be making more money than all of you put together. I'll make a killing."

The Professor, who lay nearby, said, "What kind of business were you in before you joined up, anyway?"

Numb Nuts hesitated, then said, "Patent medicines."

The men all laughed. Hunter said, "You mean hair tonic? Guaranteed to cure what ails you?"

"So what happened?" asked Dutch Hartz, who was there to have his wounded bicep examined.

Numb Nuts shrugged. "The market was bad after the war. Things will be picking up now."

"Damn right, they will," Hunter agreed. "You can sell that stuff to yourself now. You'll always have one good customer."

B Company's officers and Major Carr's staff congratulated Captain Bannerman. They knew Bannerman. He was a West Pointer, one of them. Of K's other officers, Starke was a ranker, and Conroy, the new man, was with the wounded.

Then the Major and his staff mounted. They rode after the regiment, while B's officers left to oversee their men. Bannerman and Starke were alone. Still chewing the cigar, Bannerman smacked a fist into his palm. "Well, Starke. A nice little action we fought."

"We?" Starke said.

Bannerman ignored him. "You got your wish. I let you come with the expedition. Now I expect to see your name on a letter of resignation when we return."

Starke said nothing.

Bannerman chuckled. "I don't know what Emily Hayes has on you, but it must be good. It'll be a great day for the army when you resign."

Behind them a voice said, "No, Captain. It's you who's going to resign."

They turned. It was Conroy. His bandanna had been wrapped around his wounded neck as a bandage. His once beautiful clothes were a wreck, like everyone else's. He supported himself on a staff made from a cottonwood branch.

"What are you talking about?" Bannerman huffed. "Don't be ridiculous."

"I'm serious, sir," Conroy said. He was wan and drawn. His open, youthful face had aged in the last few weeks.

Bannerman took the cigar from his mouth. "And why the devil should I resign?" he asked Conroy.

"Because last night you proposed abandoning your command. You wanted to save yourself and leave your men to their fate. I believe they call that dereliction of duty."

"That?" Bannerman said. "That was a joke."

"I'll swear that it wasn't. I'll also swear that you took n

active role in the defense of this bluff, and furthermore, that you appropriated the men's drinking water for your own use.''

Bannerman was frowning now. "Stiff charges, mister. With only the word of a junior lieutenant to back them up."

"Perhaps," Conroy said. "But my father knows the editors of this country's biggest newspapers. He has friends in Washington. If you don't resign, I'll tell him what really happened here. He'll see that the story gets in every paper in the East. There will be inquiries in Congress. Every surviving man of this company will be called upon to testify, and I don't think you'll like what they have to say. You'll be lucky to get off without a term in Leavenworth."

Bannerman worked his jaws. "Go through with this, and you'll be betraying a brother officer. Your own career will be ruined, as well."

"Do you think I care?" Conroy said. "What's the use in having an army career if I have to please people like you? There's other occupations, far more profitable ones, that I can pursue."

Bannerman shook his head. "I'm disappointed in you, Conroy. You had the makings of a good officer. But you let a bad apple like Starke, here, lead you astray."

"If he's a bad apple, there should be more like him," Conroy said. "Now, you have a choice, Captain. Retire, and I won't say a thing. People can think you're a hero. You can run for Congress. You can run for governor. You can run for dog catcher, if you want, but you're not going to stay in the army."

Bannerman pursed his lips. Beneath his heavy brows he looked from Conroy to Starke. He let out a deep breath, then turned and walked off. He threw away his cigar.

Jim Starke watched him go. For the first time, Starke saw a glimmer of hope for his own future.

Dr. Haskell had finished Numb Nuts's amputation and the other necessary operations. The wagons had been loaded with the wounded. The guidon was taken down. At last the men of K Company prepared to leave the bluff. It seemed as if they had been there a long time. They retrieved their uniform jackets and leather carbine slings. It felt funny to be wearing them again.

To the north, clouds were building. "It's going to rain," said Link. "Do you believe this?"

"A day late and a dollar short," Hunter said. "Typical army bullshit."

Lieutenant Starke watched Hunter struggle to put on his carbine sling with his unwounded left hand. Hunter's other, bandaged, hand dangled to one side.

Starke said, "How's that hand, Hunter?"

"Don't know, sir," Hunter replied.

Starke raised an eyebrow. "You haven't lost the use of it, I hope?"

Hunter tried not to smile. "Don't know, sir. I believe I may have."

Starke turned to Link. "The Major says all temporary promotions are to be made permanent when we get back to Fort Pierce, Hayward. Think you can keep those stripes this time?"

"Oh, yes, sir," Link assured him. "I'm a changed man after this, sir."

"Form up!" cried the new First Sergeant, Cronk.

The few men who were left straggled into line. Harry Winston walked toward the small formation. Blood still seeped from his wounded shoulder. The shoulder had begun to stiffen, as well. He would have to get it looked at eventually.

Then Link Hayward—Sergeant Hayward now—grabbed Harry's arm. Harry winced with pain.

Link thrust his face close to Harry's. "Mad Dog, when we get back to the fort, you buy yourself a white jacket. Get Quince to fix it, and wear it on payday." He grinned and cuffed Harry's wounded shoulder. "You're a K now."

Link turned away and joined the formation. Harry stood for a minute. There had been a time when Link's words would have meant a lot to him. Now he didn't know what they meant. He didn't even know if he cared anymore.

He knew one thing, though. God help any rookie that he found in Barker's bunk when he got back to the fort.

ABOUT THE AUTHOR

Robert W. Broomall has been a journalist, draftee, bartender, and civil servant. His main interests are travel and history, especially that of the Old West and Middle Ages.

Broomall has written several Westerns for Fawcett, including *Dead Man's Town*, *The Bank Robber*, *Dead Man's Canyon*, *and Dead Man's Crossing*, as well as the historical novels *Texas Kingdoms* and *California Kingdoms*. He lives in Maryland with his wife and children.